A More Perfect Union

A Hugo Miller Mystery

Joseph Allen

ISBN: 978-1-62420-463-0

Credits

Cover Artist: Design by Ms G
Editor: Sherry Derr-Wille

We the People of the United States, in Order to form a more perfect Union, establish Justice, insure domestic Tranquility, provide for the common defense, promote the general Welfare, and secure the Blessings of Liberty to ourselves and our Posterity, do ordain and establish this Constitution for the United States of America.

Dedication

For Rudy and Angus, who put up with my whining and don't hold it
against me
and
for Doctor Watson, Bunter and Archie Goodwin
and
for my wife, Mary, who would read this if she coul

Chapter One

Ruth and I were heading up to the Catskills to find somewhere to scatter Murray's ashes.

We decided on someplace around Kaaterskill Falls, near Woodstock, where the legendary 1967 rock'n'roll love-in and multi-day concert was held – that was why we thought it might be a fitting final resting place. Murray was the right vintage. I was driving my old Jaguar XK8 convertible. It had undeniable advantages – it was fully paid for and had very low mileage because it was a city-dweller's car. And it was sexy.

It was June last year. Murray was in a cardboard box the size of a Courvoisier carton, which seemed appropriate, but I did not make that comment to Ruth, who was genuinely bereaved. I found myself thinking as I drove across the George Washington Bridge and veered north onto the Palisades Parkway that she was lucky to have found someone whom she loved enough to be so deeply and affectively wounded by his passing.

Although I have been married twice and divorced twice, I think I have never been in love, because I always felt relieved when a relationship ended; girlfriends first, then wives. I didn't cheat on anyone, but I fomented reasons to break up eventually. Probably my insecurity, as Wife Number Two used to say. She said I wanted to fall in love, not to be in love.

I turned on the car radio fairly loud because the top was down, and Ruth's voluminous Hermes scarf was tightly tied in almost the manner of an Islamic headscarf.

"Penny for your thoughts," she said.

"I think I'm easy to read. I was thinking about my two failed marriages, and your one super-successful one, that's all. It's odd to say I envy that you miss him so much. It means you were a good couple. I married women who were deeply unsuitable for me, just as I dated unsuitable girls in college before I married Barbara."

"Unsuitable? Really? What does that mean?"

"Just nothing in common except maybe physical attraction, and too stupid to know that, I guess, but I wasn't thinking so much about me as I was about you. I think you and Murray were a love story."

She turned to face out her side of the car and I thought she was probably teary.

A silver Bentley whizzed by on the left, the windows in the back seat tinted dark. It was a Wednesday and there was not a lot of traffic as we went around the big curve that points the Thruway due north toward Albany on the west side of the Hudson after you turn from the Parkway onto the Thruway in Rockland County.

I saw a red car ahead of me in my lane, fairly far ahead, but other than those two and my Jag we had the road to ourselves as we passed the exit for Tuxedo Park, which at least used to be where they held the Renaissance Faire most summers. If I had small kids, I would have been there at least once a year. My son from the first marriage loved going to the Renaissance Faire in San Bernardino County, particularly to see the 'serving wenches' who combined jolly big breasts with low-cut dresses and no bras. My daughters were interested in seeing the 'Queen', which somehow seemed a better reason to enjoy the Faire.

"That guy in the Bentley up there is driving like a pimp."

Ruth jerked back from watching the scenery on her side and leaned forward to look at the silver car that was moving farther and farther ahead of us. "He's wobbling too."

"Yeah, that's what I meant and driving like he was fired out of a gun." I eased up on the accelerator, not wanting to get close to either car.

There was a fast flash of some kind between the cars, like maybe one car kicked up a rock that hit the other one or something like a beam of sunlight reflecting back from the chrome of the big Bentley. The red one veered right, and seemed to drive onto the shoulder and stop. The Bentley kept going or maybe even speeded up then vanished around a curve a couple of miles ahead of us.

"They didn't collide," she said.

"No. I wonder if the red car had a blow-out."

"Call 9-1-1," I said. "Tell them it looks like somebody may be hurt a couple of miles north of the Tuxedo Park exit going north on the Thruway.

2

I'll pull off and see what happened. Maybe I can help."

I slowed down and as we got close to the red car, I realized it was a sporty car, maybe a red Mustang. Nobody was getting out of the car to see what happened.

"I don't think it was a blow-out."

I stopped about one hundred feet behind the red car, put on my hazard lights. I asked Ruth to stand by the car and wave to the first responders when they got there. I walked carefully toward the red car. If there was somebody in the car who was hurt, I wanted to help. If there was somebody there who had a gun or something, I didn't want to get shot.

There was an arm hanging out the driver's side window. Dark-skinned hand. African-American or dark-skinned Latino, 'blatino' in NYC. I circled toward the edge of the roadway so I could approach from far enough away so I wouldn't scare whoever was in the car.

"You okay?" I yelled.

No response.

"I saw your car here and called for someone to come with paramedics," I said loudly.

No response.

I started to walk toward the car. It was early afternoon and the sun was overhead. The driver was slumped down and at the same time leaning back where he had been left by the now-deflated airbag. There was blood but not a lot. The airbag had probably hit him in the face when it was activated and the blood probably came from his nose. He moaned but seemed unconscious. I knew it would be dangerous to try to get him out of the car. I wondered what to do, but at the same moment I heard a siren. It was a State Police car heading south on the other side of the Thruway.

When they reached us, they slowed down slightly and drove across the grassy medium, which was a slight ditch with mowed grass or weeds. They crossed the northbound lanes with lights flashing and siren at a very high volume. A black Ford Fusion pulled to a stop in the fast lane, and another car approaching slowed behind. I stood still.

The State Police car pulled parallel to my Jag. I watched. One of the cops stepped out of the car with a bullhorn.

"Put your hands in the air and walk slowly in this direction."

3

I did as I was told.

The other cop popped out of the passenger seat and ran to put flares in the street, then ran forward with an EMT bag.

"You hit this car?" the bullhorn blared.

I could hear Ruth explaining how we saw the accident but were half a mile or so behind when it happened.

"Keep your hands up."

I did what he told me to do and kept walking toward him.

After he looked at my license, registration and proof of insurance, he said, "Sorry for that, Mr. Miller. We have to be careful."

The other cop came back wearing blue nitrile gloves, leaned into the police car and grabbed a mic, said something, then hung it up.

"Only one person in the car. He seems to be breathing but I think they're going to have to cut him out of the car. I think the frame is bent."

I said that I expected to see a dent on the side of the car, because I thought the other car side-swiped the red car or that maybe the other car kicked up a rock.

"Not that I could see," the second cop said. "Maybe just swerved and the car ran into a rock or something. Obviously totaled, probably nothing left underneath the car."

They wanted a description of the silver Bentley. No, neither of us had a clue about the license plate number. No idea whether it was a New York plate.

"He drove by us going one hundred or so. All I wanted was to drop back and let him have the road."

"And you're heading for?"

"The general area of Woodstock, looking for a place to stay for a day," Ruth intervened. She did not explain that we had her husband's ashes in the back seat.

"We're going to have to ask you to accompany us to our station in Woodbury, so we can take a statement."

I nodded.

"Nice car," he said, gesturing at the Jag.

"It's not new. In fact, it is a 2000 model," I said.

The car was British racing green with a tan convertible stop and champagne-colored leather upholstery. My version of middle-aged crazy, purchased after my second divorce, and fully paid for ten years earlier. It had about thirty thousand miles on it, and had always been taken care of at the dealer. It drove like a dream.

"What's that in the back seat?"

"Ashes of a friend who died."

"It's illegal to scatter them in water," he said.

"Thanks."

"It's my husband," Ruth said. "His name was Murray."

She did not cry.

A second siren came from the south, and an ambulance marked 'Orange County Fire Department' pulled over in front of us, near the red car.

We stared as they cut the door off the car and maneuvered the driver onto a gurney. They strapped him down, put a green oxygen mask on him, and rolled him into the back with two EMTs working on him. As I watched, they connected an IV with what was probably a bag of saline above, and they put cardiogram sensors on his chest. Blood pressure cuff. One EMT gave us a thumbs-up as they closed the door. The driver ran over and told the cops they were taking him to New York Presbyterian Hudson Valley Hospital in Cortlandt, on the other side of the Hudson River across the Bear Mountain Bridge.

We went to the Woodbury Police station and gave a formal statement that was recorded then transcribed. I signed mine and Ruth signed hers.

"Is this where all the discount stores are?" I asked.

Ruth nodded slowly. "Probably nothing good, including the prices," she said with a blank look.

"What's his name?" I asked Cheslack.

"Edward Razmus Hall, according to the ID in his pocket," the first cop, Officer Eddie Cheslack, said.

"Pa dum dum," Ruth said.

Cheslack stared at her.

"It's a joke, right?"

He said nothing, just waiting for her to explain.

"E Razmus Hall? It's a high school in Brooklyn. It's where I graduated. On Flatbush Avenue and Church Street."

"That's what his driver's license says. Hard to say if it's real or fake, but some moms have an odd idea of what names would be good when they're coming out of an anesthetic after delivering a baby," he said. "Forty-two years old, address on Prospect Park West in Brooklyn."

"I think I know his name," Ruth said.

"You said it's like your high school," Cheslack said.

"It is, when you look at his whole name. But I think he ran for congress under the name Eddie Hall a couple of years back. Or maybe it was just a primary, because he was a Democrat."

I shook my head. "I used to live in Manhattan. Now I live in Queens. Never paid any attention to Brooklyn races. Not as though there's much doubt about which way New York City will vote."

"Well, look at Giuliani and Bloomberg. Both Republicans."

"Lots of Republican mayors. Lindsay for instance. Almost zero Republican congressmen."

Ruth shrugged and looked at me. "I already told Murray he has to wait for next weekend or the weekend after that."

I nodded, shook Officer Cheslack's hand.

"We may be in touch," he said, "if we have any follow-up questions. Meanwhile, drive careful. You see what can happen."

We walked out to the parking lot and dead-headed back to Manhattan.

Chapter Two

I dropped Ruth at her place at Park Avenue and 60th Street, and headed to my digs over the Queensboro Bridge in Long Island City. It was darkling and the traffic was mild. I was home and, in my apartment, staring out the window at the Chrysler Building thirty minutes later.

Queens, like Manhattan, is made up of many different neighborhoods, many of which used to be virtually separate cities. Most of them retain their spiritual or geographic identities. So, in Manhattan, for instance, you have the old Dutch village of Harlem, the more English Greenwich Village, and the formerly mostly German Yorkville, all of which were 'out in the country' at the time of the Revolution.

Long Island City was for many years the principal ford of the East River, where goods were moved between Manhattan and what is now Queens. The Dutch called it Dominie's Hoek, which I think translates as the Lord's Spit of Land, "Lord" meaning the one in Heaven.

Anyway, today it is Queens, but directly opposite the United Nations, and my street, 50th Avenue, looks to be contiguous with 42nd Street in Manhattan, but for the East River intervening. Very pretty views, many tall residential buildings. I am lucky enough to live in one that is just across the street from the River with a park on the other side, so the view is unobstructable. Manhattanites identify Long Island City, or LIC as it is called, by an old neon sign that reads "Pepsi," which stands in a park today but formerly identified a factory where the drink was formulated or bottled or whatever.

When I turned on the computer there was a message from Ruth, who had hit Google as soon as she put Murray back on the mantel.

Edward Razmus Hall was quite the man. No, he had not run for congress, though there was talk that he would. He had been an Assistant District Attorney in Brooklyn after graduating from the eponymous

Erasmus Hall High School on Flatbush Avenue, then from Columbia and Columbia Law. He had prosecuted several high-profile cases, including charges against an NYPD officer who was accused of sodomizing a prisoner with his night-stick and causing lasting damage to the man's digestive tract. That one had been all over the news for weeks during the time leading up to the trial, which only lasted a week itself. The jury was out for less than a day before convicting. He also prosecuted a Medicaid fraud case involving a group of medical doctors who were accused of providing false diagnoses for workers claiming to have been hurt on the job, and who were subsequently awarded disability pensions and a variety of drugs in some cases.

He was a member of the AME church, but attended several local mainline Protestant churches on a rotating basis. Most interesting, he had run for and come within a hair's breadth of winning, the 40th District City Council seat, covering Prospect Park, parts of Flatbush, Crown Heights and some other relatively upper-middle neighborhoods in Brooklyn.

When he lost, he began a radio talk show where he called out weak or wrong-minded public officials, basically accused certain private citizens of being members of organized crime, and sided with civil rights leaders when the NYPD roughed up minorities. That seemed to happen fairly frequently, judging from the nightly news, but less often than in other big cities like St. Louis and Chicago or Baltimore. He was thought to be prepping for a congressional run, or perhaps for another run at the City Council.

All this under the name Eddie Hall. There were lots of pictures of Hall cutting ribbons, striding down the steps of the Brooklyn Courthouse, and in front of City Hall in Manhattan. There were pictures of Hall playing pick-up basketball games on asphalt courts outdoors with red-brick project apartment buildings in the background. He was tallish but not tall enough to be an NBA player. Because his DNA was mixed, his skin was relatively light, and his hair was curly but 'good hair' in the lingo. He had been married to a White woman, divorced, had two kids – a boy of twenty-one and a girl of thirteen, whom he seemed to spend time with. No scandals that she could find.

"Sounds like an all-round good guy," I said. "I bet it'll be all over the TV tonight."

"Already is," she said and I looked at my watch.

A few minutes after five PM. We signed off to watch TV and see what more we could find out. Made a plan to have dinner later someplace we could meet easily without my having to get my car out and end up paying for parking in Manhattan.

I tuned in just in time to hear two factoids about Mr. Hall that came out of the blue. He recently announced his engagement to a partner, Jimmy, and planned to be married in September. Even more unusual, Jimmy was from a wealthy family. They met while Eddie was running for City Council.

My cell bleeped. "Did you get all that?" It was Ruth, of course.

"What did they say about him? I tuned in too late to get the details."

"I don't remember exactly word-for-word, but they said he has been stabilized after what may have been a road rage incident in Orange County on the New York State Thruway."

"Road rage? Really? Looked more intentional to me, like a drag race. That Bentley sailed by him but as far as I could tell never touched him."

We agreed to meet at Ora di Pranzo, which belongs to friends of ours and is in SoHo—not super-convenient, but we wanted to talk to Gabriele and Dante, the proprietors, about Eddie Hall.

Ruth and I have been friends for eons, dating back to the middle of my second marriage, when I was establishing an office in Manhattan for my California-based PR company. She wasn't married then, and I was freshly separated, so we were introduced by a mutual friend who, though elderly and Scandinavian, carried on like a marriage-maker, openly suggesting that we would make a good couple.

Not. We had everything in common and nothing in common. When I met her, Ruth had a long-term squeeze in the movie business who was married, so she needed a date, being very social. I was a two-time loser who liked to go to the opera and theater and member nights at the museums, so I needed a date. Neither of us needed complications or any kind of physical relationship other than the PDAs that friends share—kiss-kiss on the cheeks, for instance, or slightly lewd comments that had no follow-up. *You look like you need a good fuck. Is that a gun in your pocket or are you just happy to see me?*

We provided each other with safety and friendship. I never wanted to have another relationship, but I have always craved other people's company. Her BF relationship eventually cracked up and she met a garmento who fell in love with her. He gave her a big diamond and they married when she was about forty-eight. I almost literally danced at their wedding.

She is an amazing person, a perfect travel companion, and most years sees everything that opens on Broadway, musical or not. She and I have teamed up to help our friend Mike di Saronno, an NYPD detective, solve a couple of cases, and we seem to have a knack for ferreting out clues. We almost never get in each other's way.

We have the same dark sense of humor. Politically incorrect, ethnic, not for an open mic. She's connected in amazing ways to the power structure of New York. She's a docent at this and that museum, a volunteer at Carnegie Hall, and has been a key fund-raiser for several politicians.

Gabriele, the uber-handsome maître d' at Ora di Pranzo, has a very checkered background, and I don't think, even after having been friends for years, that I know a tenth of his experiences, but he was certainly a sex worker at one point in his life. Gabriele's cousin Dante (they are from Capri and Naples, respectively) is the co-owner and chef at Ora di Pranzo, a chic, white-table-cloth restaurant on a side street west of Varick Street, which is 7th Avenue in midtown, a few blocks up from Canal. It is highly starred or reviewed or whatever by everyone and his cousin. Big brick pizza oven and all kinds of fish, vegetable and chicken dishes that make your taste buds dance a jig. At any normal time, there is a longish wait for a table if you don't have a reservation. Except if you're me.

I got there fifteen minutes ahead of Ruth, purposefully to do a stand-up hiya and hug with Gabriele at the bar, kiss-kiss on the cheek, etc. I also wanted to tell him about the scene on the Thruway and to see whether he sparked to the mention of Eddie Hall.

He did.

"You know I live in Brooklyn? Very popular guy in Brooklyn. TV said last night he was in a car crash with some guy when he have a fight on Thruway. Why you want to know about him?"

I explained Ruth and I were behind his car when he may have been clipped by another car and ran off the road.

"Lot of people not like him. You know that?"

"And you? Did you like him?"

"He come here many time. He sit over there," he said, pointing to a table for two next to a window. "He like pizza sometimes, but like *pollo Milanese* and *cannonau di sardegna* many time."

"A man after my own heart."

"What that mean?"

"It means he liked the same food I like."

Even as he approaches forty, Gabriele is nothing short of dashingly handsome. Black wavy hair, a high forehead, tanned complexion, green eyes, perfectly symmetrical features, small ears, broad shoulders, whatever. One of those men born to wear Armani couture.

"So, you looking for what happen with Eddie Hall car?"

"No. Just curious. No part in it."

"Signora Ruth want to know who hurt Eddie Hall?"

I shook my head no. "How is Dante?"

"Dante in kitchen. He come out in few minutes, say hello."

"You know he gay?"

"Who? Dante?"

"Eddie Hall."

"I know he gonna marry boyfriend, *si*."

"Very rich man. Jimmy van Gelsen."

"TV say he maybe run for congress."

Dante appeared in the kitchen doorway, looked at us, then shrugged and headed back to the kitchen.

Gabriele opined. "Lawyer. Help gay men. Help people get green card. Help gay men find gay girl for marry and get green card."

Ruth arrived wearing a pink and black large window-pane checked classic (i.e., second-hand) Chanel jacket with a long pair of stretchy pants that displayed her toned legs well. Three-inch heels. Kiss-kiss with Gabriele, who complimented her in Italian, of course, stepped back and made a palms-up, downward-sweeping gesture with both hands to indicate how much he approved of her ensemble.

As though there was a loudspeaker in the kitchen, Dante re-appeared. Unlike Gabriele, Dante was tall and slim, probably going on twenty years older, mostly gray but with the broad shoulders that apparently ran in the family. He had indeed been an Armani runway model before sneaking into the United States as a chef on a cruise ship.

Gabriele and Dante were cousins, although in Italy the word can indicate any familial relationship, no matter how distant. It's like the word *nipote*, which refers to absolutely any relative, even though it strictly translates as "nephew."

Dante grew up in Naples, Gabriele on the famous Isle of Capri. Anyway, they made their own *limoncello* from lemons grown on Capri and shipped over by Gabriele's mother twice a year She had a tree in her yard. *Fatt'in casa*, homemade, and only served *gratis*, due to NY state law about making your own spirits. If you make it, you can't sell it. They kept some commercially bottled *limoncello* behind the bar to serve to strangers.

Ruth plunked herself down at the bar and ordered a dirty vodka straight up with olives. I was staring at the wine list, and decided to opt for a favorite, *Puer Apuliae,* a treat from the southeast of Italy near Bari. It's a dark, dirty, berry-ish, tobacco-ish red made mostly from the ancient *uva di troia* grape that was supposedly taken to Italy by the Greek hero Diomedes after he finished tearing down the walls of Troy at the end of the Trojan War. Cool, no? A really ancient grape, a really ancient wine, and from a part of Italy that was Greek until relatively recently in historic terms. Heck, the real St Nicholas is buried in Bari in a church called *San Nicola di Bari.* The famous Christmas saint was a bishop in Asia Minor, and as the Turks began to conquer the area, the Byzantine Emperor had the bones of St Nick exhumed and sent to Bari for reburial to keep the remains out of the hands of infidels. That was in 1087, virtually yesterday in Mediterranean terms.

Anyway, Ruth got her drink before they fetched the wine, and Gabriele was goo-gooing over her clothing when the bartender returned with what was the last bottle of *Puer Apuliae*, so named after the famous, or infamous, Holy Roman Emperor Frederick II in the Middle Ages because he was born in southern Italy, of Germans of course, and actually called himself King of Jerusalem for no particular reason. Go figure.

I suggested that if we were going to eat at the bar, we should move to the end where it touched the wall, so that we could talk with Gabriele. I mentioned Jimmy Van Gelsen and Ruth lighted up.

"He's a member of the Opera League, almost never misses. Nice guy, kinda swishy sometimes but always looks like a million bucks. Funny, I thought he was involved with that television news guy, the one in the evening. But maybe he was bringing a Black guy recently. Wow, nice-looking guy too. That's the one that was on the Thruway?"

"I guess."

My cellphone lighted up. Mike di Saronno.

"*Pronto?*"

"Very funny, Hugo. How ya been? "

"Generally sitting up and taking nourishment, as they say. How 'bout you?"

Mike is a detective in the Midtown West Precinct on West 54th Street, a stone's throw from where I lived for a decade on 48th Street. We became friendly because Mike lived in the neighborhood, unlike most cops, who commute from someplace else, and because Ruth and I were able to lend a hand with a couple of relatively messy cases he worked on over a few years.

"Understand your propensity for violence put you on the scene when Eddie Hall was run off the road."

"I happened to be driving behind him about a mile, yes."

"Amazing."

"So anyway..."

"I'd appreciate if I could take a statement, since the Commissioner asked me to have a look into it. It happened outside our jurisdiction, but we have an interest, since there may have been a political angle to whatever happened."

"I heard he was going to run for office."

"I heard you were the first person on the scene, before the State Police got there."

"Yup. Ruth called it in on 9-1-1."

"My next call is to Ruth."

I handed the phone to Ruth.

"Mikey..."

She listened and made assenting noises a couple of times. "Why don't you come to Ora di Pranzo? We're just getting ready to have dinner."

She handed the phone to me. "He wants to interview us there at the precinct so he can record everything."

We agreed to meet the next morning at ten.

As the dinner hour wound down, Gabriele brought his own dinner out to the bar and sat with us. He gave us some flavor about Eddie Hall. Nice guy, very liberal, walked in the Pride Parade the last two years and was in favor of universal Pre-K for three-year-olds. Also, totally behind New York City being a sanctuary city, a place where the police or other authorities do not refer illegal residents to the feds.

"Was he in the closet?" Ruth asked.

Gabriele shrugged. "Well he not act faggy, but have boyfriend."

"And I bet he was paying child support to his ex-wife."

He shrugged again. "She rich too. Old money. Like Jimmy van Gelsen."

Ruth cocked her head. "So, he swings for the fence and hits home runs. Interesting. How about you? You dating anyone?"

"Is called '*yenta*'?"

She smiled, but repeated the question.

He nodded toward me.

I had a mouthful of spaghetti with oil, garlic and parmesan cheese. I took a drink of wine and stared at her, trying to tell her telepathically to lay off. It didn't work.

"Ugo," he said. "Si no Ugo, *nessuno*."

I started to swallow a whole strand of spaghetti the long way and felt it catch in my throat. I reached in my mouth and pulled the offending piece out and dropped it on my plate, took a drink of water and felt like I might live.

"Ruth, *mon petit chou*, can we drop this please?"

She put her hands in her lap and looked downward.

"Tell me everything you know about Jimmy Van Gelsen."

She said he came from a wealthy family, had the perfect education from The Horace Mann School to Yale. Forty-ish or maybe very early fifties. Had a fairly public liaison—that is, lots of paparazzi, on Page Six

14

several times—with a young male novelist at one point then was rumored to be cavorting with a network newscaster, though there were no photos of any kind to support that one. He worked for several liberal politicians in fund-raising, including a prominent City Councilman from my area of Queens around Long Island City who also had a Dutch name and a longtime live-in bf. He was a generous patron of Gay Men's Health Crisis, and God's Love We Deliver, which is a service that supplies prepared food, lunches and dinners, to people with cancer or AIDS or other diseases that make them unable to take care of themselves. He volunteered at Housing Works bookstore on Crosby Street in SoHo, where he ran the espresso bar two days a week, raising money for shut-ins from all kinds of illnesses and conditions.

No hint of scandal, although he had been the victim of persistent bullying as a child and a teenager. Nothing negative on social media. He posted frequently on Facebook and Twitter, referred to the Republican president as POTUS only, and retweeted substantially everything the ACLU posted.

Any Facebook page or Twitter account that might have been used by Eddie Hall had been idle since the accident, but there were various tweets that were being retweeted in significant numbers, and talk about a vigil outside City Hall.

Ruth was continually pressing keys on her smartphone and coming up with more in the way of what appeared to be a tsunami of worry about Eddie. His mother's picture cropped up several times, but without any indication of whether or not she was still alive.

My phone buzzed again. Mike di Saronno again.

"Yo, Mike. Been a while since we talked."

"I think we need to get that statement finished. I just got news that Jimmy van Gelsen was found outside his apartment building with a bullet in his head. This is now a homicide."

Chapter Three

Ruth and I called an Uber and were at the 54th Street precinct in twenty minutes. Gabriele came along for the ride, and because he wanted to see Mike. Gabriele has been part of our group for several years, and was smack-dab in the middle of solving two cases where it didn't seem there would ever be a culprit identified. Dante stayed to take care of the store. As it happened, we heard about Jimmy van Gelsen's death on the radio, 1010 WINS, on the way uptown, but of course it was just a neighborhood shooting on the radio. The vic was a wealthy, socially prominent guy who was active in political circles. They mentioned another politico, Eddie Hall, had been hurt in a car accident the day before in Orange County upstate, but did not draw a line connecting the two events.

That won't last long when they find out the two were boyfriends, or even maybe engaged to be married.

"Mr. van Gelsen was an investor in a lot of companies and real estate projects," Mike said. "We're looking over all those to see if there has been any trouble, but I kinda doubt it. We're looking for anything that might have got him in trouble—you know, bad habits, debts, gambling, whatever. Nothing so far. Linked up with Eddie Hall. It seems that Jimmy was wearing the apron in the family, so to speak."

Ruth said she knew van Gelsen from the Opera League, which is a group of opera-lovers who, for the most part, meet every Monday evening during opera season, late September to late April or early May, in the Dress Circle, aka, third balcony, at the Metropolitan Opera, wearing black tie and tiaras. Why they insist on dressing like penguins in today's world is a bit of a mystery. Not unlike kids wanting to dress up like princes and princesses.

Mike wanted to know what Ruth knew about van Gelsen.

"Well, he's old money, which is a little unusual in the Opera

League," she said. "Most of us are outsiders from the Social Register. You know, Jews like me, Italians, Irish, recent immigrants, people of color. It happened because people like us were excluded from the normal charitable organizations until the 1950's, but you don't have to be a WASP to be interested in culture or theater or whatever.

"Same kind of thing as the ladies of B'nai B'rith being the life blood of Broadway shows. Basically, you can't open a show on Broadway without their backing, not because they're some kind of monopoly, but because they just buy so many tickets. It's a real tradition, seeing all the shows that open."

"So, about Mr. van Gelsen..."

She said that he very seldom missed a Monday, even though the season was arranged so that if you went every Monday you saw the same opera more than once, potentially several times with changes of cast. "The Italians don't care how many times they see a piece. They have them all memorized anyway."

"Anybody dislike him?"

"No," she said. "What I'm telling you is that aside from being a little swishy, which is not so unusual at the opera, by the way, Jimmy was pretty much like everybody else. Older family maybe, more money probably, more political, we all knew about that because he wasn't shy about it. I can tell you almost for sure that he brought Eddie Hall on a Monday night, at least once when I was there. I admit I missed a lot of Mondays in the spring because Murray was so sick. I knew he was gonna die, but I didn't think it would happen so fast..."

I put my arm around her. Maybe she wasn't my oldest friend in the world, but at times it seemed like it.

Mike turned to me.

"Mostly only what I read in the newspaper," I said. "Both names were familiar, maybe from newscasts, but if either one of them stood next to me on the 7-train I wouldn't have recognized him. Just people in suits, you know."

"But you saw someone in a car that might have pushed Hall off the road?"

"I guess so, yes, I thought the gray car could possibly have scraped the side of the Mustang. I thought I saw a spark or a spray of sparks. Didn't hear anything, too far back. Then the Mustang tacked over to the right and off the road. You know, you've seen the State Police reports. I never touched the car when I saw all the blood and the air bag and the EMTs arrived. But there wasn't a side-swipe or scrape on it, so I guess there was no contact. I was thinking I might be able to help, but there was no way…"

Mike made a couple of notes, but the whole meeting was being recorded, so he could have it transcribed word for word if he wanted.

"So, van Gelsen was just lying on the sidewalk down in SoHo?"

"More or less."

"Drive-by?"

"No way to tell yet. M.E. said first take was that the gun was fairly close to the victim, but no powder marks. So, if that's true, probably not a drive-by. Seldom happens in Manhattan anyway, too many people on the street even in the middle of the night. License plates would be easy to get, for instance, or make and model, even the race of the driver."

"No video?"

"That I don't know about yet."

"What can we do to help?"

Gabriele was sitting quietly, but offered, "Signor van Gelsen come to Ora di Pranzo many time."

"Did he bring Eddie Hall?"

"Maybe, *lo dimentico. Forse, ma…*"

"Any Black guy?"

"*Si.*"

"Eddie Hall?"

"*Si.*"

Mike showed him a photo from a political poster. Gabriele nodded. "This one?"

He nodded again.

"You sure?"

Yes. "He live Brooklyn, like me. People in Brooklyn know him, on television, make speech sometimes."

"Do you remember anything about the man in the picture? Was he quiet? Did people go over to talk to him? Did you think he might be a celebrity?"

Gabriele stared at the picture. "People go over and shake his hand. He nice guy, always smile and maybe tell joke."

"Many people?"

"Yes."

"Let me have a look at that picture," Ruth said. She cocked her head. "I know this guy. I was looking at some pics online, but not very clear. Maybe from one of the political campaigns I worked on. Good looking, like an actor. Could be from Opera League with Jimmy."

"Maybe from television?" Mike asked. "He prosecuted some pretty high-profile cases when he was ADA in Brooklyn, which is up until a couple of years ago."

She pursed her lips together and slowly shook her head. "Maybe. I mean I know when I see Cyrus Vance on TV, or when I used to see that Indian guy who was U.S. attorney and who got fired after the election. I don't think that's why he looks familiar. Honestly, I seldom watch the news on TV anyway. Bad times. Either I'm out someplace or I'm getting ready to go to bed." She shook her head, unable to dislodge whatever memory was stuck in her pipes.

"Oh," she said, a bit louder. "I just remembered. I went to a party, probably this spring, yeah, kind of a fund-raiser for a women's rights group, at a gorgeous townhouse on the Promenade in Brooklyn Heights. All kinds of famous people mingling there, and there was a distinct boiler-room feel to it. Raising money, you know. Fortunately, they all used to look to Murray for donations, not me, or they did when he was alive. He was there, Eddie Hall, the guy in the picture. I was sitting almost next to him on a sofa, having a drink with an African-American pastor of a church in Harlem who was sitting on my right, one of those guys who is a go-to interview on CNN when the police are accused of violence with a Black guy.

"That guy, the pastor, stood up, and I turned to the other side, my left, and there was this very good-looking Black guy, and it was him, Eddie Hall. I said something like, oh you're running for City Council. He smiled and nodded, stuck his hand out and said his name. I told him I can't vote for him, live in Manhattan, but said good luck or something formulaic like that. Really good-looking. Why are the best-looking guys always gay?

Then he got up and strolled out into the crowd, patting backs and shaking hands."

"Was Mr. van Gelsen there?"

"If he was, I don't remember."

"I wonder why someone would want to take him out. I mean, van Gelsen kind of a quiet guy, not high profile. Liberal like a lot of people, but hard to believe that even as snarky as politics is these days, someone would shoot him for his politics."

"Not official, but the Commissioner told me word is that van Gelsen left his whole estate, lock, stock and barrel, to Eddie Hall."

"Well, so there's a money angle?" I said. "Do we know who in the van Gelsen family would stand to lose?"

"I think van Gelsen's got several brothers," Mike said. "Doesn't mean much though. We need to look through his connections to see if he's on any Boards of Directors, for instance. If he's on Planned Parenthood here in New York, we know that can get some people worked up."

"But even then, what kind of coincidence that Eddie Hall's upstate in a hospital and somebody shoots his boyfriend?"

Mike shrugged. "This is going to be a challenging one. If you feel like you can spend some time digging up what you can dig up, you know I'll appreciate it. Just don't get involved in the overall situation. Let me know what you find out, and keep your nose clean."

Gabriele put his hand to his nose. "Clean?"

"It's just a saying, Ri-Ri," I said, using a childish nickname that he had foolishly disclosed to me years earlier. "Keep your nose clean. It means don't get in trouble."

He wrinkled his nose and frowned at me, indicating that the Ri-Ri nickname was annoying. He had told me his grandmother called him that and, frankly, I only called him that to annoy him. Not something to be proud of, I guess.

I said that I would guess at some point the van Gelsen estate would be settled. The fact that Eddie might still be unconscious and might not even know that van Gelsen was shot. What if Eddie didn't make it? I am *so glad* I'm not a lawyer.

"He has kids. Or had kids, I guess. A boy and a girl, I think, from his second marriage. At least that's what I read online."

"You're right," Mike said. "A boy and a girl. They live here in New York with their mother, who still uses her married name, Aurora Carter Hall. Carter was her maiden name. She's White, by the way, not that it matters. The boy is Alexander, at Columbia. The girl is Matilda, high school. The girl just finished eighth grade, so she will be a freshman in September. Alexander went to Trinity, an Episcopal prep school on the west side then to SUNY Albany. Matilda has been going to Spence, which is kindergarten through twelfth grade, on the east side, in the nineties. Of course, Mrs. Hall comes from money, which helps.

"So, look," Mike said. "Changing the subject, your statement to the State Police said the second car, the one that may have run Eddie Hall off the road, was a silver Bentley. Are you sure?"

I nodded. "Yup. Well you don't see them often, and they might as well be a Rolls Royce or a Sherman tank. I think I told them that several minutes before whatever happened, happened, the Bentley went tearing by us to my left like we were standing still. And I was driving my old Jag XK8. I thought of flooring my car and showing that driver a thing or two. But I didn't. I slowed down to put more distance between us."

"But you didn't get a license plate?"

"Nah. I have a vague impression looking back that it may not have been a New York plate, but that's only because I was straining to see the logo on the trunk. Light-colored but maybe not New York. Nothing else. I'm no expert on expensive cars, but I think that one was a Flying Spur, if that's the right name. The only thing I noticed about it was that the back windows were smoked or tinted so you couldn't see in. I thought that was illegal, but maybe not. The front window wasn't, and I do remember that there was no one sitting in the passenger seat."

"The driver. Anything you can remember?"

"Not much. I think he was White, mostly because I don't remember thinking he wasn't White. Definitely a guy, not a female."

"And you knew that because?"

"He looked like a guy, maybe even had a moustache. Yeah, I think he had a moustache, and he was wearing a kind of uniform cap, with a brim like a cop more or less."

"Jacket and tie?"

"Sorry, no idea. I wasn't expecting any kind of incident, you know. People speed like crazy on the Thruway all the time. And when Ruth and I were cruising north, we were like an invitation to a drag race. She was looking like Isadora Duncan with a huge scarf, and we had the top down. Over the years there have been several times when teenagers or younger guys try to pull ahead then slow down, to see if I would accelerate. Usually not. Frequently I pull off at the next exit and get some gas instead. I've never had a ticket, by the way, even driving a fast sports car."

I looked at Ruth questioningly.

"Don't look at me. The wind was blowing in my face and I had my Holly Golightly sunglasses on. I did see the cars looked like they might be racing before the red one pulled off the road, but that's because Hugo told me to look at them. I looked up because he thought they were drag racing."

"How dumb would you have to be to drag race in a Bentley? Whether somebody got the license or not, there are so few of them that finding the owner of one has to be just a matter of sorting out colors and years and so forth. Have you figured out who owns the Bentley that roared past us on the Thruway?"

"More or less. It was reported stolen earlier that day near Atlantic City. It belongs to one of the casinos. Whoever did it forced the driver out of the car and took off. Nobody was hurt. Sounds like a joy-rider."

Gambling. Hmmm. Doesn't make sense. Just joy-riding?

"Did anybody check the Mustang to see if there was a homing device in it?"

Mike looked at me questioningly but didn't say anything.

"Well, if the guy was looking to get rid of the Bentley and grab a new car, y'know. I don't know, just curious. That Bentley went by me like he knew exactly where he was going. That's all. Makes sense that if he had already driven one hundred and twenty miles, he might have been high or whatever."

"As it happens," Mike said, "there was a passive RFID locator fastened with a neodymium magnet under the dashboard in the Mustang. It could have been put there at any time, no way to tell when, no battery power needed because all it did was to bounce off a signal when it was hit with a radio beam. It could be found by a beacon that broadcasted radio frequency beams off it, but the radius would have been no more than a few miles, probably more to help find the Mustang if it was stolen."

What made him speed up when he did?

"The RFID locator in the Mustang didn't help us find the Bentley," Mike said, "but the Bentley, as it turns out, had a battery-powered homing device of its own in the frame of the car. The casino had a big investment in it, and had no intention of just losing it. Using that, we located it in the town of Catskill, New York, brought it back to New York City and went over it inch by inch. As you might suspect, abandoned, wiped clean, although the CSI guys are all over it looking for prints and they have some partials at least. There were apparently some passengers or a passenger in the car since the last time it was cleaned. There were some bits of gum wrapper or candy wrapper that would have been cleaned up before an expensive car like that was assigned to some high-roller in Atlantic City."

It was too full of coincidences. "There must be some way all of this makes sense, just don't know how to look at it to find what really happened." I keep thinking about Sherlock Holmes. Never trust coincidences to be just accidental.

It's all about van Gelsen. Hall is a coincidence, even though we don't like coincidences.

I looked at Ruth. She had the same look on her face. A combination of overload and puzzlement.

"I think we should hit the computers at home and sleep on this," she said.

"Gotcha." I patted Mike on the back and we left. I went home after I put Ruth in a taxi.

Chapter Four

I looked up Jimmy van Gelsen, feeling sure Ruth was on the same sites, but that's okay. Two pairs of eyes see different things.

He wasn't an only child. He had four brothers and a sister who was developmentally disabled and being taken care of in Westchester County with twenty-four-hour nursing and fairly constant social stimulation, as I interpreted it. It made me think of Laura in "The Glass Menagerie," but without the overbearing mother. Well, they had in common a gay brother yes, but not living with her. And most likely no gentleman callers or jonquils.

His mother was also from an old Dutch family that regularized their name to Skylar from what presumably was originally Schuyler or van Schuyler. His father was one of five brothers, the other four of whom had a total of four boys and five girls. No danger of the name dying out, at least not for that generation. Jimmy was safe from being accused of killing the family name. In an Italian family maybe, he would have been a priest, but in a Dutch family maybe not.

Good education, check. Beautiful apartment in the West Village, check. There was a tour of his apartment dating back to a charity walk-through a couple of years earlier. Two floors of a lovingly restored eighteenth century townhome. He had the main floor and garden, and the floor below it, formerly a servant floor with an entrance under the front steps. Beautiful wide-plank oak floors with an original look to them, and several fire-places, though I doubt they were functional, looking at the pictures with flower arrangements where there would have been logs. Lots of family pictures in the hallways, two big Susan Rothenberg paintings facing each other on opposite sides of a broad doorway, one a roughed out black horse lifting a foreleg, the other an almost smeary looking black horse in what I would gather was a show stance. There was a near-life-size full-length portrait of a shepherd with a rough-hewn staff and no shirt, with hair that would have graced a fourteenth-century Florentine man; very curly in a soft halo bigger than Angela Davis's 1960s Afro.

No mention of a boyfriend, so it probably predated any liaison with Eddie Hall. There were other paintings that looked vaguely familiar, probably just from style. No, it couldn't be a Rauschenberg—that would have been in the caption. Just Pop Art, looking clean and big and comic-strip-ish. Lotsa money, check. A pair of white leather Barcelona chairs blended with a smorgasbord of styles of furniture united by upholstery in tints and color values that blended like flowers in a garden.

There had been some litigation with a past romantic relationship. A guy who felt he should get a pay-off when they broke up. Seems to have been settled without a judge, and the former partner mo ved to New Mexico. Jimmy van Gelsen helped bankroll out-of-pocket costs for good *pro bono* lawyers who had filed suits on behalf of a man whose transgender surgery went bad, apparently settled in the patient's favor.

There were a variety of lawsuits by tenants in rental buildings that were owned by a series of well-known and generally well-regarded property managers in whom Jimmy owned shares. Plumbing that didn't work, elevators that didn't work, an absentee doorman in a building where all the tenants went together to force the property manager to hire new doormen on a twenty-four-hour basis. Nothing really hostile. Fairly vanilla, all things considered. You'd have thought he might have offended somebody at some point. At least it seemed logical, knowing that he died from a bullet to the forehead.

Entirely different picture when I looked up Eddie Hall. He seemed to poke at hornets' nests pretty regularly. He went after the public housing authority, the union that represents corrections officers at Rikers Island, the MTA lines that were voted "least dependable" or "dirtiest" by the Straphangers Coalition. He regularly criticized the mayor, the Speaker of the City Council, and even the District Attorney, especially when there were accusations of police brutality against people of color.

Hall was being sued by numerous nonprofits and conservative political groups seeking to force disclosure of his election fund-raising records, and separately seeking to force an audit of a charity where he was active on the Board of Trustees, alleging that there were expenditures that were instances of corruption. That charity provided homes and education for street kids who had run away from home in other parts of the United States. Nobody accused Hall of pocketing anything, just alleging that his oversight was inadequate or that he overlooked improprieties.

He had been paid large honoraria by some New York City business icons in the investment banking business for conducting sensitivity training seminars with an emphasis on people of color, people whose sexual orientation made them targets of what might be called bullying, and on how to deal with women in the workplace without feeling like you were walking on eggs. His taxes had not been published, and there were newspaper allegations he was taking home six-figure speaking fees in years when there were no elections. His relationships with a variety of largely African-American churches were questioned by lawyers for several alt-right and conservative PACs. Were there inappropriate or illegal contributions being made? And from the left, a group of animal activists accused him of animal cruelty because he wore a fur collar on his topcoat, a shearling hat and what looked like ostrich boots. Some fairly scabrous accusations, but nothing you wouldn't imagine an up-and-coming politician being taunted by.

I decided to have a cocktail and make something simple for dinner—pesto sauce in the blender with unmeasured quantities of fresh basil, pine nuts and blanched almonds, garlic, lots of olive oil and a handful of grated parmesan cheese. The hard part for me is getting the blender to grab it all and make it into a sauce, because the basil is too lightweight and sits on top of the maelstrom below, so I have to push it down with a wooden spoon without getting wood splinters in the sauce which is not as easy as you might think.

Anyway, it's fast. All you have to do is boil some pasta in salted water then toss it, preferably with some cherry tomatoes cut in half, and the almost gritty, oily pesto sauce spreads spottily over the pasta. In my preference, I used medium shells because the shells pick up the olive oil and pesto sauce. I took my plate into the living room and turned on the big-screen television to Channel 7. My favorite news is ABC. Why? No particular reason, just that the anchors are familiar and they seem like okay dinner companions.

There was a breaking news insert that started with a visual of candles in glass canisters crowded together on a sidewalk. I never see a video of a makeshift vigil that I don't remember when Princess Diana was killed. The spontaneously built and constantly growing mountain of flowers, balloons, cards and candles outside Kensington Palace was as memorable in its way as her famous wedding at St Paul's Cathedral in 1981.

In this case, it was a pop-up vigil for Eddie Hall, and it was outside City Hall, probably because he ran for the Council and people thought he was going to run again. Apparently, there were several hundred people there, and a much bigger crowd was materializing the way that steam fills a bathroom when the shower is on.

I sent an email to Ruth that I was heading for the City Hall subway stop. Then I took off for the 7-train at Vernon-Jackson, a short three-block walk from the front door of my building. Once on the train it was one stop to Grand Central, then a quick transfer to the 4 or 5 downtown. I grabbed a 4-express, which stopped at 14th Street, then at City Hall. If I had stayed aboard it would have stopped at Fulton Street then at Wall Street in front of Trinity Church on Broadway. But I got off at City Hall/Brooklyn Bridge and headed up to the street. The crowd was taking up the entire sidewalk in Steve Flanders Square at the fence marking the front yard of City Hall.

The Flanders that the Square is named after was a journalist who had a heart attack on his way to a City Hall press conference, and in the way of New York, his sudden death earned him a place on the map. It was hard to tell how many people were there because it was crowded, but it looked like more than a few hundred, and Steve Flanders Avenue on the other side of the Square was totally blocked by mostly youngish people carrying votive candles and, in some cases, bouquets of flowers that clearly came from a corner deli someplace. It was not quiet, but it was not loud. There were vans from all the major television stations and CNN, and doubtless reporters asking people rude questions about how they felt.

I heard Ruth's voice behind me someplace, but could not see her. I stood as tall as possible, and waved my arms over my head, which, judging from the fact that I could touch the ceiling of my apartment, meant the tip-top of my reach was nearly eight feet. Soon she was pushing her way through the crowd and I could see her plaid jacket in a distinctive Chanel pattern. Hug, hug, Kiss, kiss.

I asked a tall young man who was standing near me why he was there.

"We're all here to show our support. He's gonna be the next mayor of New York," he said.

"You mean Eddie Hall?"

He nodded.

"You a fan of his?"

He nodded.

"You know he was going to marry his boyfriend in a month, before he started campaigning for a seat on the City Council?

He nodded. "So?"

"So, nothing." I vamped for time. "I just wonder why he was on the Thruway going north."

"He was headed for a liberal conference in Cooperstown, or at least that was what they said on the news. Some kind of annual retreat sponsored by some rich hedge fund managers. Everybody knew that. Lots of us were on the e-mail list for the wrap-up report on that."

"Lots of who were on the email list?"

"You a cop?"

I shook my head and answered, "No, I am not a cop, but I was at the scene of the crime completely by accident."

"You mean you saw what happened?"

"Unfortunately. I was about a mile back when it happened. I saw Mr. Hall's car, which was a red Mustang, pull off the Thruway and onto the grass. As I got closer, I pulled off behind him to see if I could help."

Ruth was nodding aggressively.

The tall kid leaned over and whispered to someone next to him. That whisper went viral and soon there were young people of all sizes, colors and economic strata facing me and staring at me.

"And what were you doing when Eddie was hurt?" a youngish blonde asked without seeming unfriendly.

"Well, we were driving up the Thruway, I'd say about a mile behind the car it turned out Eddie Hall was driving. My friend Ruth," and I gestured to Ruth, "and I were looking for a place in the Catskills where we could scatter her husband's ashes."

The blonde looked down as if in sympathy, but didn't pause. "And you are?" she said, apparently to Ruth, without looking up.

"I'm Hugo Miller," I pre-empted Ruth. "I'm mostly retired, but with an interest in solving crimes. I live in Long Island City."

"An interest in crime solving?" she repeated. "Really? Like Sherlock Holmes?"

"Yes, not a cop, but also not like Sherlock Holmes. Ruth and I have worked with the police on a couple of difficult homicide cases. We're volunteers, I guess, but for sure not cops."

Ruth spoke up. "My husband passed in the spring, and I haven't been able to figure out what to do with his ashes. I thought maybe in the mountains, I don't know. He was at Woodstock in 1967, so I thought maybe someplace around there."

I diverted my look to her, wondering if she was going to break down. Not gonna happen.

"So, do you know Eddie?" the tall kid asked me.

"I didn't have the pleasure, unfortunately. I am his kind of voter politically, for whatever that matters. Unrepentant liberal. I just don't live in Brooklyn so I'm not in his council district. I'm in Long Island City. I happened to be the first car on the scene after he pulled off the road. I stopped on the shoulder about half a football field behind him and started to try and help, but the paramedics got there before I got to the car. I thought he had a blow-out, to tell you the truth."

"Did you know Jimmy?"

"Jimmy?"

"Van Gelsen."

I shook my head. "I didn't know either one of them. I knew Eddie Hall's name from the newspaper, but I've never met him."

Ruth looked up. "I did. I knew him. Jimmy, that is. Jimmy van Gelsen was a member of the Opera League for years, and I saw him most Monday nights during the Met season. My husband was a real fan. And Jimmy was like an encyclopedia about opera. Ask him a question, and he knew the answer. Amazing."

"I knew that," a young man of medium height said, pushing into the conversation. "I'm an opera fan, and he used to let me find a seat in the Dress Circle when I bought a standing room ticket."

The kid was Mediterranean-looking, curly black hair, square jaw, slight olive cast to his skin. Big, big eyes. Smile.

"Hi," I said. "I'm Hugo." I held my hand out.

"Enzo," he said. "Actually Vincenzo, but everybody just calls me Enzo. It's better than Vinnie."

"You live in Park Slope?" I asked.

"Nah," he said, "Flatbush, but Jimmy was a hero to a lot of people like me."

"Like you? Italian?"

"Like me. Gay," he paused, "Gay and also Italian, yup."

"You ever hear any pushback about Eddie Hall with Jimmy's friends?"

"You a cop?"

"Nope."

"Just nosy?" He grinned friendly-like, and put his hand on my shoulder.

"I guess I'm just nosy, yeah. I hate it when somebody who is trying to do good gets in the way of a bulldozer. Makes it look like the motivation was maybe race or politics. Doesn't belong in New York, even though it happens. And I happened to be there almost when it happened."

"You're talking about Eddie then. Jimmy liked Black guys, if that's what you're asking me," he said. "He liked to hang out with Black guys, particularly artists and musicians. There's that place on the west side, Chez Josephine, where he used to hang out. Lots of famous jazz musicians playing piano there for free. And he was really a good guy, helped people, couldn't say no when somebody asked him for help. He volunteered everyplace. Shit, man, he ran the coffee bar at Housing Works for years, and I bet the coffee bar there makes more money than they make selling those used books."

"This seems pretty peaceful. I see some cops but no protestors."

"This is a vigil, not a political rally. We just want Eddie to get well."

Almost timed to his comment, there was a loud roar from the west side of the little park we were standing in, in front of City Hall. There were a handful of scruffy-looking men, mostly with beards, and carrying tiki torches that were lighted, of all things. A torch-lit protest outside City Hall?

"Blood and soil!" they were chanting. Police with tall, clear plastic shields formed a blockade to keep them out of Steve Flanders Square. Television reporters charged over toward Broadway, where the torches were, like neodymium magnets migrating toward a refrigerator door.

Ruth recoiled. "*Blut und Boden*," she said very, very softly.

"What?"

"Blood and soil. It's a Nazi slogan. God, Charlottesville comes to City Hall."

One by one the torches were doused or put out as the police formed a ring around the handful of protesters and took them into custody. Soon they were in vans headed for One Police Plaza, and nothing but a scary memory to us in Flanders Square. But it put a new energy into the crowd, and it seemed for a moment that the crowd would march over to Zuccotti Park, which had become a symbol of liberal protest during the 'Occupy Wall Street' demonstrations back in 2011. But just as quickly the crowd settled back down to the makeshift eulogies and occasional tears that were more appropriate to the situation.

Ruth and I headed to the subway and hopped on a 4-train uptown. I suggested if she wanted, we could go to Tournesol, a fine French restaurant in Long Island City, for a bite. She agreed and I texted Gabriele to see if he wanted to join us. He did.

Chapter Five

There is no place to wait for a table at Tournesol. It's tiny to begin with, and the bar, such as it is, is in the middle of the space instead of at the front door. So, if there is no open table, you just hang out wherever there is room, frequently basically offering your backside to someone having dinner. It's a testament to the food, which is beyond excellent, that people put up with it. The tables are crammed together like little cafes on the Left Bank, and the wait-staff are all native French speakers. If you like duck, you're gonna like Tournesol, which is the French word for 'sunflower'.

It's an odd thing when the three of us get together in a situation like this. We're like a small pack of dogs following a scent. I'm mostly retired, although I still go in to the office at times to show my name, since it's on the door. Ruth is a widow now, very socially active and influential in politics, but also a little at loose ends. Gabriele is different, he and his cousin have a successful restaurant and he works there most of the time. He's the guy in a tuxedo who makes you think he remembers you from the last time you were there. He likes the chase too, and he says he is in love with me, of all people.

Anyway, we're like kids on Christmas Eve, that kind of excitement. Can we cross the finish line before Mike di Saronno, our police detective friend, does?

As you might expect, Gabriele is very curious about food at other people's restaurants. And he usually gets comped wherever he goes and sometimes gets us comped too, wow. He wanted the *lapin*, rabbit, roasted and served with morel mushrooms and a brown sauce, wild rice and bright orange carrots steamed in orange juice. Ruth has the discipline to try something different whenever she has a chance, and opted for wild boar with Lyonnaise potatoes and *haricots verts*. Me? I'm like a kid. I want what I know I like, and at Tournesol it's a toss-up between duck confit and roast chicken. This time it was the chicken with perfect fries and a side salad of arugula and tomatoes with vinaigrette. We had a bottle of Domaine La Garrigue Vacqueyras, a wine from the Rhone area, sometimes considered a little brother of Chateauneuf du Pape and cheaper, which is also a treat.

"I think we have a road trip in front of us."

Ruth and Gabriele looked up and said nothing.

"Atlantic City. We need to find out what we can about the guy in the silver Bentley. Or at least about the Bentley itself."

"You know," Ruth said, "I barely saw it. Glad you did. Didn't Mike say they found it up the road someplace and repatriated it back to some casino?"

"I never been in Bentley," Gabriele said, with a Christmas smile like a kid with a new bicycle.

"Since there are three of us, we can't go in my old Jaguar. I think we should take one of those Chinese gambling buses. Would be interesting, not to mention cheap."

"What Chinese gambling buses?" Ruth reacted like I said something in Greek.

"No, I'm serious. There are buses that leave from Chinatown every morning, and the round trip to Atlantic City is like twelve dollars. Mostly Chinese people. You know they have a reputation for being gamblers. No idea if it is true, but the buses are for real."

Ruth did a slow burn from me to Gabriele, who was smiling and paying attention, and back to me.

"Not."

"Well, we can't fit in my car."

"So, we'll go halfsies and rent an Enterprise car. That way we can speak English, won't have to smell lo-mein and garlic all the way to Atlantic City, and we can come back whenever we find out what we want to know."

"I…"

Ruth held her hand up like a traffic cop blocking cars. "I don't gamble, in case I never mentioned it."

Gabriele looked at me, smile unchanged.

"Okay," I said. "Enterprise works. I think there's a pick-up place in the west 50s, should be easy. I need to talk to Mike di Saronno and see if he can give us a name in the Atlantic City PD to talk to."

Gabriele dug into his rabbit with gusto. Ruth stared at the wild boar when it was put in front of her, sniffing it carefully. She picked up a fork and poked at the meat as though it might move or scurry off the plate.

"Trying to wake it up?"

She rolled her eyes at me, indicating that my remark was not worth answering then she cut a tiny piece of the meat and tried it. Smile. "It's kinda gamey but good."

"Southern Europeans are all gaga about wild boar. I don't eat red meat, so I have never tasted it, but they say it tastes a lot like pork. When I was a kid, my mom would have said it tastes like chicken. She said everything tasted like chicken, including swordfish."

I pulled out my phone and punched up Enterprise. They did have a sedan available for the next morning, so I set up a pickup for ten, intending to leave after rush hour. I forwarded the confirmation to Ruth and Gabriele. "You owe me forty bucks plus half the gas when I fill it up."

The Vacqueyras was spectacular, and the roast chicken was falling apart, just the way I like it. The fries were crisp on the outside and juicy on the inside. I think the key is keeping the fries frozen until they hit the hot fat in the deep fryer.

"I stay with you tonight," Gabriele announced. "Brooklyn too far."

I nodded and waved for the check. When the waiter dropped it off, Gabriele grabbed it, put his business card in the folder, handed it back.

Sure enough, it was comped.

Gabriele and I walked Ruth to the Vernon-Jackson subway station where she could get to Grand Central in a single stop, with a trip of about four minutes. Knowing her, she would probably walk from Grand Central to her apartment at 60th Street and Park Avenue then we walked back to my apartment, where the lights of Manhattan virtually made it possible to read. Well, not quite, but they were pretty.

I did turn on the lamps in the living room and poured us each a small snifter of calvados, which is a brandy that is made from apples in Normandy. Tastes like most brandies but if you concentrate, you can taste the apple in it. Heavenly bouquet.

Gabriele sat next to me instead of at the other end of the couch like most people would do, and leaned up against me as he sipped a bit at the snifter. I put my arm along the top of the couch and he snuggled in. I had long ago become used to sitting that way with him.

For Gabriele it was a romantic experience. For me, it makes me feel closer to being a whole person, like having my son with me. A gay son, yes. But who the fuck cares? A son. I actually have a son who lives in California, and who is younger than Gabriele. Not sure how old Gabriele is really, maybe thirty-seven or so. Johnny is twenty-seven, and I haven't actually laid eyes on him since he graduated from high school, although he dutifully sends photos at Christmas, and I get the occasional email when he gets around to writing. I respond quickly, but I have been so little a father to him since his mom and I parted ways that I feel like I don't have any right to try to get to know him again. One of these days I need to fly out to California, book into a hotel near where they live, and invite him to dinner with his girlfriend or whoever he wants to bring along.

Johnny looks like me. Actually, he looks like my grandfather, but I have been told I look like my grandfather as well. I have pictures of Papa in the hallway and I stare at them sometimes. I can see my mom in my face when I look in the mirror sometimes, but Papa I do not see. Other people do. Any family resemblance that Johnny has makes it painful to see his pictures, but only still pictures.

I am usually happy-go-lucky, independent, seldom lonely, but there are times when the only way to deal with being who I am is to pour another vodka and watch television until I think I can go to sleep. Gabriele is very comforting to me, and I think I am to him. Not ever going to be more than it is right now, and we both understand that, but I am very happy to be his dad, especially when we are both tired and defenseless. He doesn't have a dad. He told me his father died when he was a teenager in Capri.

"I like Eddie Hall," he said. "I like it when he come to Ora di Pranzo, and I always send his table some *contorni,* olives, salami and hard cheese when they sit down. He like me. He smile at me. His skinny White boyfriend smile at me nice. I take them a glass of some new wine sometimes. Something Dante think maybe add to wine list. They like always ask me sit with them, but I don't. Not good for other people eating to see me do that."

I could tell he was tired and that his defenses were down. "Why don't you have a boyfriend?"

"I have boyfriend."

He meant me. I didn't go there. I finished my calvados and stood up. He did too, and put his arms around my neck. "I sleep on couch."

"My bed is big. You sleep with me. I like to listen to you breathing at night."

When I woke up in the middle of the night to pee, he was sprawled on the other side of the bed, with his leg almost hanging off the edge. He didn't move.

Honestly, I sleep better when he's there. I never asked him if it is the same for him, but I think it is.

When I woke up again, it was light outside and he wasn't there. I could hear some rattling in the kitchen. He was making coffee. I staggered out in my shorts and t-shirt, pushing my thinning hair to the side with my fingers to keep it from being in a downward icicle shape on my forehead.

"So, you are a fan of Eddie Hall?"

He nodded. "Why nice man like Eddie have to get in big car crash? And boyfriend shot?"

"That's what we'd all like to know." I stretched and could almost hear joints cracking. *God I'm getting old, but it feels so good to stretch.* "I guess we're thinking it might have had something to do with politics, but Jesus, if they start killing all the liberals in New York, we'll end up being the population of Salt Lake City."

He was smiling, holding a mug of black coffee out to me. I took it. It was very hot, so I sipped at it only gingerly. As it cooled, I started to gulp it down. Caffeine. Spark plugs for the brain.

"Bathroom's yours," I said. "Clean towel on the rack. The red one." One of my many obsessive-compulsive traits is that I adhere to very strict color arrangements so that I don't have to think about things like sheets and towels. My bedroom is red, white and blue. Period. I like quilts, so there is a patchwork quilt on the bed, a new one, made in China, but it looks hand-stitched. And the towels are either navy blue or bright red. Mix 'em, match 'em. I always have fresh blackberries in the fridge too. They go bad, moldy, very quickly at some times of the year, like summer. The humidity, I guess.

And I always have the same silver candlesticks, my grandmother's silver candlesticks, on the dining table, usually with either a runner or a full tablecloth. It's the way I grew up. I like the table without a tablecloth, but it needs to be refinished, and I never seem to get around to it.

Why am I so attached to things I remember from my childhood? Even with that, I was able to walk away from my own family just because my wife and I were at each other's throats. I can't explain it. I know I will pay for that when that great gettin'-up morning comes. Fare thee well, fare thee well.

I looked at the time. Just after seven AM. I turned on the computer and looked at the confirmation of the Enterprise car. Ten AM pickup, four-door sedan. I rummaged around in the front hall closet and found a duffel bag; black heavy weave, polyester and waterproof. Fine. I threw two clean shirts, a couple of pairs of underwear shorts and black socks, two black t-shirts. I grabbed a pair of jeans and a belt, and a pair of sweatpants that said "Champion" on them. Electric toothbrush and charger, electric razor and a couple of Bic razors just in case. Speedstick deodorant. Aspirin, Dristan, toothpaste, a couple of small traveler-sized bottles of mouthwash.

Gabriele disappeared into the second bathroom. I could hear him singing something while the water was running. He had all the notes to sing Santa Lucia. How remarkable, I thought, to be able to sing a Neapolitan barcarolle in the shower:

Sul mare luccica, l'astro d'argento ... Santa Lucia! Santa Lucia!

He managed a credible high note on the second Santa Lucia, and held it followed by what I would call an impressive mordant sliding down from that note to the conclusion.

I'm satisfied if I can sing one verse of "Turn! Turn! Turn!" or "California Dreamin'" when I'm in the shower, even with the acoustics that make my voice sound better than it possibly could sound in the real world.

"I forgot you could sing like that," I said as he wandered out of the bathroom with the red towel around his waist and thighs.

"At home everybody sing. Everybody have good voice if just sing when you feel good."

He whipped off the towel as he walked by me, revealing his rear end that looked like Greek statuary. I had to smile at the antic, even though he didn't see me do it. The next I saw he was fully dressed, carrying his shoes into the living room with a pair of socks.

"I take some socks and t-shirt from your drawer. Is okay?"

You could probably take a lot more than that and it would be okay. Just being around you makes my day brighter. "Sure," I said, "whatever it takes."

I sent a text message to Ruth that we would be at Enterprise at nine thirty.

She replied with a "gotcha."

Chapter Six

The ride to Atlantic City was humdrum, took about two and a half hours, mostly on I-95. Light traffic. Atlantic City strives to be the Las Vegas of the east coast, but depending on the state of local finances, Atlantic City has as many as seven casinos, versus Las Vegas's forty or fifty. There is an undeniable sense of fun and excitement in Sin City, Nevada, something Atlantic City has never been able to duplicate.

Mike had told me the Bentley was swiped from The Borgata, which arguably is the fanciest of Atlantic City's casino choices. I had booked two rooms easily—most of Atlantic City's visitors are day-trippers who don't stay overnight, and an astonishing number are Asian. Thus, the Chinatown buses, I guess.

I had not been to Atlantic City since I was a child, umpty-ump years back, when we went to see what my dad called the Elephant House. More appropriately called Lucy the Elephant, it is in fact a house that is made to look like a giant-sized elephant. It was built in the 1880s and it's actually not in Atlantic City, it's south of there a mile or so. Anyway, we skipped visiting Lucy and headed straight for The Borgata, an Italian-ish, Venetian-ish hotel and casino that presents a solid glass wall and airport-sized portico that could have been lifted from the Las Vegas Strip, but wasn't. One thing it shared with Las Vegas was the low price of accommodations. The two rooms were well under one hundred dollars each for the night. They were obviously expecting that we would empty our pockets in the casino.

There were in fact three silver Bentleys lined up just past the main entrance, with a liveried attendant seated at a free-standing table on the sidewalk by them. I turned the white Ford over to the valet parking guy, who unloaded our sparse luggage onto a cart, and walked over to the Bentley attendant.

"Pretty fancy cars," I offered with a smile.

"Reserved," he said, not looking up.

"How can I reserve one?"

"Talk to the Front Desk when you check in. The casino boss usually has some people he wants to show a good time."

"They hard to drive?"

"Doesn't matter. You get a driver with them if you get one."

I had figured that, wondered if that was a new thing or whether somebody mugged the driver when they absconded with the Bentley that passed me on the New York Thruway.

I did ask at the Front Desk. The man checking us in looked at my credit card and called a bellman over, asked him to take me to the Bentley desk outside.

The same guy smiled this time, held out his hand to shake. He showed me the interiors, which included a wine cooler stocked with some bottles, and a little fridge with beer in it. "We can stock it with whatever you like," he said. "Where you thinking about going?"

I demurred, just saying I had never ridden in a Bentley.

"Like just a spin around town maybe?"

I shrugged. "I heard somebody took one of these up to Albany a few days back."

"You a cop?"

"Nope, but I read the papers."

"You a reporter?"

"Nope. If I were, I'd be angling for a freebie to get you some publicity."

His face clouded up. "Well, let me know. I'll remember you. I won't forget."

I thought I detected a warning in what he said, but I turned and walked back into the lobby where Gabriele and Ruth were waiting.

"Making friends?" Ruth said quietly.

"Kinda the opposite," I said. "He thinks I'm a bad guy of some kind. Or a potential problem of some kind."

"Leave him to me if we want to make a deal. But frankly I don't have a lot of interest in joy-riding with a big expensive car like that. It's a car, right? Probably very smooth, but mostly it's like a Disney ride, over with pretty fast, and there you are, back to being a peasant again."

I nodded. "He showed me the interior. The windows in the passenger area are all smoked so you can't see in. That's what I recall when one of those raced by us."

Mike di Saronno already told us, Ruth and me, that the Borgata driver had been forced out of the car in Atlantic City itself with the threat of a gun, a gun the driver never saw. He was unharmed when he got back to the hotel where he originated.

The rental, which was intended to be for a couple of hours, was for only one person, who was a passenger. The car would be driven only by the driver employed by the Borgata. According to the identification he used, which was a California Driver's License, his name was William Samuel Smith, and he lived in Irvine, California. There was no such person when Mike's department checked, and the ID was declared by the California DMV to be a forgery, based on the absence of a hologram that was standard on all real licenses.

The driver described the thief as about forty or forty-five, six feet tall with black hair, wearing a baseball type cap with no team ID on it. Could have been White or Mediterranean. Not African-American or East Indian. Probably not Asian—too tall and maybe a little portly, or with a beer belly. He wore very large sunglasses that were of a type that fit over a normal pair of vision-correcting glasses. The driver never saw the thief's eyes or the bridge of his nose. He tried working with a police department artist, but was unable to come up with much of a portrait, nothing that would help identify a specific person.

Gabriele and I went to the room we were sharing, and Ruth checked out her digs. We agreed to meet back downstairs at the B Bar. It suffered from a bad case of gigantism, as gambling casinos tend to do. The best bars have some intimacy to them, but there was no intention at B Bar of encouraging people to relax and enjoy themselves as people do in neighborhood bars. The idea was to give them something to drink, cheap, then make them uncomfortable enough that they want to leave.

The three of us took adjoining seats at the bar. I ordered my traditional dirty Tito's vodka straight up with olives. Ruth made that two. They slapped down some potato chips and a small bowl of pretzels.

Gabriele wanted a glass of Chianti. He settled for a glass of cabernet sauvignon from California, and wrinkled his nose when he tasted it.

"I don't know why I thought we needed to come here," I said as apologetically as I could. "We're not going to learn anything, and basically nothing happened here anyway. The guy grabbed a car, headed north, pushed Eddie Hall off the road, maybe by accident because he was going so fast, and dumped the car at the next exit. We should have gone to Catskill or wherever the Bentley was retrieved."

Ruth stared at her vodka. "It's not like we took Advanced Detection 101, y'know. Don't be so hard on yourself. The vodka is fine, even if the red wine selection doesn't please somebody's palate."

I texted Mike. *Any prints from Bentley?*

Yeah, a lot. Nothing helpful.

Anybody see the guy?

Not so far, but second-story security video maybe him, no face.

"I need to do some online research." I was thinking about my tablet-sized Surface Pro upstairs in my duffel bag.

"Gotcha," Ruth said, and pulled an iPad out of her handbag. "Whatcha want?"

"Google Eddie Hall or Edward R Hall."

She did. "Lotta hits. Two just in the last few minutes."

"Really? Mind if I look?"

She handed the device to me. There were two hits that looked like almost the same hit, one from Idaho, the other from Virginia, little towns. I clicked through to the Virginia one. Hostile. *You will not replace us. Jews will not replace us. Make America great again. Give us back our America.* Then a rant about defending against *n****rs killing patriots.*

"This is strong stuff." I handed it back to her.

Ruth is normally pale, but she looked like the blood was draining out of her face as she read.

I put my arm around her shoulder. "Earth to Ruth. You okay, sweetie?"

"How can I be okay reading this crap?"

"Let's go up to my room, and I'm gonna check to see if this is just isolated crap, or whether there's a lot of it. Good God, man, Eddie almost died! Why all this?"

The three of us went upstairs and I hauled out my Surface Pro. It had a full charge, but I plugged it in anyway, signed onto the Wi-Fi service that was included in the room rate.

"If you use that people can see what you're writing," Ruth said.

"Not planning to write anything on public Wi-Fi."

So, it wasn't just the two hits. There were several that popped up in the time since I read the Virginia piece, which seemed to be from a blog that was named *AmericaFirst767676*. No names. Most of the new ones seemed to be cutting and pasting, or just sharing the Virginia piece. The Idaho piece was slightly different, but not by a lot, like two children of the same parents.

I called Mike.

"Yo, Hugo."

"Hey, Mike. I'm looking at some pieces online that are saying they are about Eddie Hall. Very strong language, very hostile. Have you seen them?"

He was looking at several himself. One of the guys in the precinct had sent him a link, and he was reading through several of them. Mostly the same.

"Have you seen the one from AmericaFirst767676?"

He had.

"Did anyone question those skinheads that tried to start a protest with their tiki torches at the memorial for Eddie Hall outside City Hall a couple of nights back?"

Mike said the protesters disbanded peacefully. Their IDs were copied on smartphones, but no arrests, nobody questioned. "They didn't actually cause any trouble. At least that's what I was told."

"We were there. They were like chanting 'blood and soil'. That's a Nazi thing from the 1930s."

"But I guess they stopped and disbanded when the cops told them to."

"The chanting did stop," I said. "I thought it was because the SWATs arrested them. It looked like somebody was taken off in a van. I thought it was them."

"I was told no arrests."

"But you have the IDs?"

"I don't. No."

"Who does?"

"Dunno. State Police maybe. Feds?" He said he would look into it and let me know. "Can't give you their names, even if I find the IDs. No arrests. Privacy."

"What happened to the old days when you could just deputize a posse and bring them inside like that?"

"You mean like back in the days when America was still great?"

"You blue-state liberals are all alike."

I imagined him chuckling. "Hey listen, Mike, we're gonna be back tomorrow morning. I think I read that there is going to be a prayer vigil for Eddie Hall tomorrow, and we should probably be there. I presume you will be too?"

"Probably. I never got why you ran off to Atlantic City. I didn't think you were a gambler."

"I'm not a gambler. When I was younger, I liked to drink and hang out at a loud craps table, but my experience is that gambling is usually a tipsy few hours that might as well be spent burning dollar bills. I wanted to see the Borgata, not to mention the Bentley.

"Turns out they have a bunch of Bentleys. I saw three, all identical to my eye, and again to me, not a professional, identical to the one that raced past me and that you found up the road a bit after the shooting. If it was up to me, I would have had a bunch of different middle-aged crazy cars instead of a conga line of silver Bentleys. Goes to show you. Mostly a no-charge perk for high-rollers, I think.

"Makes it seem more like Vegas maybe? All stocked with booze or 'whatever you want'. I guess that proves that whatever happens in Jersey stays in Jersey. No idea how or why whoever got the car here, got it or why nobody sent the cops after whoever it was when the driver walked back to the hotel after being thrown out of the car. But nothing to be done here. The ID the guy gave them was fake, apparently, but you know that already."

"So, I'll see you at the prayer vigil for Eddie Hall tomorrow? You know it's going to be outdoors, right?"

44

I told him that I read it was going to be at the Bandshell in Prospect Park. He confirmed that.

"My guys and I will be close to the front so we can see who shows up. There are going to be several speakers. I just got a bulletin that Eddie is out of ICU and stable, expected to recover."

"Later, 'gator."

Chapter Seven

The next day, a Saturday, was warm and muggy with a low layer of clouds that obscured the top of the Chrysler Building from my windows in Long Island City. I rousted Gabriele and Ruth and hit the road by seven AM, against the traffic, with clear lanes in front of us almost all the way to the Lincoln Tunnel. I turned in the Enterprise car at nine forty-five and took an Uber home, after putting Ruth into the first Uber to arrive. She was grumpy.

Gabriele disappeared into the subway. It's not difficult to get to Brooklyn Heights, where he lives in a beautiful full-floor flat in a nineteenth-century townhome on the famous Brooklyn Heights Promenade.

I decided not to wear a suit to the prayer vigil. It would make me look like a cop or a foreigner, but I decided to dress in dark colors, which comes naturally to the New Yorker in me anyway. So, I put on a pair of black corduroy jeans and an untucked, charcoal gray short-sleeved shirt. I almost always wear a baseball cap, never with a team insignia. Learned about that the hard way. I have an almost-black cap with a painted horse-like image on the front that I bought in a national park in New Mexico. Place where there were cliff dwellings called Bandelier National Monument. My favorite cap. I tucked my smartphone into my left front pants pocket so I could find Ruth and Gabriele when I got to Prospect Park.

I took the G train from a stop about six city blocks from my apartment, direct to the Prospect Park West/15th Street station, which is about a seven-minute walk from the Bandshell. I took an umbrella because it looked like the sky might open up at some point.

When I got there, it was easy to find Gabriele because he was hanging on the sidewalk approaching the Bandshell and he was looking for me. So, he just appeared. Ruth was a little more difficult, but she was on her phone saying that she was standing under a tall oak tree right near where the footpath crossed West Drive near the 15th Street subway station.

She too decided to dress in somber colors, which for her meant a black-and-white classic Chanel jacket and black slacks, with a solid black baseball cap that had 'Hermes' on the back where the adjustable strap is. Kiss-kiss.

There was a fairly large crowd assembling. Unscientifically, it looked like there were more people of color than Whites, but there was no way to know for sure, because I could only see the people who were nearby. A lot of people were carrying a flower of some kind—lots of roses, but some carnations. Some were carrying votive candles not yet lighted. There was a choir on the bandshell stage in royal blue choir robes, singing and swaying, with a choir director facing them, back to the audience.

And He will raise you up on eagles' wings / Bear you on the breath of dawn / Make you to shine like the sun / And hold you in the palm of His hand.

Clearly there were going to be speakers, because there was a podium with microphones and big speakers on both side of the stage. There were what looked like several hundred or a couple of thousand folding chairs arranged in amphitheater rows in front of the stage, but most of the crowd had brought folding chairs, towels, blankets or tarps and were sitting on the grass behind the more traditional seating. I had never been there for a concert, but it was obvious that the seating was ad hoc, depending on the situation. There were a lot of people, and an area up against the stage where many people were putting bouquets, some stuffed animals, some votive candles—hard to tell if they were lighted because it was still daylight.

The choir finished their set and exited, and a near-twin group appeared in red choir gowns, and began singing some Wesleyan hymns. Opening with a rousing version of one of the best-known Methodist hymns, "Christ the Lord is risen today, halleluiah!" That got a lot of people clapping in unison, and a man in a dark suit and tie approached the podium. I didn't recognize him, but we were standing way back.

The PA system wasn't working well, so it was hard to hear what he was saying, but I heard Edward Hall's name. "We are gathered here to pray for the full recovery of our friend, Eddie Hall, a prominent and much-loved member of our community who was seriously hurt in a car crash. We need you back, Eddie. I am glad to tell everyone here that Eddie is now stable, out of Intensive Care, and expected to recover."

There was a generalized cheer, and the PA system went out, or started to crackle.

There was a commotion behind us, and as I turned, there was a snaking line of men wearing black, walking two-by-two on the footpath to the Bandshell, carrying lighted tiki torches. They were chanting something, and waving flags and banners. The first ones were carrying what looked like Crusader flags with a "Deus Vult" cross in red; basically a plus sign with a cross-bar at the end of all four legs, almost forming a square, but without the corners filled in.

White supremacists. Ruth grabbed my upper arm and squeezed. We were not inside the Bandshell area, but were standing under some trees closer to the West Drive where cars were transiting the park. Ruth and Gabriele started shooting videos with their smartphones. I started looking around to see where the escape routes would be.

There were sirens from several directions, and a swarm of riot-dressed police appeared from behind the Bandshell, with clear tall shields and what looked like automatic weapons.

The marchers kept marching forward two-by-two, pushing aside people who were in their way. *What are they trying to do? This is a prayer service for a guy in the hospital.*

Suddenly there were vans pulling up to the curbs of West Drive with satellite dishes on them. Cameramen popped out of them like strippers jumping out of cakes. There were television reporters moving toward the marchers and toward the people who had gathered for the memorial. The sky was turning dark gray.

This can't happen in New York. Where did these goofballs come from?

The marchers were waving a blue flag with a single white star in the middle. There were a couple of Confederate battle flags, the "stars and bars." Were they singing "Dixie?" There was too much noise. People were starting to throw things at them. Bottles, maybe plastic water bottles? Pine cones, probably some rocks. The marchers kept going, and now they were chanting, "You will not replace us." Or maybe it was, "Jews will not replace us."

Ruth and Gabriele were furiously capturing as much as they could on their phones. I grabbed them both and started to move backward.

"We have to get out of here," I said loudly as the noise level was cresting to sound like a full-fledged riot.

People were throwing food: apples, oranges. The marchers were getting pelted with all kinds of missiles, some baseballs it looked like, some animal feces. They kept marching. The police formed a barrier around the back of the Bandshell, and the marchers kept coming.

Bullhorns. "Stop where you are."

The line of marchers halted and started waving their torches, which looked like they had been taken from some old-fashioned Polynesian restaurant someplace.

There was an enormous crack of lightning and a sharp smell in the air, like a gigantic klieg light flashing and exploding, then a deafening overhead clap of thunder almost at the same moment, and it started to rain. Hard.

Ruth and Gabriele were ready to get the hell out of Dodge. We backed away to West Drive then began to jog south toward the 15th Street subway station, dripping. I never even unfurled my umbrella. No point. When we got to the plaza where the subway station was, there was a yellow taxi with his light on.

Thank you, God!

I waved and he blinked his light. We climbed in. I gave him my address in Long Island City and he took off. It actually only took us a couple of minutes to be out of the area, and I asked the driver to turn on 1010 WINS. Sure enough, there were bulletins on a disturbance at the Prospect Park Bandshell. Police had made numerous arrests during a pop-up prayer service for Eddie Hall, who had run for City Council, filed papers to run for congress as a Democrat, but was badly hurt in a car crash north of New York City. No mention of James van Gelsen, sadly.

Ruth continued to clench my upper arm. I put my hand on her hand and she relaxed a bit. She was shaking. I kissed her lightly on the forehead.

"What a nightmare," she whispered.

"Did you get some good video?"

They both nodded without saying anything, started replaying what they had. Ruth stopped shivering.

"Send it to Crowdspark now!"

They both looked questioningly at me.

"Crowdspark. Look it up. It's a crowd-sourced video and photography service. They'll farm it out to the news media, and you might even get paid for it. I did some work with one of the companies they bought. It seems for real to me."

They both started tapping on their phones. Gabriele lighted up. They had accepted his video and would be in touch at his email.

"And you?" I asked Ruth.

"I sent mine to CNN," she said. "I know somebody there. It's better."

I hugged her. "You're the best, sweetie."

Gabriele smiled.

When we got to my apartment, we turned on the television. All the network channels had cameras on site. It looked like the event was over. The rain was pelting down, and reporters were summing up what almost happened. It looked like there was the potential for a riot, but between New York's finest and a sudden downpour, the danger melted.

"Maybe that's my video," Gabriele said, talking more to himself than to us as we flipped through several channels. "Yeah, I think it is. It is. I remember that tree and that guy with the red hat on."

Interesting how his English improves so fast sometimes.

I offered towels to Gabriele and Ruth, and changed my clothes for a dry pair of jeans and a long-sleeved black t-shirt. Better dry than damp. Made a big pot of coffee and the three of us watched television for the better part of an hour, flipping from CNN to Fox to ABC to CBS to NBC to the BBC, which was also carrying some of the story.

"Eddie Hall is better known now than he ever was before," Ruth volunteered. "I frankly wouldn't have been able to tell you who he was before all this. And that's even though I probably met him at some point, since I knew Jimmy van Gelsen."

"The forgotten man, van Gelsen."

I called Mike. They had nearly twenty people in custody, no idea how many were from which group, because they were all being held in Brooklyn. The marchers were all from out of state, and yes, some were from Idaho and some were from Virginia. The ones arrested were not carrying fire-arms, although several had knives in their boots. All were White. There were attorneys who showed up almost immediately to represent them; lawyers Mike said were familiar in political stand-offs. It looked like they would all be out on bail.

"I guess nothing really happened. That lightning and rain seemed to scatter people."

Mike said it apparently took a couple of trees down in Prospect Park, so it had been very close.

"Mother Nature is very effective when she decides to be. Thank God this time. It could have been bad."

Ruth called a friend, apparently from the Opera League, and asked if there had been any news about Jimmy van Gelsen's funeral. Yes, it was that afternoon at Grace Episcopal in Brooklyn Heights on Hicks Street. We decided to go.

I changed yet again, put on a navy tropical worsted suit with a dark blue tie and a white shirt. Gabriele asked if he could use one of my shirts. I said yes. He picked out a yellowish shirt and a basket-weave dark blue tie. Of course, he looked spectacular, as always. My jackets don't fit him, too long, so he put on a dark blue cotton sweater, rolled the sleeves up a little, and looked like he was ready for a photo shoot.

We hopped on the 7-train to Times Square and transferred to a Brooklyn-bound R train. From there it was about twenty-five minutes to get to the Borough Hall station in Brooklyn Heights.

We had time to eat. Gabriele showed us to the Heights Café, where we sat at the bar. Everybody knew Gabriele, kiss-kiss, hug-hug. It was a couple of blocks from his apartment, and people knew Ora di Pranzo. Celebrity sits well on Gabriele, who has a smile like a lighthouse beam. I had huevos rancheros from the Saturday brunch menu and a screwdriver with a double shot of vodka to combat the jitters that I get when the adrenalin wears off. Of course, it was comped.

"You ought to marry him," Ruth said to me, gesturing to Gabriele.

"Too young," I said, smiling at Gabriele, who was paying attention. "My son's age."

"Trophy husband," she said. "If you won't, I will." Gabriele put his arm around my shoulder to indicate his choice. She smiled in a way that indicated she was pleased, not just polite. Such a pretty smile, and it's never going to happen between Ruth and me, I was thinking.

"You could get married at Grace Church," she said. "I went to a same-sex wedding there a couple of years back. Nice. Church is gorgeous. They spent a lot of money renovating it, I think. Look at the ceiling when we go in."

I didn't look back at her, just took a bite of my eggs and salsa, and threw back another swallow of coffee. Topic closed.

When the doors were opened, we walked into the church with a group of maybe forty or fifty people who were waiting in the narthex. There was a cloth-draped coffin at the communion rail. The pall had a gold cross with the top facing the altar, on a background of white. There were two acolytes holding lighted candlesticks. There were flowers on the altar but none on the coffin.

People we assumed were close friends and relatives took their places in the first three rows. Some were dressed 'for church'. Others were casual, but the women had their heads covered and the men had taken their caps and hats off. As people took their seats, the organ began to intone an improvised introduction that after a couple of minutes morphed to the Faure setting of *In Paradisum*.

A small group of choristers filed onto the right side of the altar and sang the sweet, calm setting that starts and is dominated by the purest of treble voices, written to be for boy sopranos, but in this case sung by female sopranos who managed to erase all the natural vibrato from their voices as the ethereal beauty of the deeply calming and preternaturally beautiful music sailed higher and higher then settled down to a long held mid-voice note in unison.

Into paradise may the angels lead you. / At your coming may the martyrs receive you, / and bring you into the holy city Jerusalem

The funeral service celebrates the resurrection. Because Jesus was raised from the dead, all shall be raised. "Neither death, not life, nor angels, nor principalities, nor powers, will separate us from the love of God in Christ Jesus our Lord." This does not ignore grief. Jesus himself wept at the grave of his friend.

The choir sang the more familiar *Agnus Dei,* and there were few dry eyes in the church as the clergy processed in.

The familiar music filled the brilliantly lighted nave with its impossibly beautiful gilt and blue gothic revival ceiling, and I began to realize that although many hundreds or even thousands gathered to celebrate and pray for Eddie Hall's recovery at Prospect Park before the marchers and the rain put an end to things, Jimmy van Gelsen was getting the kind of send-off that people would want for themselves. You could almost see van Gelsen's soul rising like a dove in a light shaft up toward heaven.

There were no eulogies, just readings from the Old and New Testaments, in the ringing, comforting language of the King James Bible.

An usher put a basket of white roses on a table at the foot of the coffin. After a general blessing, and a sprinkle of holy water on the congregation and the coffin, the pall was removed, and the congregation filed forward, each picking up one rose and placing it on the coffin. After placing the roses, the congregants filed out, one by one. I was the last to leave, and thought to myself, *You chose the best part, Jimmy. You are with God and I can only hope to be there with you some day.*

There was a sign in the narthex saying that there were refreshments in the Parish Hall, and that interment would be in a cemetery in Westchester County and would be attended only by family members.

I whispered to Ruth and Gabriele that I was buying and we headed back to the Heights Café.

As we walked out of the church, Gabriele leaned into me. "I do this for you on some sad day," he said.

I hugged him hard and looked away since tears were streaming down my cheeks. He handed me a paper napkin from his pants pocket.

"Jimmy wait for Eddie in heaven?" he asked as we walked. "Maybe they hold hands and look down on you and me some day." He looked up at the sun and waved. "Then they know now how I love Hugo Miller."

Chapter Eight

"We basically have nothing," Mike said. "I mean we have some data, but very little that fits together, nothing to go on."

We were sitting in an interrogation room, drinking machine coffee from Styrofoam cups. Oddly, it tasted good. I drained mine.

"The marchers from Prospect Park?"

"What, you mean one of them stole a Bentley, drove up to Orange County, pushed Eddie Hall off the road, then disappeared, only to show up the next morning to shoot Jimmy van Gelsen in the Village?"

"Nah, nothing like that. I just wondered why they planned to show up here when nobody outside New York knows who the crap Eddie Hall is anyway."

"The internet brings us all closer together, I guess," Mike said with a wry look on his face.

"Which one do you think was the target? Or were they both targets?"

"Nothing makes sense. My guess, personally, is that the car crash was its own thing. Nothing to do with the shooting in the Village, and maybe even that was random."

Ruth listened attentively, looking back and forth between Mike and me like she was watching a ping-pong game. Her phone made a popping sound.

"Oh," she said. "That's an alert. Hold on."

She tapped at the phone, then held it up. It said one of the local television stations had an exclusive interview with Eddie Hall from the hospital. Mike stood up and motioned for us to go with him. We went to his office where he turned on the television to Channel 3.

Eddie had a bandage over his nose and both eyes were discolored, but he was wearing a shirt and sitting in a chair, facing a reporter, who introduced the segment by saying that remarkably, Eddie Hall sustained only minor injuries when his car swerved off the Thruway. He had been treated for some contusions and had been monitored for concussion, but was being released from the hospital and was expected to recover completely. The camera focused on Eddie.

"Thanks, Carl," he said. "For those of you who are wondering, yes, I'm a tough bird and I'm going to be okay, but something else has happened in my life that I can't fix. Some of you know that I was intending to marry Jimmy van Gelsen. Jimmy and I have been seeing each other for months, and we decided to tie the knot in the fall. That won't be happening." Eddie looked down and made a snorting sound that sounded like he was crying.

When he looked back up, he said quickly, "Jimmy's dead. Somebody shot him. I won't ever see him again." He turned his head and motioned to someone. A young man stepped up behind him, and the camera pulled back to show the two of them.

"This is Alex, my son. He's been here with me, and I want to tell you he's a rock. He's a young man, still in college, but he's helping me hold myself together, and he'll be coming home with me to help me recover. I have a couple of cracked ribs. That's the worst of it physically." He grabbed Alex's hand and pulled. Alex knelt beside Eddie's chair and hugged his dad.

Alex was not obviously African-American. Eddie looked like he probably was, but not everyone would assume he was.

"Yeah," Eddie said. "He looks like his mom. She's a great woman, his mom, and Matilda, my daughter, she's a great kid too. I want you to know we are a close family. My kids mean everything to me. Their mom, Aurora, and I have a strong relationship even though we have been divorced for several years now."

He turned to Alex and put his arm around the boy, grimacing in what was obviously a painful stretch.

"I'm gonna get through this," he said, "and I'm gonna be the next City Councilman from my district in the great borough of Brooklyn. We gotta lot of work to do for our kids, for our brothers and sisters, and for the people who work and live with us, who pay taxes like us, but who are just shadows in our society because the immigration laws won't let them stand up and be counted." He made a fist and jammed it up in the air. "You can take that to the bank. We're all one family here in New York. Black, White, whoever we are, all one family. One big united family. We're gonna take care of each other, and we don't need to be 'great again' either. We never stopped being great. We're the greatest city in the world."

He looked directly into the camera like a prize-fighter who just won a match in spite of getting beat up. Alex stood up and made the same fist, although he was clearly crying.

"Jimmy," Eddie said, looking up at the ceiling. "I don't know what to do without you, man. Keep your eyes on me from heaven. Stay with me. I need you."

The image went to black. The reporter signed off "from Cortlandt, New York at the New York Presbyterian Hospital in the Hudson Valley."

"Well that was something," Ruth said. "He certainly came out swinging."

"Good looking kid," I said. "Looks like he ought to be a basketball player like his dad. There are all kinds of photos of Eddie shooting hoops on the blacktop courts."

"Interesting about his wife. Good for them that they still have their family."

"She wasn't there for the interview," Mike said. "Maybe that says something."

"Well, she wasn't on camera anyway," Ruth said. "Neither was the girl. Having the son with him might send the right message about masculinity. I wonder as time passes, if they start looking more like they were a few years back, now that van Gelsen is out of the picture. They could be back to a two-parent family. Not like there's a lot of attention paid to City Council elections, but with all this happening, he's gonna have the media all over him. With those neo-Nazis or whatever they were, the ones who were marching and waving goddamn flags, that means somebody on the other side has got some skin in this game too."

"I think we're going to see a lot of Eddie Hall for a while," Mike said.

Ruth was tapping on her phone. "Lotta tweets. Scrolling by very fast."

"Well, I guess we know that it's possible to get a lot done with tweets these days."

Mike said according to the hospital, Eddie was heading for an address in Manhattan, not in Brooklyn. East 65th Street. According to Mike, the address was his ex-wife's home.

"Makes sense," Ruth said. "His son was with him at the hospital. They were married for around twenty years I think, the boy is in college after all. And she has money, so maybe she's willing to help him recuperate. Lots of marriages break up and the partners are still friends. It seems peculiar, since Jimmy van Gelsen was just buried, but maybe she wasn't shocked by that. Who knows? There have been stranger things. Maybe Matilda is a daddy's girl too. I was always my daddy's girl, probably would have been no matter what, I guess."

I was searching around on my phone. "There seems to be a new Eddie Hall website. Or maybe not a new one, but if it's the same one, it has all new graphics." I sent them both a link. "I bet his kids had a hand in this. It's really good-looking, and seems to have some motion to it."

The new domain was covered with poster-type graphics that just said 'Eddie', with a smiling close-up portrait where his eyes were looking straight at the camera, so they seem to follow you as you move around. If those are the political posters they're planning to use, they would be great in subway cars or on TV ads with the candidate always looking straight at you and smiling. There were separate mission statements about pre-K for 3-year-olds in the public schools, about universal health insurance, and about welcoming immigrants. There was a simplified program description about affordable housing. There was a link that said LGBTQ, but nothing was posted there yet.

"Seems pretty clear he's running."

I said I kinda thought he would run for congress instead of City Hall, but maybe there was no district where he could squeeze in without squeezing out somebody who didn't need to be squeezed out. Control of congress seemed to be up for grabs at every election, and the tone of politics seemed to get more strident every time campaigns broke out again.

"No charges from what happened at Prospect Park," Mike said. "Just got an email. Nobody detained. I guess they can thank the rain for keeping people out of the pokey. Maybe some on both sides. You never know who's gonna throw a punch, or a rock, in a situation like that."

I was beginning to feel naked without my tablet at least or preferably my desktop computer. I needed to do more research than I could do on the phone. My fingers are too big, for one thing, for the phone, and if I hit pay dirt, I have a hard time reading and comprehending much beyond the first few lines on the phone.

"You look like you need something," Ruth said.

"I need to go home. I'm feeling like I need to hit the computer and do some pointless searches that might lead me someplace."

Mike stood up and swept his hand toward the door.

"Can I come with you?" Ruth said softly.

"Sure," I said, "but I want Gabriele to help out too. I want to find out more about Eddie and Jimmy, or Eddie after his divorce, or whatever."

She looked puzzled.

"Look, I understand what it's like to get all banged up and feel like you're not in control. I had a DVT about ten years ago, and I thought for sure I was going to be an invalid for the rest of my short life. I'm guessing that's what Eddie feels like and why he needs to go home. For me, I'm twice divorced, remember. The temptation to be cocooned is very nearly irresistible sometimes, but at the last minute I can't do it."

I fought with myself for a minute. "But it's not the best idea, or it wouldn't have been for me. I'm not Eddie Hall, not even close, but I want to understand how Jimmy van Gelsen seems to have just evaporated from who Eddie is today. I think Gabriele will be a big help with that."

"Because he's gay?"

"Not exactly, no. I think everybody is potentially bi at least, maybe gay, just that most people never walk through that door. Some because of morality, some because of taboos, some because being heterosexual is fine for them. Some, like me, because I am deeply pessimistic about change."

I stopped, because I didn't know what I was thinking. "Gabriele has a lot of experiences in society at large that I can't come close to. Besides that, he knew van Gelsen and also remembers Eddie from Ora di Pranzo and seems to have found him attractive. I know Gabriele well enough to feel sure that if he found Eddie attractive, he has found out or figured out a lot about him. It sometimes scares me how much he knows about me. He's a born psychologist, I think. He knows what drives people when he studies them."

She stared at me.

"Yeah, he knows a crazy lot about me. And no, not because of what you're thinking, because that's not going on, what you're imagining. It's because he just figured me out. He knows what I can and can't do, and he knows he can't push me over the line. Is that because I'm not attracted to him? Maybe, but I think it's way more because I have been so fucking burned in my life that it's nearly impossible for me to make even the simplest kinds of commitments."

When we got to my apartment in Long Island City, I went after Aurora Carter Hall online. She seemed like a wild card. They'd been divorced for a while, but she apparently let him move back in with her, at least straight out of the hospital. Maybe he's headed for Prospect Heights day after tomorrow.

So, she seemed to exist mostly as Mrs. Eddie Hall. There was a Wikipedia profile, surprisingly, which seemed due mostly to her charitable activities. She is actually two years older than Eddie, which was a surprise, looking at their pictures together. She has one of those faces, at least in photos, that doesn't seem to age. High cheekbones maybe. Big smile, great sense of style. Kept her hair in an old-fashioned pixie cut, and it actually emphasized her fresh young image.

She was born to an investment banker and an art gallery owner, went to an east side prep school from kindergarten to high school graduation. She studied French and French literature at Wellesley, and had worked on a catalogue of works by Auguste Rodin while interning at the Metropolitan Museum of Art, receiving credit for her work as an assistant on the title page of the catalogue.

She met Eddie Hall at a New Year's Eve party in 1970. She was tall, but he was taller, and they stood out in every glamorous event they attended. They courted for several months, were regularly featured in the society pages and gossip pages. They were married in the Episcopal Church of the Resurrection on East 74th Street in April 1972. Alexander was born about ten months later, and Matilda followed about seven years after that.

They were a social couple, participating in a variety of charities, and always stand-outs at the Metropolitan Museum's Costume Institute Gala.

Alexander was a beautiful Gerber-baby type of toddler, matured into a highly athletic, academically outstanding Trinity School stand-out. Matilda was pretty from birth, darker than her brother, but with shiny, straight brown hair that developed a slight curl when she was in grammar school. Most people would have taken her for Hispanic.

"Kinda bland," Ruth said after we read through the lead articles on Mrs. Hall. "Surprising, because as I look at her, she looks like she has some spark. Like you wouldn't want to get on her bad list."

As we read from the oldest articles to some of the newest about the couple, it seemed, when we compared Eddie's increasing interest in progressive politics, that the couple's nearly fairytale public image began to melt as Eddie began to make more and more speeches then became identified more and more with minority communities. After a couple of years of activism, there were very few photos of the couple in the newspapers, virtually no cases where their names were in lists of attendees at glamorous social gatherings.

"I wonder if that's because as a minority politician, his supporters didn't like that he was married to a White woman, even a rich White woman," Ruth said. "Of course, Eddie's mixed-race too. All you have to do is look at him to know that, and look at his kids."

Never a rabble-rouser, Eddie nevertheless moved fairly quickly left from a basic centrist position that he stuck to as an ADA. As an Assistant District Attorney in Brooklyn, he was constantly in the headlines as a champion of minority citizens, mostly but not exclusively male, who were injured or killed during police actions. But as far as we could find, he never campaigned for anybody, never gave speeches at political rallies. He talked about equal treatment under the law, and prosecuted several high-profile cases that the newspapers characterized as 'police brutality' cases.

After he left the District Attorney's office, he started a talk radio program on an AM station that was moving from soft rock to more news and talk shows. He began to characterize himself as "progressive," which was more generally acceptable than just plain "liberal." He and Aurora moved from the Upper East Side to Park Slope in Brooklyn, still a stylish and expensive neighborhood, but nevertheless a clear separation from his no-politics history and an identification with Brooklyn instead of Manhattan. He ran for City Council in 2012, missed by a hair, losing to an incumbent who was more obviously African-American, and who had the mayor's endorsement.

Then after the election, Aurora quietly moved back to Manhattan, into the 65th Street apartment she had lived in before they married. She never sold it or sublet to anyone, and for the most part it was still fully furnished. Eddie stayed in the co-op in Park Slope. The children started going back and forth, spending every other weekend with Dad, but there was never a hint of any hostility between Eddie and Aurora.

Eddie began a series of interviews on "The Eddie Hall Show" with prominent LGBTQ personalities, including a famous female impersonator, several well-known Broadway actors, male and female, and a parade of doctors and scientists, most of whom were primarily interested in the health and welfare of the very vocal and increasingly politically active LGBTQ community.

Soon after the first few LGBTQ interviews on the radio, Eddie began appearing at fund-raisers for LGBTQ groups such as initially the largest AIDS charity in New York, Gay Men's Health Crisis in Greenwich Village. Very soon after that he expanded to a group of AIDS-focused groups, including Housing Works, where Eddie headed book donation drives several times each year for about a decade. It was apparently at Housing Works that he met Jimmy van Gelsen, who had volunteered there for several years, running the espresso bar. Although Jimmy was clearly gay and clearly comfortable being gay and had been tracked with various men in the newspapers and by gossip-mongers on social media, there was little if any coverage of Eddie with Jimmy, although they apparently began hanging out together, initially because they had similar views of society.

Then one day in 2015 there was a photo of the two men on Page Six in the "Sightings" section. Page Six started out on Page Six of one of the New York tabloids, but grew into a gossip source with tentacles in television, social media and also in print. The photo of "new couple" Eddie and Jimmy showed them sitting next to each other at a banquette at Balthazar, a garish but stylish French bistro on Spring Street in SoHo.

Aurora filed for divorce.

But the silence from the family itself was undisturbed.

Chapter Nine

My cellphone chimed in a pattern that told me it was Gabriele calling. It was eight PM.

"*Ciao bello*. I got a problem here. Eddie Hall is here, and he got a guy here at the bar and they drinking. I no wanna call the cops, but they kinda not acting right."

"You mean they're drunk?"

"Not drunk. But they kissing and people staring. And besides, it look fake."

"C'mon," I said, "This is New York, not Iowa. People aren't shocked by same-sex couples."

"They doing too much, hands all over, people gonna leave."

"Then tell them to cut it out, or put them at a table in the back."

"I help you. Now you help me."

I put on my shoes and headed to Ora di Pranzo the fastest way I knew how, on the subway. When I got there, the couple was ensconced at the bar, with at least two bar stools empty on either side of them. They were putting on a show, and as Gabriele said, it frankly looked staged.

I walked up behind them and put my hand on Eddie's shoulder. "Hey there, Mr. Hall," I said, "I'm Hugo Miller, and we met, more or less, when you got run off the road in Rockland County a few weeks back."

He jerked away from his partner, who didn't seem at all bothered by the sudden intrusion. The guy was younger, White, average looking.

"What do you mean that we met? I don't remember."

"No, you wouldn't. You were unconscious. I was the first person on the scene, but by the time I walked up to your car, the EMTs were already pulling up. You were moaning so I knew you were still alive. I have to say that, although I'm a dyed-in-the-wool Democrat, I didn't recognize you. All I saw was the blood."

That was a mood-stifling conversation if ever there was one, and Eddie wiped his mouth and tapped on his glass to tell the bartender he wanted another drink. He held his hand out to me. "Hugo? Is that what you said?"

"Yeah, Hugo. I'm a friend of Gabriele Cortese, who's a partner in this restaurant. You probably know him." I signaled to Gabriele to come over, which he did.

"I'm sorry we weren't acting more civilized," he said, looking at Gabriele.

"Hey, it's a free country," I said jovially, slapping Eddie on the back. "Mind if I sit here?" I plopped down next to him then leaned over and whispered in his ear. "That show you were putting on was getting a lot of attention. And you weren't doing the restaurant any favors either."

"Good," he said. "I got no secrets." Then he looked down at the bar. "But I wasn't thinking about the place. I just wanted to make it onto the internet or onto Page Six."

"Crissake," I said and handed him my business card. "If that's all you want, just give me a call. I can take care of that."

The company that pays my bills is a specialty public relations agency, specializing in sports, but what the heck? A politician is easy to place too, especially a young, good-looking, queer one.

"This is Billy," Eddie said by way of introducing the young man he was with. "He's an actor."

I tried to look surprised. "So, this was a stunt?"

"Kinda."

"Why? For heaven's sake?"

"Because I want whoever shot Jimmy to take a shot at me. God's truth, Jimmy was the best of the best. I loved him," he said *sotto* voce, but so that Billy and Gabriele could hear it.

I put my arm on his shoulder and signaled to the bartender who started pouring vodka into a shaker with ice. "With you on that one, bro."

I took a drink of the vodka and turned back to Eddie. "Why?"

"Why what?"

"Why decide to put on this act? Why not just do an interview on one of the weekend shows? Or why not talk about it on your radio show?"

"I dunno. It seemed more fitting this way. I made a commitment to Jimmy, and I have a commitment to the gay community. Solidarity, man!" His fist shot up as he said that. A flash went off from somebody's cellphone.

"See?" he said. "People understand."

Gabriele slid into the seat on my other side, and grabbed my arm with both his hands.

"Could be you and me."

"You mean dead like Jimmy?"

He let go. "No, I mean we could be making each other happy."

"It's not the same, my friend. I'm almost twice your age, and I have a lot of mileage on me. You're young and you need a young partner."

We had been over the same turf over and over and over. The unspoken truth was that although I have always been fascinated by Gabriele, love spending time with him and although I considered him my friend, I have no interest in any kind of romantic relationship – no matter male or female. Three strikes, you're out, and I already had two strikes.

I couldn't get the same question out of my mind, though: *Why would somebody want to kill Jimmy van Gelsen? Is money the answer? But there wasn't anything stolen.*

But here was Eddie Hall, looking to make some headlines about his relationship with Jimmy. Page Six? Why?

Because he's running for office, and he wants to establish his credentials with some special-interest groups. LGBTQ is one of those, and gays turn out to vote in big numbers, or so they say. Oh well, in for the kill, as they say.

"Hey, listen, Eddie. From what I know about you, and I read up about you after I happened on the accident where you were hurt, I'm in your camp politically. I have a really good friend who is an excellent fund-raiser, and also a bleeding-heart liberal like you and me. I would love to get together with you and Ruth, that's her name, and see how we can help you either get on the City Council or maybe the State Legislature, or even congress."

He looked at me like my grandfather looked at a heifer he was thinking about buying. I had a fleeting feeling he would check my teeth.

"Billy's welcome to come too," I added with as much enthusiasm as I could muster.

Billy waved at me. "Not political here, just wanted to help out Eddie. We're friends, and, besides, I think he's hot."

I nodded and shrugged. "Well, you'd be welcome either way."

Eddie jerked his head back ever so slightly. Then he held his hand out to me. "Deal," he said, "as long as you can get Mr. Cortese to come along too."

"I know this sounds corny, but Gabriele and Ruth and I are like three musketeers; have been for years."

"You gay?"

"Me? Put me in the 'Undecided' column. Truth is I think I'm just plain too old to start over, but I love Gabriele. I happen to think it's more fatherly, but he thinks it's more gay. Who knows? He may be right. I might as well be gay, but to tell you the truth, I really am attracted to Ruth, who's a widow now, and I know how well we get along, but it might be a toss-up."

He looked doubtful.

"I don't feel like defending my position on the fence, but I think you've been on both sides of this subject, so I have a feeling you know where I stand." It was a gamble.

He stared for a minute, then smiled. "You're okay, man. Hugo, is it? I want you on my side."

Gabriele tightened his grip on my arm with his left hand and picked up his wine glass with his right hand and made a 'Salut!' gesture before taking a big gulp. I did the same with my vodka in the left hand. Eddie toasted us with whatever he was drinking, and Billy joined by downing the dregs of his wine glass.

We traded phone numbers and agreed I would set up a time the next day for us to get together.

"Gotta be at the radio station at two o'clock," he said. "I'm on the air at two thirty, and I need to talk to the guy in the booth, chat a few minutes with my guest, who is a City Councilman from Queens, and do a little prep work."

"What's the subject matter?"

He said they were planning to talk about the new branch of the Queens Public Library that was opening on Center Boulevard in Long Island City. "First time for something like that in Queens in a long time, and kinda big budget too. But we're going to talk about the impact it ought to have on the community, with PS1 just a few blocks away too."

PS1 is a 'branch' of the Museum of Modern Art that was opened in an old unused school in Long Island City when MoMA was remodeling its base in Manhattan. It's a red brick, late-Victorian building that a lot of people find charming, but looks like a prison to me. So old-fashioned that it has separate entrances marked for Boys and Girls. It has been an art space since the 1970's, but officially became part of the MoMA family in about 2000. It gets a quarter of a million visitors a year, according to the numbers they publish. They show a lot of local artists. Great place to spend the shank of an afternoon; the exhibitions never fail to be interesting.

"So, after the show maybe. It could be hard to get the gang together real early."

Deal. Shake. Drink. I kissed Gabriele on the forehead as he smiled wanly, and left. I saw Billy stand up and start gathering his jacket, but Eddie and Gabriele sat where they were. *Good,* I thought. *Eddie thinks Gabriele is hot. That helps.*

Chapter Ten

I listened to the radio show. It was interesting because he had other guests than the Library official. In fact, the guests were Billy and Eddie's kids, Alex and Matilda, both of whom had apparently been on Eddie's show in the past as well. They ended up talking at length about Harry Potter books. The Harry Potter books, as they came out, were devoured by kids all over the world, including the U.S., and were said to be causing a renaissance of reading in elementary, middle-school and even high school kids.

I later found out Aurora was there too but not in the broadcast booth, just observing from the other side of the glass and encouraging the kids in their comments from afar. It seemed to me Alex and Billy were really hitting it off, and I wondered if Alex knew Billy was in some way entangled with his dad.

Ruth pretended to be annoyed that I had made plans for her without asking, but she dropped it quickly. She was interested in Eddie, in the mystery of what happened, and, truth be told, she loves working with me, and she finds Gabriele endlessly interesting. They couldn't be more different, but opposites attract, or so I'm told.

Knowing that Gabriele would need to be at Ora di Pranzo by six or so, I suggested we meet at my apartment in Long Island City at four. That worked. I told Eddie to go to the Vernon-Jackson station on the number seven subway, one stop east of Grand Central. Easy, a two-block walk, no sweat, and very close to the new branch of the Queens Library they had been talking about on the radio.

As it turned out, it was raining cats and dogs, so they arrived shaking their umbrellas and stamping the water off their shoes. I spent most of my life in southern California, and I never fully get used to the fact that it rains in the summer in New York. Summer is bone dry where I grew up.

Beach weather. No humidity. No mosquitoes.

The three of them showed up, including Billy but minus Aurora and Matilda, within a few minutes of each other. I had made a big pot of Darjeeling tea and had a tray of cookies on the dining table. I figured we could just sit and chat, get to know each other. The apartment was a simple floor plan with a large square living room. I had cordoned off about a quarter of it with a dining table that had belonged to my parents, and a low buffet that acted as a room divider. It probably wasn't the best layout that anyone could have come up with, but it worked for me. I like having a dining table. Eating dinner off a coffee table in front of the television doesn't work for me unless there is breaking news that's interesting instead of just plain scary.

It's a little odd having dinner at the dining table by myself. I used to share my old apartment with an old friend, Carl, who finally decided to get married to his longtime girlfriend and moved out, of course. That's when I moved from Manhattan to Long Island City, which is just opposite the United Nations on the East River. Kind of 'honorary' part of Manhattan for us in LIC, but Manhattanites still act as though they need a visa to cross the river. Like they ought to pack a lunch and have a yellow fever shot to go to Queens, except the airports, of course, which are also both in Queens.

I have to admit I was the same way. I went to BAM, the Brooklyn Academy of Music, sometimes if there was absolutely no alternative in order to see something I didn't want to miss, like a fully staged version of an eighteenth-century French opera-ballet by Rameau that had never been performed in North America before. And there is a section of Brooklyn right on the river that has a reputation for being interestingly *avant-garde*, called Williamsburg. I went there a few times to catch hard-to-find acts like the Tiger Lilies, a really weird, slightly nightmarish musical group that sings hilarious ditties that are either shockingly blasphemous or that violate commonly accepted norms for the treatment of naughty children.

Except for the occasional outer-borough adventure such as those, when I lived in Manhattan, I considered it the island at the center of the earth, as most Manhattanites do. I think there's a book by that name, not sure. For sure there is no place else in the western hemisphere that has the quantity and quality of cultural assets and places of sheer beauty all packed together on one small island. Of course, if you go to Rome, you can dwarf Manhattan's cultural assets in a few blocks, but let's be real. Rome's in Italy.

Anyway, I had put a pad down on the table so I could make sure if any tea got spilled it wouldn't spot the teak tabletop then put an old calico tablecloth on, one that had belonged to my grandmother. I went up the street to the deli and bought some flowers and put them on the coffee table, so it looked like someone actually lived there, instead of just renting it furnished.

Eddie lives in Brooklyn, so he only has part of the Manhattan attitude. He used to live in Manhattan, but even he looked around at the apartment and seemed to be surprised to find that otherwise normal, cultured people live in Queens, which, on a scale of acceptability, ranks just above Staten Island.

His stated goal was to run for City Council from Park Slope/Flatbush. The rationale is that it usually only takes just under twenty thousand votes to be elected, primarily because the voter turnout for City Council elections is very slight. In a recent election, for instance, the now-retiring City Councilman for District 40 was re-elected with a vote of about fourteen thousand, capturing sixty percent of the votes cast in the fairly populous district.

Ruth was all about going for something bigger. "You're a very attractive candidate. Lots of reasons," she said. "First, you're not European genetically. I don't know the statistics, but I think that's true of the majority of us, at least downstate in the City and the 'burbs.

"More important, you're a good speaker, a man with a head on your shoulders, and you have an impressive background as an ADA in Brooklyn looking out for the rights of the little guy."

He listened without interrupting but signaled at the end of the discussion that he did not want to spend his life raising money and catering to people who wanted influence in Albany or Washington DC.

"That's why you need a group of people working with you," she said. "Look, I've worked on mayoral campaigns and a couple of congressional campaigns. It's not easy, and yes, there is some pandering to people who can write checks, but mostly you look to the party to help you fund your campaign. After all, the party needs the seats to be filled with Democrats, right?"

He nodded, smiled, and shrugged. "The issues I care about are very local."

It was her turn to shrug. "Like what?"

"Like somebody shot the man I was going to marry on the sidewalk in front of his apartment, and the cops have no leads, no motive, no persons of interest. That wouldn't be so if there were more security cameras deployed. Look at London. They can find any terrorist because they have them all on camera footage. You can't go anyplace in London, at least outdoors, where you're not on camera."

"And Big Brother?" she asked quietly.

"I'm not nearly as worried about Big Brother when it comes to finding murderers, as I am about not finding murderers. That's probably the DA in me. I want to see the bad guys caught and taken off the street, and I want to know who killed Jimmy van Gelsen."

"That's not a platform," she said. "Not even for City Council. You'd be running from Prospect Park in Brooklyn, and Jimmy was killed in Manhattan."

"I believe there are something like nine thousand unsolved murders in Manhattan. That goes back a couple of decades, but it's not like there's a suspect in every death. There are one hundred and fifty or two hundred cold cases every year, and that's a citywide problem." He was getting up a head of steam.

"Just because I have a personal interest as a gay man in the murder of my husband-to-be Jimmy van Gelsen does not make me a dirty bird. I have a history, like you said, of helping to put bad guys away. I can't do that in Albany and I can't do that in Washington DC."

"And," Ruth said quickly, "you can't do it from a seat on the City Council either."

"I don't want to be the DA, and besides the DAs are all good at what they do. They don't need to be replaced by me. But the police and the DAs need support from the mayor and the City Council. I have a radio show that a lot of people listen to, don't forget."

Gabriele raised his hand like a student in a classroom. Eddie nodded toward him. "You're part of what we're doing here. You don't have to ask permission to speak."

"I know Jimmy van Gelsen. He come to Ora di Pranzo often, not live far away, I think. Nice guy. You and Jimmy, you love each other?"

"Of course, we did."

"Not always people get married for love."

He stared at Gabriele.

"You not gay," Gabriele said flatly.

Eddie just stared at him. "Define what you mean by 'gay'. Of course, if I was going to marry a man, I'm gay."

"I'm gay," Gabriele said. "I want have sex with man, now only this man." He pointed to me. "This man not gay either. He not want have sex with me. But if he ask me, I marry him, even without sex. I need this man for live."

I could feel myself flushing, and Ruth was staring a hole through me.

Gabriele never looked at me. He said to Eddie," You and Jimmy, you have sex?"

"I don't see what business that is of yours."

"Good for you. Sex not everything. Many mens love each other but no sex. Like I love Hugo Miller with no sex, and he love me with no sex."

"So, what's your point?"

"You not gay. Is only point. You want help gay, but you not gay. You want find who shoot Jimmy because you love him. But you not gay. Other people will know that, not just me."

"Where did you get so smart?"

"I escort for many years, have sex with men for money. When I come from Italy, I have no money, but I have good body and I like men sex. I make money and I learn many things. Then I meet Hugo Miller and all change because I find what is like to love one man." He looked at me and smiled. "Even man who always tell me he too old for me. He can put his foot on me when he sit in chair if he want. He old man, I young man, is work out good."

"Whatever you say, I loved Jimmy."

"Is good. You have good soul, Eddie Hall. Good soul. I help you however I can help you."

Eddie looked at me. "Is what he said true?"

I nodded.

"You should marry him."

"You're in no position to be giving advice on that."

Eddie smiled and stood up. I stood up. He walked around the table to me and hugged me. Ruth watched like it was the bottom of the ninth, three balls, two strikes and the pitcher was throwing a fastball over the plate.

I turned to Gabriele. "You know I love you. I have always loved you. And you know who I am, what I can do and what I can't do. And you still love me, even with all that I can't do for you." I get teary easily and often. Softy, softy, I can hear my brother saying. "You are more precious to me than gold or diamonds. I don't have to tell you that, because you know it already. But I am telling you that in front of these people. You know I love you."

Billy was clearly uncomfortable.

"Hey, Billy, take a deep breath. We're off the subject anyway. We're supposed to be talking about how to help Eddie win an election."

Billy sat back but looked doubtful. Eddie walked back to him. "Yes, I like you. It's not fake. Relax."

"Look, I was married to a woman for a long time. Mostly we were happy. We have kids and I love them like a father loves his kids. But that doesn't stop me from being attracted to men. So, am I gay?" He turned his palms up in an I-don't-know gesture. "I am sexually attracted to men sometimes. I have a hard time with that personally. But I know it about myself, and I'm trying to come to terms with it. That's one of the reasons I want people to think I'm gay. Because I think I am gay."

Ruth blurted out, "Gay may be something that characterizes you, but it is not who you are. It's an aspect of Eddie Hall, and since you are a politician, at least prospectively, it may not even be the most important aspect."

"It's what makes me different."

"I disagree, and so will voters. You are different from everybody else totally aside from whatever your sexual preferences are."

"Gays are progressive, like me."

"J. Edgar Hoover was gay and he wasn't progressive like you."

"I thought you were here because you're on my side."

"You were right. I am on your side. I just want you to know that there is a heck of a lot more to Eddie Hall. You won't get enough votes if you just run as gay. You have to run as who you are, what you believe, what your priorities are. You've been building that up all along. It's the most important part. Hey, the LGBTQ vote may be important, and you may have a leg up on getting it, so to speak. And you may get some campaign funding because you are presenting yourself as gay. If you do, it's because you're running in New York, and not a few hundred miles south of here."

"I don't know if I agree with you."

"Do you think Barney Frank was elected because he was gay?"

"Maybe, yeah. Maybe originally," Eddie said slowly, "but he became more important than just being a gay congressman."

"I understand, I think, where you're coming from, but I gotta tell you, you are electable no matter what your sexual preference is. You are eloquent, obviously strong, and you have a fund of energy that seems bottomless to an observer. How much better does it get?"

I stepped in. "We want to help, but I think we would like to see you run for either state office or national office. Why? Because we think you could win, and you could make a difference."

He threw me a thoughtful look, like he was weighing things on a mental balance.

"I'll think about it. Can't tell you how much I appreciate what you've said." He turned to Ruth. "And you think you can help me raise enough of a war chest to run for congress?"

She nodded.

He grabbed his cup and saucer and said to me, "Where can I put this?"

I told him not to worry. He, Alex and Billy left.

Chapter Eleven

"So," I said to Gabriele, "what was that about Eddie not being gay?"

"He not gay. He know. He say yes, when I say that."

"Why would he pretend to be gay if he's not?"

Gabriele shrugged.

"You've met men who say they're gay when they're not?"

He nodded.

"Why do they do that?"

"Most times just have sex."

"They are gay, right? If they want to have sex with a guy? Or at least bi?"

"No. *Forse* they just want something that girlfriend not do, like blowjob. Long time ago, I meet up with men that watch straight porn while we have sex. *Pompino* mostly," he said, using the Italian term for oral sex. "Lotta men just wanna feel good, relax, and wife or girlfriend too much trouble, or they talk all the time or wanna kiss when guy just want to finish up and go to sleep."

I was scanning through some social media on my tablet while we talked. Ruth got up and went into the kitchen, came back with a glass of orange juice.

"Wait," I said. "There's something going on. Look at Twitter."

Ruth screwed up her face a little and sat down beside me on the couch, leaning over to look at my screen.

Oddly, although we had just been talking about Eddie Hall's apparent sexuality versus what he admitted his real sexuality was, there were hundreds of tweets scrolling by that took him at his word. Words like "fag," "queer," "cock-sucker" and "pervert" were scattered in hostile tweets with racial epithets, some of which were disguised a little, but most of which were in-your-face offensive. The "N" word over and over, with asterisks in place of the vowels, to keep computer cops from seeing the offending words in scans. No White supremacist rants as far as I could tell, but Twitter rules keep pretty brief what you can say.

"Twitter's gonna pull those down, you watch," Ruth said.

"Whatever Twitter's gonna do, that's not what these people are doing. These are like those guys at Prospect Park, but all talk, no torches this time. "

Then the Eddie Hall search froze and that little bird cartoon took up the whole screen with a balloon above it saying "OOPS."

"I told you," Ruth said, as Gabriele sat on the arm of the sofa and stared at my screen from the other side. "When it comes back, that whole string is gonna be gone."

She was right. Totally washed away. Whiter than the whitewash on the wall, as the old song says.

I got an alert on my cellphone. From the ping I heard, so did Ruth. So did Gabriele.

There had been a shooting in the Times Square area, although no one was hurt. Apparently, a gunman who had not been identified fired a shot at a pedestrian, but the bullet didn't hit anyone, except a mannequin in a show window.

"There's always a crazy around every corner," Ruth said. "What kind of idiot would fire a gun in Times Square, where you could almost never tell who was going to get hit?"

My phone rang with a call. It was Mike di Saronno.

"Hi, Hugo, did you see that alert that went out about a shooting in my area?"

"Yup."

"Well, the target could have been someone you know."

I didn't respond, just waited.

"It looks like it may have been either Eddie Hall or a guy he was walking with, William White."

"Hold on." I covered the phone's mic and said to Ruth. "That shooting that we got the alert on was pointed at either Eddie or Billy."

She screwed up her face in puzzlement. "For what?"

"Any idea who it was or why?" I asked.

He asked me if I could come over to the precinct. Of course, I said yes and told him Ruth was with me and we had just met with Eddie and Billy at my apartment.

"I bet they were on their way when they left my apartment," I said.

The three of us took the 7-train to Times Square and the 1-train to 50th Street then walked up to 54th Street to the precinct, which was between 8th and 9th Avenues. Mike was waiting for us at the top of the stairs. His office was on the second floor.

"It seems pretty obvious that whoever it was, he was firing at either Eddie Hall or the guy he was walking with, who was a younger guy..."

"Named Billy White. He's an actor, and he was also on Eddie's radio show today, talking about Harry Potter books, as I recall."

"You were listening to the show?"

I nodded. "We met with Eddie—and Billy—last night at Ora di Pranzo. They were causing a bit of a scene by sitting at the bar and necking, but Gabriele called me and they stopped when I got there and basically interrupted them by saying I was the first one on the scene when he had that car accident. They weren't trying to cause a problem. Eddie was apparently trying to get picked up for Page Six."

"Well, he was successful, I guess. At least he was in the print version this morning. No photo though."

"I didn't know. Not a Page Six reader," I said as Ruth nodded and pinched her nose as though there were a bad smell.

"Page Six is pure trash," she said. "People who read it are morons."

Gabriele disagreed. "Good for business for Ora di Pranzo. Page Six mean more people for us."

"Were you at Ora di Pranzo last night too?" Mike asked Ruth.

"We went to a birthday party last night. The answer is no, I was not, but I was at Hugo's apartment this afternoon for a discussion of whether or not Eddie was gay, mostly."

"Whether he was gay?" Mike looked puzzled. "He was getting ready to marry a man last I heard. Then his boyfriend was shot."

"Not gay," Gabriele said, "but want to look gay, maybe for get in news."

Mike didn't react.

"So, we were theorizing that it might be a way to get elected," I said. "When we were at my place, he was talking about New York City Council from Prospect Park. District Forty I think?"

"Seems like a long way to go to win an election," Mike said, "but I wonder if it persuaded somebody to take a pot-shot at him."

"Are you sure the shooter was trying to get Eddie?"

"No way to tell, and that's the truth," Mike said. "So far we don't even know where the shooter was, although the CSI's will probably be able to give us some more intel on that because they were able to retrieve the bullet from a mannequin in a street-side window."

"What if it was somebody after Billy?" I asked. "After all, somebody shot Jimmy van Gelsen, and he was the previous boyfriend."

"So, you think Billy is the boyfriend now?"

"No idea personally."

"They act like it, but they not. Billy say he actor. *Forse*. They going at it too much, like on stage."

"But if they were in Page Six, who would know that?" Mike wondered.

"It just seems like a longshot to me," I said. "Have you talked to Eddie? Or Billy?"

"Not yet. We're officially not even sure they were the intended victims."

"That seems like no reason not to ask them to come in and let you know if they had any idea what was going on."

My phone bleeped, indicating that a text message had come in. It was from Eddie Hall.

Hey U have time to get together?
Sure When
Now?
I'm in City with NYPD friend.
Hour or so? Ur place?
Sure

I told Mike and Ruth it was Eddie and showed them the texting string.

"Am I invited?" Ruth asked.

Yes. I nodded.

"Mind if I come along?" Mike asked.

I shrugged. "Lemme text Eddie and ask him."

I did, and it was okay with Eddie.

The four of us jumped on the 1 then the 7 and were back in Long Island City a little more than fifteen minutes later.

Chapter Twelve

"I gotta tell you, I have no idea what's going on," Eddie said when he walked in the door. He was alone. "Zero."

Mike uncrossed his arms and put his hands in his pants pockets. "Keep talking."

"People don't shoot other people for no reason, but I have no idea why somebody would want to shoot me."

Ruth responded, "Could it have anything to do with the Page Six article this morning about you and Billy?"

"Well, they both happened the same day, so I guess the answer would be yes, but the why part? I can't figure that one out."

"Some people don't like gays," I said. "Not defending that, but we all know there are gay-bashing stories that crop up in the news all the time. There was a kid in the Bronx who stabbed some classmates because he said they had been bullying him for years because he was gay. I just don't think it's that uncommon. You don't expect it in New York because New York is so inclusive usually.

"Also, Mike tells me that there is no real proof that someone was shooting at you, just that there was a shot fired. Where were you?"

"On 8th Avenue about 45th Street. There's a lot of construction and we were on the west side of the avenue walking to the yellow line at 42nd Street to Prospect Park."

"And you heard a shot?"

"No, I didn't hear a shot, but I saw people around me hitting the deck, ducking and covering. So, I did the same, and so did Billy."

"What makes you think someone was shooting at you? Somebody else could have been a target, or the shooter could have just shot wild. Right?" Mike was not putting any undue emphasis on anything.

I ducked into the kitchen and returned with a coffee pot. There were some mugs on the dining table. I gestured to them. "Coffee anyone?"

Eddie nodded.

"Take off your hat and stay a while. "

"What? Not wearing a hat."

"Nah, sorry," I said. "That was something my mom used to say. Take off your hat and stay a while. It just means relax, have a seat, be comfortable."

So, we all sat down, Gabriele and Ruth in arm chairs, Eddie and I on the couch, Mike in a straight chair pulled over from the dining table. Everyone had coffee.

Mike said quietly, "I feel like I walked in late to a movie. Back up a little and tell me why you and your friend Billy were in Page Six. It's the worst kind of gossip rag usually."

Eddie set his coffee on the coffee table, put his head forward in his hands. He was clearly choked up. "Look, somebody shot Jimmy, and I was in love with Jimmy. Everybody knew about that, or everybody I know anyway knew about Jimmy. We were going to get married, even had the church and a date picked out. Alex and Mattie were going to be in the wedding."

Mike cocked his head to indicate puzzlement.

"Alex and Matilda are my kids. You may already know that I have political ambitions. I have wanted to be elected to the NY City Council and was planning to run. Now, because of these nice people, I'm considering running for something with a bigger constituency, like the state legislatur e or maybe congress."

Mike nodded.

"So, I have a lot of LGBTQ supporters. I met Jimmy at a political rally about three years ago, and it seemed like he knew every gay guy in the city. I met some lesbian politicians, and that multiplied. I met a couple of trannies, and then suddenly I knew a lot of trannies."

Mike put his left hand to his mouth, resting his index finger on his upper lip.

"Everybody assumed because Jimmy and I were getting married, that I'm gay."

"Not a reasonable assumption?" Mike asked.

"Yeah, reasonable. Just not accurate."

"But you never told anyone it wasn't accurate."

Eddie shook his head. "No, and maybe it got Jimmy killed."

"Who would have been so upset that they would shoot Mr. van Gelsen?"

Eddie shook his head again. "It's a big city. No idea. But I didn't want to cut and run, so Billy was helping me stay in the game, so to speak."

"Is Billy gay?"

"I don't think so, but we haven't really discussed it. There was never any intention for us to get intimate, just to be lovey-dovey in public."

"Was Mr. van Gelsen gay?"

"Yes."

"But he was going to marry a divorced straight man?" Mike asked. "Sounds like a recipe for being unhappy—both of you."

"Well, like I said, I loved Jimmy. He loved me. We never had sex and probably never would have, even after we got married."

Mike stared at Eddie.

"A lot of marriages are platonic," Eddie said. "Aurora and I never had sex after Mattie was born."

"How long was that?"

"Almost fifteen years."

"Did you have affairs?"

He shook his head. "I never stopped loving Aurora. Still do. But we couldn't live together. I'm too selfish. I wouldn't give up on politics. It's too important for me to give up, and she couldn't stand it. Couldn't stand my friends. Couldn't stand the conversations. Refused to go to the parties and rallies. When I ran for City Council and lost, it was like she won the Lotto, she was so happy. I was furious."

"So, you haven't had sex for a long time? Not any at all?"

He nodded. "Not any at all."

"And your wife? Did she have affairs?"

He shook his head. "I don't think so, no."

"Mr. van Gelsen?"

"I think so, yes." He looked up and wiped his eyes. "Wait, let me explain. Jimmy had been in several relationships with men. As far as I know, no women. But he wasn't feminine, not a queen at all. I don't know if I could have been so friendly with him if he was a flamer."

"You don't want to be with feminine men but you were willing to be married to a man?"

"That's what I said, yes."

"To walk down the aisle in a church and say 'I do' to a man?"

"Yes, of course."

"I admire you," Mike said, and held his hand out to shake.

Eddie grabbed his hand. They didn't shake, but Eddie held his hand for a long moment and looked at Mike straight in the eyes. "That would take a lot of guts, and a commitment beyond what most people could give."

"But somebody doesn't admire me if they were willing to shoot Jimmy and take a shot at me. Somebody hates me."

"Why does that have to be tied to the fact that a lot of people think you're gay? You were an ADA in Brooklyn and put a lot of people away for a long time. There have to be people who hate you totally independent of your politics or your sexual preference."

Eddie nodded. "Could be. I tried never to destroy anyone's dignity, even when I prosecuted them. Even that cop who sodomized the Puerto Rican prisoner with a night-stick. I tried not to walk on anyone's self-respect unless there was no other way. Most defendants know what they did was wrong, and my biggest hope with bad guys always was that they would find a way to be rehabilitated. Can't do that if someone has ruined your sense of self-respect. I never got any threats that I remember, and I would remember if I had been threatened. I just wanted the bad guys to be convicted, that's all. I think they knew that."

Mike shrugged. "Gotcha. I feel the same way about guys I arrested and got sent away, but a lot of them hate me anyway. Some people are just bad to the bone. All I'm saying is we don't know for sure that your seeming to be gay was the reason behind either shooting. and there's no such thing as a prosecutor that convicts like."

Eddie didn't say anything. It was clearly something he thought about a lot. His gaze didn't look uncertain.

Gabriele spoke up. "Eddie not only straight man live with gay man. I know *coppie*, how you say, *couples* like that. Happy people. Straight man and gay man fit together. Maybe not sex. Who care? I not have sex in long time. I believe Hugo not have sex for long time."

Eddie looked like he was going to tear up again.

"You miss Jimmy," Gabriele said. "Me too. I not know Jimmy except at Ora di Pranzo, but he nice man. You lucky man to be with him. Just not lucky what happen to him."

"Look, I didn't tell you this before, but the CSI's figured out where the shot came from on 8th Avenue. It came from the second floor of a building under construction on the corner of 8th and 46th Street. Whoever did it knocked a hole in the glass because that part of the building was already closed in."

"And that means what?" Eddie asked.

Ruth perked up.

Mike explained that meant they found the place from the angle that the bullet came from when it hit the mannequin. There were fingerprints all over the glass, but no obvious evidence of the shooter. They were vetting all the fingerprints, and checked the door on the ground floor that was unlocked. No prints there.

"What that means," he said, "is that the shooter was most likely not shooting at you specifically. To do that he would have to know you would be walking by there when you did, and remember he broke into the building to get in position. Maybe he accidentally pulled the trigger before he intended to. Maybe he was after somebody on the second floor of the building you were walking by. But the idea that he was sitting in that window waiting for you when you happened to walk by would never fly in a courtroom. I mean this is not like Lee Harvey Oswald waiting for JFK's car to drive by the Texas School Book Depository. There was no way for a shooter to know where you would be—or when. If it happened outside your apartment in Park Slope, that might be different, but it didn't."

"Well I suppose that's a load off," Ruth said, looking at Eddie.

"Hey," Eddie said. "I meant to say. Tomorrow is the Million Woman March. I'm going to be marching toward the front of the parade, and I wonder if you would march with me. You have to wear something pink."

"I already agreed to march with a group from my synagogue, but thanks," Ruth said.

I put my hand up like a student. "What time? Where? I'm there."

Gabriele signed up too. We were to meet Eddie on 59th Street somewhere near the statue of General Sherman near the corner of 5th Avenue.

"They're going to stack us up to enter the parade in a certain order at the top of 6th Avenue. Plan already made. Just find me and we're okay. And wear something pink please."

Chapter Thirteen

The Million Woman March was just kicking off the next morning at the top of 6th Avenue, heading south, the opposite direction of normal traffic on 6th Avenue. But there's nothing so odd about that. The St Patrick's Day Parade goes north on 5th Avenue, same thing, going in exactly the wrong direction relative to the normal flow of traffic on 5th Avenue, where cars can go south only.

I had no problem finding Gabriele. To tell the truth, he found me when I got off the N train at 5th Avenue and exited up the stairs at the back end of the Plaza Hotel. The street was mobbed. I was wearing a raspberry-colored linen shirt, closest thing I could find to pink in my closet. Gabriele was wearing a hot pink short-sleeved shirt, which of course looked like it belonged on him against his tanned skin.

We managed to hook up with Eddie, who was, it turned out, easy to find standing right next to General Sherman. Hug-hug, and he introduced us to a bunch of people, mostly women, but also the governor of New Jersey and a couple of male New York state legislators. *Probably up for election,* I thought. Gabriele was taking it all in, and managing to stare at Eddie in the process.

Eddie looked even more athletic than usual in a fairly tight-fitting, pink V-neck t-shirt. Big biceps, and, as with Gabriele, his swarthy complexion fit the pink shirt to a tee. Billy White was walking alongside him with a pink bandana around his neck and a straw cowboy hat, looking a little like a parody of a rodeo performer.

Predictions were for two hundred and fifty thousand women to take part, protesting pay gaps between men and women, sexual assaults and harassment in the workplace or in schools, and in general the abridgement of civil and human rights for women. The forecast was for a full million women marching in Washington DC on Pennsylvania Avenue. There was an "anti" march downtown in the financial district.

Social media was full of well wishes but pock-marked with very negative and extremely hostile remarks, some of them verging on real threats. There were calls from a variety of people or groups with names that included "freedom," "liberty" and "traditional values". But many of them picked up phrases and graphics with frightening historical implications. There were burning crosses in illustrations, swastikas, stiff-arm salutes, and dare-you phrases like "White nationalism," "Jews will not replace us" and "Blood and Land".

As a result, the parade routes in most major cities were thick with law enforcement. Nowhere was that truer than in Manhattan.

Because there was the potential for a clash of opposing groups, television stations were dotted around the parade routes and international television gathering agencies were grabbing grandstand positions in midtown; national news agencies like Agence France Presse, NHK World Radio Japan, TASS, Al Jazeera and of course the grandest of all, the BBC World Service. If there was to be a clash of opposing groups, it would make perfect television. Audiences would be glued to their screens like they were on September 11, 2001, when people watched the same footage of planes hitting buildings over and over and over.

The official plan was for several alt-right groups to stage rallies in the financial district, far from the Million Woman route which started at 59th Street, Central Park South then by Herald Square just outside Macy's, continuing as far as 23rd Street but not below. So theoretically the groups would be at all times a couple of miles or more apart.

There were prominent men marching in the Million Woman March. The mayor of New York marched at the front, as did the governors of New York, New Jersey and Connecticut. The New York governor was wearing a pink stovepipe hat, which made him stand out even more than usual. Senators from both parties from Pennsylvania, Delaware, New Jersey, New York, Connecticut and all of New England were marching, some in Washington DC but many in Manhattan, where the media coverage was likely to be very heavy. We were about a block behind the real VIPs, but the prediction was that the parade would cover twenty blocks as it moved south, so we were pretty close to the front.

The media didn't promise they would actually count the marchers in DC to see if there were a million women pounding the street pavements. Of course, there would be various reporters or networks who would do exactly that—use helicopters or camera-drones to take pictures from the sky, and banks of computers to calculate precisely how many people were actually marching, city by city. The numbers were almost guaranteed to be precise.

There had been a clash of estimates at a presidential inauguration one year, with the incoming president proclaiming it was the biggest crowd ever on the National Mall, and several television stations estimating it was not even close to the biggest crowd to witness an inauguration. The organizers of the Million Woman March were clear in saying that the word "Million" meant a big crowd and was not a forecast of a specific number.

No matter. Reporters and cameras from around the world were watching and waiting for a fight or a slip-up. There were commentators from both ends of the spectrum, so controversy was almost guaranteed.

The early estimates in New York, all helicopter-based, were for the number of marchers to exceed two hundred and fifty thousand. The women were wearing pink wherever they could. Pink scarves, pink ribbons, pink clothing, waving pink banners and flags. The marchers carried signs and placards indicating "The Time Is Now" and "No More Glass Ceilings" and "No Means No."

There was a blocks-long contingent of beefy guys on very noisy motorcycles, each of which was flying a pink flag from a flexible pole attached to the back of the seat. There were two lines of high-kicking chorus girls with pre-recorded music. Several marching bands with pink themes but comprised of both male and female musicians were scattered between blocks of marchers, because who would stand and watch a parade that didn't have music?

There were a few marchers carrying twenty-foot long banners held across the street by five or six women in a row, decrying the villains of sexual harassment, many of them from the movie or television industries. There was a well-known Black comedian, a Hollywood producer with a pronounced five o'clock shadow, an actor who revealed an open secret that he was gay but was accused of having manhandled several women while he was working on some very famous movies as well as a formerly beloved newscaster who was summarily fired from a highly rated morning show for refusing to take no for an answer.

In general, most of the spectators were standing but some were more comfy in bleachers that had been set up at strategic points where television cameras were able to scan them, picking out some famous faces from Broadway and Hollywood.

The downtown marching crowd was largely, but by no means entirely, male. It was, however, almost completely white. I watched a replay of some of the coverage later that day, mostly out of curiosity about the downtown contingent.

The largest female group were "sister wives" who marched with their children in granny-type floor-length dresses and head-covering bonnets with placards praising the virtues of polygamy. Right up there with them was a variety of religious groups who made it clear they were Bible-based, believing the world was created in seven days and Eve was constructed from one of Adam's ribs. This group dressed more like women you might see on the streets of New York, beautiful fabrics and flounces, high heels, gloves, hats, and they waved signs praising "traditional" femininity, with slogans on how rewarding it is for them to do as they are told while a man makes all the decisions.

There were hundreds or thousands of t-shirted men with leather vests carrying tiki torches, reminiscent of the scene in Prospect Park a few days earlier. And as the chanting, torch-bearing parade approached Zuccotti Park where the "Occupy Wall Street" siege was carried out, the spectators were ten or twenty people deep, and their chants spread through the sidewalks.

The mood downtown was not so much celebratory as almost military. The marchers moved along more quickly, and there was no music other than the chanting torch-bearers.

The torch-bearing contingent didn't carry any signs. They chanted things like "You won't replace us" and "Jews won't replace u s," peppered with "White Lives Matter" and "America for Americans."

In the spectator groups there were caricatures of Black and Hispanic politicians and civil rights leaders, as well as derogatory chants about

LGBT people, immigrants, people of color and non-Christians.

Uptown the mood was upbeat. As we walked, we talked. Gabriele was staying close to Billy. I could tell he was studying Billy, but Billy seemed to be talking all the time. We were all waving to the people on the sidewalks, and they were waving back, cheering and applauding. There were as many signs and placards on the sidewalk as in the parade. I didn't see any that were hostile, but I can't say I saw them all.

Eddie was smiling big, lots of teeth, and going up on his toes to wave, and occasionally to point someone out on the sidewalk for a special wave.

"You're as much into women's rights as you are into LGBTQ rights," I said, though it was a question.

"More," he said. "There are more women than gays and lesbians, and they have been suppressed and mistreated for all of history, I think. History is mostly about men, you know. Mostly about White men. My people have probably suffered more in some ways, but women have been suffering for thousands of years." Waving all the time.

A reporter from an independent television station in New York was waving at Eddie. He quickly side-stepped over to where she was standing, and said a few words into the camera and microphone, then quick-stepped back to where I was.

"Channel 1," he said. "Not the biggest audience, but every little bit helps. I need for people to know who I am if I want to win any election."

He looked at me and slowed down slightly, causing the woman behind him to nearly bump into him.

"I'm thinking about what you said. That I should set my sights higher than just New York City. That would mean I need to have a larger constituency. The radio show helps too. I'd like to interview you and Ruth in a day or two, to talk about your experiences walking in this parade."

I shrugged an aw-shucks shrug. "Never been interviewed," I said. "You might do better with someone who has some experience, but I'll try my best. It's live, right? No editing?"

He nodded, grinned at the sidewalk and waved at someone in particular.

"Somebody you know?"

"Nah," he said. "Just somebody flashing a V for Victory sign and looked like she was looking at me."

Off to our right, and over the sound of the parade and the crowd, there were sirens, lots of sirens, it sounded like. Maybe Times Square area? Hard to tell. Traffic accident maybe.

My cellphone bleeped. I pulled it out and looked. It was a text message.

Police action Times Square. 7, Bway no vehicles. 43 to 47 closed completely 9 to 6 Ave. Avoid area.

I showed Eddie, who stared at it, briefly looked puzzled then went back to smiling and waving. I pressed the internet button and went to CNN.

Terrorist Activity in Times Square was the headline. The article said several people had been arrested in a van carrying explosives in the Times Square area. No casualties. I showed Eddie. He nodded, kept waving and smiling.

The groups ahead of us stopped abruptly and I could see over the heads that a line of police had formed across 6th Avenue at about 43rd Street. They were in riot uniforms, with tall transparent shields. Mounted cops with bullhorns were riding up 6th Avenue on each side of the marchers, saying that the rest of the march was cancelled due to police activity in Times Square. All participants and spectators should quickly and calmly leave the area. Best to go east, since most of Times Square was closed off. Subways were all running.

The parade began to melt away, as people in pink and spectators with cellphone cameras moved east. Some ran for 42nd Street to get into the subway at the Bryant Park station, which had 7 trains, B, D, F and M trains. Upshot is that you could get to uptown or downtown Manhattan from there, or to Queens or Brooklyn, and some places in the Bronx, like the area around Yankee Stadium. I grabbed Gabriele and told Eddie I was heading for Grand Central to get on the 7 there. Too many people at Bryant Park. They came with me, and Billy followed Eddie too. Eddie could get the green line at Grand Central, which would take him to Prospect Park. Gabriele could get to Brooklyn Heights.

Truth was I wanted to go to Grand Central because there is pretty good broadband there and I wanted to know what the heck was going on.

Also, there are television screens at various places in the station. I was surprised when we got to Grand Central though. There were people standing on Vanderbilt Avenue waiting to get into the cavernous station. You can't tell a half-million people on 6th Avenue to go to the east side without creating a logjam.

Eddie and Billy pushed their way across 42nd Street to a subway entrance on the downtown side of the street. I expected Gabriele to do the same, but he stayed close by me.

"I going with you," he said. "Not want go to Brooklyn alone. 7-train faster anyway." He was right. If we could get a 7-train that we could squeeze onto, it would only take five minutes to get to my station stop. I took out my smartphone, which was at less than fifty percent of battery life. Video would drive it down faster. I felt in my pockets and yes, there was a charger there, if I could find an electric plug.

I tuned in CNN. There was footage of the Million Woman March disbanding in New York, but that was followed by video of over one million people marching in Washington DC. Then there was footage of the downtown "protest" march by the alt-right. They were looking confused, and many were peeling away from the march. There were no sister wives marching any more, for instance. Police had made the male marchers extinguish the flames on their tiki torches, and those for the most part were no longer held high.

A lot of the downtown marchers were looking distressed or frightened. There were no spectators, and there were signs littering the streets and sidewalks where people dropped them before dashing away from the scene.

Cut back to Washington DC, then quickly to Times Square, which was on lockdown after what was probably an attempted terrorist attack that the police caught before it happened.

"Midtown Manhattan looks like it's been evacuated," the reporter said, as a camera panned across crowds running across 42nd Street toward the Bryant Park subway then looked back up 6th Avenue, with not a soul in evidence more than a block or so up from 42nd Street.

"The Million Woman March disintegrated when the alert came out," he said, "and everyone was told to go east because of potential terrorist activity in Times Square. There were an estimated three hundred thousand marchers on 6th Avenue, including a lot of well-known politicians. Probably an almost equal number of spectators and well-wishers on the sidewalks. Hundreds of cops.

"Right now, 6th Avenue looks deserted. Lots of signs and trash on the street and sidewalks. No cars or trucks. Virtually hard to see anybody on the street.

"The downtown march in protest to the Million Woman March fell apart too. The police have been on high alert, and there are mounted police in all the crowd areas.

"We can't get into Times Square, but when we can we'll be bringing that to you."

He signed off. Gabriele was looking over my shoulder. He put his hand on my waist and I felt a twinge of wanting to hug him, but I just went back to my main screen to see if there were texts.

Avoid mid-town Manhattan was an alert text from a few minutes before, while I was watching CNN.

You okay honey? from Ruth. *I'm home. So far so good.*

I texted back, *OK w Gabr. E & B to Bklyn green line. AOK. LIC when 7-trains have room.*

Can't get inside GCT. Going to subway Mad btwn 42 & 41.

Watching TV. What a mess. Glad they got those guys.

There are more bad guys than one we're looking for. How's Washington march?

OK good more than million

Cool. Later.

Chapter Fourteen

When we walked into my apartment, Gabriele turned to me, pulled his shirt off, and hugged me. He was frightened. I hugged him back.

"You're okay," I said. "You're with me."

He let go and backed away about a foot. "Ugo,'' he said.

I walked into the kitchen, reached into the cupboard and pulled out two Waterford juice glasses from a set that was part of what was at one time a huge Waterford collection my grandparents had. He was Irish, and there was something magical about Irish crystal. The glasses dated back nearly one hundred years. I threw an ice cube in each one from the icemaker in the freezer, and grabbed a bottle of blended scotch, poured a couple of fingers into each one and splashed them with water from a Brita container. I handed one to Gabriele and held the other.

"To safety and good friends," I said and held my glass out to be clinked. "And courage." He stared at me. "And love." He tapped my glass with his and drained the scotch in one motion.

I matched him. The scotch felt hot going down, but it was smooth. The trade-off with blending whisky is that you lose the individual personalities of the components, and those are so different one from the other that even an amateur can recognize label after label in a blind tasting. But the blends are smooth as silk. The burning feeling that a "neat" single malt can inflict almost disappears in a good blend like Dewar's or Johnny Walker Black. Then I grabbed him and hugged him the way he had hugged me. He went limp, and when I let go, he turned and walked into the living room and plopped down on the couch.

"News on television?" he asked, picking up the remote control.

I nodded.

"Which channel?"

"Doesn't matter. Not Fox, not CNN. One of the locals."

We sat in the middle of the couch, our hips touching and my arm stretched out behind him on the couch. He was recovering his *sang froid* as the drink moved into his bloodstream, but he slouched back into my arm. I grabbed his far shoulder in an almost-romantic hug.

I muted the sound. It was all the stuff we already knew, but at least now there was some footage of what happened in Times Square. "The Crossroads of the World" was empty except for police, with garbage trucks parked across each street opening onto the great open space. A white van with a passenger-side door wide open sat outside the Marriott Marquis Hotel, apparently the vehicle the police apprehended.

I unmuted the television in time to hear the five men arrested admitted their complicity. Two had suicide belts in the back of the van, among package after package of C4 plastic explosive.

Then the picture morphed to the scene downtown as the alt-right march disintegrated then to a camera view of the street where the tiki marchers had been. Placards lay everywhere, and there were more than forty tiki torches on the pavement where they had been abandoned. It was a study in abandoned action, stretching from Times Square to Zuccotti Square. And then there was 6th Avenue, which looked like Times Square at one AM on January 1, litter everywhere, more trash than twelve garbage trucks could hold.

My cellphone beeped, indicating a new text message from Mike di Saronno.

Van Gelsen brother lawsuit to overturn will

I dialed Mike's cellphone.

"That was quick."

"Why is it important? Or why did you text me about it?"

"Apparently he changed his will a couple of months ago, maybe when he and Eddie decided to get married, and he left everything to Eddie Hall."

"I assumed he was wealthy because of what I read about him."

"Interesting. No indication of what he was worth, but I'm guessing double-digit millions."

"So, the brother doesn't want Eddie to get the money?"

"The brother wants the artworks and family heirlooms that Jimmy had, but if the will is overturned, the likelihood is that the estate would revert to the brothers."

"Brothers plural?"

"Four."

"But if Jimmy had money, don't they have money too?"

"No way to know that for sure, but you might think so. Not everybody is able to hang onto whatever they have, I suppose."

Mike said he had invited Ragnar van Gelsen, the brother who filed the lawsuit on behalf of the family, to meet at the Midtown West Precinct to discuss the ongoing investigation of James van Gelsen's death. Ragnar accepted and would be there at five PM today.

I looked at the computer, which theoretically had the most accurate time. It was minutes after four.

"Is it okay if Gabriele and I come over too?"

Mike said it was okay, but we might not be able to participate in any meeting.

I took off my raspberry-colored shirt from the March, and put on a black t-shirt.

"Now you look more like you," Gabriele said.

We fast-walked to the Vernon-Jackson subway station and a train was pulling in just as we cleared the turnstile. We arrived at the top of the stairs on Mike's floor on the stroke of five PM. Mike was standing at the entrance to his office and walked over with his hand out to shake.

"He's not here yet. When he gets here, I will introduce you, tell him that you have helped the NYPD in the past, and ask him if he minds if you sit in on the conversation."

"And if he objects?"

"Then you'll have to wait in my office. We will not be talking about any legal issues. There is no violation of the law in anything we will be discussing, but I may have to promise him confidentiality on some issues. As you know, everything in the interrogation rooms is captured on video and sound."

Mike's office is almost all glass, and Mike saw a man in a suit and tie walking in his direction. He opened the door and said, "Mr. van Gelsen?" The man nodded and held out his hand.

"Bud van Gelsen."

"Ragnar?"

"Yup, but everybody calls me Bud. Ever since I was a kid."

He introduced Gabriele and me, adding "Hugo and Gabriele have been very helpful to the NYPD on numerous occasions, and we've asked them to keep their eyes open with regard to the death of your brother, James."

He shook our hands and Mike gestured to the other side of the floor. "Not enough room in my office, so we can use one of the Interrogation Rooms over there if that's okay?

Bud shrugged and nodded an okay. "What do you guys do other than help the police?"

"I'm retired."

"I have a restaurant," Gabriele said.

"Anyplace I would know?"

"Ora di Pranzo."

"Oh, I've been there."

"Maybe with brother Jimmy. I think I see you before."

Bud smiled slightly. "Good food, Ora di Pranzo. Yeah, went there with Jimmy. We were close. You're okay by me if you were a friend of Jimmy."

"Jimmy good man, come to Ora di Pranzo many time."

We walked over to the interrogation room closest to the staircase, and Mike held the door for us. I sat next to Mike and Gabriele sat next to Bud.

"So, Mr. van Gelsen, you know we're trying to make some headway, trying to find out what happened to your brother."

He stared at Mike, waiting.

"Do you have any idea who might have wanted to do that to him?"

"I've thought about that a lot. I honestly don't think Jimmy had any enemies."

"He had ex-boyfriends."

"Yeah, a couple, but they were nice guys, and Jimmy never had a bad break-up. In the first place, he didn't tomcat around, ever."

"So, the lawsuit to invalidate the will had nothing to do with any suspicions you might have?

He wrinkled his brow. "No, of course not. We want to supersede the will because we know that Jimmy intended to marry Eddie, but he didn't live long enough."

Mike sat silently, waiting.

"You wondering if we, I had a problem with Eddie Hall? Never, nothing. He spent last Christmas with the whole family. Great guy, we all were happy for Jimmy because he was obviously happy with Eddie."

"Did your brother leave a large estate?"

"Depends on how you look at it, I guess," he said. "Not a lot of cash, stocks and bonds, if that's what you mean. I think his co-op is probably worth a good amount, maybe two-three million, but what I'm concerned with is that our parents and our aunts and uncles gave Jimmy a lot of things we grew up with."

"Like?"

"Paintings."

"Those modern masters that are in the apartment?"

"A Rauschenberg, yeah, and we would give that to MoMA. Also, the other significantly valuable pictures. Not much interest in those. There was an oil painting our Dad painted on vacation up in Canada one year when we were kids, and Jimmy had Mom and Dad's silver. No point that not staying in the family. Same for china, the Thanksgiving table settings, for instance." He was tearing up.

"Did you talk to Eddie about those things?"

I wanted to say something, but I held myself back. I wanted to say *Eddie wouldn't want anything that was part of somebody else's family. He's a family man himself.*

Now he was dripping tears. "I didn't want to talk to anybody about that except the family."

Mike looked at me. "Hugo, you look like you want to say something."

I almost started blurting things out, but took a breath and counted to five. "I don't know Eddie Hall very well, but my impression of him is that he's a softy. He didn't get anything or apparently ask for anything from his wife in the divorce, and she's got a hefty bank account. That's all. We marched with him in the Million Woman March yesterday."

"So, you are good friends?" he asked.

"No. I barely know him, although Gabriele knew him from the restaurant, apparently. I happened to be driving behind him on the Thruway when he ran off the road and was taken off in an ambulance, but I didn't know him and I didn't know his name either. And that was only a few weeks ago."

"But you're a quick study," he said.

"Maybe," I said. "I liked him instinctively. Partly maybe that's politics, because I'm in his camp on that."

"So am I," Bud said. "So are my brothers. So was Jimmy."

"I just think hitting him with a lawsuit may have been more harsh than asking him if you can have the family heirlooms back. That's all."

"But you marched with him in the parade."

"He asked us to, and my friend Ruth too, but Ruth was already marching with some gal-friends."

"Why?"

"Long story, but I met him at Ora di Pranzo. He was sitting at the bar with Billy White, and Gabriele introduced us. I told him I was first on the scene when he ran off the road, and we started talking. That night we agreed to get together the next day or so after that, and we did, with Gabriele and Ruth, one day when he was doing his radio show. They were talking about the new Queens Library branch in Long Island City, which is where I live."

"When was that?"

"Day before yesterday, I guess. It was the day before the March, and the March was yesterday. That's how long I've known Eddie Hall."

"You want to broker a meeting between Eddie and me?"

"Maybe Gabriele would be better, since he knows Eddie better than I do."

"Okay."

Eventually the meeting was set up, and Gabriele was to be there too. Referee, I guess.

Chapter Fifteen

"It didn't seem like Bud had any animus toward his brother," I said.

"Agree," Mike said. We were on the phone together. "I wasn't convinced about his feelings on Eddie Hall, but nothing I can put my finger on."

My phone bleeped, indicating a message was waiting.

Gabriele: *Meeting set Bud & Eddie 1pm U coming?*

I relayed the info to Mike, who said "Go." Then before he hung up, he added "Take notes."

Where?

Ora di Pranzo

I could have guessed. Gabriele always wanted to be on his home turf if he wasn't at my place.

I left my apartment in Long Island City at noon, took the 7-train to Times Square, then the R train downtown, got off at Prince Street in SoHo and walked to Ora di Pranzo. I got there fifteen minutes early. Gabriele offered me a glass of *nero d'avola*, a Sicilian red and one of my faves. I accepted it, but only took one sip and put it down on the bar. Gabriele slipped away to greet a couple just arriving.

The maître d's job is to make everybody feel like they just came home. I'm so glad I don't own a restaurant.

Eddie showed up first, spotted me and sat down at the bar on my right. A few minutes later Bud walked in, smiling, saw Eddie, and the two of them did a comfortable-looking one-armed hug and pat. Bud sat on Eddie's right.

Gabriele came over and beckoned us to follow him. He took us to a corner table in the back of the restaurant, as close as you can get to privacy in a crowded restaurant.

"I keep hoping I'll run into you with the kids. I miss Alex and

Joseph Allen

Mattie. Great kids. You must be ideal parents, you and Aurora."

Eddie smiled, a little uncomfortable. "One of these days then, we'll get together, maybe a bike ride?"

Bud nodded.

"I got the papers on your lawsuit."

Bud looked down at his hands. Three glasses of wine arrived at the table with a runner, who also put a plate of cheese, olives and sliced meats in the center of the table, with some hot bread and a small dish of olive oil.

"I shouldn't have done that. I've been kinda screwy on some things since Jimmy…"

Eddie put his arm around Bud's shoulder. "You don't think I had anything to do with that, certainly?"

Bud shook his head. "I just can't stop thinking about poor Jimmy on his way to the market or going for a walk or something, and suddenly he was dead."

"We all feel that way."

I was taking mental notes, but didn't say anything.

"Anyway, I read the papers, and you can have whatever you want. I'm okay and there's nothing that will bring Jimmy back. I know he had all the Christmas decorations and the silver and stuff. It's yours, of course, your family's."

"And his other assets?"

"I don't even know what his other assets are."

"There's a pretty fair amount of stocks and bonds, some cash and the apartment, which he bought for cash. I'd guess a total of around eight million dollars. The paintings are worth money too, but I'd like to donate those to MoMA or the Guggenheim or the Whitney."

Eddie shook his head. "He left all that to me?"

Bud nodded, but stiffened up a bit, from where I sat. Eddie sat up straighter too. Money has a peculiar effect on people.

I found myself wondering if these two men might be on opposite sides of an argument. I signaled to the bartender, who refreshed their wine glasses. Bud took a big slurp and Eddie ignored the refill.

"Bud, there is nothing that belonged to Jimmy that ought to be mine, except maybe just some things to remember him by. I didn't want to marry

Jimmy for his wealth. I wanted to marry him because I loved him and he loved me. I'm not so lovable that lots of people want to marry me. My wife divorced me, remember. Please, send me something to sign, and I will sign it, saying that I prefer not to accept any bequest from Jimmy van Gelsen."

He took a gulp of the wine. He looked forward and put his hand under his chin. His eyes were glistening. "I hope you will let me have something that I can keep close to me. Could be neckties or his watch. We weren't the same size, so there's nothing I could do with his shirts or clothing. Maybe that mantel clock from the living room, the one with the arched top that chimes all the hours."

Bud turned to Eddie and reached out to touch his face with his napkin, wiping one eye's tears away. "We all love that clock. We grew up with it, but take it, man. If that will remind you of my brother, take it. We want you to be part of our family, an honorary brother-in-law. And I can't tell you how ashamed I am that I filed that lawsuit instead of just talking to you. Honest to God, if I could do it over…don't want you to hate us, or me."

"I don't hate anyone, especially anyone with Jimmy's last name."

My cellphone rang. I looked at it. Mike di Saronno.

"Have you heard of the big marches in Boston set for the weekend?"

"What are you talking about?"

"There are news announcements out from Citizens for the Republic, which is ultra-conservative, and from United Progressives, which is ultra-liberal announcing marches in Boston for the same time on Saturday; at ten AM, and both of them say they're starting in Copley Plaza and marching to Post Office Square. At the same time."

"Gotta be a mistake. Can't you find out from the Boston PD?"

"They tell us there are no permits for either march."

"Hold on a minute. I'm gonna talk to Eddie for a minute."

I asked Eddie if he knew about the United Progressives announcement of a march in Boston.

"News to me."

"Would you normally know if there was going to be a march?"

"Usually. I can't remember a time in the last three or four years when I wasn't on the list for something like that."

Bud van Gelsen was looking puzzled.

"I wonder if it's fake," Eddie said.

Back to Mike. "Eddie says he never heard of it. He just said to me he wonders if it's fake."

"Both of them?"

"All I asked him about is the United Progressives march."

"Ask him about the Citizens for the Republic march." I did.

"That's insane! There would be a mass fist-fight if those two groups were in the same place at the same time. The police are going to have to be in riot gear for the whole length of the march," he said. "I bet it's a spoof, but not a funny one."

"He says it's, and I quote, *insane,*" I said to Mike. "And he said he thinks it's a, his words, not mine, a *spoof but not a funny one.*"

"Look, forget what I told you. I'm gonna see what I can find out from Boston PD. This doesn't make sense."

"I'm not a believer in fake news," I said, "but if there is such a thing, this is probably it."

Click.

I tuned my phone to CNN. Nothing on Boston marches. I texted Mike, *Nothing on CNN.*

I looked up the Fairmont Hotel on Copley Plaza, dialed it, asked for the Front Desk. I asked them if they had a special rate for the marches tomorrow.

"This has to be the tenth call in the last few minutes about some march from Copley Plaza tomorrow. We know nothing about it."

Click. I texted Mike. *Fairmont Copley Plaza never heard of this, but said there have been a bunch of calls in the last few minutes.*

Mike texted back. *News starting to break now. Marches bogus, no such thing. BPD agrees.*

Eddie was staring at me. I showed him Mike's text.

"This is so not funny," he said.

He whispered something to Bud, who looked surprised but nodded vigorously then stood up, asked for a tab, handed the bartender a credit card, signed and was out the door within two minutes. Never said a word.

I switched to Facebook. My time line was alive with Boston

marches talk. Twitter, same. I went back to CNN, and they were now headlining "Breaking News" in Boston.

They all agreed it was fake news.

Eddie was on his phone, booked a seat on the Acela Express to Boston from Penn Station. I called Ruth and told her to turn on the TV. She said there were Breaking News banners on all the major channels, as she flipped around.

"Eddie seems to think it's bogus," I said, "but he booked a seat on the next Acela to Boston."

"I'm gonna go too," Ruth said. "If there's going to be a bash of some kind, I want to be there. The alt-right bullies with the tiki torches aren't gonna sneak away into the night. They're gonna be watched."

"Hey," I said. "Book me a seat next to you, let me know. Maybe airplane shuttle?"

"Call ya back," she said. I could hear her keyboard clicking. She hung up.

Chapter Sixteen

Ruth had pulled the right strings, and we were seated together in the front row of the six thirty AM plane from LaGuardia to Logan Airport in Boston. It was raining when we left New York, and it was still raining when we landed at Boston-Logan. *Not great parade weather, but I kinda doubt there's gonna be a parade anyway.* Of course, what was going through my mind was the fiasco that started off as opposing marches in New York a few days before. We were only footsteps from where two pressure-cooker bombs blew up at the finish line of the Boston Marathon in 2013, killing and maiming runners and spectators at random.

We checked in at the Fairmont on Copley Square. Depending on which hotel you go to, it might be called Copley Plaza, which is what it was called in the "fake news" announcements of the parades, or sometimes Copley Place. But on the maps, it is Copley Square. It's bounded by Boylston Street, Clarendon Street, St James Avenue, an extension of Huntington Avenue but more hoity-toity, and Dartmouth Street, betraying the super-Anglo background of the city itself. Boston may Irish be by reputation, but the layout of the city itself was, and is a little bit of England in Massachusetts.

Ruth chose the Fairmont which is called the Fairmont Copley Plaza because she thought it would have the best views of Copley Square, just in case there was a donnybrook to be seen. The hotel was built by the architect who designed the Plaza Hotel in New York City, and opened in 1912 as the Copley Plaza Hotel. Sometime later, it became a Sheraton hotel, then a Wyndham hotel, and when Wyndham was bought by Fairmont, it became the Fairmont Copley Plaza. Bostonians have a soft spot for the building, and everyone in Back Bay will tell you that then-Mayor John F Fitzgerald cut the ribbon at the opening. That's the same Fitzgerald who was the grandfather of John Fitzgerald Kennedy.

But the operative part for Ruth was they have a gym on the rooftop, and from the gym, you should be able to see the Clash of the Marchers if it happened. I had been in favor of finding a hotel at Post Office Square, which was the putative end of both marches, and I thought that might be the best show.

"If it gets there at all," Ruth said. "If not, Post Office Square will have a normal, suit-and-tie day in the financial district of Boston. B-O-R-I-N-G."

Off and on in my life I have been a gym rat, sometimes sliding into gym slacker, but put me in a hotel and I will haunt the gym. My former wife always wanted to eat her way through anyplace we visited. If there was a gym where we stayed, or within walking distance, that's where I would be. I love having an open-ended gym visit. Usually, I am in and out in an hour or an hour and fifteen. The ultimate in luxury to take my time, drink more water, relax and recover between different weight machines then the ultimate in gym pleasure—a steam room that cleans all the pores and makes you feel younger than when you walked in.

By the time we got checked in, it was a little after nine o'clock. We were staying in the same room, because neither of us expected to stay even until dark, much less overnight. We had a view of the Square, and as far as I could see, there were indeed some burly guys who looked like slightly pudgy body-builders, with tattoos and white t-shirts, milling around. The progressives don't have a "look" that would identify them, but there were twenty or thirty scruffy younger people mixing with some skinny older people who all looked like runners.

"Could be progressives," I said, pointing toward the scruffy lot. She was walking on a treadmill looking out the window with five-pound weights in each hand, pumping them up and down as she walked. She was glistening a bit, breaking a sweat.

"They could also just be MIT or Harvard people."

"Isn't that the same thing? They say you're liberal when you're young, and get more conservative as you get older."

"Whoopee," she said rather quietly. "That means I'm still young."

"I think in our case, it just means we're incorrigible."

"Look," she said, pointing to her right and down in the square.

"Over there. That person look familiar to you?"

"Eddie?" I almost whispered it. "It could be," I said. "It could be Eddie Hall." Ruth hauled out her cellphone and starting taking pictures.

I waited to see what would happen next. The 'Eddie' person moved toward the scruffy 'progressives'. They seemed to recognize each other, and two of the tall skinny boys or men broke away from the pack with arms outstretched, and ran toward the newcomer.

At just about the same time, all of a sudden there were sirens outside. It was hard to tell what direction they were coming from because we were up high and behind glass, but I decided they were coming from the left, up Huntington Avenue. We were facing north, so that means they were coming from downtown. I pointed to the left and down, and Ruth, who was higher than I was because the treadmill was slanted up, strained to look down the street.

"Lots of flashing lights," she said. "Can't tell much more."

A train of police vehicles was moving slowly on Huntington Avenue toward us. When they got to about a block to our left, they stopped, but the sirens kept blaring. The doors seemed to open all at the same time, and out came a thousand cops. Not a thousand, but a lot of cops. They blocked off all traffic on Huntington Avenue and began diverting all vehicles in other directions. Some were told with circling gestures to turn around.

They did and before you could say 'Jack Robinson' the street was totally clear. Two blackish armored trucks pulled up ahead of the first police car, slowly. When they were sufficiently clear of the lead police car, they stopped and the doors slid back. It was a SWAT team with tall see-through Lucite shields and what seemed like Kevlar everything.

The group of men who looked like bodybuilders were focused on the police. The scruffy crowd, and there were no more than fifty of them at most, stayed in place and watched. I took a lot of pictures I hoped would turn out in sequence. My cellphone was down to forty-seven percent battery life. I stopped taking pictures and turned off the light on the face of the phone.

"How's your battery?" I asked. She looked at the phone, and said, "It doesn't matter, I have two portable chargers in my gym bag. Don't even have to find a plug." She kept snapping pictures as the police fanned out, clearly targeting the "alt-right" and "alt-left" groups.

There was the noise of a bullhorn, but I couldn't understand what it was saying. Both groups backed up and turned around, walking slowly in opposite directions.

The televisions in the aerobic exercise room sprang to life with 'Breaking news' and what we could see below became clearly visible from street level. There were obviously television cameras in or just outside the lobby of our hotel.

"Well, look at that," I said. "It's Eddie for sure."

Eddie was waving his hands above his head in a signal that he wasn't armed. A cop stepped forward and motioned to him to approach. When he got near, two cops frisked him carefully, and wanded him with a tool that looked a little like a tennis racquet with no webbing. Clearly the signal was 'no weapons found', because the cops stood down and allowed him to pass to where some senior-level cops were standing behind the front line.

No way to tell what was going on. Ruth reached up and turned the volume up on the television in front of her treadmill.

"This was all some kind of massive practical joke," Eddie was saying to the cops, clearly within hearing of the television mics, but he was talking to the cops, not the cameras. "We started hearing what we thought was 'fake news' last night in New York. I came up here to try to talk to whoever showed up, but it seemed impossible that any real marchers would actually show up." He waved his arm back at the scene. "And they didn't. These people are lookie-loos. I know some of those university types over there. They told me they just wanted to see what was happening. They're as puzzled as we are."

He gestured to the tough-looking crowd. "No torches, no chants, no marching. These guys are just curious," he said, clearly aware he was on television, because he began looking straight into the camera.

The phalanx of cops fanned out into the crowd at the east end of the block in front of the semi-Romanesque Victorian turreted semi-castle called Trinity Church with its mock-Gothic spires surging upward from a reinterpretation of a façade reminiscent of half the old-old churches in Italy.

There were five people in black cassocks standing at the top of the steps in front of the church with their arms stretched out, palms up, clearly in prayer. The cops were obviously telling everybody to go home. "Nothing happening here."

It was surprising how quickly all the people in the square vanished. Almost like a wizard waved a magic wand and made them disappear.

Ruth hopped down from the treadmill and motioned to me to follow her. I did. We made our way to the elevators, and a late-middle-aged hotel official motioned us into a car, inserted a key in the control panel, and took us straight down to the ground level.

Ruth virtually exploded out of the elevator car when the doors opened, and ran, in her Lycra® tights and sports bra, toward the front door. I followed her, wondering what would happen when we got outside.

There were cops with bullet-proof vests and semi-automatic weapons at the ready about every eight feet on the Fairmont side of the avenue, the south side. Standing in front of the hotel, you couldn't see down Huntington Avenue, which cut diagonally back at the east end of the square. When it turned onto the square, the name of the street changed, and it was St. James Avenue. You were officially in the Boston Back Bay. The price of everything was higher, even the air smells chic.

There's no place in Manhattan where the whole appearance of a street changes from one block to the next. Maybe if you go up Mulberry Street, starting off in Chinatown, then going into the Mardi Gras lights of what is marketed as "Little Italy," it's about as abrupt when you cross Canal Street. But going from Huntington to St. James, you go from Beantown to a Boston version of Via del Corso in Rome or Rue du Faubourg St Honoré in Paris.

Ruth was taking video of the street-level scene as the crowd dispersed. She reached into the gym bag that was slung over her shoulder and retrieved a phone-sized black box with a cord, plugged that into her phone, and regripped the phone. It was the kind that had another twenty-seven hours of talk time in it. I was taking snapshots and worrying about my battery life.

She walked without hesitating toward a clump of cameras and high-held mics, elbowing her way in. I slipstreamed her and slid through the wake she created.

She stopped, smiled, and I could see over her that she had found Eddie.

"Ruth!" he said, and looking at me, "Hugo!"

"We decided we wanted to see if the whole thing was a hoax or what."

Eddie answered a couple more questions then told them he had other business to attend to and walked off with us.

"How about a drink?" I offered.

Eddie flashed a thumbs-up. We went into the Fairmont and bee-lined for the Oak Long Bar, which calls itself a restaurant, but is basically one of the best bars in Boston.

We found three places at the bar. Ruth was on one side and I was on the other.

The smile dropped off Eddie's face, and he said, "You know, this sort of thing is more dangerous than if there had actually been some kind of face-off between toughs and nerds."

"Why so?" Ruth asked.

"Because somebody we don't know and can't identify was trying to start a fight, a political fight, that could have been another step into the abyss for Americans, especially voters."

"Kinda like the bully who keeps telling a drunk 'You're not gonna take that from him, are you?' Trying to get someone to take a poke at someone else."

"I guess, sure, but even in that case, you know who's doing it." He paused and sucked his lips inward. "Who do you think did this? Why are we here? Who set us up to be here?"

"Well, you know there was a lot of talk a couple of years back about Russia trying to do things just like this," I said. "Trying to deepen the hatred between the far right and the far left."

Ruth shook her head and looked down at the bar.

"You're saying no?" I asked.

"No, I'm not saying no. I have no idea who would pull a stunt like this, but I'll tell you something for sure. If this sort of thing happens again, it's a perfect issue for a candidate to work with." She looked at Eddie.

"I'm wondering if whoever gamed this started the fracas in Prospect Park when Eddie was still in the hospital after the car crash."

"Nah," Ruth said. "That was too organized. Look around here. Nothing happening, just some spectators waiting for a bomb to drop. Which it didn't do."

Eddie sipped the scotch he ordered. He cocked his head and nodded simultaneously.

"You've worked in campaigns before, right?"

Ruth nodded. "Some Republicans and some Democrats."

"No political position of your own?"

She smiled. "I work with people I trust. I think trustworthy people of almost any political stripe are good people to be in government."

She kept the smile on her face, but began to speak seriously at the same time. "I always remember the close friendship between Orrin Hatch and Teddy Kennedy. It would be hard to find two senators further apart on a lot of big issues, but they respected each other. That's important. That's what makes me want to help."

"You interested in working with me?" His upper teeth met his lower lip as he waited.

"I'm inclined to say yes, but there are a couple of things."

"Shoot."

"First of all, I don't think I would want to go all out on a City Council district race."

He nodded.

"Second, I think you're going to run on the issues," she paused pregnantly. "If you were going to run on race or sexual orientation or feminism like the Million Woman March, I think I might be less interested."

He stared at her, waiting for a third point. "I'm ready to take your advice from when we talked before, and run for congress. I want to make a difference. I'm usually good at bringing people together, and maybe that's getting more important every year."

She nodded and smiled a new smile, a friendly one.

"The other thing. I'm Black. My mom was White, but I'm Black, like Obama.

"I'm a family man but am more comfortable living in a gay environment these days. As you and Hugo realized, I'm not gay in a sexual sense, at least not yet. But I can tell you I loved Jimmy van Gelsen. I'm not going to run as a gay man, but I intend to campaign directly to the LGBTQ community. On the other cutting-edge issues, like marijuana, like breaking up families by deporting a parent, like healthcare for people who can't afford it, I tend to be on the liberal side of those arguments, but I can tell you I'm not going to the mat to defend recreational marijuana. I was an ADA long enough to know both sides of that one."

"So where does all that lead?"

"I need help deciding how to handle a lot of things," he said, looking at me while he said it. "I was a good DA. I'm not afraid to take a stand, but I frankly haven't worked through all these things yet."

Ruth held her hand out. He took it. They shook.

"So, you want to work with me?" he asked quietly.

"Give me a day or so," she said, looking at me.

As we took the elevator back upstairs, she came clean. "Look, I like him. If he runs for congress in my district, I'll vote for him, but if I work with him, I'll have to stop working with you. When I was working for the Mayor, I threw myself into everything one hundred percent."

"What is it that you want to do working with me?"

"I want to find out who shot Jimmy van Gelsen. I want to get your texts at all hours of the day and night, and have drinks with Gabriele."

I took her hand and squeezed it. "I don't have any good idea who shot Jimmy."

"I know," she said. "I want to be here when the light goes on."

"Lots of times it's you who flips the light switch, my dear."

Chapter Seventeen

Eddie was all over the news that night. He was on screens in Boston because the non-marches happened there and they broke out the SWAT team. He was on screens in New York City because he's a New Yorker and in the national spotlight. He was on screens in Washington DC, and made the nightly news on all the networks. He was featured on the BBC, and his picture was on more newspaper front pages than Carter had pills. A well-known silver-haired newsman interviewed Eddie on CNN in a worldwide hookup.

"Well," Ruth said, doing an almost statuesque pose of a woman thinking, with her chin in her cupped hand. "Well," she shifted and then dropped it.

"Well?"

"Well," she started again. "He said he was going to run for congress. Pretty clearly, he meant that. I've never seen anybody do a trifecta on television like that. It would have been almost impossible to watch the news last night anyplace and not see Eddie Hall looking like a candidate."

"Something tells me that's going to make things more difficult for us in some ways."

"Meaning?"

"He's going to be campaigning for the next three months."

"That's how it works."

"I know, but you and I are going to get a lot of exposure just hanging out with him."

"I'm pretty good at disappearing in a crowd, but you're too tall," she said walking up to me and looking up at my face in a comically exaggerated stance.

I didn't respond.

"One thing for sure, I am not going to go to work on his campaign."

"Why?"

"I told you I want to work with you. You and Gabriele and Mike di Saronno and I are going to find out who shot Jimmy."

I told her I was finding that I look forward to helping Mike solve things. I didn't know that the first few times. It seemed like I fell into things by accident. "But now I think my disorderly mind gives me an advantage when I line up the clues. Maybe I'm kidding myself."

She pulled me over to the couch and sat down, patted the cushion next to her. I sat down.

"I watch you when your mind is in gear and buzzing," she said, holding my hand. "You're not clever like a stand-up comic, but you can put the pieces together better than I can. Better than Mike can, usually." She smiled in a friendly way. "There's a reason why Mike calls you, you know, and it's not because you're pretty."

"I'm not pretty?"

She gave me her disgusted-mommy look.

"I've been wondering why we keep chasing after Eddie instead of the people who any cop would say is the most likely to have been involved."

"Meaning?"

"I don't know. Family. People with a financial interest. People with a bitter taste in their mouths."

"I'm very literal. Give me an example."

"I don't know. Maybe a former love interest of Jimmy's. Somebody who can't stand that he was happy being with that Black guy with the radio show."

She stared at me.

"Or maybe it's even more basic. Somebody from his family who resents Jimmy willing his treasures to an outsider."

"That wouldn't be Bud, from what you said."

"I didn't say Bud. It's a big family, I think."

I decided I needed to hit the computer and do some serious research on the van Gelsen extended family. I offered to Ruth to kibbutz and help or just to check what I was doing to make sure I was going in the right direction. She decided to go home and put her feet up instead.

After I walked her to the curb and hailed a cab for her, I headed back upstairs and launched a browser, in this case Internet Explorer, but I tend to alternate with Chrome.

At first, I was just searching for obvious descriptors like "van Gelsen," "James van Gelsen," "Jimmy van Gelsen," "van Gelsen shooting." I found a link to a Facebook page that wasn't there when I tried to click on it. Facebook had apparently taken down the page when Jimmy was killed, or when the news of his murder broke. There was a LinkedIn page that was intact, and indicated that Jimmy was experienced in working with nonprofit charities, mentioned that he had worked in the food service operation at Housing Works for the last fourteen years. Nothing new had been added in the time since he was shot, but the page was still there.

Wait. What I'm looking for is information about Jimmy's family or close friends.

There are several genealogy apps. I chose the most obvious one: www.ancestry.com. It was born as a service to the Mormon Church, as I understand it. Mormon scholars had been in the lead on modern genealogy for decades, because it had a religious value for the Church.

Possibly because van Gelsen is a distinctive name, or because it is uncommon, or both, this was a much more productive search, though it was clear to me after about an hour that it would be endless as it expanded the boundaries of the family by moving up the family tree and increasing the number of cousins, second cousins, third cousins, fourth cousins, and so forth.

The way it works is that you enter a name, and a second name from the same family. I guess ideally that would be a parent, but in this case, it was Ragnar van Gelsen, a brother. The pair of names kicked off a chain reaction that first established the parents, John Albert and Martha Elizabeth. Then as the internal search engine chugged along, the screen started to sprout 'leaves', which are adapted from the concept of a family *tree*, which would customarily have leaves. Each 'leaf' appeared on my screen as a graphic, and when I clicked on them, they added family members, previous generations, or lateral relatives.

My cellphone beeped. Gabriele texting.

Getting off R train 49 St OK to come over
Sure I'm working on van Gelsen family tree.
Tree?
I'll show you when you get here.

About five minutes later, the concierge called the house phone to let me know that Mr. Cortese was on his way up. That was approximately simultaneous with the doorbell ringing.

Hug-hug, cheek-kisses.

I took Gabriele into the office room, actually the third bedroom, but for me an office and TV room. The television was tuned to CNN, but the sound was muted, so the only real product of that was a flickering light from behind my chair.

I showed Gabriele the Ancestry research. "Trying to learn something about the family. Relatives tend to be suspects in a situation like this, especially anybody that might have a financial interest in whatever the dead person left in the way of money or valuables."

"You mean somebody that want Jimmy money?"

"Maybe. Maybe more than just money. There are some valuable paintings and antiques, and his apartment is probably worth a fair amount. Could be two or three million dollars, maybe more, depending on whether there are other places like it for sale at the same time. And who knows what kinds of other investments he might have had."

"Eddie in hospital when Jimmy killed."

"Clearly not Eddie. He has a perfect alibi and lots of witnesses that he was in Westchester at that hospital where they took him after he got smashed up in the car."

"Eddie not killer anyway. Eddie care too much about people."

"You're probably better at things like that than I am. Ruth too. You two are both intuitive."

He gave me a puzzled look.

"Intuitive. It means somebody who knows things about people before there is any evidence that somebody like me would believe."

His brow was still wrinkled.

"It means you know things about people without having to figure it out. You can tell when you meet somebody."

He nodded slowly.

"I can't do that. I have to look at all the evidence, and even then, sometimes I don't know."

I went back to the screen.

"So, there are five brothers. Jimmy and four others. Ragnar we met at Ora di Pranzo. Then there is a John Mark, an Augustus Herman, and a Christopher Edward." I pointed out all the names on the screen, then scrolled up.

"Here are the parents," I pointed. "and the grandparents."

He squinted at the screen then pulled up another chair and sat at the same level to my right. He touched the screen where the brothers were listed.

"Yes. John, Augustus and Christopher are married, according to this. Or at least were married when this research was done. I have to look those three up separately to see what I can find out about them."

"I use tablet?"

I nodded, and grabbed the tablet from its docking station, then hooked its keyboard onto the bottom, where it was magnetized to go. I put the password in and handed it to Gabriele. He launched a browser and pushed his chair back, put the tablet in his lap with the left foot propped on the right knee, creating a backstop for the tablet screen.

I went back to looking at cousins, anybody Ancestry listed as being alive.

Unfortunately, I was not able to print anything out without paying a fairly substantial fee to Ancestry, but I was able to save it so that I could get back to where I was if I lost the signal or ran out of time or energy and needed a break.

"There are a lot of them, this family," I said out loud but without directing it to Gabriele in particular. "Also, lots of family names, and most of them not Dutch. Spinnaker seems to be one branch that is pretty big, but there doesn't seem to be much of a young generation of Spinnakers." In fact, as I looked at them, most of the names had two dates; birth and death.

I need to narrow my scope. The third cousins aren't going to have any claim on Jimmy's estate.

I went back to the married brothers. Their wives were listed, and all three of them had children, most of them looked to be ages eight through about eighteen.

Gabriele stood up and stretched. He handed the tablet back to me. He found LinkedIn and Facebook information on the three married brothers, and on Ragnar. All four had advanced degrees from good schools. John from Wharton, Christopher from Tufts, Augustus from NYU Stern. Ragnar had a law degree from Cardozo, which is part of Yeshiva University. Three, John, Christopher and Augustus, worked for companies that were easily recognizable. Bud (Ragnar) was listed with a large law firm with a reputation for Wall Street work. He probably made the most money. Jimmy, the youngest, went to Harvard, but no post-grad degrees that I could find. *Maybe the best grades?*

How can I find out if anybody in the family would have hated Jimmy for his sexual preference? Not something that's going to be online. Maybe Bud would know.

Text from Ruth: *Any progress?*

Lots of information, working on Ancestry.com, tons of stuff, most of it extraneous to what I want to know. The grandparents, parents, all except the mother dead, are not part of Jimmy being shot.

Dead end?

No, we now have the brothers, three of them married with kids, maybe living in the New York area.

Persons of interest?

Not yet, no reason from what I can find online, that any of them would want to shoot their kid brother. But maybe Bud can help.

???

He might know if there was any bad blood.

And he's going to tell the cops?

Maybe not, but between you and Gabriele, you can probably tell what makes him uncomfortable.

Gabriele stretched again, showing off his arms and shoulders, hands clasped behind his head, working the shoulders and elbows. Biceps bulging.

"You hungry?" I asked, changing the subject.

"Sì."

"Let's go someplace that's not Ora di Pranzo."

He looked offended.

I explained that I just wanted to be able to talk without being interrupted. He shrugged Mastroianni-like. I smiled, didn't have to say I found that amusing. Gabriele laughed, reading my face.

We went downstairs and walked the four blocks to the Vernon-Jackson subway station. Took the 7-train to Times Square. Both Gabriele and I felt at home in Times Square. It was where I lived when we met, and it was where Gabriele and his cousin Dante helped us figure out who killed a musician who fell seven floors from above Carnegie Hall onto 7th Avenue.

We walked from the 43rd Street exit from the Times Square subway station to La Masseria on 48th Street near 8th Avenue. It is in the building I used to live in, and I generally get VIP treatment there. Great food, especially great seafood, because the chef is from Bari, on the Adriatic Sea at the bottom of the 'boot' of Italy.

As we walked across 48th Street, there were two bulky, over-muscled men in white skintight t-shirts and jeans who eyed us as though they were trying to memorize something. I shivered when we walked by them, and Gabriele made an evil-eye sign by holding up his hand with the index finger and pinky extended upward and the thumb folded over the middle finger and ring finger that were bent down into the palm. He refused to look back at them, and without thinking about it, grabbed his testicles with the other hand.

I frowned at him. He looked at me and said *maloke*, which I know from experience is Neapolitan for *malocchio* or evil eye.

Hug-hug, kiss-kiss as we walked in. They seated us in the back-right corner of the restaurant, the quietest place in a rather noisy environment. Immediately a plate of cheese, salamis and olives arrived, accompanied by French fried julienned zucchini and a bottle of *Il Falcone*, a deep red wine from the area around Bari, theoretically descended from the time of Holy Roman Emperor Frederick II, who reigned from 1220 to 1250. No way to disprove that, and no way to prove it either, but the wine is top-of-the-line in my book.

"What do you suppose that was about outside?" I asked Gabriele after the waiter opened the Il Falcone bottle and poured two glasses.

"*Maloke*," he said.

"I got that," I said. "I wonder who they are and what the deal is about you or me or both of us."

He shrugged, meaning he had nothing else to say on the matter.

"What they looked like to me is the toughs who were at Prospect Park when we were there at the prayer vigil for Eddie Hall while he was in the hospital," I said. "We were saved by a thunderstorm that day."

He stared at me and muttered something in Italian. I didn't get what he said, and knew it would be pointless to ask him to repeat it. His real first language is Neapolitan, which is not even close to the Italian I learned when I took a total immersion course years back from the State University of New York at New Paltz, on the west side of the Hudson River and about forty miles north of the Tappan Zee Bridge.

"Maybe they'll be gone when we leave."

He rolled his eyes in a cinematic slow burn. *Good luck*, he was saying.

We talked about the van Gelsen family a bit while the food was brought. *Zuppa di pesce* for Gabriele, like a shellfish stew that looked like enough food for three adults. Spaghetti with oil and garlic and *rapini* for me. Lots of grated cheese.

Gabriele was on his phone looking something up. He turned the phone to me and I read that Christopher Edward van Gelsen is a resident of San Francisco. He returned the phone to where he could see the front and kept tapping. He showed it to me. John Mark van Gelsen lives in Briarcliff Manor, up in Westchester County, north of the Bronx.

"And Augustus?" I asked.

"Manhattan."

"I guess we start with Bud and Augustus. Maybe we invite Bud to lunch and ask him if he can bring Augustus. That way we can just talk about Jimmy over lunch. That way we won't look like we're prying into family secrets. Who knows, maybe John can join us too. Especially if he works in the City."

We spent the rest of the meal talking about food. Gabriele has a huge appetite and never seems to gain an ounce. He ate his way through the whole *zuppa di pesce*, which I found virtually mind-boggling. I can never eat more than half a serving of pasta, and pasta isn't nearly as filling as a bowl of lobster, shrimp, clams, mussels and calamari.

Having consumed more food than a family of five could eat, as well as a bottle of Il Falcone, the smiling maître d' sent us two snifters of *Vecchia Romagna* brandy, which we also made short work of.

As we left, the two toughs were still there, waiting across the street. They stared at us, but made no motion in our direction, and when we got to Broadway, I looked back and they weren't there.

Chapter Eighteen

Bud thought he could get both Gus and Johnny to join us for lunch. I suggested that we meet at Joe Allen, a popular tavern on West 46th Street on 'Restaurant Row'. The home of what some people consider one of the best hamburgers in New York City. I don't know about that. I haven't eaten red meat in nearly thirty years.

When the day came, I told Bud that the reservation would be in my name at one o'clock in the afternoon. Joe Allen is a comfortable eatery, crowded at lunch, crowded before and after the theater, with a huge joke going on constantly. Hotel concierges constantly send tourists to Joe Allen for the comfort food and hefty drinks.

Here's the joke. There are theater posters all over the dining room, but they are for shows nobody has ever heard of. Why? Only total flops make it onto the walls of Joe Allen. No hits, thanks very much. Only flops. Gus and Johnny stared at the posters with puzzled looks. I short-stopped it when they sat down by explaining the joke. Then they were insiders, and they could be superior watching the out-of-towners trying to figure out what was going on.

Bud made the introductions. I saw no shared family features. The three men sitting with us didn't look like they were related. Johnny was my height, six foot four and Gus was five foot nine, the height of a normal-sized woman with high heels on. Gus had a full head of hair. Johnny was balding; the top of his head was already mostly shiny scalp.

They sounded alike when they laughed. Bud was dark-haired, John had auburn-brown hair on the sides, and hazel eyes. Gus was skinny with faded blond hair and brown eyes. It was a perfect demonstration of the geographic location of the Netherlands, at the crossroads of northern Europe, a melting-pot of genetics. Europeans normally say that the Dutch are the tallest people in Europe. Gus wouldn't fit. Bud wouldn't fit, being about five foot eleven, though he almost towered over Gus. Line them up and they would be a staircase.

"I want to come clean before we get to know each other," I said. "Gabriele, Ruth and I are friends of Eddie Hall." I paused.

No comment from the three men.

Ruth spoke up. "Speak for yourself, Hugo. I knew Jimmy from the Opera League. He almost never missed a Monday night. Everybody liked him, and that includes me. I am a fan of Eddie Hall, by the way, not really a friend, and Eddie came to Opera League Mondays several times with Jimmy. I was fond of both of them. Never really got to know Eddie until the last few weeks, when we talked about whether he would run for office or not," she said. "I am really happy to meet Jimmy's brothers." She shook hands across the table with each man in turn.

I was taken by surprise by Ruth's speech. My usual reaction to something like that is a smile, and I felt the corners of my mouth turning up without my telling them to do so.

"Anyway, guys, we just wanted to meet you. I never knew your brother, but I went to his funeral at Grace Church in Brooklyn Heights. Beautiful service, very calming and sympathetic. I met Eddie Hall because I was the first person on the scene when he had his car accident on the Thruway. I wish I had met Jimmy."

Gabriele stood up. "I am Gabriele Cortese. My cousin Dante and me, we own Ora di Pranzo, ristorante in SoHo. Jimmy van Gelsen was very soon in Ora di Pranzo. Everyone like Jimmy. He eat with good appetite and smile all time. I meet Eddie Hall at Ora di Pranzo too, with Jimmy. Nice men, nice together."

John looked like he didn't want to join the conversation, but he offered, "Jimmy and I were close as kids. Everybody in the family knew he was gay, because he told everybody. We knew his boyfriends. Was it hard at the beginning? Yes, I guess so, but I loved Jimmy. I wanted to take care of him. He loved my children and Sonia, my wife. I met Eddie. I liked him. I was very happy for Jimmy, watching him smile and put his arm around Eddie. They were obviously in love. That's all."

Gus nodded, but didn't offer anything additional.

Bud spoke up. "These three people are helping the police as they try to figure out what happened. Who, um, shot, um, Jimmy. We should help them any way we can."

"Have you found out anything?" Gus asked.

"We've been trying to put together a map of Jimmy's friends and family. We're making some progress, and we could use your help." I stopped and looked at them.

"You know there was no video of anything that happened that night. It happened where there were no cameras, at least none that was actually recording anything. There are almost always drones, fake cameras that are intended to scare burglars away.

"So far we have no leads." I said slowly.

"What can we do to help you?" Bud asked.

"Tell us who might have had a problem with Jimmy. Anybody he didn't like or didn't get along with. Anybody who owed him money. We're not looking to point fingers at people, but when we run into a situation where nobody admits to ever having had an argument with a victim, it leaves us totally in the dark."

"I can give you a list of people who owed him money," Bud said. "I've been over all his books. There are a couple of personal loans, but not big ones. The other people who owed Jimmy money are with companies where he invested in bonds or notes."

"Your brother, Christopher. How long has he lived in San Francisco?"

They looked at each other. Bud answered, "About six years, I'd say. He went to work for Wells Fargo in New York, and they wanted him to go to the home office after a while. So, he did. It's easier to live in San Francisco. No snow, no cold weather. Occasionally earthquakes of course. but no huge storms like the nor'easters that fly up the east coast and cause havoc everyplace they hit. Like Superstorm Sandy, Hurricane Maria, or any of the great blizzards we've lived through."

"Would it be right to guess that Christopher, if he likes San Francisco, is okay with gay men marrying gay men."

They all nodded. "Look," Gus said. "The family is not all one religion. A few are Catholics. Most of us are Lutheran or Reformed Church, but we generally all try to live and let live. It's the way we were brought up."

"Is it possible he had a bad relationship with one of his neighbors?" I asked. "His apartment is a co-op. Is it possible that he was having trouble with something and complained about it?"

They looked at each other and each one shrugged in turn. No responses.

"Does that mean you don't know if he was having a rough time with someone in the neighborhood?'

Three nods.

Gabriele spoke up. "You ever see him kiss Eddie?" He paused. "Big kiss?"

Gus held his hand up and nodded then Bud did the same. Not John.

"It make you angry if he kiss man?"

John answered. "We're not a very demonstrative family. We don't hug and kiss in public, so it might make us look away if they kissed like that, but would be because we don't do that, even with our wives. Not because we think Jimmy was doing something wrong."

"What if he kissed Eddie when your children were watching?" Ruth asked.

"Same," John said. "Not something we're used to, but we definitely want our children to understand that love is love, whether it's a man and a woman, or two women or two men."

There was silence.

"You have to understand," Gus said. "This is not new. Jimmy was always gay. We always knew. He danced with his boyfriends in high school. We had family pictures with Jimmy and several different men. We went skiing and Jimmy shared a sleeping bag with a guy. Just kind of an everyday thing."

"And not a problem with that?" Ruth asked in a smallish voice. "I don't have children, but I think if my brothers were kissing men in front of their children, it would make me uncomfortable." She looked at her hands and pursed her lips slightly.

"I don't eat meat," I said, "but I have been told many times that the hamburgers here are really good." I waited two Mississippis. "And I don't mind if you eat meat, even though I don't."

John laughed out loud. "Exactly right!" he said.

There was a relaxation of shoulder muscles all around the table. I raised my wine glass. "To Jimmy's brothers!" They held their glasses. "It's okay. You can drink to yourselves, or you can drink to me."

I could see out the window in the front of the restaurant, even though we were a half-story below sidewalk level, having walked down a few steps to the door. There were those two goons who were at La Masseria. I motioned to Gabriele, who looked and nodded. He did the horns gesture.

"Evil eye?" Bud asked.

Gabriele pointed at the two men.

Bud flashed a badge.

"What's that?" Ruth asked.

"Honorary cop, Upper East Side, twenty-third precinct on 102nd Street" he said. "I'll get us all by these goofballs."

"Looks like the tiki torch guys from Prospect Park," Ruth said.

"The what?" Gus asked.

"There was a prayer vigil in Prospect Park in Brooklyn for Eddie Hall when he was still in the hospital," she said. "There were these Charlottesville neo-Nazis or whatever who tried to break everything up."

"What happened?"

"Nothing. It started to pour rain and thunder, and everybody ran for cover. Mother Nature saved the day."

The six of us walked out together and when the two took a step toward us, Bud pulled out a badge and just flashed it at them. He said nothing. The pair backed away, turned and walked toward 9th Avenue as we walked toward 8th Avenue.

"Thanks," I said.

"*De rien*. It was nothing," Bud said with a big grin. "I love doing that."

"Hey, a favor," I said to Bud. "I may try to either talk to your brother, Christopher or even go out to San Francisco and meet him. I need to know all the players so I can report back to the detective who runs us."

He stared at me.

"If you don't mind, maybe you can tell him I'm okay to talk to, not trying to do anything to anyone. Just want to find out who shot Jimmy van Gelsen."

Bud smiled and nodded. "And next time, I'm buying," he said.

Chapter Nineteen

"I'm going to San Francisco to meet Christopher van Gelsen."

"And you want me to go with you?" Ruth asked.

"Well, I think we both have a better chance of being upgraded if you're my seat-mate."

"Honestly?" she squinted at me as though the sun were at my back, but it was evening. "You have enough miles to do whatever you want in the way of upgrading."

"Maybe, but I can only spend mine once, and you're permanently golden."

"What about Gabriele?"

"I don't think it would be fair to ask him to go with us. He'd do it, of course, but that would strand Dante at Ora di Pranzo alone, and they'd both be miserable," I said slowly. "Although I have to admit it would be fun to watch the streetscapes in San Francisco when Gabriele hit town."

"Anyhoo, you thinking tomorrow?"

"I have to call Christopher van Gelsen and make sure he's available. Bud said he'd help pave the way."

"No time like the present. They're three hours earlier."

I called the number Bud sent me and Christopher answered after one ring. Yes, Bud had called, and yes, he would be happy to get together when I was in town.

"If I can get the right flight, how about tomorrow early evening?"

That would work, he said. He was very close with Jimmy, and wanted to be helpful in any way he could be, to find out who did it. I told him my friend, Ruth Jensen, would be traveling with me. We agreed that I'd call when I checked into my hotel and we could meet up for a drink or whatever, provided I could get a seat on an early flight. Otherwise it would be the day after.

Ruth told me she'd call me back when she spoke to the airline.

I linked back to the Ancestry research I had been working on. Maybe something would jump out at me. I decided to look into the wives' families. Nothing interesting, and they were all from out of town. Connecticut, Massachusetts, Delaware. Like looking at a brick wall.

I picked up the phone on the first ring. It was Ruth. She had arranged super-APEX fares on the ten AM flight, and they upgraded us both ways to Business. Flying west takes longer than flying east because you head into the wind, so if we took off at ten, we'd be to San Francisco by about one PM Pacific Time, because we gain three hours flying west. She also had two rooms at the St Francis Hotel for one hundred and fifty-nine dollars each per night. Like the miracle of the loaves and fishes, but this was the miracle of the plane and hotel.

I clicked out of the Ancestry research and had a quick look at Facebook. Not a lot there. My political friends were up in arms, some one way and some the other, about the latest Washington DC shenanigans. For some reason I have some of the extreme loonies as Facebook "friends" too. I think I just clicked "connect" without checking, totally mindless. I typically hit "Hide Post" when one of them appears. What I ought to do is "unfriend" them, but I haven't done it yet. I keep thinking I will get the jump on the latest conspiracy theory if I let them blather on. So far, not. One day soon I'll clean house, most likely.

Because I am a Nervous Nellie about flying, I got to JFK at eight AM, the recommended two hours ahead. I know they fly three classes on transcon flights; Cattle, Business, and First. I have only flown First once that I recall, at least on a longish flight. Business is my preference, even though they give you nice pajamas and a bigger selection of wines in First and they have those little cubicles that are like separate roomlets. The seats in Business on the larger planes recline to totally flat, and they hand out comforters that are very puffy and comfy.

The food is airline food, bumped up a couple of levels, but still not something you'd order in a restaurant. Whatever.

I checked in at the First-Class booth, which is okay for Business passengers, because we're *almost* First Class. They gave me a pass to the airline club, where there was a reasonable facsimile of a Greek diner breakfast selection on a help-yourself buffet. Ruth wasn't there yet. I know Ruth, last-minute Ruth, golden Ruth the Queen of the Upgrade, most likely because she and Murray always used to fly "real" First Class on their vacations to places like Argentina, South Africa, Sri Lanka, Bali or Rio. Drop a bundle like that on an airline, and you are a friend for at least a year, maybe longer. It was probably about to expire, since Murray was in a cardboard box in Ruth's living room.

I helped myself to scrambled eggs, hash browns that looked like the ones at McDonald's, some toast-it-yourself rye toast with gobs of butter, a cran-apple juice in a ten-ounce bottle, a peach yogurt and a black coffee. I doubted they were going to serve breakfast on a flight leaving at ten AM, after all. I seated myself at a desk with an electric plug and tuned in using the Wi-Fi from the club.

True to form, Ruth came running in like a herd of turtles at about nine thirty. Like me, she never checks luggage. ("I have had too many suitcases that went to Chile when I was going to San Diego—never again.") I carry a small black duffel that I can pack with a suit, four shirts, four ties, four pairs of socks, four t-shirts and boxer briefs, a long-sleeved sport shirt, a spare book, a Dopp kit, an electric razor and two spare chargers. That lets me wear jeans, a black t-shirt, a V-neck sweater and the only pair of shoes I travel with a pair of penny-loafers in cordovan, which goes with anything. Ruth uses a roll-aboard that probably has just as much crammed into it as my duffel does.

We hustled out to the gate, just as they were getting ready to call group one, Coach but slipped in while they were still boarding Business and Military. We had two seats in the middle, separated by a very large console that had "my" television screen tucked down and into it. Maybe the best thing about Business Class is that the overhead bins are never crowded, and pretty much everything is clean-looking and in working order. We also have two restrooms for our cabin. I had my shoes off faster than you could say "Jack Robinson," preparing to doze off while the pilot taxis.

I don't actually let myself fall asleep until the plane levels off after the take-off. One of the problems with air travel is that the flights are never long enough to get a good sleep, but I give it a run for its money. I was reading yet another history of Constantinople. It never gets old for me. But even with my glasses, reading while reclining makes my eyes sandy, and soon they want to close.

Ruth hissed at me.

"Was I snoring?"

She nodded. "I would have shoved you like I used to do with Murray, but I couldn't reach far enough over the console, the dishes, your book and the rest of that stuff."

I looked at the console, which had a tray of food on it. *When did that happen?*

"The flight attendant didn't want to wake you up. I told her you are vegetarian, so she left you some pasta."

I held an upward arrow down on the arm of my chair and the motor sat me up. I looked at my watch. Noon.

"We've been in the air two hours?"

She shrugged and rolled her eyes. Well, at least she wasn't an imposter; she was the real Ruth.

"I'm not a vegetarian."

"I know, but it's the easiest thing to say in order to get something you'll eat."

I opened my tablet and managed to connect to the airline's Wi-Fi, which charges nine dollars and ninety-five cents per twenty-four-hour period. Goes directly to my Amex card. Went to Ancestry to look at the last page I was on there. All kinds of leaves blinking at me. Mostly further and further back in time. *How do I explain to them that the nineteenth century doesn't matter?*

Ruth was watching a movie. I couldn't see what it was because of the angle. So, I decided to watch something on my little TV screen. I defaulted to 'Big Bang Theory', and watched several episodes back to back. None of the movies turned my crank.

As my watch told me it was getting to be mid-afternoon, I realized I needed to set it back by three hours to be on the right time in San Francisco, and as often happens to me because I love being in the air, the gradual descent began as the nose of the plane slanted ever so slightly down. I knew that if I had a tennis ball, it would roll to the First-Class cabin if I put it on the floor in the aisle.

Then we were touching down. I looked at my watch: one o'clock on the nose. I pulled out my phone and checked it for messages, because once on the ground, it's okay. It took a while to get to the gate, but we disembarked almost first, First was first, of course, and before it seemed possible, we were meeting our Uber car driver, whose name was Joaquin, in a black Toyota Highlander.

"St. Francis Hotel," he stated without a trace of accent and looked at me in the mirror. I nodded.

Everything went smoothly and I was in my room by two thirty. I called Christopher van Gelsen, who said he would meet us at the bar in the Clock Bar, a comfortable, old-fashioned looking room with Art Deco tables and chairs, and subtle indirect lighting. I told him I would be wearing a light blue shirt and jeans, and that I am tall. My friend Ruth would be looking more stylish, and most likely a 'classic Chanel' jacket, since she seemed to have a fixation about second-hand Chanel clothing. A throwback to Grace Kelly, I guess, or a young Catherine Deneuve. Long time passing, as the song says.

I am always surprised by Union Square in San Francisco. It's smaller than I expect it to be. I lived in Los Angeles for a while, and Union Square is about like Pershing Square in LA, and it also has a subterranean garage under it. Union Square is more strollable, possibly, but postage-stamp sized. San Francisco is pretty no matter how you look at it, though. This trip was a milk run. We'd meet Christopher, have a quick sleep then catch a plane back at eleven AM, connecting through Chicago and arriving around ten thirty PM at LaGuardia, instead of JFK. Not even time to have dinner at one of the famous restaurants in the City by the Bay unless Christopher was in a hurry and left us before dinner time.

Christopher had more than a passing resemblance to John Mark van Gelsen, the tall, bald brother from our meeting at Joe Allen on 46th Street. He was smiling when he walked in, and held his hand out to shake. I introduced him to Ruth, who was wearing a white classic Chanel jacket with black windowpane checks on a slightly nubbly-looking textile, almost like the fabric had been repeatedly snagged on something. Pretty, and it was one I hadn't seen before. I've never been in Ruth's bedroom, but I have always fantasized she would have a closet that was more like a small room, with floor-length mirrors, and possibly an automated clothing rack so she could stand and run clothing by until she got to what she wanted. Like a dry cleaner.

We had a much more informal-feeling talk than we had with the other three brothers in New York. Christopher said everyone called him Kip, so we did.

He said that Jimmy had spats fairly regularly with his boyfriends in the past, when Kip was still living in Manhattan, before Wells Fargo transferred him to the home office.

"Like fights?" Ruth asked. "Or like pouting?"

He didn't know, because he never witnessed one, but Jimmy would complain to Kip, because they were only a year apart, and growing up they had been inseparable. He most vividly remembered Jimmy complaining about Raul a few years back. Raul was a celebrity chef who opened his own restaurant near the meat-packing district, one of those places where there is a line halfway down the block of people waiting to get in. Raul and Jimmy lived together for over a year, and it seemed like they were in Page Six every week, photographed with lavish PDAs frequently.

But it hadn't been a bed of roses, apparently, because Jimmy regularly called Kip to complain about Raul, who spent money like water and was always in debt. He drank a lot, although he didn't seem to be a drunk.

"How about Eddie Hall?"

"Jimmy seldom said anything negative about Eddie. I have to say I never met Eddie, never even saw them together, except in snapshots on Jimmy's Facebook page. I think I am still friended with Eddie on Facebook, but Jimmy's page is in digital heaven these days. Probably being written over by somebody new. All gone."

"Seldom said anything negative," Ruth asked, "but when he did, what was it likely to be?"

"I remember one rant about Eddie. Jimmy was tired of talking about politics, and he said that was all Eddie thought about. I asked him if he and Eddie were on the outs. He chuckled and used some colorful language to say no, they were good."

"But with Raul, they actually fought or argued."

"Raul was in trouble with his restaurant. The food critics loved it, but he was losing money I think, although Jimmy never actually said that. When they closed it down, Raul moved to Florida fairly suddenly to work at some restaurant in the Miami area. That was it. Jimmy never said he missed Raul. I had the impression that they never even spoke or emailed or texted. Jimmy just stopped talking about him."

"How do you think things were going between Eddie and your brother?" I asked.

"Well, like I said, I never met Eddie Hall, although I saw him on television with that business in Boston. That march that never happened? Good-looking guy. Jimmy was head over heels for him. I had never known Jimmy to be that much in love."

"And you don't know anyone that Jimmy would have been having a financial argument with? The most common motives are money and family. That's why the spouse is almost always a suspect. In this case, no spouse, and Eddie was in a hospital a county away after his car swerved off the road. So, we know it wasn't Eddie."

He looked up in thought, and shook his head. "Jimmy didn't talk to me much about his investments. He would sometimes ask me to explain something, like the difference between yesterday's closing price and fair value but nothing specific, at least nothing that I remember."

We switched to small talk. "You and your brothers don't look as much alike as some brothers and sisters do," I said, "but you look a lot like John."

"Because I'm tall and bald."

Ruth chuckled.

"I'll take that for a yes," he said.

Ruth gave him some play-by-play descriptions of what happened in Boston. "It seemed like some outside party was trying to start a riot," she said. "It didn't work, but it did get the Boston PD out in riot gear, and a couple of squads of SWAT cops. Better safe than sorry, I guess."

"Maybe like what people were saying Russia did in the presidential election?"

"I suppose," I said. "I don't think we're ever going to know how this one rolled out. I remember seeing the initial announcements of the two opposing marches when they hit my screen. I have Google Alerts set for things like that. They came out minutes from each other, and they had almost exactly the same wording about where and when. We all thought it looked like a prank or a practical joke, like something one of those night talk shows would cook up to be funny. Could have been a high school hacker, I suppose, or it could have been the Kremlin or some other unfriendly government. Cuba? China? Maybe the NSA knows, but I don't."

Kip shook his head. "The things that happen these days. Hard to figure out."

"Well, it came very soon after that terrorist attack in Times Square caused the Million Woman March to disperse on police orders, and there was a protest march downtown at the same time. So, the Boston thing looked like someone was trying to get the same effect."

"Did you know that Eddie Hall's radio show is carried on a listener-supported station here?"

"Really?" I was caught totally off guard. "I wonder if anyone listens to it, or if they do, why they listen to it. Eddie is all about New York most of the time."

"I listened to it once. Just happened to be in the car and the radio was on that Pacifica station that carries it. When I heard that it was Eddie Hall, I wanted to hear what he had to say. I think they were talking about a new library opening? I have to say I thought Eddie was a born emcee. It moved along well."

"One of the kids he was interviewing was his own son, Alex. Good kid, basketball player. High school."

"And the other kid?"

"Somebody that Eddie found, I guess. Older than Alex, maybe college."

Chapter Twenty

"What did you take away from meeting Kip?" Ruth asked me as we were riding back to the airport.

"I suppose the sour relationship with the former boyfriend is something that goes on the bulletin board. It's just a guess, but I think we're looking for someone who had a beef with Jimmy about something. Not his brothers."

"A beef about what?"

"Love or money usually."

"No shit, Sherlock."

"Watch it," I shook my index finger at her playfully. "He's my hero, you know. Sherlock, that is. Not Jimmy."

The flight back was actually shorter because the jet stream was pushing us along, but it seemed longer, because it was dark by the time we got to the Mississippi River. The pilot said it was down there, and we were over St Louis, but all I could see were some city lights. Might as well have been Bakersfield or Omaha. We got in at about eleven PM, and called an Uber. He could drop me in Long Island City and then skip over the 59th Street bridge to drop Ruth off.

The entrance to my building is on 50th Avenue, which looks like a continuation of 42nd Street where it ends at the East River. Addresses in Queens are in large part on numbered Avenues, Roads and Streets, which makes it seem like there is a grid like Manhattan, but there isn't. Just because there is a 1st Avenue and a 50th Avenue, does not mean there are all the normal numbers between them, and very few are through streets that actually go more than a couple of blocks. My cross street is 2nd Street, and the next block is 5th Street, for instance.

When New York City was consolidated on New Year's Day in 1898, the area we know as Queens was a large group of small communities, all of which were in Queens County, which was a partner with the county that Brooklyn was in, called Kings County. Queens County was one of the twelve original counties that were created in 1683 just after the British took over New York from the Dutch, but it was a county, not a coherent city. As much as it has grown, it has never become a coherent city, and all of the old communities and neighborhoods retain their names, some of which are still Dutch, like Flushing, which is named after a town in the Netherlands named Vlissingen, which the English shortened to Vlissing, and pronounced 'Flushing'.

Anyway, I got out of the Uber just before midnight and used my keycard to get in the revolving front door of the building. As I curved around the doorway, I realized there were people behind me, and when I got in, I looked back. It was those two goons that I nearly clashed with a couple of times in the past. They were standing outside, not trying to push their way into the building. I went around the corner and into the elevator to get to my apartment.

When I stepped out on the balcony, there they were, looking up at me from the sidewalk. I went back inside, took a bottle of vodka out of the freezer, which is where they belong, in my mind, and poured some into a martini glass. I added a teaspoon or so of olive juice and a nice plump olive, and drank it. Not in a single gulp, but also not sipping like I'd imagine a British gentleman in a centuries-old club in London would do.

Well, there's no question they know who I am and where I live.

I pulled out my cellphone and sent a text message to Mike di Saronno. *2 toughs outside my bldg. OK, advice or help? Met Jimmy bro @ SanFran w Ruth.*

Text to Ruth: *2 toughs waiting at apt bldg. Lemme know you ok pls?*
No prob here. Want me to call Mike
Alredy dun

When I pressed 'Send" the phone on the kitchen pass-through rang. It was Mike. I explained best possible. He said he had sent a posse to clean things up. I turned out the lights and walked out onto the balcony again. Sure enough there was a black-and-white and a cop asking for ID, and taking notes on a tablet. The two toughs turned and quick-walked toward the subway station.

"Can you come to my office tomorrow?"

"Sure, just gotta get some sleep first. You think I'm okay here, or am I going to get visitors again?"

"Check outside."

The squad car was sitting at the curb.

"They're gonna stay out front of your building for a while, but I already had word from my guy in the Vernon-Jackson station that two bodybuilder types in white t-shirts just got on a Manhattan-bound 7-train and are already gone."

"Thanks."

I took a hot shower, turned up the A/C, and climbed into bed with a book on Elizabeth I, a lead-pipe guarantee that there would be very little that was new. I've been reading books on the Tudors since I was in college, umpty-up years back. I love fact-filled but boring books that help summon up my mind's ability to generate alpha waves. It wasn't long before my eyes started to close, and I put the book and my reading glasses on the other side of the bed, pulled up the quilt I use in the summer, and that was all she wrote.

The sun was shining on the windows of the building next door, and beaming a shaft of sunlight directly onto me. There was a moment of panic—what time is it? But it was just after seven, so I was safe. I put on jeans and a black t-shirt, athletic socks and sneakers and headed out to get a subway to Times Square then transferred to the 1 train, took that to 50th Street and walked the four blocks to 54th and across 8th Avenue to the Midtown North precinct, formally the Eighteenth precinct, which is chiseled into the granite above the door, but nobody ever calls it that. I could have done it with my eyes closed because I lived right near the precinct for ten years.

Mike was waiting for me with an empty Styrofoam coffee cup. We walked over to the machine and filled my cup, and topped his off.

"I wish I had something to tell you that would shed some light on Jimmy van Gelsen's end, but so far I haven't found anything much." I explained that Ruth and I had met with the four surviving van Gelsen brothers, three at Joe Allen and one in the St. Francis Hotel in San Francisco.

"They all seem close to destroyed about Jimmy's murder," I said. "And Ruth's nose says none of them had anything to do with it. Christopher, who we met day before yesterday in San Francisco, said that Jimmy regularly had fall-outs with his boyfriends, especially a Raul Vasquez, who used to run a restaurant in the meat-packing district called Sapori."

"Oh, yeah, it closed up a few years back. I think the chef was broke and actually ended up stiffing the landlord. Food was good though. Really fresh bread, as I recall."

"Christopher said Raul left in a hurry and moved to Florida to work with a friend who had a restaurant someplace. He said they had cut things off already anyway, and Jimmy seemed relieved that he was gone. I got the impression there may have been some substance abuse going on."

"No problems with the co-op board where he lived?"

"None of the brothers knew of anything, but other than that, I don't know how to even check that part out. I'm sure Bud, Ragnar van Gelsen, is in charge of selling the co-op, so maybe he would know."

"So, they weren't pissed off that Jimmy was leaving everything to Eddie Hall?"

"Never got a straight answer to that exact question. Eddie was there when I was talking to Bud, uh, Ragnar, and he defused it immediately. Said he didn't want any of Jimmy's estate, except something to remember Jimmy by."

"I wonder if he knew Ragnar was sore about that."

"I'm sure he did, because he had been served with papers on a suit to invalidate the will."

"So, are they pursuing the suit?"

"No. I think it was dropped because Eddie didn't want anything. I think Eddie is comfortable. He has that radio show, and he made pretty good money for a long time with the Brooklyn District Attorney's office, and his ex-wife comes from a family that made sure she was comfortable. I think she helped Eddie with his political ambitions for a while, but they eventually cracked up because of politics."

"Were they divorced?"

"Well, Eddie was getting ready to marry Jimmy, but I don't know anything about the divorce. Nobody refers to her as the ex-wife. If they are still married, she would have stood to inherit part of a pretty healthy amount of money."

"I haven't met her, but from what everybody says, she was happy to just be back on her own, after Eddie ran for City Council and lost."

"Kids?"

"One of each. Alex is in college and Mattie is about middle school, like eighth grade going into high school. Perfect kids, good manners, clean and polite. Eddie dotes on them. Alex was on one of his radio shows while Ruth and I were there. Very well-spoken, almost shocking for a kid his age."

"They live with him?"

"No idea, but he spends a lot of time with them. I'd guess they live with Mom on the east side. She has a townhouse in the east sixties between Madison and Park. I think Alex was at Trinity, now in college, and Mattie is at Spence."

"So, Mom is supporting them, I'd guess."

"Maybe, but since Eddie is African-American, so are they, and they may get scholarships."

Mike sat back and took off his glasses. "We did some poking around. Not everything was peaches and cream with the co-op board in his building."

"Do tell."

"We subpoenaed any correspondence between Jimmy and the Co-op Board. It arrived a week or so ago, and we've been reading our way through it," he said. He pointed to a cardboard box on the small conference table in his office. "Jimmy wanted to buy the apartment above him and he wanted to put a staircase in. The Board wasn't enthusiastic, and I think the papers referred to some engineering problems. That building dates back to the twenties, and the Board thought it would be a real challenge to cut a staircase through the ceiling without destabilizing the place. Plus, Jimmy was in the process of listing his apartment for sale. Could have found a bigger place. After all, he and Eddie were getting married."

"Lotta times the agent that lists the old place also handles the new place."

Mike said that would be Ellison, one of the major residential brokerages catering to the high end.

"On it," I said, thinking *this is a job for Ruth the Sleuth*. "I bet Bud has some input on this. You mind if I talk to him about it?"

"No boundaries. Use your judgment."

I look cautiously out the front door of Midtown North to see if there were two bruisers out there waiting for me.

Not that I could see.

I pulled out my cellphone and found Bud van Gelsen in the Contacts. Pressed 'Dial', and listened to the ringing.

"Mr. van Gelsen's office," said a youngish woman's voice.

"Hugo Miller here for Bud van Gelsen."

"May I tell him what this is about?"

"'Fraid not."

A couple of clicks later Bud picked up.

"Kip is a fan of yours."

"That's nice. I'm a fan of yours, and your brothers seem like salt of the earth too."

"What can I do for you?"

"I'd like to slurp down some coffee together and see if you can help me piece some things together about your brother Jimmy's apartment."

We agreed that I would walk over there and we would adjourn to one of the two Starbucks stores in the building. *Two* Starbucks in *one* office building. I rang him again when I got to the front of the building, a moderately tall office tower that stayed within the envelope of the neighborhood. It was called World Wide Plaza. He said to meet him in the Starbucks at the corner of 49th and 8th. I walked the thirty or so paces to the entrance. He was already there.

"How'd you get here so fast?"

"I was already here, your call got relayed to my cellphone."

I got a grande Colombian, black, no milk, no sugar.

I explained about the boxful of correspondence between Jimmy and the co-op Board.

"He told me he wanted to buy the place upstairs and shift the front door up a floor, so that the apartment he was living in would be like a cellar."

"Sounds easy enough."

"I haven't read all the documents. Probably never will. But the Board didn't want him to unify the two apartments with a new staircase. They said there were structural problems.

"Jimmy talked to me about it. He didn't understand why they were giving him a hard time. He had hired an architect and an engineering firm, and they told him it would be pretty straightforward.

"I think it went on for a while, and the Board never budged. Jimmy told me he was going to sell the apartment and find a new place."

"Did you represent Jimmy on the transactions?"

"Transactions plural?"

"Selling the old place and purchasing the new place?"

He never sold the apartment, so he never made a firm offer on the new place."

"Do you know where the new place was?"

"Sure, it was in TriBeCa on White Street, right near a kind of avant-garde theater group called 'The Flea'."

"And it was bigger than the old place?"

"I presume so. Never saw it. Remember he never made a serious offer for it. He probably took Eddie Hall for a walk-through though."

That's interesting. If he did see the apartment, wonder why he never mentioned it?

"I'll ask him about it when I see him. I was just wondering, though, whether there was a buyer for the old place or a seller at the new place who could have felt burned when the deal didn't go through."

"You mean somebody with a gripe that would lead them to kill my brother?"

"Yeah."

"Then no."

"Nobody that wanted the apartment and wouldn't want it taken off the market?"

"You mean angry and stupid enough to shoot Jimmy so the apartment wouldn't be taken off the market?"

"I guess it doesn't make sense when you put it like that. I just meant someone who was pissed off about something, anything, about either of the apartments." I paused and struggled for some words. "Look, most violent crimes are committed by either a family member or someone with a financial motivation. Love or money, as they say."

Bud looked puzzled.

"No, I didn't mean that someone in the family did it. I was trying to see if there could have been a financial reason, somebody who either stood to profit by shooting your brother, or somebody who was just pissed off about a financial situation. Maybe whoever owned the apartment upstairs, and the co-op board wouldn't authorize the construction. Removing Jimmy from the transaction might not help, but revenge can be totally self-destructive as well as the damage it does to others."

"Look, Hugo," he said. "If anything you said caused even a spark of something, I would tell you. I worked with Jimmy on most or all of his legal issues." He raised his hands, palms up, arms partly extended, and said, "I just don't know what to tell you. Nothing rings a bell of any kind."

Chapter Twenty-one

Afterward I decided to go for a walk. I find that I think better when I am doing something that amounts to busywork. Vacuuming. Playing solitaire. Walking a couple of miles and just breathing the air. Swimming laps. Almost anything that takes no real thought process but that keeps me busy.

I walked east on 50th Avenue toward the village-like commercial strip of my part of Long Island City. I was heading for a watering-hole named Dominie's Hoek, which is a name that was used of this neighborhood when the Dutch were still in control before the English ships from New England literally sailed into New York Harbor and threatened to burn the city to the ground if the Dutch didn't capitulate.

The Dutch capitulated, and "Peg-leg" Peter Stuyvesant gave the keys to the city to the English commander. On September 8, 1664, a scant four years after Charles II was restored to the English throne, the English took over all of New York, and the entire length of the Hudson River. New Amsterdam became New York, and an upstate fort became Albany named after James Stuart, Duke of York and Albany, the brother of Charles II.

Later, in 1685, when Charles II died, James Stuart became king of England as James II. Three years later he was thrown out because he was Roman Catholic, married to a Roman Catholic, and they had a Roman Catholic baby son. The English named the flight of James II the 'Glorious Revolution', and James's Protestant daughter, Mary, became Queen Mary II, and her husband, William of Orange, became William III. The university in Virginia, William and Mary, is named after them. So, in a way, the Dutch took over again for a time, although they had no children, and Mary's sister, Anne, became the last of the Stuart monarchs of England.

I was thinking about what the area we call Long Island City must have looked like back then. What would it look like if you swept out all the crowded-together buildings, dug up all the roads, and let the area go 'wild' again? Oh, and bring back the native Americans who had lived there from time immemorial.

Then the two toughs were standing in the middle of the sidewalk ahead of me, between me and Dominie's Hoek.

"Buy you a drink, guys?" I tried.

It was a busy sidewalk, lots of people everywhere. I thought I'd give it a try.

They said nothing, but one grabbed my arm and turned me around. The other made it clear he had a gun in his jacket pocket. I thought briefly *I ought to ask you the questions I was asking Bud van Gelsen,* but they were almost dragging me, although I kept moving my feet as though I were walking, and so that they wouldn't actually drag me. We walked right past the police precinct and I yelled at the top of my voice "Help!"

Two cops appeared in the front door of the precinct building, and the two toughs let go of me and quick-walked ahead, turning right on the first street and breaking into a run.

I tried to explain what was going on to the two cops. They frisked me and found nothing other than my wallet, which had my driver's license saying that I lived at 201 50th Avenue.

"You live in that building?" he said, pointing at my building.

"Yes, officer."

"What were those two guys doing?"

"I don't know what they were going to do, but they were dragging me someplace, probably to a car, after they grabbed me on Vernon Avenue."

"Do you know them?"

"No, but they have been hanging around, and I have no real idea what they want. I am working with Detective Mike di Saronno at the Eighteenth precinct, Midtown North in Manhattan. He is investigating a murder from about a month ago. I have worked with him before and he asked me to lend a hand on this case."

"You're a snitch?"

"No." I gave him a strongly disapproving stare.

"Then what?"

"I'm basically a volunteer and I work with Detective di Saronno," I said, fully aware that the police don't have a lot of volunteers, unlike some fire departments. "If you call him, he'll tell you the same thing I told you. He has helped me stay out of range from those two guys before, as a matter of fact just two nights ago, here at my apartment building. Maybe they have something to do with the case I'm helping Mike with, but they've never said anything to me, so I don't know."

They took me inside and talked to the Sergeant on duty. Somebody called Mike, who fortunately answered his cellphone when it rang through from the office phone system, and did, as I predicted, say that I was working with him on an investigation. He didn't specify what kind of investigation apparently.

"He says he's working a homicide case," the Sergeant said audibly.

Apparently, Mike verified that.

"What do you want us to do, Detective?"

The upshot was that he asked them to keep an eye on my safety while he arranged a safe place for me to stay. Two uniforms walked with me to my building then to my apartment on the tenth floor.

"You got a lot of paintings here," one of the men said. He introduced himself as Marek Stenkowski.

"Do you live in Greenpoint?" I asked him. Greenpoint is a section of Brooklyn that borders Long Island City, and is famously Polish.

No, he grew up in Greenpoint, but it was getting too expensive, and he and his wife lived in Sunnyside, a section of Queens, that also borders Long Island City, but to the east, rather than the south, like Greenpoint.

"Each painting has a story," I said. "Meaning a story about how I happen to have it, not a story about the picture itself."

"There's no place that doesn't have a painting on it," he said, smiling and walking from picture to picture. "What's that?" he said, pointing to an assemblage on a metal sheet that is supposed to depict Atlantis sinking into the ocean. So, there are wave and flames, and a jumble of modernish-looking buildings collapsing. Sounds grisly, but it's very pretty and very colorful.

I told him what it was supposed to be and that I bought it at a gallery in Laguna Beach, California. He said he knew about Atlantis.

"A lot of my friends think my apartment looks like a garage sale."

I told them I was going to sign onto my computer,

I told them to look in the fridge, that there were some fruit juices and a container of iced tea.

"How long are you going to stay here?" I asked.

They indicated that they were going to stay until the Manhattan detective got there.

"Mike's coming here?"

They nodded and wandered into the kitchen. I signed onto the computer to see if there was any email. There was a note from Ruth saying she was coming over, had talked to Mike and heard that some goons were bothering me.

"You gonna punch them out?" I asked playfully.

"They better hope not," she said with an air of finality.

I didn't pursue it, but I would have believed if she had said she was a black belt in karate. I've learned over the years that she has a lot of secrets, and they could be almost anything, from spiral peeling a potato with the whole skin intact, to skydiving in the Rockies.

As it happened, they arrived within a few minutes of each other, and they had spoken about next steps, something that Ruth hadn't mentioned.

"Pack a bag," Ruth said. "You're coming to stay with me for a while. I don't want something happening to you when I'm counting on you to help me find a place for Murray when we have time to go for a drive."

"I don't want to leave my apartment."

"Nobody's suggesting that you move out," Mike said. "I just want you to vacate your place for long enough for us to pick up the goons who were doing whatever they were doing."

"How you gonna do that?"

"We have some video of them from outside Joe Allen," Mike said. "We've been running some facial recs on them, and we think we know who they are."

"Look," Ruth said. "I've got what they call a classic eight. That means I have three bedrooms and three baths, in addition to the rooms you've seen at the front of the apartment where you come in. You can have all the privacy you want, and there's a television in each bedroom, with good Wi-Fi everyplace."

So, it was settled, and I packed my duffel with shirts, underwear, a Dopp lot with shavers, my dandruff shampoo, my tablet computer and charger, a couple of books to help me go to sleep, and a small bottle of my blood-pressure medicine, Amlodipine Besylate.

"Let's go have dinner at La Masseria," Mike said. "On me."

"You know, these two guys haven't ever said anything to me, so I don't rightly know what kind of a beef they have."

"Their timing is just too coincidental not to be related. They didn't show up until you had been seen with Eddie Hall, by hundreds of people at Prospect Park, and by whoever was standing on the sidewalk or watching on television at the Million Woman March. That's circumstantial, but it's good enough for government work."

It seemed to me that they were probably connected, but without confirmation of some kind, it just didn't seem like a slam-dunk to me.

Ruth was edging closer to the front door.

"I'm coming," I said. I looked at Mike.

"Your bag?" Mike was looking a little impatient. "Unless you want to stay here and wait for those two guys to show up again. When? A couple of hours after we leave maybe?"

I grabbed my keys off the peg in the kitchen, picked up the duffel, and we left. Mike had a black-and-white downstairs idling at the curb. He got in the front seat with the driver. Ruth and I were in the back, and I threw my duffel in the trunk.

When we got to La Masseria, it was a little early for dinner, according to the way I live, but I can usually always eat something. I had some chewable Dramamine tablets in my pocket. Sometimes I feel like if I eat, I may be nauseous, and the chewable Dramamine seems to banish that. My sister says she wishes she felt nauseous when she was eating too much or too often. I tell her, no, she should not wish that. She laughs.

They put us in the back in a corner, at a table that they think I prefer. I actually prefer being in the window at the front where I can watch people walk by. No biggie.

Mike is a trencherman. He likes to eat, although he doesn't appear to be overweight at all. Must have a high metabolism. Ruth almost never eats much, at least not when she's around me. She tells me about foods that she overeats on, "The four food groups: cookies, ice cream, pizza and chips." She's slim and wears her clothes like a model, probably looks good in a bathing suit. Although she's no spring chick, she has a great sense of style and always looks like a million bucks.

Mike was not interested in trying to do a status meeting over dinner, but we did talk about where things stood.

My contribution was basically that we had interviewed all the van Gelsen brothers and three times with Ragnar/Bud. There seemed to be no motivation for any of them to have felt hostility toward their youngest brother. I had not run Dun & Bradstreet ratings on them, but I had no reason to believe that any of them was hard-up for money. They had probably inherited equal or approximately equal parts of their parents' estates, and Jimmy's net worth most likely was similar to his brothers' net worth. If it was not, it was because Jimmy never sought out a job or had a regular earned income. His brothers all worked for prosperous companies in executive positions.

Unless there was something we were missing, there were no persons of interest in the van Gelsen family.

I had also determined that although Jimmy had put his co-op apartment up for sale, there had been no serious bids. He had been interested in an apartment in TriBeCa, but had never made a bid so there were no deals being busted, and probably no one with a serious financial beef, at least with regard to real estate. The rest of his estate seems to have been largely passively invested that is, invested by investment managers, a couple of hedge funds, and a bond fund. He wasn't a sugar-daddy to any company, not as far as we could tell, a "robber baron" of any type.

Mike said that the way he was killed probably indicated the shooter was someone Jimmy knew. There was no sign of a struggle. No one reported any loud yelling. One lady heard the gun fire, and thought it was a firecracker. Unless Jimmy was caught completely unaware, he knew whoever shot him, and since he was shot in the forehead, it seemed likely that he was looking at the shooter when the gun was fired.

"That means it could have been a neighbor, a friend, a relative. In any case, someone whom Jimmy didn't feel was dangerous. Otherwise he would have probably turned to run away, or put his hands up to protect himself," Mike said.

"And let's not forget that Eddie Hall was in a hospital in Westchester County when it happened," Ruth added.

"Have we interviewed Eddie's family?"

Mike observed that Eddie didn't seem to have any close relatives. His parents were dead, no siblings. He had two children and an ex-wife who seemed to have no ill feelings, and who actually took him in when he was released from the hospital. It seemed to have been a strong relationship.

"This is out of left field, but has anyone talked to Eddie Hall about exactly what happened when he was run off the road?" It was Mike, with his left hand loosely touching his mouth and chin.

"I don't follow," I said.

"You said you didn't think the Bentley you saw actually bumped or touched the red Mustang that Eddie was driving. We should find out what he actually remembers about what happened."

"Okay, I'll bite," Ruth said. "Why do you say that?"

"Well, if Eddie was trying to set up an alibi, nothing would work better than being hospitalized upstate when somebody shot Jimmy van Gelsen."

"Are you suggesting," I asked, "that Eddie could have wrecked his car at high speed in order to be hurt and prove that he wasn't anywhere near Jimmy van Gelsen?"

"Not exactly, no. Just wondering whether he was distracted by something, or whether maybe he saw someone he recognized in the Bentley. It would take a stunt driver to wreck the car and not risk being killed."

"Good," I said. "Because if he wanted an alibi for some reason, there are a heck of a lot less dangerous ways to do that. Like he could have pulled off the Thruway at any town, and gone to the local PD to report a dangerous driver on the Thruway. That would have created a paper trail, with cops who would have verified his identity when he filed the complaint."

"Hugo, calm down. I don't want to theorize about what could have happened if anything. In other words, not trying to explore alternative reality. Just suggesting that we should find out more about what Eddie remembers. After all, he was engaged to be married to the dead man."

Ruth looked down at her hands on the table. "I think you're tilting at windmills."

"It wouldn't be the first time if I am," he said, "but as Hugo knows, once you have eliminated the things that didn't happen or were impossible, what remains is probably the truth. We need to figure out which questions we haven't asked, because they have to be there, unless what we are investigating is in fact a perfect crime. I don't believe in perfect crimes."

"Arthur Conan Doyle," I said, nodding. "It's from 'The Adventure of the Beryl Coronet.' Sherlock Holmes says, 'When you have excluded the impossible, whatever remains, however improbable, must be the truth.'"

"The adventure of the what?" Ruth was sitting up, looking incredulous.

"Beryl Coronet. Beryls are semi-precious stones. The story is about a British earl who is killed, and his coronet is found in the hands of his son, with some stones missing from it. The police decide the son is the culprit. Things happen and it turns out that the son is in love with his cousin, who is actually guilty, working with a criminal she happens to know. I'm not doing it justice, but it's a Sherlock Holmes short story."

"And you just happen to know the plot?" she asked, wide-eyed.

"I've read all the Sherlock Holmes stories and books, most of them several times. When I was a kid, I was sick a lot of the time, and I read the same books over and over at my grandmother's house. She had all the Sherlock Holmes books and all the Hardy Boys books – and they solved crimes using the same rules of detection as Sherlock Holmes. Life-shaping times for me."

We had worked our way through plates of pasta, although Ruth typically ate very little of anything except snacks and sweets.

The waiter brought us each a fresh cannoli and an espresso. Smiles all around as they cleared the dinner plates away. There was still some wine left in the bottle, and Mike poured it in my glass. I never turn that down.

No goons when we walked out of the restaurant, and Ruth wanted to walk to her apartment, from the theater district to Park and 61st Street. Mike shook his head and hailed a cab. He walked over to the black-and-white that was idling in front of the restaurant. The driver popped the trunk and Mike grabbed my duffel and handed it to me.

"Discretion," he said with a smile as he closed the taxi door. He waved and turned to walk to the precinct.

Chapter Twenty-two

"That was bizarre," Ruth said, dramatically miming wiping her brow.

"What was bizarre?"

"Mike hinting that Eddie could have staged the accident to create an alibi."

"I think we both misunderstood him. What he was trying to say is that we have never found out what Eddie knows, or what he remembers about that day. We never asked him, for instance, what happened the night before. Did they go out to dinner? Did they have a fight? Did Eddie see something that made him turn off the road? Like the driver of the Bentley maybe?"

"Then why did he say maybe Eddie staged the accident?"

"It was an example of something we haven't considered. We haven't considered anything about Eddie, simply because he was in a hospital upstate when Jimmy was killed. That of course does not mean Eddie knows nothing that would be helpful in figuring out what happened. Maybe they stayed home that night, and Jimmy told him about an argument he had with somebody at Housing Works that day."

"Okay, okay."

"What's wrong, dearie-pie?"

"I like Eddie, that's all. It is pretty clear that he had nothing to do with the shooting."

"Well, it is theoretically possible, I suppose, that he hired a hitman then drove upstate to be out of the picture."

She looked at me like I was crazy. "Eddie didn't hire a hitman. Think about what you're saying before you say it."

"I didn't mean to say he hired a hitman, just that we never investigated it. Just like we never asked him what happened the last time he saw Jimmy. Anything Jimmy said to him could have a hint at what happened when Jimmy was walking down the sidewalk and somebody he knew stepped out of a shadow and shot him in the head."

"Okay, I'll give you that one."

The cab pulled up in front of Ruth's building. She started to get out.

"Don't," I said. "Let's look around before we get out." I was putting the ride on a credit card.

"No goons that I can see."

"Sometimes it is a spotter who monitors things then calls the goons when the target appears. Could be exactly what happened with Jimmy."

"Except it couldn't have been a goon, because Mike thinks whoever shot him was someone he knew, or at least wasn't afraid of."

"That's an interesting way to put it."

She rolled her eyes, very Ruth-ish.

Ruth got out her keys and we opened the door, got out of the cab, and quick-walked to the entrance of the building, where a liveried doorman opened the door for us, and offered to take my duffel. I thanked him and said I was okay.

Ruth's apartment was on the ground floor, with the square footage of a whole floor apartment, minus the lobby and elevators. So that meant that she didn't have a library, she had told me, but that wasn't a problem. It also meant that they had no butler's pantry, which *everybody* else had, but when you see an apartment that is twenty seven hundred square feet with three bedrooms, three and a half baths, it looks enormous.

"What did you mean, it was an interesting way to put it?"

I told her that she had pointed out something else that we hadn't thought about.

"What? I just said what Mike said."

"No, you added that it could have been someone he simply wasn't afraid of, not even necessarily someone he knew. Like, just for example, a senior in a wheelchair, or a post-office letter carrier with a satchel full of mail. I think there was a movie about a post-office killer. Something like 'The Postman Always Rings Twice'."

"I saw that one. Late-night television. Lana Turner in pure white dresses, looking innocent when she was guilty as sin." She pointed at me.

"But letter carriers in the real world are seldom delivering mail in the middle of the night."

Sometimes the best answer is no answer at all.

I held up my duffel. She beckoned me and walked down the hall, pausing in front of a door. "I don't think anyone has ever slept in that bed," she said. "I bought it last year, but then we put it in storage and put Murray's hospital bed in here."

"So, this was Murray's room?"

"No, but I put a hospital bed here for when he came home." She winced. "Only when he came home, he was in that box that's on the mantel in the living room."

I hugged her. "We'll find a perfect place to scatter Murray. I promise."

She was slightly teary. She really loved him, even though they didn't marry until she was in her late forties and he was over sixty. I don't think anyone ever loved me that much, except my mom.

I put my duffel on a chair and zipped open the top, took out the two books, one on the Tudor dynasty, and the other on the lost landmarks of Constantinople. Either one is good going-to-sleep material. If you hit a spot where one of Henry VIII's wives is begging the executioner to be fast, I just flip the page then she's already dead. It's not as though there's any suspense about Anne Boleyn or Katherine Howard and how they died. My favorite of his wives is Anne of Cleves. She and Katherine Parr are the only wives who survived him, the only ones who were still alive when he died.

I put the contents of the Dopp kit around the sink in the bathroom, which opened on both sides to two bedrooms, the other of which was empty, of furniture as well as of people.

"I'm planning to convert it into an office," Ruth said. "I've always envied you the office in your apartment, and now I'm going to have one. Maybe I'll write a book. You never know."

I pulled out my tablet and put it on the little desk that was probably intended as a vanity table for a woman, but there was a plug just to the side of it, and I hooked up the power cord and converter, and plugged it into the wall. Ruth was watching me and said the Wi-Fi name was Murray and the password was Ruthsleuth.

"Awww, how cute," I intoned, with what I imagined would sound like a parent-to-child speech pattern, exaggerating the vowels.

She rolled her eyes and said she would be in the living room. I wandered back out to the front of the apartment, following her down the hallway. She was pouring a nightcap. She looked at me and gestured with a scotch bottle.

"Yes, please."

"Ice?"

"No, just neat, please."

"You want to watch TV?"

I looked at my watch. Ten minutes to eleven. "News?"

She nodded. "Any particular flavor?"

I shrugged, "Channel 7, unless you have a favorite. Doesn't matter. I'm usually as interested in the weather forecast as the news itself. And yes, I look at Accuweather on my computer too, but I like the schoolmarmy teaching of the Channel 7 weather team."

She turned on the television and scooted down the hall. Just about the moment that the urgent seventh chords that make up the theme music for the news, she walked back in with a silver tray that she put down on a coffee table in front of the couch. Crackers and various kinds of cheese with a cheese knife and some gelatinous small bricklike thing on the side.

"What's that?"

"Quince paste. Try putting it on a cracker with some of the cheese."

I did. It was great. I gave her a thumbs-up and mumbled something while chewing, with my hand in front of my mouth.

She smiled. "Me too."

"So how do you think we ought to go about interviewing Eddie about what he remembers?" I wondered.

"I think we call him and ask him if we can talk to him about the days just before the night that Jimmy was shot. Tell him we talked to Mike, and we'd just like to find out what he remembers about any conversations they had."

"I think I'll send an email to that effect, give him a chance to respond after he thinks about it. Don't want to just hit him in the face with it."

After I hit SEND, I started paying attention to the news. There was a story about alleged sexual harassment of a woman in a City Department, who was not identified but had accused various elected officials of making off-color remarks to her and occasionally touching her sexually, without her permission. The commentator chosen by Channel 7 was Eddie Hall.

Reporter: *As a former ADA in Brooklyn, what can you tell us about these accusations?*

Hall*: As an ADA, it was my job to prosecute people who had been indicted for a crime. But even a prosecutor must never forget that each person is presumed to be innocent until proven guilty. That is true of a person accused of sexual harassment as much as any other crime.*

Reporter: *So, if a man is accused by a woman of workplace harassment, he should be considered innocent?*

Hall: *Before the law, absolutely. And we should remember that the accused has the right to face his accuser, and not to be accused by someone who stays anonymous.*

Reporter: *But what if his company fires him when he is accused?*

Hall: *That would have nothing to do with the presumption of innocence under the law. If the man chooses to sue his employer, he might well prevail, but if he is convicted of harassment, that might not do him any good.*

Reporter: *Thank you. That was Eddie Hall, who served as an Assistant District Attorney for nearly ten years, and will be running for congress from the Flatbush-Prospect Park area of Brooklyn.*

"He's good, you know?" Ruth was smiling and shaking her head. "Really good. And credible. And he seems normal, not like some stuffed-shirt lawyer."

"But when the governor points out that someone on his staff says he is innocent after he's been accused of punching his wife, then you would say he should be fired anyway. Right? Hashtag Me Too?"

She stared at me. "Look, Hugo. I'm a woman, have been all my life, and I have been pinched and felt up many times. I think most women go through the same thing, no matter what they look like, or how they dress. Nobody would pull that crap with me now, and if they did, I'd break their nose." She made a pushing gesture with the palm of her hand. "Like that, just push the nose back into the head, push upward, like that."

"I understand. All I'm saying is that the presumption of innocence is not something we can take for granted. Vigilantes and lynch mobs are the most extreme violation of that, but firing a man for an anonymous accusation is on the same continuum, in my opinion."

"When you say it like that, sure, but when some idiot snaps my bra on the subway, I'm entitled to smash my knee into his crotch."

"Of course. If he does it, you don't have to presume he didn't do it, because you know what he did, and you're entitled to protect yourself, to strike back."

She stood up and picked up the lowball glass she had poured the scotch into. She made a gesture asking if I wanted another one.

"I'm okay. And yes, I think Eddie will be a killer candidate. I'd pity anyone who tried to debate him, for instance. Or for a Town Hall type meeting, the other candidates should probably bang in sick."

My phone bleeped. It was a response from Eddie. "Speak of the devil," I said.

Sure. How about lunchtime tomorrow?

I relayed the response to Ruth, who nodded. "Someplace where we can be off in a corner."

"Oyster Bar at Grand Central?"

She was okay with that, and poured herself another two fingers of scotch over the remains of the ice that she had put in some time back.

I responded. *Noon at the Oyster Bar in Grand Central? Ruth will be with me.*

I texted Mike to let him know.

Chapter Twenty-three

The Oyster Bar is a fairly grand space, and, for Manhattan, gigantic. It was opened in 1913, and is the oldest business at Grand Central, which actually opened to train traffic and passengers in 1871. The Lower Level wasn't a food court like it is today; it has twenty-six track platforms, and the Upper Level has forty track platforms, more than any other train station in the world.

The Oyster Bar is architecturally significant because of the fancy vaulting that forms its ceilings, but it is a checkered tablecloth, casual dining restaurant. It has a section of lunch counter where people can have a quick platter of seafood without having a reservation, and a large old-fashioned saloon tucked away at the back to the far right after you go in through the front door. It's popular because the seafood is fresh and plentiful, and because the waiters never hustle you out. You can sit there for hours and talk after you've finished eating, and because it's so large, it's frequently possible to be seated away from the madding crowd. They usually have the biggest selection of oysters in the whole city.

Eddie showed up at just before noon. Ruth and I were already seated, and had asked for the last table in the far corner of the dining room. At that point, nobody even close to us. He was wearing jeans and a slightly garish Mexican or Hawaiian shirt. Sandals without socks. A mostly crumpled open-weave cowboy hat. He hadn't shaved and was looking fashionably scruffy, but clean.

After the hellos, Eddie opened the conversation. "Tell me what you want to know."

"We're not exactly the PD," I said. "We're not going to record anything, just want to get some outlines of what you remember. If there's something that Mike considers worth following up, he'll ask you to go to the Midtown North precinct on 54th Street and go through it again."

"And then he would record the interview on video, right?"

I shrugged. "Usually, yes, but like I said, we're not PD. We're volunteers, and we've worked with Mike several times in the past. We're like extra hands and feet for Mike, at no cost to the City of New York or the PD itself."

He asked where we wanted to start.

Ruth answered. "Hard to tell. Can you tell us when was the last time you saw Jimmy?"

"The night before I had the car accident. The night before he, um, died." It was clear from the crack in his voice that this was not going to be easy for him.

I asked, "Quiet night at home, or did you go out?"

"We went out, went to the Aquagrill on 6th Avenue, not very far from his apartment."

"You had a reservation?"

"No. We went there often, because both of us liked seafood, and they knew us. Jimmy was a big tipper, I think."

"Did he usually pay the tab?"

Eddie gave me a questioning look. "We usually alternate. One night me, the next night Jimmy. Neither of us wanted to split the tabs, and," he paused and swallowed, "we were together a lot." He had a slightly lost look about him.

"Do you remember what you talked about?"

"We talked about the Metropolitan Opera's production of 'Turandot', and whether they would replace it with something corny and tacky like the new 'Tosca' with two sleazy hookers in Scarpia's palace."

"I've seen it several times," I said, "and I want it to last long enough for my grandchildren to see it. It's like the old 'Walküre,' the one with storybook sets and costumes. Somehow the storybook quality of that production made it more believable, but that's not all you talked about?"

"Jimmy told me he still wished he could remodel the apartment. He wanted to put a staircase up to the apartment on the floor above us, and double the size."

"Bud mentioned that," I said.

"Bud was the lawyer for everything Jimmy did."

Ruth stepped in. "What did he decide to do instead?"

"It wasn't a new subject. I knew his problems with the co-op board. I offered to help him deal with them, but he didn't want me to. They thought the original structure of the building wouldn't allow that kind of alteration. It's an old building, I guess. There are columns here and there that look like they are load-bearing, not decorative."

I told him Bud told us Jimmy was looking at other apartments, and had put his apartment on the market to sell. "Did you ever see the apartment that Jimmy was looking at? I think Bud said it was in TriBeCa."

"It is in TriBeCa. I think it is on White Street, just two short blocks downtown from Canal Street. That restaurant, Petrarca, is on the corner. Cool neighborhood."

"Bud said he was looking for something bigger."

"Yeah, it was a whole floor in an older building, probably used to be a factory, lots of big windows. Could have been nearly twice the size of Jimmy's place. Hard to tell, because it was empty, like a shell, not even any walls to partition off rooms."

"Were there any offers for his apartment?"

"I don't think so, but I tried not to poke my nose into things. He seemed a little sensitive if I asked about projects like that."

"Projects like that? What kind of other projects?"

He looked at me oddly and shrugged. "He was remodeling the kitchen to have a cooking island in the middle. I offered to help but he didn't take me up on it, so I backed off. I've been married before, you know, and I understand that both people need some space of their own."

"Was Jimmy a cook?"

"Yeah, well he had been with Raul Vasquez, who was a chef. I think Jimmy started being interested in kitchen stuff and cooking because of him. He cooked fairly often when he had people over for dinner."

"Like dinner parties?"

"Usually more impromptu than a dinner party. Like he'd be talking to somebody on the phone and invite them over, and then call a couple of others and say he was making some red sauce, and c'mon over. Sometimes there would be eight or ten people for dinner, and he would be whipping up a meat sauce all afternoon. Yeah, I'd say he was a good cook. He could roast a chicken as good as any bistro, and he had a deep-fat fryer, so we had crisp Julia Child-quality french fries too."

"But you didn't eat in often?"

"Not often. He didn't seem to want to cook dinner for two. He liked to cook for a roomful of people if he was going to cook."

"That last night, he wasn't upset about the apartment situation?"

"We talked about it, but I think he had kinda moved on to the idea of starting from shell space and building absolutely everything out from the floor up."

"But you said he still wished he could put in the staircase. Bud said that too."

"He didn't let go of things quickly, even when he decided on some other alternative. He pined after a painting in one of the SoHo galleries for months, even after it had been sold to somebody else."

"Why didn't he offer to buy it from the party who bought it?"

"He wouldn't have done that, but he did once in a while say something like, 'That painting with the soldiers in it, would look great over on that wall.'"

"Soldiers? Did you ever see it?"

"I don't think so, no. I think it pre-dated me."

"But you didn't think he was agitated about anything that night?"

"Hey, listen, I was a prosecutor. I've been over all this territory myself. Everything I can remember from that night, or from a while before, I've been all over it. And no, I don't think he was upset or angry about anything."

Ruth started to ask another question, but Eddie interrupted her before she said anything. "I'd kinda like to just leave this subject alone for a while." It was apparent that he was feeling very emotional, talking about Jimmy.

"Sorry, just one other thing. When that Bentley buzzed by you, did you have a chance to see the driver?"

He blinked and looked down at his hands. "No. I just thought he was going to hit me and I swerved."

"He? So, it was a guy?"

"Oh. Yeah, I guess so. Yeah, maybe bald or shaved head. White guy."

"You loved Jimmy, didn't you?" Ruth asked softly

"I told you I did, and I still do. There's a big empty place inside me where he should be. The bleeding has stopped, but I'm not healed, and I'm not moving on yet. Can we be finished now?"

I signaled the waiter for a check. When he handed me the folder with a check in it, I put my Amex card down on the folder without looking inside. He was back quickly, and we were free to go. Ruth and Eddie had walked out the front door into the walkway outside the Oyster Bar, which is on the Lower Level of Grand Central. Each one was facing into a corner of the beautiful Guastavino tiled foyer. They were whispering to each other. That place is a whispering gallery. If you face the corner and whisper, the person facing the opposite corner can hear you clearly. It never gets old.

Eddie smiled when he turned around.

"You get what you wanted?"

I smiled and nodded. "We'll summarize the conversation for Mike, but I doubt he's going to want to interview you formally. At least not from what I know. No telling if he has something else he wants to ask you."

He nodded several times quickly, shook my hand, kissed Ruth on the cheek, turned on his heel and walked briskly up the ramp toward the street level.

"Kind of a dead end," I said to Mike on the speaker of my cellphone so Ruth could chime in.

We were sitting at an isolated table in the saloon back room of the Oyster Bar. I felt like a vodka, and Ruth voted yea on that too. The place was, surprisingly, almost empty, maybe because people don't hang out in the saloon in the middle of the afternoon, and my phone registered plenty of signal for a phone call.

"I don't think there's anything hiding inside Eddie," Ruth said. "He is righteously sad, and I don't think he remembers anything that was bugging Jimmy before that night."

Mike asked if we talked to him about the car accident. I told him that I had just asked him if he saw the driver. He said no, he hadn't, but he thought the guy in the Bentley was going to hit him and he swerved. "I asked him if the driver was male, and he said yes, shaved head, White guy.

That was all."

Ruth jumped in again. "We mostly just talked about Jimmy, trying to find out if he knew of any arguments or fights that Jimmy was engaged in. It was crystal clear that he didn't think there was anything upsetting Jimmy. He did say that Jimmy kept his own projects close to the vest, didn't want Eddie's or anybody else's help on things like remodeling the apartment."

"Did you get the impression that he might remember more about the accident than he's been letting on?"

"Maybe," I was thinking back on what was said, but it seemed to me like he remembered seeing the driver of the Bentley when I prompted him. He looked surprised when he said what he said. I think he was a little shaken, like he had been over it in his head, and never remembered that part."

"It was right after that when he asked if we could stop talking about all this," Ruth said. "Didn't think about that exactly until just now."

I suggested we duck downstairs to the subway and take the 6-train to 59th Street then walk over to Ruth's place.

"We see any goons, I scream bloody murder. And I can scream loud, baby."

The ride was uneventful, normal subway straphangers, nobody paying any attention to the silver-haired guy and the lady in the fancy checked coat. Nobody making eye contact.

When we got to Ruth's apartment, I checked my phone. Text from Eddie: *Now I remember more about the Bentley. Can I call?*

I showed Ruth and answered Eddie in the affirmative.

My phone buzzed. It was Eddie. I didn't put on the speaker, just held it to my ear.

"I don't know exactly what happened, but when you asked me about the driver of that car, it suddenly made me remember things that I didn't know I knew."

"Like?"

"Like I did see the guy, and I didn't remember seeing him before."

I asked if he remembered anything more than the shaved head.

"I think I might have recognized him, but I can't bring up a picture of him in my mind, and I don't think I could place him even if I could remember exactly what I saw. I know that doesn't make sense."

"Don't worry about making sense. If you have memories coming back, you have to relax and let them come. Was his window open?"

"Yeah it was. How did you know that?"

"He drove by me before he drove by you. I was pretty annoyed by the way he was driving, weaving around like he couldn't control that big car. I paid attention."

"I think I saw him coming up behind me in the rear-view mirror."

"You think you did? Or you remember seeing him?"

"I remember. He was scowling, like I was in his way.

"So, when he pulled up next to me, I looked at him. Now I remember his face. Maybe late forties, White, tanned, white t-shirt and big biceps. A tattoo of some kind."

"What color was the tattoo?"

"Green."

"A picture of something?"

"Sorry, I don't know."

"You said you recognized him. Was that when you saw him in the rear-view mirror or when he drove by?"

"I think when he was behind me."

"If you close your eyes, relax and look in your memory to see if you can remember more."

He was silent. Ruth was trying to make sense of just hearing my side of the conversation.

I mouthed *L-A-T-E-R*.

She nodded.

"I recognized him but I didn't know him."

"Explain what you mean."

"I think I had seen him on TV, but I don't think I ever met him."

"Any idea what kind of TV show? Situation comedy?"

"I think a news show. That's what I tend to watch anyway."

"Like a news show or a talk show?"

"I don't think I would recognize somebody who was just making a comment on videotape for a newscast. I think he must have been on a panel of some kind."

"What news channels do you watch?"

"Depends on what's going on. I sometimes watch Fox to keep up to date on the right and the alt-right. I watch CNN, but there's too much of it, and it's too speculative. They go on and on about the same things and keep guessing what *might have happened*. Sorry, that's just not news. Sometimes I watch CNBC if there's something going on in the market or the Fed or whatever. Like when I wanted to see what companies were saying about the big tax cut the Republicans pushed through. It gave me some perspective that I would never have had. It never occurred to me that companies would bring back all their sheltered cash from Ireland and wherever else it was stashed, but a lot of that happened. Goes to show you that those of us on the left have blind spots just like we accuse the right of having."

"Okay. Where do you think this guy was?"

"Probably Fox."

"Talking about what?"

"No idea."

"Would you work with a police sketch artist to see if we can get a sketch that looks like the man in the car?"

"What good is that going to do? Wouldn't have anything to do with Jimmy."

"It tells us something that you had forgotten. Maybe there are other things."

He agreed. I asked Eddie if I could put on the speaker because Ruth was with me. He said it was okay.

"So, I gather from what Hugo was saying that you remembered something about the driver of that silver Bentley."

"Yeah. It's very odd to suddenly remember something that you didn't think you knew."

"Disorienting?"

"Yeah."

"Did anyone tell you that the Bentley had been stolen from a casino in Atlantic City, so it was hot."

"I didn't know that."

166

"So that means the driver might have been taking the car someplace where it could get chopped up and sold for parts," Ruth said.

I summed up that Eddie was willing to work with a PD sketch artist to try to get a picture of the guy. Then they could run facial rec on the picture. I shook my head in a fairly exaggerated way to get Ruth off that subject. She nodded.

I told Eddie that I was going to call Mike on another phone and bring him in on what we had been talking about.

"Can you show up at Midtown North this afternoon? It's on 54th Street just west of 8th Avenue. Just ask for Mike di Saronno. I'll probably be there too."

"Just tell me when. I'll be there."

Chapter Twenty-four

Mike shifted things around and arranged for a sketch artist to be there at three o'clock. I sent Eddie a text. He confirmed. I asked Mike if he wanted me to be there. Yes. Ruth? Okay if I want, but not necessary.

I got to Mike's office at just after two thirty, in case he wanted me to go over the interview with Eddie. As it happened, he was in an unrelated interrogation, and didn't emerge from that until almost three. No harm, no foul.

"So," Mike opened the conversation when Eddie was seated in the interrogation room closest to the staircase. "So, you remembered something that you had forgotten?"

Nod. "Yeah. Hugo asked me a snap question and I answered it, and he realized my answer had some information in it. He quickly asked me a follow-up question, and all of a sudden I remembered seeing the guy in the car that I thought was going to hit me."

"From the side you saw him? Or was he looking at you?"

"Well, from the side when he was passing me, but I now remember seeing him in the rearview mirror when he was pulling up behind me."

"You could recognize him if you saw him again?"

"Yes."

Mike picked up his cellphone and tapped a couple of numbers. A minute later the door opened and a young Latin guy came in.

"Eddie Hall, meet Carlos Bernat. Carlos is a sketch artist. He helps us create a likeness of someone we don't have a photo of, using the memory of someone who saw that person. "

"Yeah, I'm familiar with the process. I was an ADA in Brooklyn for over eight years." He held his hand out, and shook with Carlos. "Nice to meet you, Carlos."

"Carlos is going to take you to his work space and you guys can get started."

Carlos beckoned Eddie, and the two of them left.

"Tell me what happened after we talked when you and Ruth had been talking to Eddie."

"Well, Eddie seemed kinda bummed out, talking about Jimmy and the night before he was killed, and he begged off, asked us if we could be finished with the subject. Then he got up and left."

"And then..."

"We were at the Oyster Bar having lunch. When Eddie left, Ruth and I went into the saloon and took a table away from anybody else so we could talk about what happened. My phone buzzed and it was Eddie, sounding a little out of breath or something.

"He said when I asked him about an offhand comment, he made about the guy who was driving the Bentley, he started remembering things that came back to him, kinda from nowhere, I gather. He said my question made the memory come back."

"Then he remembered?"

"Yeah, he started remembering a bunch of stuff. He remembered seeing the driver of the Bentley pulling up behind him, and saw in his rearview mirror that the guy had a kind of angry look on his face."

"Angry?"

"I don't remember if he said 'angry,' but an intense look anyway. But that's not the interesting part. He also remembered recognizing the guy he saw."

"Who is he?"

"Well, he couldn't remember who he was, but he thought he saw him on television."

"An actor?"

"I asked him what kind of TV show, and he said mostly he watches news or talk shows, and he thinks it may have been a talk show on Fox, but he can't place the man. That's why I ask him if he would work with a sketch artist, because if he can get a good likeness, maybe facial rec software will be able to bring up some likely people. Right?"

He stared at me without looking at me, like he was staring at the wall behind me. He nodded. "Yeah, right."

"Eddie said he watched Fox fairly often to keep tabs on the right and alt-right people and what they were talking about. He watches CNN for the left, but he's part of the left himself, so that wouldn't be as much of an effort as learning about the right."

"I can't be interested in the politics of what he does," Mike said. "Alt-right, alt-left, whatever. As long as there's no rabble-rousing it's all the same to me."

"Really?"

"Really. I'm a cop. Cops aren't judges. We try to keep the peace. If somebody is a super-liberal, or a crypto-fascist, it doesn't matter, as long as they don't break the law."

"Even so, Eddie is a politician, and what I took him to say was that he watches television to keep track of political thought across the spectrum. He's going to be running for congress, after all."

"I know, I know. I just don't want to be talking about who's right and who's wrong. Not even in private. When I go to vote, then I can vote the way my heart and mind tell me to vote. For now, right and left are the same for me."

He sounded a little defensive to me, and the sermon-like quality of what he said made it sound like he was setting up a defense. Then I realized that we were sitting in an interrogation room and everything we said was being taped.

"Gotcha," I said, hopeful that none of the video cameras could see the relief I was feeling. "Anyway, I thought if we could get a sketch, it might give us enough information that Eddie could figure out who the guy was."

"What do you think that would have to do with the homicide of Jimmy van Gelsen?"

"No idea, Mike," I said. "You wanted me to find out what Eddie remembered about the car crash. So that's what I did. What if somebody did try to run him off the road? That might have something to do with Jimmy getting shot, right?"

"I suppose so, but the likelihood of someone knowing where Eddie was on the thruway and being in a Mack truck like that twelve-cylinder Bentley to push Eddie off the road—that's pretty goddamn far-fetched."

"I did what I thought you asked me to do."

"You did the right thing. I'm just trying to sort this all out. I tend to think that there was no connection between the car crash, as you call it, and the murder of Jimmy van Gelsen that same night, a hundred miles away."

"I wonder if he remembers more about the accident, maybe he could remember more about Jimmy?"

"That would be helpful."

"Maybe you have a psychologist who could work with him?"

"Maybe, but you seem to be doing a good job already. I think we should just keep going in that direction. If there was something going on in Jimmy's life that would have something to do with why he was shot, the only keys might be Eddie and Brother Bud."

"And they're both lawyers, so they know how to talk around things."

"I find myself wondering if it's possible that Jimmy was shot by somebody who fired a gun by accident," he said. "That could be why Jimmy didn't turn and run or put his hands up or duck, or whatever. He apparently just stood there while whoever it was killed him."

"Is that unusual?"

"Unusual? I've been in homicide for twenty years and I've never seen anyone who was killed by a bullet without trying to avoid it. Sometimes people are unconscious when they're shot, but Jimmy wasn't. Sometimes bullets ricochet off something and hit someone who's not expecting to get hit, but the CSIs couldn't find any evidence of a ricochet, and the slug wasn't misshapen by hitting a granite or steel wall before it killed Jimmy. And a ricochet would most likely have hit him at an angle instead of straight on from the front."

"What about someone who fires a gun in the air then it falls to the ground and hits someone?"

"Well, theoretically that's possible, but practically speaking it's close to impossible unless the gun is fired straight up in the middle of a crowd like Times Square on New Year's Eve. Then it stands to reason that it would hit from the top, not from the front."

"So, what are we left with?"

"After we remove all the things that are impossible, what's left is probably the truth. He was shot by someone he wasn't afraid of. A friend, a relative, an old lady in a wheelchair."

I asked if there were any unusual results from the autopsy.

"He had alcohol in his blood, not near the zero-point zero eight percent that would make him intoxicated. I'd guess he probably had a couple of drinks or maybe a drink and a glass of wine. He also had what may have been metabolites of cannabis, but they didn't send that to the lab for analysis because it had no impact on the cause of death. He also had some interesting contents in his stomach, including urine, which he must have swallowed. But nothing that would indicate that he was drunk or incapable of defending himself. He could have been driving and wouldn't have been anywhere near a DWI level."

"Are we going to find out who the driver of that Bentley was?"

"Goddamn right we are."

We got up from our chairs in the interrogation room and walked back toward Mike's office.

"How about some coffee?" he said.

"I'm good, but if you want some, I'll walk with you. After all, we have to wait for Eddie and Carlos."

Mike said that Carlos is usually fast. Some sketch artists work slowly, but the ones who work fast usually get better results. Eye-witnesses get confused if you change the image too many times while you're working on it.

"What if," I mused, "what if the driver of the Bentley recognized Eddie when he drove by Eddie. Not following him, but recognized him then sent somebody after Jimmy to finish things off."

"That makes more sense than somebody tailing Eddie and pushing him off the road. The odds against being able to find somebody on the Thruway without using roadblocks are almost absurd."

My phone buzzed. It was Gabriele texting.

Where are u

Mike's office

I'm at Joe Allen

Come on over

K CU

"Gabriele is coming over. He's on 46th Street."

Mike smiled. "Great guy, and he can read people as well as anybody I ever met."

Eddie and Carlos appeared at the door. Mike led the four of us back over to the interrogation room we were in before.

Carlos pulled out a sketch from his folder. It was of an angry man with a steering wheel obscuring part of his face.

"So, we went this way. What Eddie remembered best was the way the driver looked in the rear-view mirror. So, what we're looking at is a mirror image if it's at all correct."

Mike pursed his lips. Thinking, thinking.

Carlos pulled out a second sketch of the same face, relaxed, or looking like a mugshot. "When Eddie told me the first sketch was close, I made this one up by relaxing the brow and frown lines. I made an assumption he was clean-shaven, since nobody told me he had a moustache or a beard. And that's this picture.

Eddie picked up the sketch. "Yeah, now he looks more familiar, and I feel fairly sure he was on a Fox talk show."

Gabriele arrived. He knocked on the interrogation room door. I looked out the peephole. "It's Gabriele." Mike made a c'mon in gesture.

Gabriele was all smiles, hugged me, kissed Mike on both cheeks, left cheek first, and shook Eddie's hand. He looked at Carlos and introduced himself. They both said "nice to meet you." Gabriele sat down next to me. He put his hand on my thigh. I stared at it and he moved it to his own thigh.

"You just happened to be in the neighborhood?" Mike asked.

Gabriele explained that he was looking at the video cameras around Joe Allen. "When we there with Jimmy brothers, two wise guys look for us outside. I want see if video camera see them.

Mike perked up. "We did that too, and we got several shots of them. We were able to identify them, and when they tackled Hugo in Long Island City, we took them into custody. So, we have mugshots now, and fingerprints."

Thunder stolen, and Gabriele sat back in his chair, something he seldom does. I think of him leaning forward in chairs, sometimes elbows on the table. He was slouched back.

My attention went back to the relaxed sketch. "Is that clear enough for you to run through facial rec?"

Mike nodded. "It should already be at facial rec, right Carlos?"

Carlos nodded. There was a knock on the door. A uniform cop with a piece of paper that he handed to Mike.

"We got a hit on the sketch." He looked at the paper. "Augustus Thomas Lee, age fifty-four, home address in Elmira, New York, occupation not stated. Mr. Lee was taken into custody in Syracuse, New York in 2017 in a march protesting Sharia Law. Disturbing the peace, demonstrating without a permit. Taken into custody in Charlottesville, also in 2017, during the Unite the Right demonstration in 2017 and was released with the notation that he was carrying a loaded handgun for which he had a permit from the State of New York."

Eddie lighted up. "Yes, now you say the name, he is part of the so-called New York Light Foot Militia, a kind of private army upstate. They march in all kinds of demonstrations. Surprised he's only been arrested twice. A lot of these guys want to be arrested, like badges of honor."

"Does this jog your memory about why you recognized him?" I asked.

"Yeah, he was on a Fox talk show about something called 'peaceful ethnic cleansing,' to re-establish the White race in America." He said he remembered him because he was so calm about the way he talked about White supremacy, something he termed, "America First. Like I'm not American because I'm not White."

Mike said, "Maybe we should have a talk with Mr. Lee about where he got that car. I believe it had been stolen in Atlantic City that morning."

"We went down to Atlantic City to have a look, and that's what they told us at the Borgata, which is where they had four Bentleys for high-rollers. I think we also found out that they recovered that Bentley near the Thruway that same day, maybe just on the shoulder. Keys in the ignition. So maybe it served its purpose, or maybe it just got too hot, so Mr. Lee found other means of transportation."

"Just need to let Atlantic City PD know what we found out."

I stayed on message. "Was this the first time you had a run-in with someone from the alt-right?"

Eddie shook his head. "Probably not, but most of these over-developed White guys with Kevlar vests don't announce themselves when they whack a Black guy with a baseball bat. I know I've never seen this guy in person, just on that television show. Burns me though, makes me want to call Al Sharpton. Makes me wish I had named my son Malcolm X instead of Alexander."

"I wonder how big this Light Foot Militia is, how many members."

Gabriele was looking it up on Wikipedia. "Don't say how many in Wikipedia. But it say they 'neutral peace keepers' in Charlottesville."

"If they were, they didn't get the job done, because it was not peaceful, not even close," I said. I looked at Mike. "Were those two goons you arrested in Long Island City affiliated with this Light Foot Militia group?"

"If they are, it didn't say anything on the arrest report. They were released on their own recognizance about an hour after they were taken in. Mailing addresses in Sharon Springs, New York. Farm country."

Chapter Twenty-five

Mike was on the phone to the Atlantic City PD as soon as he got back to his office. I waved at him, he waved back. Eddie, Gabriele and I left together.

"Buy you a drink?"

They both nodded.

"Good," I said. "Then you can buy me one after we finish the first round."

We walked south on 8th Avenue until we got to a multi-story bar called Social that was largely built over a very well-lighted porn store. What the heck. They pour a good drink. I was feeling an adrenalin rush since we identified Augustus Lee as the guy who may or may not have tried to run Eddie off the road.

True to form, even before five o'clock it was mobbed. We walked up two flights of stairs, and the crowd thinned out enough for us to find three seats at the bar. I ordered Johnnie Black on the rocks with a splash. Gabriele looked at me strangely and ordered a dirty vodka straight up with olives, my usual drink. Eddie ordered a cran-apple. I asked for an order of hummus. I'm not the sort to drink a cocktail without having something to gnaw on at the same time.

When we all had our drinks, I turned to Eddie, who was sitting between Gabriele and me. "Tell me, in your words, what the alt-right is," I said, "and keep in mind that I am not a political junkie. I tend to be liberal on social issues like women's reproductive rights, and more conservative on tax-and-spend issues. I think of myself as middle-of-the-road."

"Well, to start off, for the alt-right I'm Jesse Owens."

"Okay, a famous Black runner and long-jumper. Does that mean you can run fast enough to get away from them?"

He smiled and straightened up. "It means that I am the symbol of what they don't want to happen in their country. Jesse Owens was the star of the 1936 Olympics, which were held in Berlin. The Nazis hated him. It could only have been more humiliating if Jesse had been a Jew in addition to being Black."

"Okay, you're Jesse Owens," I said, "but other than that, how do you define them, the alt-right?"

"From my point of view the alt-right is built on the idea that Europeans civilized America and descendants of Europeans ought to own it and run it."

"Meaning?"

"Meaning White supremacy, the return of the dispossessed White people to positions of authority. Nobody whose ethnicity is not European should be here. Nobody whose religion is not European is acceptable. No Muslims, no Jews—well, both groups are Semitic, right?"

"You know that sounds ludicrous the way you put it, right?"

"I probably put it in ways that the alt-right wouldn't like or approve, but I think if you boil it down, it sets up an 'us and them' battle between Whites and everybody else. So, Hugo, you're an 'us' and I'm a 'them.' Ruth's a 'them' because she's a Jew. Gabriele is a 'them' because he's gay. Mike di Saronno is an 'us.' It has the advantage of being simple. You're White or you're not White. Easy. On the one hand you have Thomas Jefferson. On the other hand, you have Sally Hemings. Owner on one hand. Owned on the other hand."

"Where Mariah Carey fits?" Gabriele asked.

"'Them.'"

"Hugo, you're a scholar," he said to me.

I blanched when he said that, suspecting the worst to come.

He continued, "The great Ferdinand and Isabella didn't just send Columbus to find the New World. They started the Inquisition and found Torquemada to run it, by the way, a converted Jew himself. They sought out Jews and Muslims who had continued to practice their old religions while pretending to be Christian. They called it *limpieza de sangre*, or 'purity of blood.' If you were unlucky enough to have been polluted by impure blood from your parents or grandparents, you were consigned to the Inquisition for judgment and punishment, which could mean just being banished from Spain, could mean perpetual imprisonment in the dark with torture and starvation, or in the worst case, it could mean death by strangling or being burnt alive at the stake. The Nazis didn't invent antisemitism or pure "Aryan" blood. But the Inquisition was not an invention of the Church either. It was a brainchild of Ferdinand and Isabella; it was a political follow-up to the Spanish monarchs chasing the last Muslims out of Granada in that famous year, 1492, when Columbus sailed the ocean blue."

"And if you were Augustus Lee, what would you say you stand for?"

"Oh, no idea. You'd have to ask somebody who cares more about White nationalism. Something about getting back what the White race had stolen from them, I guess."

"Okay, no worries. Do you think this whole thing has anything to do with who shot Jimmy?"

Eddie looked up at the ceiling, and then at me. He took a drink from his cran-apple glass and signaled the bartender, who hustled over. "Vodka tonic with lime." He stared at me while the bartender poured vodka over the ice in a lowball glass, and shot some tonic water into it from the bar gun. When he brought it, Eddie drank half the glass in one long gulp, swallowing three times.

"No," he said. "No, probably nothing to do with Jimmy getting shot. They'd have all the hate they could muster because he was gay. That alone was enough to send you to a concentration camp in the 1930s., but not now. And besides if somebody attacked him, Jimmy would have tried to get away. He apparently didn't try to get away, so he probably just watched while somebody shot him in the middle of the forehead."

"I think I remember that Mike said there was alcohol in his blood, and maybe urine in his stomach?"

"Yeah? Really? Urine? Was he drunk?"

"Not enough alcohol to make him confused if somebody pointed a gun at him. Something like zero-point zero four percent as I recall. And you have to be zero-point zero eight percent or more to be intoxicated in New York."

"And the urine?"

"What about it?"

"Human?" Gabriele asked.

"Don't know. Probably."

"Anything indicating he had sex?"

Not that I could recall.

"But if he had sex, maybe he had someone with him in the apartment and could have been walking with him outside."

"Could be, but the CSIs didn't find anything in the apartment to indicate he had a visitor. One lowball glass with traces of whisky, one wine glass with some red wine stain in the bottom. One plate, one fork in the sink with some bits of food."

"Was he the sort who would have been playing around with other guys?"

"Well, it's no secret from you that Jimmy and I didn't have a sexual relationship, even if other people thought we did."

"I mean, do you think he was having sex with guys?"

Eddie was uncomfortable, pretty clearly wanting to stop the conversation. "Probably."

"Anybody regular?"

Shrug. Negative head shake.

"You mean no? Or you don't know?"

"Don't know."

"Don't care?"

"What's the point in caring now?" He was looking at the ceiling.

"When I first heard that Jimmy had been shot, all I heard about him said he was a perfect kind of guy, easy to get along with, wealthy and open-handed, open-minded and tolerant."

"That was all true."

"He was also persnickety, secretive and stubborn."

Eddie stared at me without moving his face. He was asking me what I meant.

"I mean, even Bud said Jimmy wanted everybody to butt out of things he was trying to do, like the new apartment he was looking for."

He still said nothing, just stared at me.

"Eddie, I'm twice divorced, never had a good relationship with any girlfriend. Great relationship with Gabriele, but it's not what you and Jimmy were talking about. Gabriele and I are not going to get married. We've never had sex and we most likely never will. It's not the way I'm wired, but something I learned over the years is I get along better with men than with wives. Of course, wives and I have a zero-batting average. I think that's something you and I have in common—that we're more comfortable with men in lots of ways."

No movement.

Gabriel was taking it all in, looked like he was taking notes in his mind.

"Anyway. I just feel like Jimmy was a much more three-dimensional person now than when I first heard about him."

He smiled slightly and shifted in his chair. "I didn't just get along better with Jimmy. I loved him."

"I believe you. I think I love my Gabriele in lots of ways, although with two marriage strikes against me, I can't imagine I'd ever take that third swing, male or female. Maybe a cat if my relatives weren't allergic."

He shifted again and looked back at me. "You were asking me if Jimmy played around. I avoided the question. Yes, he did. I know he did. He told me. It was okay, because that was not what our relationship was about. We had both been in love before. I was in love with Aurora. He was head over heels for Raul Vasquez, even though they fought a lot. I was looking for a platonic relationship, maybe like your man, Sherlock Holmes, and Doctor Watson. He was fine with that. I wouldn't have wanted to date on the side, because I could never have done better than my marriage to Aurora. It was all I wanted. She left because she didn't want to go the way I was going with my career. She hated politics and politicking. We're still close, but of course we don't have sex any longer. We have Alex and Mattie. I wanted someone to live with, and so did Jimmy. Does that make sense?"

I nodded. "Yup, it makes sense to me. I don't want someone to live with, but if I did, it would be a guy. Sex for me is overrated as the basis for a long-term partnership. Not only am I disillusioned, though, I'm also a lot older than you are."

He stared at the horizon. He shifted to look at Gabriele. "Watch out, young man. I might be after you one of these days."

Gabriele smiled ear to ear. "Hugo own me."

I didn't want to pursue that line. "Not wanting to be offensive, do you have any idea why there would have been urine in Jimmy's stomach?"

Eddie put his hands out in front of him and looked at them like he was inspecting his fingernails. "I'm attracted to politics and most people aren't. He was also attracted to some things that most people aren't. Can we leave it at that?"

Gabriele stood up and patted me on the back.

Enough said.

Chapter Twenty-six

We split from Eddie outside Social. He took off toward the A train station at 50th Street, two blocks up. Gabriele and I walked straight across 48th Street to the R station at Broadway and 47th. Didn't try to talk until we were on the platform.

I went first. "You want to come over? You can stay if you want. You know I love you. I watched Eddie suffer when we were talking about Jimmy, and imagined how I would feel if you were suddenly not here anymore."

He hugged me and whispered in my ear. "*Ti amo.*"

I put my arm around his neck and pulled him to me while we walked. I'm sure people wondered what that old guy was doing to that young guy.

When we walked into my apartment, the mood changed.

"Jimmy like rough guys," he said.

"You knew that already?"

"He bring to Ora di Pranzo many time."

"Same guy each time?"

"No, different. Never same, not even one time same."

"Why didn't you tell me this before? You know somebody killed him."

He shrugged. "Is private. Escorts. I not talk about them, get them in trouble."

"He was paying them? All of them?"

He nodded. "If he pay, he tell them go when he want. If he not pay, can't do that."

"If he really liked rough guys, it could be one of those that shot him."

"Escorts not kill john."

182

"Never?"

"Sometimes johns hurt escort, but escort not want trouble."

I had been very mean to Gabriele when we first met. I treated him like a chess piece. Didn't insult him, but I tricked him, basically made him feel like a fool. He made me feel like a fool too.

I hugged him tightly.

"You matter to me, Ri-Ri," I said, knowing how much he hates that babyish nickname that his mother called him.

"So, tell me about the rough guys that you saw Jimmy with."

"Mostly Latin guys, short, maybe tall like woman," He made a sign with his hand at about the level of his shoulders. Gabriele is about five foot ten, so he was probably showing a height of five foot four or five foot five.

"But rough?"

"Big muscle, tattoo, long hair." He waited for that to sink in. "Rough."

"You think they would hurt him?"

"If he want. If he like it."

"You ever do that?"

"To Jimmy? No, why you ask?"

"No, I meant to anyone."

He said maybe but he couldn't remember. *"Forse, ma mi sono dimenticato."*

"Doesn't matter. Pretend I didn't say that."

"Escort no have gun, no shoot, not want trouble. Jimmy escort not have visa, not have green card. Run away, not be in trouble."

I pulled out my cellphone and sent a text to Eddie. *Jimmy like rough guys?*

He responded very quickly. *Yeah Never saw one but saw bruises*
U gotta tell Mike di S If I tell him it'll look bad
Bud probably knows something, paid credit-cards and kept bank statements
Talk to Bud don't use me LMK what you find out

I asked Gabriele to tell me about what rough sex is. He was uncomfortable but gave me some examples. Could mean spanking, beating, punching, handcuffs or ropes, hot wax, clamps. Maybe urine. Fifty shades of whatever.

"Any idea what Jimmy was into?"

"Not see any hurt. He walk okay, eat okay. Maybe just want master slave things. Dog leash maybe." He really didn't want to talk about it. "Maybe he want Raul come back."

"You think Raul was into that?"

He shrugged and said he didn't know. *"Non lo so."*

"C'mon. You have an opinion, and you know more about this than I do."

Gabriele was clearly at the end of his patience. He announced he was going to cook something, walked into the kitchen and opened the fridge to see what he had to work with. Then the freezer. He found some frozen chicken thighs and some vegetables. The pantry had a lot of tomato products: crushed tomatoes, whole peeled plum tomatoes, tomato sauce, tomato paste. He grabbed several cans and put them on the counter.

"Garlic?" he asked.

I pointed into the pantry. He looked back and found it in an open-weave basket on the top shelf.

So that was the end of that.

My phone bleeped, indicating a text message.

Mike di Saronno. *Whats this rough sex crap*

Not crap Jimmy was into some kink

The phone rang. Mike

"Yup?"

Gabriele looked up. I mouthed "Mike." He nodded.

"Eddie called me and I smelled you all over it."

"What's that supposed to mean?"

"Eddie calling me and laying this egg on me. It didn't seem like something that he woke up thinking about. What did that leave? You."

"Well, it wasn't me. It was Gabriele who told me that he thought Jimmy was hanging out with some rough escort types. I asked Eddie, who said, something like 'Oh sure, I knew about that'."

"And?"

"I told him to call you and not to use my name. Now that we're talking, I'll tell you that Eddie had nothing to do with it. Whether you knew it already or not, Eddie and Jimmy didn't have a sexual relationship, or so Eddie tells me."

"I think you or Ruth told me something that added up to that. Eddie says he's still carrying a torch for his ex-wife? Right?"

"Kinda. Not exactly, but kinda. Believe it or not, I try not to pry into other people's sexual habits. What else did Eddie tell you?"

"That's pretty much it."

"Then he forgot to tell you that he thinks Bud van Gelsen handled all of Jimmy's credit card accounts and balanced his checkbooks, so he could possibly shed some light on who was involved."

Mike didn't say anything.

"I can hear you thinking, Mike. You're thinking that Bud won't tell you anything."

"Okay, smarty pants."

"Maybe you can get a warrant so you can have your people look over Jimmy's expenditures for recreation."

Gabriele was hearing my end, but not Mike's. He kept peeling and chopping garlic cloves. When I do it I more or less dice them, just chop them into highly irregular small pieces. When a trained cook chops garlic cloves, he or she slices them into very thin segments that maintain the shape of the whole garlic clove. I was watching him and thinking it looked like a lot of trouble for relatively little reward, and besides, my hands are not steady enough to do what he was doing.

"Yeah," Mike said. "I'd prefer to have all the records. Not just what Bud decides it would be okay to give us."

"I doubt Bud knows or cares what's there. If he is just there to pay bills and balance checkbooks, he may not know what each expense is. You match the receipts to the bills. When you have them, then you check to make sure the other charges are signed for by your client. He's not an accountant or a tax preparer, doesn't have to decide what's deductible and what's not."

"Did you know that Jimmy was adopted?"

"What? Where did you hear that?"

"When the M.E. did the autopsy, they populated it with all the information the State had about Jimmy. He was adopted when he was about a week old. I read it on the autopsy report, but it can't have been a secret."

"Odd that none of the brothers mentioned that when you met them."

"They had to know, right? I guess that's why they really didn't look much like each other."

"Two of the other van Gelsen boys, John and Christopher, were also adopted as infants. They were full brothers, but no indication of who the parents were, just like Jimmy. Bud and Gus were both natural children of Mr. and Mrs. van Gelsen. As far as we know there was no genetic or blood relationship between the van Gelsen family and John, Kip or Jimmy."

I found myself thinking that there were a lot of secrets in that family. Interesting that they were all tight-lipped, not just one or two. I had the feeling that Bud was the one who knew where all the bodies were buried, so to speak.

Gabriele was acting like he felt like he ought to go home. He stopped chopping onions and garlic and scraped what he had been working on into a plastic baggie. I put my arm around him and he snuggled a little but pulled back. "What we do?"

I told him I wanted to see if we could get together with Eddie again. I felt like we were missing something that Eddie could tell us. Not that Eddie was concealing anything on purpose but just that there was some glue that would hold the story together, and we didn't have it.

"Not at Ora di Pranzo then."

I called Eddie and he answered on the second ring. "How about we finish our conversation over dinner?"

He seemed amenable. I suggested that he pick a place in Park Slope so it would be convenient for him. We agreed on a Pan-Asian place called Talde on 7th Avenue that Eddie said was one of his favorites. I asked him if he could take care of a reservation, and Gabriele would be joining us. He was up for that, and said he would meet us there in forty-five minutes.

I put on a fresh shirt and washed up. Gabriele looked perfect as always, and just stared at me worrying about which shirt I should wear. I ordered an Uber and we went downstairs to meet the car.

It was a nice space, super-imposed on an older space with fancy cast-iron pilasters framing a big corner door. The style of the building said it was probably built late in the nineteenth century. A lot of the SoHo area in Manhattan is cast-iron facades. I have always loved them. The interior had a slightly fancy-looking Chinese restaurant air to it. Pagoda-like architectural flourishes, but basically plain wood booths that were roomy enough to be comfortable.

After we were seated and the waiter brought some drinks, Eddie looked like he was waiting for me to start, so I did. "Did you know that Jimmy was adopted? So were two of the other brothers, John and Kip."

He reacted with a slightly dropped jaw and a vague, questioning look.

"Mike told me. It was on the autopsy report."

"I never saw an autopsy report, but of course, there would be one, since he died on a sidewalk. Public place."

"You weren't a relative. I'd guess Bud has a copy. You were an ADA, so you know that autopsy reports are not light reading, and the photography can be unpleasant at least. Maybe Bud would have put it in a drawer on purpose."

"I should have been closer to Jimmy. He needed me to take care of him."

"Are you sure of that?" I asked.

Gabriele was shaking his head, not so much in disagreement as just in puzzlement.

I said that it seemed to me that Jimmy was a very private person. A guy with a lot of secrets. "When I went to his funeral at Grace Church, I envied him the dignity and majesty of the ceremony," I looked up at the ceiling and then down at Eddie across the table. "I felt like I could feel his soul flying up to heaven."

Eddie's eyes started to look wet and shiny. Gabriele elbowed me.

"But there were sides of him that were more like a normal human being. I feel closer to him because he had feet of clay, like me, or maybe like you."

"What it mean, 'feet of clay'?" Gabriele asked.

"It means he had a bad side if you looked for it, even though he seemed like a good guy. A side that had problems, that had secrets. They call it 'feet of clay'."

Eddie looked at me. The waiter brought some appetizers that Eddie had apparently ordered. We said nothing while the waiter put the dishes on the table. Something that looked like Pad Thai but had oysters in it. I helped myself to that, and asked for a Tsingtao beer. Eddie and Gabriele both wanted Singha, a Thai beer.

"I was not trying to be difficult, Eddie. What I was trying to say was that I saw Jimmy as a man on a poster, or a statue in a niche on a wall. Now I am beginning to see that life is the same for everyone. We have things we keep to ourselves, and other things that we let the world see."

Eddie nodded.

"Problem is that if we don't dig into the part that wasn't there on the surface and easy to see, we may never find out what happened that night."

I wondered if I should just shut up, but I kept going. "Mike has subpoenaed financial records from Jimmy's estate. We need to find out if he was seeing any escorts, or if there were financial transactions that might indicate something about Jimmy that we don't know. Maybe something that even you don't know."

Eddie stared at the table, picked up a spoon and put it back down. "I'm sure there was a lot I didn't know. There was probably a lot about me that he didn't know. We both knew we were agreeing to a compromise when he agreed to marry me." He looked up at me then at Gabriele.

He cleared his throat. "I knew he was seeing guys who didn't fit my idea of people I wanted to get to know. He was frank about being attracted to tough-looking men. For me that was as easy to understand as being attracted to a man in a suit and tie with an advanced degree. I was attracted to Jimmy, not the same way he was attracted to his rough guys, but in a real way. He was strong in some surprising ways, and he was fiercely committed to his charities."

I didn't feel like we were getting anyplace. Eddie was morose and clearly upset. I decided to turn it over to Mike.

Chapter Twenty-seven

Mike was in an interrogation room, surrounded by several cardboard boxes, and with a stack of papers in front of him. He was not in a good mood.

"What's that?" I asked.

"It's the files we copied from Ragnar van Gelsen's office."

"Don't you have some kind of forensic accounting expert who can look through that?"

"Not right now, no."

"Anything I can help with?"

"No, this is all confidential at the moment. You're not approved to look at any of this."

"So why am I here?"

"I wanted to know what you found out from talking to Eddie Hall."

"Give me an idea what you're asking about."

He fixed me with a dead stare.

I tried to summarize the conversations we had with Eddie at Social, on the phone and later at Talde.

"Can you skip to the end?"

"Tell me what you took away from these talks you had. Don't try to reconstruct all the conversations."

"What I took away was that Eddie wasn't surprised by anything. He knew that Jimmy was playing around with some pretty rough characters. He knew that Bud was taking care of paying all the bills. He knew that Eddie had no intention of being married in a physical sense. He was surprised that Jimmy was adopted. Not that what he knew or didn't know helped in the final analysis, of course."

"What do you think I should be looking for in these boxes."

"It seemed to me that Mr. van Gelsen's checkbook and his credit cards might have some clue as to the identity of the escorts he was seeing."

"You think an escort shot him?"

"No, not necessarily, but it is possible that he was outdoors that night either because he was meeting someone, or he was walking with someone. Since we are learning that he hired escorts, it seemed reasonable that if we could look at his credit card slips for that night, or maybe at his ATM withdrawals for that day and evening, it could help point us in the right direction."

"Okay, that's what I thought. That means we don't need to go over years of records. Possibly just the time right before the shooting."

"I couldn't say about that. I'm a civilian, not trained. Just seemed logical to me that if he was hiring men for sex, and he liked it rough, the two things might be connected."

He shuffled through the papers on the table.

"By the way, did the autopsy tell you how far away the shooter was?"

"Not very precise. What we know is the shooter was not standing right in front of him. But whether the shooter was six feet or twenty feet away, I don't think we can tell."

"Did you look at the scene and measure what was six feet away or twenty feet away? Was there some bushes or trees that someone could have been hiding behind? I mean, I think you said that whoever shot him was right in front of him, but could he have turned to see what was going on behind a bush that was moving and been right in front of the shooter that way?"

"And maybe we would find a cigarette butt that had DNA on it, and we could run that through the DNA library and come up with something?" Mike was being sarcastic.

"C'mon, Mike. I'm not the enemy. I'm just trying to run some possibilities by myself. If you've already covered all of this, then tell me I'm all wet."

He picked up another box and opened it. "Here, these are more recent." He looked at me. "You're not all wet. I just didn't plan on having to look through all this crap myself."

"Wish I could help."

"I doubt we're going to find anything, but it was a solid idea."

"Why wouldn't you find something?"

"If he was hiring escorts, do you think he would put the charges on a credit card? I don't know, but I'm guessing that an escort would want cash. From my experience as a cop, a lot of escorts are either illegal or they're working under an assumed name. I doubt a credit card or a check would do most of them a lot of good."

"Maybe. Or maybe there was a middleman who was taking care of laundering the money."

"Meaning a pimp?"

"I guess. I was thinking of an agency like a place that has masseuses for hire."

"That's the sort of thing I would be looking for, Hugo. I just doubt I would find out about it. I bet if Jimmy knew his brother was going to pay the credit cards, I don't think he would want to charge something to Big Mary's Escort Agency or whatever."

"I'm going down to Thalia. I have my cellphone. If you want me to help or to run errands or whatever, just call me."

He stood up and held his hand out. "Don't know what I would do without you and Ruth and Gabriele. Honestly I don't."

I left and walked down 8th Avenue to 50th Street and into Thalia, a restaurant with the largest bar of any similar place anywhere on 8th Avenue. Party central as a result. I stood outside and called Ruth, who said she was on her way. She got there frighteningly fast "The magic of Uber," she calls it.

The bartender had barely brought my dirty vodka straight up before Ruth was sitting down next to me at the bar.

"Make that two," she said to the bartender. Then to me, "So, bring me up to date."

I did my best, not sparing any language and not hiding anything that might have embarrassed Jimmy or Eddie or Bud. "And Mike's in a bad mood."

"Sounds to me like you might have been on to something."

I smiled and we clinked glasses. I took a gulp and ordered a refill.

Suddenly, Mike was standing next to us. I was startled but Ruth saw him come in the front door. She tapped the bar and rolled her eyes toward the entrance. I didn't pick up the hint, so I was startled when I heard his voice behind me.

"I gave up," he said. "I'm going to wait for the forensic guys to look at the records."

He pushed into the bar between Ruth and me, and one of the runners slid an extra bar stool in so he could sit.

I asked when he thought they would do their thing and let Mike know what, if anything, they found. He said they had picked up the boxes and taken them to One Police Plaza, and he expected to meet them the next day. He clearly wanted to mend fences, so we asked the hostess if she could put us at a table.

"No business," Mike said. "We're friends, first and foremost." He signaled the waiter and ordered another round of what we were having at the bar. The drinks arrived promptly, with a plate of assorted oysters, accompanied by mignonette sauce and a small container of freshly grated horseradish with some lemon slices and a tiny bottle of Tabasco sauce. The waiter said the oysters were on the house.

True to his word, Mike never brought up the subjects of the van Gelsen family or the Eddie Hall political campaign. As a matter of fact, since Mike lived about four blocks from Thalia, and I had lived two blocks from Thalia for nearly ten years, we talked about the huge changes in the neighborhood over the last decade. The old Gristede's market disappeared and was now a ladies- apparel store, while a fancy, two-story Food Emporium had sprung up in a former restaurant space on the same block as St Malachy's Roman Catholic Church, known in the neighborhood as "The Actors' Chapel."

Ruth kept looking at me as though I should change the subject. I stayed with Mike's play-list. We ended up talking about the long-running musicals that were still drawing tourists after their umpty-umpth cast change. I have never been a fan of Broadway musicals, but I admit to having been sucked into some over the years because of the stars or because of the number of Tony awards they'd won.

When I was a kid, I loved musicals, but that was when the leads in musicals were real singers; men and women who could belt out a song so that you could hear it in the back row of the top balcony of the St James Theater, which was, and is, the largest musical theater in the Broadway district. Sometime after "Flower Drum Song" was there, at the St James, and before the revival of "Gypsy" with Patti LuPone as Mama Rose, Broadway leading ladies and leading men had become smaller and better-looking, and they had sprouted microphones that hung down from their hairlines into their temples, and that turned what had once been a human voice into an amplified, inhuman braying that seldom carried a tune because the concept of melody had disappeared anyway.

Not so with Mike. He was a Broadway baby, born and bred, although he grew up in Queens. He had spent his whole adult life in the theater district, and tried to see every musical that opened every season. I never went to the theater with him, but I could imagine him jumping to his feet for a 'Standing O' after each tour-de-force belting or dancing number. The inherent silliness of a standing ovation for a singer with a mic made Mike seem closer to a normal human.

"Do you keep all your Playbills?" Ruth asked him.

He nodded.

"They're gonna be worth a fortune someday," she said, and waved at the waiter for a glass of sparkling water with lime.

Oddly enough, and unpredictably, we broke up to go to our separate apartments without ever discussing police matters.

Mike called me at ten the next morning and asked me to come over to his office. He had received the report on the van Gelsen financial records, and it was time to caucus. He met me in an interrogation room and informed me that the meeting would be videotaped and that there would be an audio recording as well.

"Sorry," he said. "I have to have a record of what I'm telling you, and I have to ask you to acknowledge that the information I am passing along to you is for your use and that of your two colleagues, Ruth Jensen and Gabriele Cortese, in assisting my office in gathering information about the homicide murder of Jimmy van Gelsen."

I did as he asked, and acknowledged that I was going to receive privileged information.

"And you may not discuss this information with anyone except the two colleagues, Ruth Jensen and Gabriele Cortese. If you are summoned to be a witness in a trial, you will inform my office."

Agreed.

He told me he would not be showing me any of the report from the forensic accounting group, and that I would not be given access to the report but that he would summarize certain of the findings to help us move the investigation forward.

I agreed.

There were several things that jumped out at the forensic accounting team. The first was what appeared to be a series of wire transfers to a bank account in Bermuda that aggregated about sixty thousand dollars in seven different transfers, each under ten thousand dollars. They were attempting to track down the recipient of the money, but there was no notation in the records of a use of the money. The Bermuda account that had received the funds was in turn owned by an account in Grand Cayman. It looked like it would take a lengthy process to find out who the ultimate beneficiary was.

The second was a pattern of ATM withdrawals on late evenings around midnight, some of them as often as once a week. These withdrawals were each of about one thousand dollars. They speculated that these were used as pocket cash withdrawals, but the pattern began a little over three months before Mr. van Gelsen's death, with nothing similar prior to that.

Oddest of all, though, there was a single payment of just under two hundred thousand dollars to an insurance company. The payment covered full payment for a life insurance policy that would, on the death of Mr. van Gelsen, pay one million dollars to Housing Works, a not-for-profit charitable organization that ran the bookstore where Mr. van Gelsen worked several times a week and that concentrated on providing services for shut-ins suffering from AIDS and a variety of types of terminal cancers. The services were largely provided in the way of delivering readymade meals, stocking refrigerators with juices and bottled water, and paying for broadband and cable television services. Most of the recipients were eligible for government-paid medical aid as well, and any medical expenses would have been covered by Medicaid. The payment would be made when the Medical Examiner determined the cause of death of Mr. van Gelsen. It would be invalid in the case of suicide during the first two years of the policy, and would simply result in the rebate of half the initial policy payment. Housing Works had not been notified of the policy, nor of the pending payment.

I asked Mike if I was allowed to share this information with Eddie Hall.

Negative. No discussion with anyone other than Ruth and Gabriele, or with Mike di Saronno.

Chapter Twenty-eight

I called a mandatory meeting of the Fab Three, meaning Ruth, Gabriele and me. I told them I would be making eggplant casserole with turkey sausages, and asked Gabriele to bring a couple of bottles of *nero d'avola*, since I was fresh out.

I seldom make eggplant casserole, because it takes several messy steps. First, I had to peel two big purple eggplants, slice them, flour them, dredge them in beaten egg and coat them with bread crumbs that have been liberally augmented with oregano flakes and rosemary. Then you fry them in a big cast-iron skillet in about an inch of vegetable oil until they are crispy looking and brownish, and move them to a rack to drip dry. Once they are no longer hot or wet, you pour some tomato sauce in the bottom of a nine by thirteen by three casserole dish and spread out a layer of eggplant overlapping like shingles on a roof. On top of that a layer of provolone slices and a sprinkling of shredded mozzarella and a thin layer of torn-up basil leaves. Then another layer of tomato sauce, a layer of roasted sausages cut the long way and sliced up then another layer of eggplant, etc. When you run out of eggplant, you pour a final layer of tomato sauce over the whole thing, sprinkle with mozzarella and a healthy dose of grated parmesan or Romano cheese. Bake for a while at three hundred and fifty degrees until it bubbles. Take it out and let it cool down. Serve warm but not so hot it burns the skin off the roof of your mouth. Lots of crispy bread with a plate of olive oil for dipping. Kinda like a family-sized version of eggplant parmigiana with more cheeses. Makes a near-total wreck of the kitchen.

Gabriele brought six bottles of wine, comprised of two consecutive vintages of *Tancredi*, a Sicilian blend by a vintner named *Donnafugata* ("woman dismissed").

I had made some *crudités*, being celery, carrot sticks, cauliflower and broccoli florets. Gabriele opened the most recent vintage of Tancredi and poured three tulip-shaped glasses from the kitchen cupboard. We sat in the living room and sampled the earthy-tasting, delicious dry wine with crunchy vegetables dredged lightly in a plate of sea salt.

As we sipped, I ran over the three big points of the forensic accounting inspection of Jimmy's checkbooks and credit-card statements. First the sixty thousand dollars in wire transfers to Bermuda, second the pattern of withdrawing one thousand dollars at a time from ATMs late at night, and third, the life insurance policy for Housing Works.

"Odd, I would have thought he would buy a life insurance policy for Eddie."

"As I understood it, Jimmy had left his entire estate to Eddie, but Eddie told Bud he didn't want it."

"Who knew?" she said.

I asked them if anything occurred to them about these three aspects of the van Gelsen finances.

"Well," Ruth said, "we knew he worked at Housing Works. So, the life insurance policy makes sense, if he wanted to leave them something when he passed on."

"A month before he died?"

The timing seemed off-color to me. Not sure exactly why, but who goes out and pre-pays a life insurance policy for a charity then gets killed a few weeks later. Premonition of death?

"*È strano*," Gabriele mused, right hand rubbing his neck.

"Strange?" I translated. "I thought so too."

"Now that you mention it," Ruth said, voice trailing off. She wrinkled her forehead.

"Do the three fit together?"

"Maybe not," Ruth said. "He was wealthy, right? So maybe it's not odd that he was sucking cash out of the ATMs in the middle of the night."

"Midnight suppers?" I looked at Gabriele questioningly.

He made a 'who me?' gesture. I nodded. "Not at Ora di Pranzo. If he come in, I see him. Regular customer I make sure I send glass wine and some *contorni*.

"Lots of places to eat within walking distance of where he lived. St.

Luke's Place, right?"

I nodded.

"Jimmy like drink."

"You mean he drank too much?"

"Too much? *Non lo so.*"

"I wasn't asking for a moral judgement," I said. "Did he get drunk?"

Gabriele shook his head slowly. "Not drunk."

"But almost drunk?"

He nodded.

"So maybe he went out drinking," Ruth said.

"Or maybe he went to a hustler bar and found a companion," I suggested.

Gabriele nodded slightly. "Maybe."

"How much would he have to pay for an escort?" Ruth asked in a matter-of-fact tone of voice. She was looking at Gabriele.

He shrugged.

"Guess," she said.

"Five hundred."

"Credit cards?"

He shrugged. "Not Mexican, Mexican want cash. Not visa. Not bank."

"But the sixty thousand to Bermuda?"

Ruth shook her head. "No idea. Golf club membership?"

I hadn't thought of that. "I don't know if he was a golfer, but if he wanted to buy a club membership wouldn't he just write one check or send one wire?"

"I guess," Ruth said, "but that would be true of anything he was buying. Why would he send seven wires instead of one?"

"Money laundering problems?" I suggested.

"What that mean?"

"All the wires were under ten thousand dollars," I said. Wouldn't trip any alarms at the banks."

"So, you think maybe he was buying drugs?" Ruth asked, looking doubtful.

"Nah, he could do that here, no need to go through Bermuda."

"But something he didn't want other people to know about?"

"I don't know. It just seems odd, so I find myself trying to figure it out. He could have been investing in something that was just getting started, I suppose, and dribbling money into it to help it along. But no reason to hide it, in that case. Bermuda. What's Bermuda about?"

"Pink sand?" Ruth said with a tonal upturn at the end to make it a question. "Insurance companies?"

"I'd be willing to put my money on tight-lipped bankers that know how to keep secrets."

"You're thinking about Grand Cayman."

I could feel us bumping up against the proverbial brick wall after we pigged out on the eggplant and bread. "Who wants ice cream?" I blurted out.

It looked like it might rain as clouds were piling up in front of the Chrysler Building, which was clearly visible from my living room window. We grabbed some umbrellas (I always have a lot, because I forget mine and have to buy new ones when it rains) and went to a family-owned ice cream stand that sold through a window onto the sidewalk of 49th Avenue. I always get pistachio, but they sometimes have twenty or thirty choices, and they claim they are all home-made.

I walked them to the subway station at Vernon-Jackson. The platform is always crowded, twenty-four-seven. All the new high-rises have increased the traffic to a choke point.

When I got home the message light was blinking on my VoIP phone. Mike had called. I pressed Call Back. It was Mike's cellphone. No answer. I left a message. "Hi, it's Hugo, returning yours. I'm at home."

I used the alternative remote control and pulled up a movie service. I wanted to see a movie from the year before about World War II. Netflix? Nope. Plex? Yup. I settled back, but couldn't sit still and went to the computer, looked up 'Bermuda bank secrecy'. Yup. Not foolproof, but the secrecy there is pretty tight. Tight enough for a bank to forward money to another location where secrecy is closer to sacred. Grand Cayman, like Ruth said. Money laundering crept back into my mind. I turned off Plex, and poured myself a couple of fingers of Oban, a light blond single-malt that goes down smoothly after ice cream.

Chapter Twenty-nine

Sometimes I can't sleep. I get something racing through my mind, and it starts making loops, going by over and over. It's not like counting sheep. It tends to make me feel like my heart is racing. Being a confirmed hypochondriac, that gets me out of bed and into the shower. More Oban. I decided to go for a walk by the river.

The two goons were smoking cigarettes across the street, of course. I was not up to teasing them, so I went back upstairs and sent a text to Mike telling him they were there.

The phone rang. "Hey, Mike," I said quickly.

It wasn't Mike. It was Eddie, and he had been drinking, not slurring but talking too carefully and in a slightly pinched voice.

"Hey, buddy," he said, not picking up that I called him Mike.

"Hi, Eddie, what are you up to?"

"At a bar near you, buddy."

"Where is that?"

"Vernon Avenue. Whatsa name of this place?" he was talking to someone there.

"Domino's Hook? That ring any bells?"

Well, my two goons know where that is. So do I.

"Whatcha celebrating?"

"I'm thinkin' about jumpin' in the river."

"How'd you end up in Long Island City? It's late." Figured it was best to ignore the river swim.

No response.

"Why don't I come over there? You gonna hang there for a while? I can be there in a few."

There is a side entrance to my building through a place where they have senior housing that's more or less attached to where I live. You can't see that entrance from where the goons were standing, smoking, at the front of the building. I could quick-walk up a couple of blocks and I'd be at the bar where Eddie was.

He hung up.

I was already dressed, so I just took the elevator down to the garage level and took the side staircase to the street. They weren't anywhere in sight. I made a fast right and hustled the two long blocks to Vernon. Dominie's Hoek, or Domino's Hook to Eddie, was lighted up and there were people on the sidewalk smoking cigarettes. No smoking indoors in public places in New York.

I still am attracted to cigarette smoke. Haven't smoked for decades, but that smell always reminds me of good times, like when you could sit at a bar and drink scotch, smoke too much and always find somebody to talk to. I paused outside and looked in the window, inhaling some second-hand smoke, appreciating the slightly muggy night air. There was Eddie, sitting at the bar. There was a martini glass in front of him with something whiskey-ish in it. Maybe a Manhattan. Doesn't take many of those to get pretty happy, or pretty sad, either one.

I walked in and sidled up to Eddie, not sure of what state he was in. Didn't want to get punched.

"Hey, Eddie," I said, still more than an arm's length away.

He jerked around, big smile. "Hey, Hugo, what're you doin' here?"

"We were just talking on the phone. We're right near my apartment."

"Goddamn right," he said, lifting his martini glass and taking a gulp at it. "To Jimmy," he said, and finished it off.

I smiled at him and moved closer, put my arm around his shoulder.

"Didn't know you were a drinker."

"Everybody's a goddamn drinker sometimes." He scrunched up his face into something like a grimace.

I backed up a bit to get more than an arm away again. The bartender took the martini glass away and replaced it with a fresh one, with a cherry and an orange slice.

"That a Manhattan?" I asked the bartender.

He nodded.

"Make me a Rob Roy?" I asked.

He smiled and nodded. "Gonna have to shut somebody down though."

"Gotcha. We're gonna see if we can get some fresh air. Maybe half a gallon of coffee."

"You know that doesn't really help. All it'll do is keep him from goin' to sleep."

Made sense.

I drank the Rob Roy and then guided Eddie back to the side door of my building. No goons. I used my card to get in. Fortunately, Eddie wasn't into singing or yelling. He was concentrating on walking without tripping.

"Hey, I been here before," he proclaimed to the empty living room when we got to my apartment. "I gotta pee."

I showed him the hall bathroom and waited outside the door in case he had a problem. He came back out but there was no sound of flushing. I looked in; the toilet bowl was fizzy-looking and yellow. I hit the flush and walked after him back to the living room.

He stretched out on the couch. I have a thing about people sleeping on my couch. I don't allow it. The couch is wide enough to sleep on, but it's light-colored, and people – especially drunks – drool when they sleep. I don't fancy having to get my couch shampooed to get saliva stains out of it. Much less vomit stains. Besides, I have good oriental rugs, same thing for getting vomit stains out of those.

I took him by the hand and stood him up. He walked with me into my bedroom. I have a king-size bed, plenty of room for two, and that way he wouldn't be wandering around the apartment. I put a blanket over him when he was flat on the bedspread, and put a pillow under his head. Whatever happened, I could wash the bedspread, and if I had to get a new pillow, that was easy too. He started to snore right away. I pushed him and he turned on his side. I got an old quilt and lay down on the door side of the bed. Since I'm not really used to anyone sleeping with me, other than Gabriele when he camps out, I thought I would have a hard time sleeping.

Wrong. When I woke up, he was still where I put him and it was light outside. I had sweated through my shirt, so I got up and put on a black t-shirt and brushed my teeth. No sound from Eddie, other than breathing.

He's gonna have a heck of a hangover, I thought. Well, I've been wrong often in my life, and this was another time. He woke up like he had been sleeping at home in his own bed. Sat up and hung his feet over the side of the bed and looked around. I was still flat on the bed under the quilt. I shut my eyes as he turned to look around. He jostled me.

"How'd I end up here?"

"I brought you, seemed like you needed to crash."

"Did you molest me?"

"What?"

"It was a joke."

He stood up and stretched. I got up and wandered into the kitchen and switched on the coffee maker, which I had loaded up before I fell asleep. Just out of deviltry I put on a CD of "Rhapsody in Blue" with a young British pianist thonking the keyboard like he was trying to kill it.

Eddie was all smiles. I handed him a mug of coffee and he looked around the room. "Do you take sugar or milk?" He nodded, but had already started to drink it. I pulled out the sugar and a container of milk from the fridge, and he dosed his coffee heavily.

"You look like you're feeling okay."

He looked puzzled. "Thanks, I am okay. Oh," he said, looking at his feet, "I drank a lot last night. Hope I wasn't gross and horrible."

"That's a blessing directly from God, that you don't have a hangover."

He nodded. "I don't seem to get them. Probably means there's something wrong with me."

"I don't usually either, but if I have a lot to drink like I think you did, I have a major case of the fuzzies the next morning."

"I was missing Jimmy," he said, with an air of finality. "A hangover would have completed what I did, I think."

I asked him if he could eat some eggs and he nodded eagerly. I handed him a towel and pointed him toward the bathroom. Then when he closed the bathroom door, I took a box of Morningstar Farms sausages (soy, not meat) and threw them in a skillet with some butter and cracked six eggs into a bowl, doused it with milk, threw in a pinch of salt and a tablespoon or so of dried oregano with a generous sprinkle of black pepper.

He emerged from the bathroom just as I was taking the veggie sausages out of the skillet and putting them on a pair of plates. I whisked the eggs vigorously and dumped them into the brown butter left in the skillet from the sausages. I looked at him and thought how old I have gotten. He's trim and hard all over like a runner who works out several times a week. Me, well, the years creep by and my young body was something I could see in old photos but couldn't quite figure out where the softness started and where it ended. I'm not fat, but I'm also not young, or even middle-aged. Oh well.

I dumped the eggs onto the plates, slightly overlapping the sausages and took them into the living room and set them on the dining table (no real dining room, 'shit happens' as that movie guy said) and handed him a fork. I put a waxed container of orange juice on the table with a pair of Waterford juice glasses that I had grabbed from my aunt's apartment when she died. "These are juice glasses," I announced, "but my grandfather used them as noggins."

He stared at me, clearly not understanding.

"Oh," I said. "Noggin is an old word for a little glass of whisky. Something you have before you go to bed."

He ripped through the sausages, though he clearly didn't know what they were made of. "Pork?" he asked.

"Soy," I said. "I don't eat red meat, and my father used to say that sausages were made out of lips and assholes anyway, so I go veggie on sausages."

"Coulda sworn they were real sausages."

"Hey, Eddie. Can I change the subject and ask you something personal?"

He nodded solemnly.

"You must have known that something was going on with Jimmy."

He nodded. There was an uncomfortably long silence, and then he said, "I was very selfish with Jimmy. I decided that the way to be happy was to find a more perfect way to live. It was stupid."

"More perfect?"

He explained that he never understood why he and his wife broke up. "We never had a fight. She just left."

I patted him on the shoulder. "Women," I said. "Can't live with 'em and can't live without 'em."

He shook his head.

"I decided I needed to live with a guy, didn't want to start dating women again, because I knew it would never be the same."

"And that was more perfect?"

"No, it was a dumb-ass idea, but I wanted it to work. Jimmy loved me and he knew I wanted it to work, and he went along with it."

"Okay," I said. "Then what?"

"Well, I asked him if he wanted to have kids. We were sitting on the side of the bed and it was morning. He said yes then I asked him if he wanted to have kids with me."

"What were you thinking?"

"I was making it up as I went along, to tell the truth. I knew a same-sex couple could have kids. They could adopt. They could find a surrogate to carry a baby. I don't know. I was just talking. He hugged me and he said yes with a real finality. Then he said it several more times, like yes-yes-yes-yes."

"And then?"

"I said, well, then we should get married." Eddie looked at me with tears in his eyes. "He fucking said yes again."

"And?"

"That was kinda the end of the conversation. He knew better than to try to kiss me. He knew I felt creepy kissing a guy, and he knew not to touch me like, well, like, down there."

His eyes began to drip tears but he didn't sob or make crying noises. He wiped his nose with his right index finger.

"I haven't ever told anybody this."

I patted his shoulder again. He didn't pull back.

"He said to me it'd be like we were Shakers. I thought I would look it up later, but I thought a shaker was something that held salt or pepper."

I poured him some more coffee.

"You got any vodka?" he asked me softly.

"Is the Pope Catholic?"

I grabbed a bottle of vodka out of the freezer, which is where I keep vodka, because nobody drinks it without it being chilled. I handed it to him. He poured an inch or so into the bottom of the noggin and filled the rest with orange juice.

"It hurts so bad that I did this to him and all he wanted to do was to make me happy."

I didn't know how to ask the obvious question, so I just flung it at him. "So, you and Jimmy never had sex?"

He shook his head and actually started to sob quietly. He choked a little and pushed out some words. "I knew he was hiring guys to have sex, and I knew that was wrong. Wrong on me, not wrong on him, but there I was, wanting to marry a nice man to have a perfect marriage where things couldn't go wrong."

"He was doing more than hiring escorts."

He looked at me quizzically.

"He paid somebody in Bermuda sixty thousand dollars in seven payments under ten thousand dollars."

"You mean he was laundering it?" There was a stricken look on his face, like somebody had just told him he had cancer. A frightened look, but he pushed it off his face.

"I don't know what he was doing, but he wasn't providing scholarships for choirboys, for sure."

"He liked to drink, and he could go a drink or two farther than he should, but he wasn't the type who would get in a car or cause some kind of disturbance. He never got in trouble. I'm fairly sure he wasn't taking any drugs. Maybe some grass, but I don't think even that. So, he wasn't buying drugs."

"And he did create a disturbance finally."

Eddie poured another vodka and OJ and threw it back. "Yeah, he did. He got himself killed."

"People tell me it's unlikely that an escort did that. Just so you know."

"I was a prosecutor. I can read the tea leaves. If he had died from an overdose it might be different. It might have been an accident, but a bullet in the forehead wasn't an accident."

He stood up and held out his hand. I held my hand out and he grabbed it and shook it. "You're a good friend, Hugo, and you are a gentleman to have helped me this way. I won't ever forget this."

Eddie scooted out the door shortly after the handshake, and I felt wobbly, like I had seen something that I didn't understand, but that scared me.

I got dressed and hurried to the 7-train, got to Times Square about fifteen minutes later, and took the 1 train to 50th Street and walked up to the Midtown North precinct. Mike was there.

I told him as faithfully as I could every bit of the conversation with Eddie.

"What do you think he's going to do?" I asked.

"I think he's going to try to get to the bottom of what happened, and he knows a lot of things that we don't, so he may get there before we can."

"What a dumb-ass idea," I said.

Mike cocked his head, waiting for me to finish what I was saying.

"Trying to design a marriage like what he described." I went back to something he said. "Shakers? Do you know what Shakers are?"

"Were, not are." He sat down at his desk. "They were a pacifist religious group that believed in remaining celibate, so of course they mostly died out."

"And now Jimmy is dead and Eddie is out to get whoever did it."

"Probably."

Chapter Thirty

I called Gabriele. I told him I needed to talk to him, meaning not on the telephone. We agreed to meet at Ora di Pranzo. He was working and would be there when I got there. I explained that I was not dressed for dinner but looked respectable and told him that I had been with Mike.

I grabbed an E train at 50th Street. Since there's free Wi-Fi on the platforms these days, I called Ruth, who was happy to get herself down to Ora di Pranzo. I told her I would wait to go through what happened until she got there, fully aware that she was likely to be there before me, just because she rode a broom and skipped all the traffic lights.

She did not in fact get to Ora di Pranzo before me, but she walked in on heels that looked like stilts from the back, about five minutes after I got my drink. Dirty vodka straight up with olives. No big surprise there. Gabriele sat next to me. It was after lunch and before dinner, so the bar was only sparsely populated. He had a shot glass of Dewar's scotch and smiled. A platter of grilled veggies materialized from the bartender and Ruth tottered in.

"How can you walk in shoes like that?" I asked, as Gabriele frowned at me. *Bad question.*

She gave me a slightly acidic smile and motioned to the bartender that she would have what I was having. Kiss-kiss. Also kiss-kiss with Gabriele. We were sitting in the corner where the bar met the wall, so I was able to talk to them both at the same time without talking across either one. I told them approximately what I told Mike, but tried to make it a little quicker.

When I finished, Gabriele said without a pause. "He go Bermuda and see what happen with money."

Ruth shook her head.

"Si, he go Bermuda. I know."

"Oh," she said, "I agree. I was just thinking what a hare-brained idiot idea he and Jimmy had about getting married." She excused herself and went to the ladies room.

Gabriele moved closer to me. "This not like you and me, Ugo. We different. Don't think about that. You and me, we okay."

Before I could think of something to say, Ruth came back and squeezed between us and into the chair she had been sitting in. "But you're right, Gabriele. For sure he's going to try to find out what happened. All those years he was an ADA probably gonna do the driving now." She downed the rest of her drink and signaled for another. "I bet his first stop will be to talk to Bud, and Bud knows more than we think he knows. Eddie is the man to find that out."

"Look at you," I said, gesturing down.

She put her high heels into a fuzzy bag with a shoulder strap on it. She had changed into a pair of black sneakers.

She smiled, shook her finger slightly at me, then took out her phone and started tapping on it. "Lots of hotel rooms available in Hamilton," she announced.

"Are you suggesting that we should go over there ourselves and step on Eddie's toes when he gets there?"

"Not the toe-stepping part, no. But I think you already know what the bank is, right? If we go over there, we can at least find out what kind of an operation the bank runs. I bet it's basically a router that redirects money someplace else and takes a cut when it passes by. Could even be as simple as just a machine."

"Have you ever been to Bermuda?" I hadn't.

Ruth looked at me as though I were a freak show. "Of course. It's the quickest way to get away from winter. And Murray had dealings with the insurance companies there, something about insuring shipments coming from Asia or something."

I had called up a map of Bermuda on my phone. "It looks like a keyhole with one side blasted open."

"Hundreds of little islands and most of them have their own beaches," she said. "It's a little like Nassau, but prettier."

"I been there," Gabriele chimed in. "Was *Febbraio*. Not cold for walk or ride bike, but ocean very cold. Too cold for swim."

"If you were there in February, no surprise it was cold. I doubt that would be a problem now, in the late summer. But I don't see any reason to go there. No banker is going to talk to us. Eddie can probably make a few calls and get some cooperation from the local police. If I just want to go someplace for a few days to relax, maybe Santa Fe. And if I want to go to an island, I would go someplace where they never get a hurricane. What are those islands off Brazil?"

"Fernando de Noronha? Brazil has lots of islands, but it rains holy heck a lot of the year. Great for snorkeling when it's not raining. Looks like a movie set too, but it takes forever to get there, and trust me, there's nothing special about the food or the hotels."

"Si, I been there," Gabriele chirped. "*È molto più bello di Bermuda.*"

"Prettier than Bermuda? Maybe. Probably. But no help finding out what happened to Jimmy van Gelsen's sixty thousand dollars," Ruth harrumphed.

"Like I said, we're not going to find out anything from a bank in Bermuda. What do you think would happen if you went to your very own Chase branch in New York and asked for information on a wire transfer that wasn't yours? And that branch would be a place where you have some pull."

"In Bermuda, I have all of Murray's insurance guys to talk to."

"So, talk to them on the telephone. If it turns out there is a reason to go to Hamilton, we'll go, but Eddie will have been there and gone by the time we can find out anything useful. Mark my words."

"What is mean 'mark my words'?"

"*Stai attento,*" I translated.

"He's trying to make up to Jimmy for all the stupid, asinine things he did," Ruth said, changing the subject.

I nodded to Ruth as Gabriele wandered away to greet a couple who had just walked in. Kiss-kiss. A great maître d' makes everyone feel like they've just come home. I was watching him when Ruth touched my arm.

"It's different for you and Gabriele. You're not Eddie and Jimmy."

I pulled back. "What? Did Gabriele tell you to say that? It's what he said to me before you got here."

"He was right." She sipped on her new drink, picked up a grilled asparagus spear and bit the end off. "He loves you the same way Jimmy loved Eddie, but he doesn't expect anything between the two of you."

I didn't respond. Just shook my head.

"From what you told me, Eddie was inventing some kind of let's-pretend game with Jimmy, and Jimmy was going along with it."

"Or pretending to."

Gabriele came back. I patted him on the shoulder. He leaned in toward me like a cat does when you pet it. *He's more important to me than I admit, even to myself.*

We agreed that Ruth would try to get in touch with some of the people that she knew, or that Murray had known, in Bermuda. I gave her the name of the bank so that she could ask around. It was getting to be dinner time and people were filling up the tables.

I asked Gabriele if he was going to have a table for us, and if he could sit with us.

Yes, about the table, negative about sitting down with us.

His look said it all. *Of course not. I can't just pretend I'm somebody else and ignore the people coming in.*

"What if we went someplace else?" I asked.

He cocked his head and nodded. He said he would meet us outside.

We took a short walk over to Aquagrill at Spring Street and 6th Avenue, to my mind the best seafood in Manhattan outside the Oyster Bar at Grand Central. Of course, they seated us right away, since everyone in SoHo knows Gabriele. On top of the minor miracle of being seated at dinner time without a reservation, there's an icing on that cake. Everyone in Manhattan comps Gabriele and his party, so dinner is always on the house, although we always leave a lavish tip for the server.

So, I made the mistake of having yet another dirty vodka and ordering a bottle of *aglianico del vulture,* an earthy deep red wine from Basilicata, which is the instep in the boot of Italy. Ruth joined me. Gabriele ordered two fingers of Auchentoshan, a particularly smooth, sweet single malt whiskey that's distilled near Glasgow. No ice. 'Neat'. The right way to drink it.

I realized I was hungrier than I had thought, and raced through a platter of eighteen Fanny Bay oysters from Vancouver, each with a spot of fresh chopped horseradish and a dip of vinegar. No pieces of shell in them, good shucker in the kitchen. Ruth was staring at me, watching me eat.

I offered her one.

She shook her head and smiled. "Traif."

"Since when?" I had been with her when she had eaten as many oysters as I did, non-kosher as anything could be.

"Since Murray passed."

I decided to jump in, and said to them that I was worried that Eddie was going to do something rash. He was upset when he realized that he had set Jimmy up to fail. He wanted to make somebody pay for what happened to Jimmy, somebody other than Eddie Hall.

"Are you thinking what I'm thinking?" Ruth asked me.

There was no answer for that, so I just waited for her to finish.

"I'm thinking Jimmy paid sixty thousand dollars for a hit man to kill him."

No, I hadn't been thinking that.

I shook my head. "I never met Jimmy, but from what I have learned about him, it doesn't make sense to me."

"It does to me," she said. "I think they call it 'suicide by hit man'."

"So that would be why there were no defensive wounds?"

She nodded.

"I suppose it's a possibility, and it would make sense as to why he would have sent the money in so many different transfers so that the government wouldn't pick up on it."

She nodded again.

"No," said Gabriele. "Jimmy come to Ora di Pranzo many time, sometimes with escort boy, sometimes just Jimmy, sometimes with brother. Not gonna kill himself."

"Why do you say that?"

"He not unhappy man."

"How do you know?"

"He drink a lot and he never be sad, always want good time, and he nice man too, good to servers. Everybody like when he come and sit at the bar. He buy drinks for the bar sometimes. He smile at everybody, always hug me and feel my butt. Not unhappy man."

"I saw him change when he and I were talking at my apartment this morning."

"Not kill self."

"How would you prove it anyway?" I asked. "If he paid someone to fly to New York from someplace outside the country, and shoot him, how would you find who it was?"

"You'd trace the payments," she said.

"From bank to bank to bank until the trail disappeared."

"Why do you think it would disappear?"

"Let's just assume for the moment that you're right, that he did want to hire someone to shoot him. So, he buys a life insurance policy for Housing Works, because he wants to do something nice for them. He could have just given them the same amount of money they would get from his death, of course, but he does it. Then he goes looking for someone to do the dirty deed, and he finds someone. They agree on sixty thousand dollars and it gets wired to Bermuda. Then we know it was wired from Bermuda to someplace in the Cayman Islands, but we don't know who got it there. Maybe it was a bank, and they then wired it on to someone else. Or maybe it was a bank and they gave the proceeds to Mister Hitman. Who is Mister Hitman? Did our millionaire victim not have enough brains to find a way to conceal what he was doing?"

Ruth listened without a muscle moving in her face until I was finished. Or until I stopped talking anyway then she opened her mouth to say something.

"I just don't think," I decided to append to my analysis, "that if Jimmy wanted to conceal what he was doing, he would have done a sloppy job of it."

"Or maybe he didn't care."

"No matter," Gabriele said firmly. "Jimmy not kill self. Not find man with gun to kill him."

I decided to skip over what he said. "We agreed before that Ruth will call her contacts in Hamilton to find out what she can about the wire transfers to Bermuda, which we already know were sent on to the Caymans.

If there are some breadcrumbs left, we can follow them."

"Bread crumbs?"

No reason he should know about children's stories in English. "It was part of a story called 'Hansel and Gretel,' about two children who were kidnapped by a witch and who dropped pieces of bread to mark their trail, but when they tried to go home, the birds had eaten all the bread."

"*Si, Hansel e Gretel. Briciole di pane.*"

When we left, Gabriele asked if he could come home with me. I told him yeah.

"Why are you so sure about Jimmy?"

"I know Jimmy. Smart man, happy man, very happy about Eddie Hall. Not want to die."

"You're sure of that?"

"Si."

"Did you sleep with Jimmy?"

He glared at me. "No."

"Okay. I didn't mean to insult you. Just that when people are lovers they know more about a person."

"Jimmy love Eddie Hall, not me or other person."

"Raul?"

"Not love Raul. He tell me about Raul when he drinking. Not want Raul again."

"Could Raul have hired someone to kill Jimmy?"

"Why?"

"Money?"

"How he get money if he kill Jimmy? Raul live in Florida."

I didn't have a comeback for that. When we got off the subway at Vernon-Jackson, I wondered if we would see those goons. I saw two guys who could have been them about a block down the street, but we were walking a different way, and the two guys I saw weren't as buffed up as the goons, who looked like they could break bricks with the sides of their hands. As it happened, they never materialized.

I was tired. When we went upstairs, I handed Gabriele a clean towel and pointed him toward the hallway bathroom, and I took a steamy hot shower in the bathroom off my bedroom. I padded out to the kitchen wearing a thick cotton bathrobe, toweling my hair. He was already sitt ing on a stool on the living room side of the kitchen pass-through.

"You want something? Orange juice? Ginger ale?"

He said nothing, but shook his head. I drank a tumbler of tap water.

We went to bed and I dropped off quickly. My experience of Gabriele has always been that he no sooner puts his head on a pillow than he is asleep. I slept very soundly, but sweated through my t -shirt, so it was clinging to me when it was still dark. *Damn alcohol anyway.* I took off the t-shirt and put on a fresh one. He was asleep, didn't move.

When I woke up, he was already awake, staring out the window at the Chrysler Building. Those gargoyles on it glint in the morning sun and can be almost hypnotic. It makes them look like they are moving. He leaned over and kissed me on the temple lightly.

"Is okay. We can love each other the way we already know how to do. Not have to do more."

"You're a young guy, Gabriele. You need a partner who you can sleep with and have sex with. That wouldn't happen with me. I am attracted to you. You know that. But the sex part just isn't part of me. I have been divorced for years, and I don't have a girlfriend or a boyfriend. I like to hug and be close, but not the sex part."

"Ugo," it sounded like a rebuke. "You know me. I already have enough sex when we meet few years ago. I have too much sex. Me too, just not need sex. Better be close and not need sex. See? Easy."

I didn't know where to take that conversation, so I changed the subject. "How about some eggs and biscuits?"

He smiled and nodded.

"Good. You set the table and I'll make the biscuits." My grandmother used to make biscuits every morning for breakfast when I was a kid. No recipe, no measuring. I measure the flour but for everything else I play it by ear. Sometimes I use avocados for shortening, and I did that with Gabriele. Biscuits don't look any different, but you want to butter them more before you eat them.

He poured some juice and folded two cloth napkins into soft pyramids. We sat there in our t-shirts and shorts and ate without talking. We smiled a lot.

Chapter Thirty-one

I kept thinking about the Shakers. Gabriele went home after breakfast, and I felt as though we had, at least for a while, resolved things between us.

I texted Eddie. *You there*
Yup
Where
Park Slope
Gabriele was sure you were going to Bermuda
Why
Find out where Jimmy's wire transfers went
That's dumb not gonna fly to Bermuda to hear about privacy I meant why did he think that
Dunno, he said he thought that
Somebody told him there were wire transfers that went to Bermuda
I guess, that came from me
Can I see that
I don't have it saw at PD w Mike. Ruth and G know too
How can I see it
Talk to Mike I guess but forensic team compiled it after Bud turned files over
Wanna meet for lunch
Nah busy
Wanna meet for lunch at Thalia and then walk over to see Mike
Okay

We agreed to meet at twelve thirty, and I called Mike to see if he had time for us at one thirty after our lunch or if he would like to meet us for lunch at Thalia.

He said he'd meet us at Thalia.

What is it about a meal or even a drink that makes difficult talks easier? I think it's because eating is a leveler, sitting around a table in a room full of people all doing the same thing at the same time. We all have to eat, and when we gather around a table and talk, there is a feeling of equality that helps awkward conversations be useful and even relatively friendly. Mike knew that. I didn't. I watched what happened, knowing that Eddie was potentially depressive and with some buried anger.

There we were, a career police detective with a streak of creativity, a former ADA and political candidate whose gay fiancé was a murder victim, and a retiree with a knack for snooping. One the son of immigrants, the second a mixed-race lawyer who was the first one in his family to go to college, then me, a mutt with ten or twelve national backgrounds and an undying need to do something to balance my disastrous private life. But all housebroken, which also helps.

In spite of that we weren't going to be drinking. It was lunch and one of us was a cop.

Mike is a genius at getting a conversation started, getting people to relax. Eddie Hall is a former prosecutor who wants to get to the bottom of things, no time wasted. I go with the flow, frequently try to be invisible. (That's the old public relations guy in me. The PR guy is supposed to be invisible, wear old-fashioned clothing, drab colors, etc.)

Eddie opened the conversation with a thrust, like throwing a one hundred mph fastball right over the plate for the first pitch. Almost always get a strike out of that. "So, I hear that you were able to extract some interesting information from Jimmy's bookkeeping materials that Bud had."

"Depends on what you think is interesting. A couple of puzzling things. No way to know if they will turn out to be interesting in terms of trying to find out who shot him. Maybe not." *Touché.*

"Try me."

"He wired some money to an unknown party through a bank offshore. No notation what it was for, and he took out a life insurance policy with the beneficiary being Housing Works."

"He was very devoted to Housing Works," Eddie said.

"But we think he made regular donations to Housing Works. Why a life insurance policy?"

"Gabriele Cortese said he thought I would want to go to Bermuda. I figure that's where the offshore bank you mentioned is?"

"When did he say that?"

Eddie gestured at me. "Hugo told me, don't know exactly when he said it."

Mike smiled. "Hearsay."

"Sustained," Eddie smiled.

"Look, I'm gonna stop being cute here. If Jimmy sent money to somebody in Bermuda, you can take it to the bank that what he was doing was on the up-and-up. That's who he was."

Mike dropped the smile. "You were a prosecutor. If someone sends seven wire transfers to a bank one after another, each wire for under ten thousand dollars, but with the total adding up to sixty thousand dollars, what would you think?"

"If that's all I knew, I would wonder if he was trying to launder the cash for some reason."

"Bingo."

"But that's not all I know, and I don't think he was laundering anything."

"The funds were then transferred to a bank in the Cayman Islands."

"Again, same thing. But this is a man I think I knew fairly well, and he didn't do things that had to be concealed. If he did that, he was just trying not to leave a trail pointing to what he was doing. We all know the banks in Bermuda can be persuaded to cooperate with governmental agencies, so if Jimmy was trying to hide something from law enforcement, he was deluding himself."

Mike didn't respond, kept listening.

"If he was to conceal something from Bud or from me, in order to keep an element of surprise, that might make sense."

"I don't get where you're going," Mike said.

"I don't get where you were trying to go either," Eddie said.

"The seven wire transfers to Bermuda are part of the evidence we're looking at in a homicide case."

"How do you think they connect?"

"What if Jimmy was interested in murder for hire?"

"I wondered if you were going that way." Eddie glanced down, then up, formulating what he wanted to say. "I thought the same thing briefly." He looked directly at Mike.

"Briefly?"

"Just not Jimmy. A real church-goer. A real believer. Just wouldn't do that. First of all, suicide is sinful, and second, swindling insurance companies is also sinful. For a wealthy man like Jimmy, it just doesn't compute. He liked to surprise people, got a kick out of watching people smile when he gave them something."

"Why Bermuda then?"

"I dunno. He talked about having a vacation home in the Caribbean for when it's snowy and nasty in Gotham. Probably something like that. I don't know. Could be a sports car. Could be anything. He had a lot of money, and a lot of times he bought things on impulse. We may never find out what he had up his sleeve."

I could tell looking at Mike that he wasn't buying what Eddie said, at least not completely. He's too good a detective and psychologist to ignore what Eddie was saying, but he also wasn't swallowing it whole.

"So, if he was buying a condo, wouldn't there be a receipt or something to prove that he paid the money?"

"I don't know. Ask Bud. The only real estate I've ever bought is my place in Park Slope, and I got a ream of paper when I bought it. I had cancelled checks for the down payment. I'm a lawyer, but I have no idea what it takes to buy a condo in Grenada or St Lucia."

He's not blowing smoke, but he's debating. No way to tell what he thinks. That's what Mike's thinking.

"You're not a suspect, you know." Mike threw him a curveball.

Eddie made a slight jerking movement with his head to indicate he didn't follow.

"Obviously you were in a hospital when Jimmy was shot, so we know you were simply not there. I know that if you knew something, you'd tell me. Right?"

Objection. Sustained. Withdrawn. But now it's been said, and it can't be unsaid.

"What does that mean?"

"It means we're not on different teams. We both want to find out what happened. I just find myself wondering if your memories make it difficult for you to fully consider all the possibilities."

Eddie took a deep breath. "I am emotionally involved. That does not mean my opinion about what Jimmy would or would not do is wrong. Ask Bud. I bet he would say the same thing."

"But Jimmy's not here to tell us what really happened, and it's my job to try to put the pieces together. I didn't say he hired someone to shoot him. As a matter of fact, it seems unlikely to me too. Not because I knew Jimmy, because I didn't. Just because there is nothing to point in that direction except the wire transfers. And you're right, the wire transfers could have been a birthday surprise for someone who wanted a beachfront condo someplace, but we know somebody shot him. He didn't shoot himself, and he wasn't shot by someone he wanted to run from. Not a thief, not a stranger most likely."

In my head I was hearing Gabriele tell me the same thing, that Jimmy was a happy guy, would not have done something like that. If there's one thing I have learned about Gabriele, it's that his intuition about other people is usually right on the mark, and Gabriele had apparently known Jimmy for quite a while.

Mike signaled for the check. Eddie started to say he would get this one, but Mike wasn't hearing it. I said nothing. Mike paid, stood up, shook hands with both of us and said he needed to get back to his desk.

Eddie looked at me when Mike was gone. "I really don't think Jimmy would have done that, but somebody did. Not necessarily a hit man either."

"Raul?"

"Jimmy very seldom said anything about Raul. I think they were okay with each other, but neither one wanted to go any further with their relationship, and Raul was working his way into a restaurant in South Beach."

I said Raul would have to be on the list. He agreed.

"And the family."

"The brothers? You've met them. Does that make sense to you?"

No, it doesn't. "They'd go on the list. How about his sexual partners? Like the escorts?"

He nodded, but in an offhand way that meant he thought it was wrong. "I think it's more likely that it was somebody in his everyday life. Somebody he saw virtually every day. That's why he didn't think anything was wrong. He just stood there and let whoever it was shoot him."

"Housing Works?"

He shrugged. "That doesn't sound right. I've been over there several times when he was working. Seemed like he was buddies with everybody; people that worked there, people that were browsing through the books and drinking his espresso, but I guess we don't really know what kind of daily interactions he had with people. Could be there was somebody he was rubbing the wrong way."

"What about your political opponents? People who would want to create some scandal around you?"

He looked at me quizzically.

"I mean, look at those toughs who were marching through Prospect Park when there was a kind of prayer vigil for your recovery. Like Charlottesville, with tiki torches and Nazi slogans. Or like the downtown crowd the day of the Million Woman March."

"I wasn't there at Prospect Park, as you know. I was still in the hospital. That was the night that it rained so hard and broke everything up, right?"

I nodded. "And those two hoods who have been following me around. They look like they were carved from the same wood as the Prospect Park marchers. Dumb as dirt too."

"It was a handgun that killed him," Eddie mused. "My grandfather always said rifles were for killing animals and handguns were for killing people. That's why he wouldn't let a handgun in his house even though he had a display-case full of rifles and shotguns. I bet a lot of people have handguns in their bedside tables these days."

"Do you?"

He shook his head. "I have a handgun, yeah. Haven't even looked at it in years, much less fired it. I got it when I was a prosecutor in Brooklyn.
"

"What kind?"

"Ruger Police Service Six. Could take three fifty-seven Magnum, but I only had thirty-eight. I used to go to the firing range to practice, but don't have any need for something like that. Never fired it except at the firing range."

"Where is it?"

"In a packing box someplace in the basement in Park Slope. It's in a safe box that needs a combination. I don't think I even know the combination any more. I may have written it down someplace. I'll have a look."

"I think you ought to tell Mike you have that. I think the bullet that killed Jimmy was a thirty-eight. I don't know the difference, frankly, but I think that's what Mike told me at some point."

"The difference is a three fifty-seven is a lot more powerful than a thirty-eight. The NYPD has never authorized cops to use three fifty-seven's, because they can go right through somebody and hit whoever is behind them."

"But it's a single-fire gun, right? Pull the trigger and it fires once?"

He nodded. "Whatever killed Jimmy was single-fire too. CSIs didn't find any other bullets."

"How do you know that?"

"I still know some people."

"Did Jimmy have a handgun?"

"I don't think so. He was very anti-gun, anti-NRA. It's another reason I don't think he would have done what Mike was saying."

I told him he ought to tell Mike about all this. "Not that it makes any difference, because we know you were in a hospital room when it happened."

He nodded.

"I'll send him an email and tell him as much as I can remember about what we talked about. And I'll copy you, so feel free to add anything you think is important."

Chapter Thirty-two

I think Mike had grabbed onto the idea of a hit man being hired with the sixty thousand dollars Jimmy wired to Bermuda. But he's a savvy guy, and I think what Eddie said and maybe what I told him Gabriele said soaked in.

Eddie did send him an email, and as far as I could see, it accurately reflected what we had talked about.

Mike said the disconnect in his mind was between the life insurance policy and the idea of a hit man. "No reason for him to try to cheat an insurance company if he was planning to take his own life," Mike said. "Might as well just leave them a bequest."

I was sitting in his office with Ruth. "I wonder how many friends Jimmy had that he could have run into on the sidewalk that night."

"I'm guessing," Ruth said, "he was on his way to someplace where he could have a couple of drinks, maybe meet a date. So, he could have been cruising every guy that walked by."

I suggested the neighborhood where he lived was *tres gai*. "Gabriele said that Jimmy went to Ora di Pranzo, even late, and sat at the bar. Also, that sometimes he would be there with an escort. If Gabriele is right, he was partial to Mexicans and some tough-looking Black guys."

"Or, you know," Mike said, "he could have been going to meet someone specific, maybe someone that turned out to have a gun." He said that the lack of information on what Jimmy did with his free time made the investigation difficult. No servants. He lived alone. He didn't keep a journal, didn't spend time on Facebook or Twitter or LinkedIn.

"People in the neighborhood knew him," he said, "but he didn't seem to entertain, like having parties or fundraisers at his apartment, even though he gave a lot of money to charities. As far as we know, he didn't have a hangout to sit at the bar, have some drinks, and talk to his friends.

Turns out he went to the opera most Monday nights during the opera season, like Ruth told us, but apparently didn't socialize outside the opera with people he knew there."

"Is it possible to say that in spite of being a good guy, he was kind of a loner?" Ruth mused.

I had to put my two-cents worth in. "Not exactly. He had everyday good friends at Housing Works, and let's not forget he was head over heels about Eddie Hall."

"Did he get along with Eddie's kids?" she asked.

"No idea," Mike said, and made a note. "He was heading for being a step-dad, I guess, so he probably spent time with them."

I said I had met them, seemed like normal kids. My first experience of them was on the radio show. "Alex is a good talker, and he was very friendly with a young friend of his father's who was obviously gay, or at least was playing that part. Matty didn't say a lot, but she was in a good mood."

My phone buzzed. It was Gabriele.

"What's up?"

He said he was at Jimmy's apartment. Bud let him in, because he wanted to look at Jimmy's computer.

"What for?"

"See if anything look like it help."

I asked Gabriele if it was okay if I put him on speaker.

"Si, okay."

I put the phone on speaker and told Gabriele that Mike and Ruth were with me. "Did you find anything interesting?"

"*Forse*," he said. I translated for Mike and Ruth, "Maybe."

He said Jimmy was using Outlook for his emails. Office 3 65. "But computer not new. Not old, *ma* no new, and little bit slow."

I explained to Mike and Ruth that Gabriele was, like a lot of people his age, a computer-savvy kind of guy.

"Is lot of emails," he said. "I not read all, not open. Not need password."

"So no password, not secret?"

"Si."

He had found an email in the Outbox. It had apparently not ever been sent. He forwarded it to me.

Hi E, I didn't want to say anything until I knew it was ready to go, but I just found out everything is working out the way I wanted. We're going to have a bolt-hole kind of condo in Antigua for when we want to escape. Wedding gift. Hope you like it. Love you, J

"So E is probably Eddie and J is probably Jimmy."

It was date-stamped the day Jimmy was shot, at six twenty-one pm. A good four or five hours before he went outside and met whoever it was that killed him.

"So, he would have been in a good mood," Ruth said. "Maybe not looking to be careful wherever he was going. Anything go out after that?"

Gabriele said that the 'sent' mail was dated earlier.

"If he was in a good mood and talking about a wedding present, he couldn't possibly have been expecting to be shot by some hitman," I said.

Nothing from Gabriele.

I asked Mike if it was possible that was the explanation for the sixty thousand dollars. He nodded and shrugged at the same time. I asked what that meant.

"It means it could be, there's no way to tell. All this says is that he got a small condo in Antigua for E for a wedding present."

"If he was notified that the condo deal went through, wouldn't there be an email or a snail-mail someplace that said that?"

"Don't ask me," Mike said. "The CSI's didn't find anything like that."

"Could've been a quick phone call from whatever real estate person was helping Jimmy with this," Ruth said.

"Even so, there would have been a follow-up, right? Something to sign maybe? Any balance owing?"

I asked Mike who had been picking up the mail at Jimmy's apartment. He said he thought it was Bud, but he didn't know.

I asked Gabriele if Bud was still there. "Seems like he would have to lock up after you leave, right?"

A new voice sounded on the cellphone, a little gravelly and for sure older. "Yeah, this is Bud."

"Have you been gathering up any mail that might have been delivered for Jimmy?"

He said he had all the mail that had come, other than catalogs and ads, in a cardboard box in Jimmy's living room.

"Did you notice any postmarks from Antigua?" Mike asked. "Or someplace in the Caribbean? Or Bermuda?"

"Tell you the truth, I don't know," Bud said. "I opened anything that might be a bill, so I could pay it, but I don't remember anything like that. Could be something I just didn't open, I guess, but I don't remember that kind of stamp. I got a stack of death certificates so I could close accounts if there were any that were monthly or whatever."

"Could you go and have a look?" Ruth asked. "Please?"

Gabriele indicated that he was going into the living room with Bud, so we just waited.

"There's not a lot of stuff in this box, because, like I said, I threw out the ads and stuff like that."

Some noises. "Wait, here's something from Luxury Atlantis Realty," Bud said. "Should I open it, or do you want me to get someone to bring it to you?"

Gabriele volunteered to be the delivery boy. "*E sciuscià, Gio?*" He spoke fast, and what he said stumped Mike.

I explained that *Gio* is what kids called Americans in Italy after World War II. "It's pronounced like Joe, not *Gee-oh* like Americans think. It's an Italian nickname for somebody named George, which is *Giorgio* in Italian, but it sounds like GI Joe. And *sciuscià* is more or less what it sounds like, a shoe-shine. Growing up around Naples, Gabriele knew kids offering to shine shoes for 'rich' Americans. Nowadays a shoe-shine boy in Italy is a *lustrascarpe.*"

"Bravo." Gabriele said. I did a formal style bow to Mike and Ruth.

"I'm impressed," Ruth said.

Mike smiled. "Gabriele, can you bring the whole cardboard box of mail up as long as you're coming?"

Mike asked if we'd like some coffee or something while we waited for Gabriele to deliver the mail.

As we walked over to the coffee vending machine, Ruth said to

Mike, "The more we find out, the more it seems like it was a random shooting."

He shook his head. "Nothing random about it. We just don't know what happened, so we're inclined to want to tie the loose ends up by depending on it being a coincidence of some kind. Like Jimmy had been hit by a meteorite. Maybe a bolt of Zeus's lightning on a clear night."

Ruth did not roll her eyes, and I could sense the self-control that took.

We sat quietly in the first interrogation room, and surprisingly quickly Gabriele walked in with a packing box with the top taped shut.

Bud wasn't kidding when he said there was not a lot of mail in the box. The envelope from Luxury Atlantis Realty was right on the top, unopened. Mike put on blue latex gloves, took two pictures of the envelope front and back, and then opened it.

The letterhead featured top center a group of buildings in what was supposed to be classical architecture with a huge tidal wave about to hit it. The word 'Luxury' was to the left of the city, and the word 'Atlantis' was ghosted over the artwork. It proclaimed that Luxury Atlantis was affiliated with a large American real estate company, and that it was a member of the National Association of REALTORS. Mike took pictures of the single sheet of paper, front and back.

It was a confirmation of the down payment of sixty thousand dollars on a house in St Paul Parish, with three bedrooms and two baths, twenty-four hundred square feet, with one hundred and thirteen thousand dollars remaining to be paid before title would transfer. The full purchase price was one hundred and seventy-three thousand dollars. There was a photo of a lemon-yellow squared-off house with a green hillside behind it, red shutters by the windows, and very elementary landscaping, including a flagstone walkway from what appeared to be a crushed rock road to the front door. There was a sizable car-port on the left as you looked at the picture. No interiors.

"Not a palace," Ruth said, looking at the photo with some surprise on her face.

I was busy with my phone, calling up a map of St. Paul Parish. "It's at the other end of the island from the airport."

"I wonder if he ever saw it," Mike said. "but the truth is that a lot of buildings in the Caribbean are made from cinderblocks so that they'll survive hurricanes."

I said we couldn't tell what Jimmy had seen or not seen. "We also don't know that Jimmy's idea of a vacation house was any grander than what we were looking at."

"His email referred to it as a condo," Mike said. "This doesn't look like a condo."

"When I was in Hawaii," I said, "we saw a lot of housing developments that looked like a normal single-family community, but was being sold as condominiums. The idea, I think, was that they could be rented out when the owners were not using them, and the real estate company representing the development was also the property manager. Could be the same, I guess. It's not shabby, but it's also not what I would expect of a vacation home in one of the fanciest islands in the Caribbean."

"I wonder what Bud will do about it," Mike said. "I doubt he's getting a refund on the down payment."

I found myself thinking the whole thing might be a scam. We could call the American 'parent' company and check with them. I started to say something, but Mike cut me off.

"I'll have somebody get in touch with Twenty-first Century Realty and ask them about their Antiguan affiliate," he said. "This is a bit of a wrinkle."

The conversation seemed at an end. "I'm buying," I said, looking from Gabriele to Ruth to Mike. They all stood up and smiled.

We trekked over to Thalia, which had a standing-room crowd inside, so we kept walking another block downtown to Social, that multi-storied bar-bar-bar that got louder and louder as the hours got later and later. Fortunately for us, it was the quietest time for this 'happening' venue. The extremely long bar on the street level was sparsely populated, and we were able to find two seats on either side of a corner, so we could almost sit across from each other.

Ruth ordered a dirty vodka with olives. I made that two. Gabriele made it three. Mike ordered a chardonnay but didn't drink it. He chugged a glass of water though. The bartender put a bowl of pretzels and a bowl of unshelled peanuts in front of us.

"Liberally salted," I said, pointing at the snacks. "Guaranteed to make you want another drink."

"So," Mike said, "I suppose there could be some dissatisfaction with the condo, but we don't know about that. I'm inclined to say this has no connection with Jimmy van Gelsen's death." He stood up and announced he needed to be back in the office then he was gone.

We gave in to the salty snacks and ordered another round.

Chapter Thirty-three

My cellphone buzzed. It was Eddie. I had just put some coffee on and was feeling like I needed some. It was gray outside, but not raining. I had left the bedroom windows open, and it was almost cool. Better than air conditioning.

"That cop friend of yours served me with a subpoena about Jimmy's death. He wants to ask me about my service revolver."

"Service revolver?"

"That Ruger handgun I mentioned to you and told him about."

"I guess that makes sense. He has to tick all the boxes, and since you were fixing to marry Jimmy, that would include you."

"I know that. I'm a lawyer, after all. And a prosecutor."

"And it sounds like you are pretty annoyed about this."

"Well, it means I have to go through all the junk in the storage area of the basement."

"I'm sorry. Do you want me to help? I'd be happy to."

I could hear him breathing. After five or six Mississippis, he said, "Well, I thought about getting Alex to help me, but that might not be a good idea."

"Why?"

"Well, he knows Jimmy was shot, and if I ask him to help me find my revolver to give to the police, he might take it the wrong way. He's just a kid. He may look like he's almost an adult, but he's still a kid."

I told him I'd be happy to help, or just to keep him company while he looked through the basement.

He thanked me, and we agreed I'd get there as soon as I could. I could take the G train all the way to Park Slope from Long Island City, but those trains are all locals and they don't run very often. I gulped down some coffee, took a quick shower and slipped into my normal "uniform," jeans and a black t-shirt, black sneakers, Met Museum baseball cap.

I sent Gabriele a text telling him where I was going, since I had a feeling he might want to talk.

As it turned out, a train pulled up almost as soon as I walked into the 21st Street station, so I walked out of the Park Slope station about thirty minutes later. When I got to Eddie's building, Gabriele was idling on the sidewalk.

"Well," he said, "I just come from Brooklyn Heights. Not take long time."

I put my arm around his neck and walked him down to the corner, where there was a deli. We got some coffee and a bagel with a shmear, sat down in the postage-stamp-sized eating area. "I need to tell Eddie you're gonna be with me. I didn't say anything to him about you. I just sent that text to you because I thought maybe we'd get together later today and I didn't want you to think I disappeared."

"I go home."

"No, it's good that you're here. For some reason I think it would be good if there was a third pair of eyes in Eddie's basement this morning." I texted Eddie: *Gabriele is with me. That okay?*

Cool.

10 minutes.

"Hey, boys," Eddie said when he opened the door. "Thanks for coming over. Coffee?"

"Already had some," I said.

Eddie's apartment took up most of the third floor of the old brownstone, and was a "railroad" layout; one room behind another with a narrow hallway on one side. He gave us a quick tour. Living room. Kitchen. Small bedroom. Master bedroom with bath *en suite*. Second small bedroom. Bath at the end of the hall.

High ceilings, lots of reddish-brown old wood in the front room with crown moldings that had some kind of plant motif, maybe ivy, carved into them, or maybe they were plaster with glossy paint to make them blend with the wood walls. A big bay window with leafy trees partially obstructing the street view, but probably keeping the apartment relatively cool. In the winter it would be sunny with the trees bare of leaves.

Railroad flats have good air circulation as long as all the doors stay open, and the high ceilings are a blessing in hot weather. There were ceiling fans in all the rooms except the living room, but the living room had what appeared to be a real fireplace with a stone mantel and an old-fashioned wind-up clock.

He produced a box of blue latex gloves from under the sink in the kitchen and pulled out two gloves for each of us. "Very dusty down in the basement. We probably ought to wear surgical masks, but I don't have any. Sorry."

We ambled down the stairs to the street level, then took a steeper staircase that began at the back of the building to the basement, which was entirely underground, no ground-level window slits like there are some places. The basement had two washing machines and two dryers, and much of the rest of its floor space was divided into five storage areas that were sectioned off with hurricane fencing with gate like doors fastened with padlocks. The third one back was Eddie's. It was stacked to the ceiling with boxes, and just enough room to step inside.

"Sorry, I told you this was not something I wanted to do," he said.

When he took the padlock off the door, Gabriele pulled the door open and walked in. He stood on his toes and just reached the bottom of one of the boxes on the top row, slid it forward with his latex-gloved hand and as it tumbled down, caught it. He put it on the floor and used a box-cutter to slice the tape holding it closed. Eddie pointed to a tape device hanging on a hook on the fencing. Gabriele nodded. Turned out to be full of file folders.

"No, the box we're looking for will be heavier, and it will have a large metallic box with a combination lock on the top, probably nothing else in the box as I recall, but it's been six years or so."

Eddie re-taped the box and moved it to the narrow hallway outside the enclosure. He reached up and retrieved a second box, opened it. Photographs or small pictures in frames. "From my grandmother's house," he said. "Not what we're looking for." On top of the box in the hallway. Gabriele started to cough. Eddie said he would go back upstairs and find some cloth scarves that we could cover our faces with. He scampered up the stairs and was gone.

He came back with three flowered scarves, all of them looking and feeling like cotton. "My wife's," he said. We tied them on like rustlers with bandanas in an old cowboy movie.

It was slow going, and the hallway started to get close to impassable, so we had to shift some of the opened boxes to the laundry area. None of the machines was in use. The air was full of dust particles that glinted in the light from the naked bulb hanging from the ceiling. I could feel the dust in my chest, and the temperature, in spite of being below ground level, was high because of the heat we were generating. Sweat dripped down my arms. We found boxes of old clothes, some of them women's clothes, most of them children's. There were boxes of toys, two boxes of old vinyl records. *"I gotta get rid of some of this crap,"* he said. Lots of smaller boxes packed with books.

As we worked our way to the back of the storage unit, the number of boxes dropped and dropped. There was some old furniture; a highboy dresser, a couple of end tables stacked up. Some boxes marked "Fragile" that had glassware and some ornate serving dishes *"Grandmother,"* he *said.* Two bicycles appeared in the back, and what appeared to be a six- or eight-man toboggan *"I should take that upstairs and give it to the kids for winter,"* he said, *"they'd have fun with it. When I was a kid, we tied it to the roof of the car and drove upstate to Westchester County to find some good hills."*

I gave up and said I needed some air and a big glass of water. Eddie took me up to the apartment and I coughed up some grayish mucous. "I don't know how much more of this I can do," I told him.

We took a couple of Poland Spring bottles downstairs with us. Gabrielle looked like a troll, his bountiful hair looking like he was escaping from a mining disaster. He made the water disappear, hardly pausing between the two bottles.

We could see the wall in the back of the storage unit. Very few boxes left, and as it turned out, none of them was what we were looking for.

"Son of a bitch!" Eddie said, not very loudly.

We started putting the boxes back into the storage unit, stacking them back in what we remembered was the order we took them out. The way we did it, there was a lot less room when we got all the boxes back into the enclosure, even with the big toboggan in the hallway.

"Go figure," I said, gesturing as I put the last box back on top of the front row. "Now what?"

"I'm pretty sure it's not in the apartment, but I'll have a look. Otherwise, maybe it's still at Aurora's place. I was sure I took everything though."

He wiped his face with a latexed hand and it streaked, making him look like he'd been filling a coal shuttle in a rainstorm.

We went back upstairs, Eddie dragging the toboggan, but carrying it like a long, long briefcase under his arm as he went up the flights of stairs. We all had to pee and wash. I looked in the mirror and decided I was hopeless.

"The least I can do," Eddie said, handing us each a clean, folded black t-shirt. He said to use the towels in the two bathrooms. "They're clean. My housekeeper was here yesterday."

Gabriele and I drifted down the hall to the back bathroom. There was a tub and a shower stall. I stripped and turned the water on in the shower. Water never felt so good. The stall door opened and disclosed Gabriele holding a washcloth over his crotch. He stepped in. It was crowded and we each endeavored not to touch the other, but the water felt so good, and the soap smelled so good, I'm not sure we were successful. I sidled to the door and grabbed a towel. Gabriele was still showering.

Eddie's t-shirt was a size too small for me, so it fit tightly and barely extended over my belt when I got the jeans back on.

"You getting belly," Gabriele said with a grin, looking at the t-shirt stretched over my torso. "Nice belly."

"Thanks," I said, "but that's not something you should say. No man wants to have a belly."

"I like you belly," he said. "Is okay for me to say. You know how I feel for you."

We wandered back down the hall to the master bedroom, where Eddie was standing, naked, toweling his hair.

"Eddie no belly," he whispered to me with a shit-eating grin. "Maybe when he grow up he have belly."

"When is Mike expecting you to show up with the gun?" I asked.

"Today," he said, "but obviously he's going to be disappointed. I'm letting him know," he said, as he tapped at his smartphone.

"Can we help you look through the closets here?"

We started at the front of the apartment which, like a lot of old residences, did not have many closets. We looked in cabinets, under furniture, even up inside the chimney "It's not real," he said. "Can't have a fire in it."

Nothing. Nothing in the pantry or under the beds or in the wide drawers at the bottoms of the two armoires in the small bedrooms.

"Must be at Aurora's," he said.

"Is there an attic in the building?" I asked.

"Not that I know of. Upstairs from here is another apartment, and one on the fifth floor too. I think the basement is it for storage."

"Trunk of your car?"

"My car was wrecked when I drove off the road. I haven't bought a new one yet, but even if it had been in the trunk, which it wasn't, the car was in impound upstate when Jimmy died."

"I wasn't thinking the gun was involved, just thinking about getting the gun to Mike."

"Can you look through your wife's apartment today?"

"I don't know, probably could, but I can't because I have a gig later. I'm talking to a group of progressives for drinks and buffet in Brooklyn Heights, maybe raise some money for the campaign. Can't really change that."

Gabriele looked at me meaningfully.

I asked him if he was going by cocking my head to the side. No words.

He nodded.

I rubbed my fingers together to indicate money, with another slight head movement.

Again, a nod.

"You do have a green card, right? Because if you don't, I think it's illegal for a candidate to accept a donation from you."

A third nod.

"Is Ruth working on your campaign?" I asked Eddie.

No.

I was too pooped to pop after sweating in Eddie's basement, and breathing in ten pounds of dust. I was like a phlegm factory and alternated between throat-clearing and coughing all the way back to the 21st Street station at Hunter's Point. From there I walked home, and since it was flat, I didn't have a coughing fit. When I got home, I took another shower, and changed my clothes starting with underwear and socks. Then I fell backwards onto my bed and closed my eyes. No idea what time it was.

I woke up to my phone buzzing. It was Gabriele, but by the time I tried to answer it, the buzzing stopped. I figured he would call back, but he texted me instead.

TV now

Chapter Thirty-four

I turned on the living room television, which was set on Channel 7. There was a 'Breaking News' story being covered from Brooklyn Heights. I switched to Channel 10, then all the other channels up to 12. Basically, the same view from the same place on the same subject.

There was a good deal of noise in the background, like people yelling, and there seemed to be something going on over the reporter's right shoulder. I could see Gabriele next to the reporter when the camera moved back. I could also see a bunch of black-shirted men with black pilots' caps, holding tiki torches. It looked dark. I looked out the living room window. There was a red sky, so it was between eight and eight-thirty, I calculated. If I looked out the balcony window, which faced north, the sky was dark— not the inky dark of night-time, but dark.

There were also a disorganized bunch of younger people, probably college-age, some with placards and some with rainbow flags.

"You can hear them chanting," the reporter said.

I could hear a noise but couldn't distinguish what they were saying.

"Black fags go home," the reporter said, knowing she probably shouldn't be saying it word-for-word. "They're demonstrating because former Brooklyn Assistant District Attorney Eddie Hall is meeting with Democratic donors in one of the houses over there." The screen split and showed a photo of Eddie looking like he was yelling or singing, mouth open anyway, white teeth flashing against his dark skin color. "Mr. Hall was engaged to marry his rich boyfriend, but that guy was shot and killed on the sidewalk a few weeks back in Greenwich Village."

C'mon. While Eddie was in a hospital upstate after a car accident. Say it.

The camera panned around the scene. There were certainly hundreds of people crowded onto the Brooklyn Heights Promenade, with the Brooklyn Bridge as a backdrop.

I bet my two thugs are there. I was straining to see any faces, but the camera was panning to the student protesters, who had placards that said things like 'Orlando, Never Again' and 'Nazis Back to Idaho'.

The reporter said they were starting to throw bottles and maybe rocks, and turned the story back to the main studio in Manhattan. I put it on mute and flipped through the television stations up to 12 and then to CNN. Same, same, same. A couple had cameras trained on what looked like it could be a melee if there weren't enough cops there to handle it. There was a line of cops with see-through riot shields and helmets, but no guns were drawn.

I rang Gabriele. He answered. There was too much noise in the background to hear what he was saying then the call cut off. I decided to take the G train back to Brooklyn and see if I could find him.

My phone buzzed. Gabriele had moved to someplace where it was a bit less noisy, and he was talking as loudly as he could. "Eddie stuck in house with rich people. *Grazie Dio forse* now rich people want to give more money for elect Eddie." Then he cut off.

I hope he finds that gun, and please God it's not the one that killed Jimmy. I hadn't had that thought before, but all of a sudden it was running through my head like the news tickers around Times Square. *Pore Jud is daid. Pore Jud Fry is daid. Rod Steiger. Could be about Jimmy, or could be about Eddie's political career.*

The phone buzzed again. It was Mike.

"What the fuck?"

"No idea, man. I'm at home. Gabriele is there in that melee. He lives there, y'know. He just called, and I saw him on camera. He said Eddie Hall is in a house there with a bunch of rich people. A fund-raiser for his campaign." I told him that Gabriele and I had helped Eddie sort through the stuff in his basement this afternoon, and Eddie had mentioned he was going to a fund-raiser in Brooklyn Heights. "That's all I know."

"Did you find the gun?"

"He says it's probably at his ex-wife's in the attic or something."

"So, the answer is no."

"Yes. The answer is no. We took every scrap of everything out of that storage unit. Nothing like a gun. Not even a kitchen knife."

The phone buzzed. It was Gabriele. I told him I was talking to Mike.

"Gabriele sounds like he's all right. No word on Eddie."

"I'm trying to get through to Eddie on his cell," Mike said.

"Maybe I'll take the G train down there and see if I can find out anything."

"Not a good idea, Hugo. Stay where you are. Try to get through to Eddie and get him to call me."

Click.

I called Gabriele and asked him if he had spoken to Eddie. He hadn't.

I texted Eddie. *WTF???? Riot in Bklyn Hgts?*

He texted back almost immediately. *Silver lining*

Money?

Campaign

How did Thugs Inc know you'd be there

??

Leak?

Newspapers and TV

??

Progressives for Peace and Justice

Very 60's

You trapped there?

Cellphones can make donations from anywhere, even here

Mike wants to talk to you

I know, he's been pinging me

He wants to know about the gun

I'm trying to find it. Going over to Aurora's when I leave here

Phone buzzed again. Ruth. *Hold on sweetie, talking to EH.* Then I realized Eddie was gone, line dead.

Ruth said she'd been watching Twitter, and the tweets were going by so fast she couldn't read them. "If I stop to read one, then there are one hundred and seventy-five new tweets in the meantime."

I asked if she had looked at Facebook.

Not yet.

I grabbed a jug of vodka out of the freezer and poured an inch or so into a martini glass, added some olive juice and a couple of big green manzanillo olives from Spain. Nectar of the Gods. Chugged it, then put the sound back on the TV and started flipping around.

Gabriele was on two stations at once. *I wonder where all the news satellite trucks are parked that are transmitting this.*

Channel 5 said all the streets in Brooklyn Heights were barricaded off. Residents only allowed in and out.

Channel 7 said estimates ranged from two thousand to five thousand people demonstrating on the Promenade. Hard to believe that many people could squeeze in that space. I was just thinking about pouring another vodka when the concierge downstairs called to say that Gabriele was on his way up.

I opened the door and threw the deadbolt so it wouldn't fully close, then went back to the living room to stare at the television. He let himself in and found me in the living room with a martini glass in my hand, heading to the kitchen. I motioned toward the martini glass and he nodded. I got down a second martini glass from the cupboard and poured about three fingers into each glass. I added about a teaspoon of olive juice from the olive jar and dropped two big manzanillo olives in. We clinked and sipped.

"You know, you and I aren't so different from Eddie and Jimmy," I said bluntly. "Just that we're not looking to get married, but we own part of each other, I think."

For once, Gabriele had no come-back. I was almost proud of that moment, but then he said, "No, we not like Eddie and Jimmy. We already married, and we happy with it. If you think I want sex, you not paying attention." He threw back the rest of his vodka and held the glass out to me. I refilled it, halfway up the glass.

He told me about going to the Progressives for Peace and Justice cocktail party, which was in the home of a wealthy gold dealer right on the Promenade. It was a normal day and he walked over from his apartment, which was only about two blocks away. Although all the guests were undoubtedly wealthy, they were dressed in everyday clothing: jeans, sherbet-colored chinos. untucked wrinkled-linen shirts, sneakers, sandals, wheat-colored sport jackets, simple cotton shifts.

When he got there, there was no sign of a demonstration, just another summer evening on the Promenade, with that magical Wall Street vista stretched from the right to the Statue of Liberty straight ahead. But a few minutes after the bar opened at the party, there was a sudden uproar. He had gone to the window, and there was a double line of men in black carrying torches, and a crowd of protesters streaming onto the Promenade from the side streets.

Like they planned it that way, he told me.

"Did you give money?"

Nod.

"I probably will too, if he stays in the race. No way he would be on my ballot though, in Queens."

He shrugged. "Not make difference if he in Washington. He vote for Black, immigrant like me, gay, old people, women. He vote for schools, good hospital, what we need."

"So, what finally happened? How did you get here through all those people I saw on TV?"

He said the noise died down and he looked out the window again, and saw a line of cops pushing the demonstrators south down the Promenade from Montague Street toward Remsen Street. "I go north, t hen south to Hoyt Schemerhorn subway and take G train here. Easy."

"No sign of trouble where you were walking?"

"Many television trucks, maybe mean trouble. No black t-shirt, no torch, no big noise. Many posters on ground." He pulled out his phone and showed me some pictures of placards from both sides, obviously flat on the sidewalk.

"Strange how much protesters know about how to work the media these days, and how they beat it when the media start to lose interest."

"Like in park when we go there and it rain."

Yes, like that. How do they know when to show up? How do they have printed cardboard posters on sticks? Both sides?

"It's got to the place where you get elected on how smart you are with publicity."

Gabriele looked puzzled, but he smiled at me. "I come here to tell you we better than Eddie and Jimmy. We both happy. Jimmy maybe not so happy."

"You're happy?" I asked.

He hugged me, patted me on the back the way I pat him when we hug. He was smiling. "More drink, little." I took the glass and he disappeared into my bedroom. As I was pouring the drinks, I heard a flush.

"I had to pee."

"Something we have in common, a need to pee."

He allowed it was something we had in common with every other human, not just with each other.

"I was just thinking we talk about our differences, not the things we have that are the same."

What I said seemed to puzzle him, and I wondered if it was a linguistic issue, so I started to rephrase. "What I meant was ..."

"*Lo so*," he said. "I understand." He cocked his head like a puppy. "We have us. Always us."

"Like Eddie and Jimmy?"

He waved his index finger back and forth in a negative. "Not like Eddie and Jimmy. We not need more, is okay. *Te amo, Ugo. Sono felice.*" He said he loved me and that makes him happy. I blew him an air kiss with a smile and a tear oozing from my eye.

I handed him the 'little' vodka he asked for and brandished mine for a clink.

Chapter Thirty-five

We went up the street for a quick dinner at the French restaurant on Vernon Boulevard. I had a salmon paté and then *moules frites*, which is not fried mussels, but mussels with fries. He had roast chicken with green beans. We had a bottle of reasonably priced Vacqueyras. We watched a couple of innings of a Yankee game two time zones west when we got back to the apartment, and he fell asleep leaning into the corner of the big sofa. I draped an old quilt over him, one that my great-grandmother had made about a hundred years ago, and put a pillow by his head, which he grabbed like a teddy bear without waking up.

I have always been an early riser; that morning was no different from other mornings. I tip-toed into the kitchen and turned on the coffee maker. I looked around the corner at him on the couch. No movement, but as I went back into the kitchen, I saw him wander by, dragging the quilt and carrying the pillow, headed for my bed.

Good, I thought. *I can have my coffee and watch the morning news*, but it didn't turn out that way. Mike popped up with a text on my cellphone promptly at seven o'clock.

Any word from Eddie?

I almost didn't answer, figuring I could claim to have been asleep.

No

I need to know about the gun

You do remember he was in a hospital upstate when Jimmy was shot, right?

I don't consider him a suspect, if that's what you're thinking

Why then?

I need a ballistic test on the gun

Why?

Because I think it's missing if he doesn't know where it is

You think it might be the gun that shot Jimmy?
No
And?
I need to prove it's not that gun
Call Eddie then
Click.

A regiment of thoughts tramped through my head. Who could have the gun if it doesn't show up? Somebody stole it from the storage unit in Prospect Park? Too far-fetched, and the boxes were in perfect order when we opened the unit. Nothing disturbed. He said it was probably at Aurora's in the attic. The weather report on the morning news said we might have a thunderstorm in the afternoon. Par for the course late summer in New York.

I heard the shower turn on, and checked the coffee maker to see if there was enough coffee left for Gabriele. Yup. I got a mug down and put it on the counter.

Mike again, but this time a voice call.

"I want you to talk to Eddie and explain to him that it's important we get that gun and test it. If I call him and tell him that, it'll go in the folder. No need for it to be in the folder. Call him."

Click.

I looked at the clock. Nearly eight thirty. *Is Eddie a late sleeper? Probably not, he was a prosecutor.*

I touched my contacts, touched H for Hall, and then touched Eddie Hall. Dial.

"Hugo, what's up?"

"The sky, Eddie."

"V.F."

I explained that I had talked to Mike, and he wants to put the gun through a ballistic test.

"He thinks it's the murder weapon? That's crazy."

"He wants to prove it's not the murder weapon, so he can get on with the rest of the investigation."

"Well it's got to be at Aurora's."

"I thought you were going to look for it last night after the Progressives for Peace and Justice."

"Last night got late faster than I thought it would. I was basically stuck at that house on the Promenade for a while, couple of cops came and wanted statements from most everybody there."

"So, you never made it to her place?"

"I just talked to her and told her I need to look through her attic because I think I might have left a few things there. And I'm trying to put together a financial statement that everybody is going to want me to file when I'm officially a candidate."

"Aha." Pause. "Can I help you?"

"Ummm. I need to let Aurora know."

"Okay. Tell her Hugo and Gabriele will both be coming over. The more sets of eyes we have, the better."

"Gabriele spent the night at your place?"

"As though that was any of your concern."

"Hey, I've been there."

"At my place?"

"No, in your shoes."

"Just tell your wife that a couple of friends will be coming over to help you look for whatever the fuck you're looking for."

"Okay."

"Meet you somewhere near her place, then we can go over together."

"Mexican take-out place on 3rd Avenue right near 61st Street."

We agreed to meet at ten o'clock. Gabriele and I could take the 7-train, transfer to the 6 at Grand Central, and be there pretty fast.

'The Mexican take-out place' turned out to be a national chain that specialized in healthy fast food. I was glad to see that, because I was hungry. Only had coffee for breakfast, and a stale biscuit from the day before. Good thing I like stale biscuits, buttered and toasted in the oven.

Gabriele wasn't surprised and was up for whatever. I explained to him what I had talked to Mike about, and told him not to say anything to Eddie, even if Eddie asked him a direct question. "We're working with Mike on this."

I had some black beans and rice in a corn tortilla wrap with some butter. Gabriele shrugged and took the same thing. "What this is?" he asked.

I told him and he said he wanted *peperoncino,* the Italian word for what we call 'pizza pepper'. I explained that we would get *salsa picante,* which would make it hot and spicy.

That was okay. Eddie had a chicken wrap of some kind with avocado, maybe some bacon.

We sat at a semi-clean table outside and washed down our food with bottled water. It was tasty and filling, just what I needed. Gabriele gave it a thumbs-up. We each paid for our own at the register before we sat down, so we were free to go as soon as we bussed our trays.

Aurora's home was a nineteenth-century town-home with a surprisingly large back yard featuring several trees that reached up to cover the windows on the third floor with a leafy sun-strainer. The original woodwork had been preserved, maybe restored, but the furnishings were sleek and modern, most of the tables glass-topped, including a Noguchi coffee table in front of one of the couches.

We didn't dawdle, walked up several flights of stairs and into an attic that was almost the same size as the floors below it, but with a set-back in the front so that it was not visible from the street. It was very different from the storage area at Eddie's apartment, clean-looking and clean-smelling, with the wooden floor apparently sealed with polyurethane like a parquet floor in a fancy modern condo.

Aurora was apparently not at home. We were shown up to the attic by a woman named Peggy in a long-sleeved, over-the-knee gray uniform with a small white apron. Alex met us on the third floor, which was apparently where his room was. Eddie introduced us, but Alex said he remembered me from after the library radio show.

"Mom told me to help," he said to his father.

He had a key to the attic on a big metal ring, opened the door and held it open while we went in. There were not only adequate lights, but they were in fixtures, not naked bulbs like many attics in more plebeian places. "What are we looking for?"

"My service revolver," Eddie said. "It's in a gun safe, so it's fairly heavy."

Alex said he knew where it was and pointed to a far corner of the attic where there was a towering but neat stack of boxes several wide.

"Where over there?" Eddie asked.

"I don't remember, but I'm fairly sure it's over there."

Gabriele walked over and started moving boxes.

I was breathing easier. Eddie wasn't surprised.

"I really thought it was at my place, but when we didn't find it, there was only one other place it could be. Here."

Gabriele was opening boxes. Some with books, some with file folders, a couple with old clothes.

"Wow, look at all the ties," Eddie said. "I remember that one," he said, grabbing a yellow tie with honeybees on it. "I'm gonna take that one with me."

In spite of the fact that the attic was clean and fairly well organized, it took us a while to work through the stacks of boxes, which were deeper than it appeared. Alex and Gabriele did most of the lifting. Alex recognized Gabriele, after Gabriele said something.

"Ora di Pranzo, right?"

Gabriele gave him a big smile and nodded.

"This is a real honor," Alex said, although you could tell he was nonplussed.

Odd how someone accustomed to meeting famous people could still be intimidated by someone as friendly and quiet-spoken as Gabriele.

"You have kids?" he asked me.

I nodded and said, "They live in California."

"Cool," he said. "You know any movie stars?"

A kid, like most kids.

The black SentrySafe gun safe was about the size of an attaché case that an auditor might carry to a job. It was in a cardboard box all the way at the back of the stack. Gabriele dragged it out and opened the cardboard box.

"*Ecco la!*" he said. I felt a wave of relief when I saw that it was there, and it was heavy, like Eddie said. It had a digital combination lock, and a keyhole.

I asked if it needed a key and a combination. Eddie said no, the keyhole was an override, but the key had been lost years before, when he was still at the District Attorney's office. He asked us all to turn around so we couldn't see him put in the combination. The gun was where it was supposed to be inside. Eddie closed it back up and spun the lock, tried to open it and showed us the lock was fully engaged.

"How did you know it was back here?" Eddie asked Alex.

"The things that belong to you are all over there," he said. "Mom wanted to be sure you could find anything you needed. I think there are some law books, couple of boxes of them." Eddie hugged the boy and thanked him for his help.

"There were three boxes with books," Gabriele said.

"So, we're off," Eddie said. "I'm gonna call Uber so we can be sure we have a ride without standing in the street and waving our arms around."

I texted Mike that we were on our way with the gun in a gun safe. Gabriele headed for the subway and said he was going home. Mike was waiting for us by the elevator, which was next to the staircase. We walked up the staircase and came up behind him. Eddie had put the safe back in the cardboard box it had been stored in. He offered it to Mike.

"Let's go into my office and I'll get you a receipt," he said.

Everything was clearly being done by the book. Mike asked Eddie to open the gun safe, put on a pair of blue latex gloves and picked up the gun, held it on flat hands and put it carefully back into the safe. He engaged the lock, then asked Eddie to open it again, which he did. He also wrote down the combination on Mike's spiral pad. There was an evidence clerk there who made out a receipt and stamped it with something that looked like a notary's seal. It was itemized.

"Is there an override key?" Mike asked.

"That disappeared years ago, no idea where it went, but it was when I was still working in the DA's office. I probably could have gotten a replacement, but I never did because I had no use for the gun anyway. The only times I ever fired it was at the firing range. Target practice. I actually intended to take it to a police station to turn it in, then I couldn't remember exactly where it was."

"Any ammunition?"

"Maybe not. I didn't see any. If there is some, it must be in another box."

Mike told Eddie they would run the ballistics test on it then would offer to give it back to him. "Then if you want to turn it in, you can just do that here, and you're home free."

Chapter Thirty-six

It wasn't to be. The ballistics test was inconclusive, but indicated that the gun might be compatible with the bullet that killed Jimmy van Gelsen. It might be the murder weapon. It had apparently been fired recently and not cleaned after it was fired. The actual ballistics comparison made it look possible for the gun to be the murder weapon, but not to prove that it was.

Eddie Hall was a not a person of interest. He was clearly hospitalized in the Hudson River Valley when van Gelsen was killed. The gun was clearly not in his apartment in Brooklyn, and he clearly didn't know where it was.

If Eddie's gun was indeed the murder weapon, somebody had to find it on the fifth floor of Mrs. Hall's townhome, remove the gun safe, open the gun safe with a combination that was not written down anywhere, use it to kill Jimmy van Gelsen, then replace it in the same attic in the gun safe, in the cardboard box it had been stored in behind a stack of boxes in a corner. The complexity of all that militated against Eddie's gun being the murder weapon.

According to Mike, however, that meant that the fickle finger of fate was pointing at Aurora Hall, a paragon of social proprietary and supporter of countless charities, who had nursed Eddie when he was released from the hospital. We were at his office. I was drinking coffee. Eddie was just staring at his cup like was hoping it would warm his hands.

"She's never fired a gun in her life," he said.

"How do you know that?" Mike asked without looking up.

"She told me a hundred times. She is a total anti-gun person, although I think her dad used to go deer hunting when she was a kid. She was angry even to be in the same house with a pistol."

"But your son knew exactly where the gun was, so your wife

probably did too."

"No sane prosecutor would take that case," Eddie said with certainty. "It's a hundred-percent loser, and there's no indication of any kind of motive."

"Jealousy."

"You don't know her. First of all, she left me and took the kids with her, but her door was always open to me. I had dinner with them as often as not, and we shared custody always."

"A woman scorned."

"Not for nearly two years after we split up. She never once mentioned getting back together, and she knew that Jimmy and I didn't have a physical relationship. She didn't want to be a politician's wife. Ask her. You'll see."

Mike didn't want to question Mrs. Hall, at least not at present, but he brought up the non-traditional nature of the Jimmy-Eddie partnership.

"A married couple that doesn't have sex?"

"We didn't have a chance to get married, you know."

Mike looked frustrated. "Why would you want to get married anyway if you weren't in love?"

"We wouldn't have been the only couple that didn't have sex, you know. Even lots of traditional marriages are sexless. You just can't tell looking at them from the outside, and who says I wasn't in love with him? I just wasn't into the sex part, that's all."

"Most couples get married because they're in love physically. Lots of couples stop having sex at some point, but not usually at the giddy-up."

"Maybe not usually, but it happens. You don't have to consummate a marriage to make it legal. Not like it was a few hundred years ago."

"Okay, whatever." A shift in the way he was standing indicated he didn't want to talk about that any more.

"Did you ever take your son to the shooting range?"

"Of course not."

"What does that mean?"

"He was a kid when I was going to the shooting range. A little kid. I'm gonna take him to the shooting range? Give me a break."

"Did he have any interest in firearms?"

"No. Not that I ever heard anything about. He's his mother's son. Anti-NRA. Anti-gun."

"How about your daughter?"

"What about her?"

"Is she interested in guns?"

"Why are you asking me that? Of course not!"

"Calm down, Eddie. You were a prosecutor, you know the routine. I have to ask you all the questions that are relevant. All of them. I'm taping all of this, and I don't want anybody to think I took shortcuts just because you have a law enforcement background."

I could tell Mike was not expecting to get any helpful answers, but he was painstakingly going through all the questions an interrogator might think up. I stood up and excused myself, stepped outside and called Ruth. I summarized for her what had happened looking for the gun and gun safe at Eddie's place in Park Slope then at Aurora's home in Manhattan.

"Sounds like a dead end," she said.

"Seems that way to me too," I told her, "but the ballistics test apparently didn't rule out that the gun could have been the murder weapon."

"How could that be?"

"Well, as I understand it, the test didn't say it was the murder weapon, just that it could have been. Don't ask me; I don't know what the test is meant to measure."

"But if it was buried in a pile of boxes in the attic, it seems like it almost couldn't have been, right?"

"I don't know. Mike understands all this sort of thing a lot better than I ever will. I know Eddie is having a hard time with this stuff. Not that you'd expect anything different. He seems to be cooperating the best he can."

She suggested maybe she'd come over and we could grab some lunch after. I thought that was a good idea. I went back to Mike's office.

"Sorry," I said. "Had to return a call to Ruth. I think she may be coming over here."

There was a soft chiming sound and Eddie pulled out his smartphone to read a text. He stood up, looked around and said he had to leave. Mike asked if everything was okay.

"I don't know. Aurora says she can't find Alex, and he apparently left his cellphone at home when he went out, so she can't call him."

"Has he disappeared before?" I asked.

"He didn't disappear, just went someplace and forgot his cellphone, so Aurora's panicked."

"Moms worry about their kids," Mike said.

"Dads worry too," he said, side-swiping me with a hostile look, "but Alex is over twenty-one. He can take care of himself, even if he still acts like a dingbat sometimes. Aurora thinks he's a child, but he's not."

"When I was that age, I was equal parts kid and grown-up," I said. "Can I come with you, in case you need any help?"

He shook his head. "I just need to calm Aurora down."

He left just as Ruth arrived. Mike said he didn't have time to talk more right then, so Ruth and I went to an Afghan restaurant on 9th Avenue for a bite. They make a very tasty chicken and rice dish that is a favorite of mine, and, unlike what might be expected from a Muslim country, they have some nice red wines. Ruth ordered lamb and we shared a split of wine.

I tried to bring Ruth up to date on the situation, but I found myself wondering about Alex, who had seemed so self-possessed on the radio show.

"What are you thinking about?" Ruth reached across the table and put her hand on my arm. "You haven't heard a word I've been saying."

I realized I had been off in the wild blue yonder. "I was thinking about Alex Hall, Eddie's son. I don't know him well, but he seems so grown-up to me, even though I know he's only early twenties. He knew exactly where the gun was that we were looking for, and Eddie said his ex-wife doesn't know where Alex is."

"I thought you told me Eddie wasn't worried."

"That's what he said."

"But you think he was worried?"

"I don't know."

"You have kids. Would you be worried?"

"I don't know. I never had to worry about where my kids were. I'm sure Alice did her share of worrying, but they never ran off or disappeared."

I thought for a minute. "And there were never any murders to worry about either."

She said she thought Eddie was a well-balanced guy, not someone who would ignore danger or pretend things were okay when they weren't.

"I'm not worried about where Alex is, or whether his parents can find him. I'm just wondering if Alex knows something about the gun or what happened to Jimmy van Gelsen. It never occurred to me, but I was amazed when he knew exactly where the gun was."

"Exactly?"

"Well, he didn't say it was in the back of that heap of Eddie's stuff, but he for sure told us in general where it was. He said that was because everything that was Eddie's was in that part of the attic."

"That sounds reasonable."

"Yeah, it is reasonable, but it doesn't stop me from wondering if he knew more than he was letting on."

"Are you saying he might have shot Jimmy?"

"No, that's not what I meant, but I guess he could have. Anybody could have. We don't really have any clues about that. Except we think whoever shot him was somebody he knew."

"I thought you said there was no proof Eddie's gun was the murder weapon."

"No proof either way. No thumbs up, no thumbs down."

"So, you just have a hunch?"

I didn't know how to answer her, so I just made a noncommittal I-don't-know face.

"This wine is tasty," she said. "Chewy; perfect for the lamb."

"I couldn't stand lamb even when I was still eating beef and bacon burgers. It has a smell to it that makes me want to run the other way, but the wine is a nice dark red with what I think of as the smell of dirt or peat moss. That's a good thing. I think that has to do with the tannins, because they change as the wine ages."

"The bottle says this is three years old."

"Whatever. Grapes from places like Afghanistan are probably old ones, old vines, old types of grapes. I like it. I like this place." We were sitting at a table that was up against the front window of the little restaurant on the west side of 9th Avenue.

"Nice day out."

I called for the check, paid it, and suggested we go for a stroll over to the park, to walk off the meal.

We walked the few blocks up to Columbus Circle and crossed into the park there. It was a slightly muggy afternoon with some clouds that could mean thunder and lightning, which happens almost daily in the late summer.

My phone buzzed. It was Mike texting me. *Guess they found the boy ok*

Did they say where he was

Didn't ask

I told Ruth as we were walking past Sheep's Meadow, which was covered with sunbathers on towels.

"See?" she said. "It's okay."

"I wasn't worried about them finding him, just if he knew something about the gun or about Jimmy that he wasn't telling anybody."

"Forget about it. Mike knows what he's doing."

We walked up to the Boathouse and got in line for a rowboat. The wait wasn't long, and before long we were facing each other in a rowboat, and I had the oars. No sooner had I got us out to the middle of the pond we were in, when my phone buzzed. It was in my rear pants pocket, so I had to stop rowing to get it out.

It was Eddie, texting.

Alex okay

Good. Mike told us. Happy 4 you

We need to talk

I told him I would meet him whenever he wanted, told him Ruth and I were in the park in a boat, so it would take a while for us to get back to the dock and walk out of the park. He said no problem, and said he would meet us at the restaurant part of the boathouse. Ruth rolled her eyes and said something to the effect that we'd have to stand in line for an hour to get in.

We already ate

Then we drink, he texted back.

I showed the texts to Ruth, forwarded the string to Mike, and we headed back to the dock. "Shortest boat ride of the year," she said.

We turned the boat and the two life jackets back in, and walked over to the restaurant that is virtually next door to the dock. As usual there was a line out the door and onto the sidewalk. We got in line, and within about ten minutes, Eddie was striding up to us.

"You must have been close when you said to meet you here," I said.

"Aurora's place."

"Alex is back home?"

He nodded, but didn't look happy. He excused himself, saying he'd be right back, and walked up the line to the door. A couple of minutes later, he stepped back out the door and waved us to the door. Being a politician has its perks. The maître d' showed us to a table that had obviously been squeezed in between two others. VIP treatment. It's notoriously impossible to get a table there.

We ordered drinks. The waiter brought us some tortilla chips and salsa.

"I'm worried about Alex," he said bluntly.

"Why?" Ruth was doing her mother-hen thing.

"Where was he?"

"Oh, he was wandering up Madison Avenue, going into shops, drinking some coffee. He was okay."

"But you're worried about him," Ruth said.

"He's obviously afraid of something."

"Like what?"

He shook his head and shrugged.

"How can you tell he's afraid of something?"

"First of all, because I'm his dad and I know him. I can tell when there's something wrong but mostly because he has a scared look in his eyes."

Chapter Thirty-seven

Eddie explained that Alex had been a real trooper after the car accident, when he was staying with Aurora and the kids for those few days after he got out of the hospital. He had kept his chin up when Jimmy was killed, but something had got to him, and Eddie could tell that his sense of being secure at home was gone.

"Do you suppose it was because of us going there to find the gun?" I asked.

"Not just that, no, but that must have been part of it, because that was when he seemed to crack."

"Maybe he's just worried about you. Kids believe everything bad that happens is their fault," Ruth said.

"You don't have kids, do you?"

She shook her head. "But I come from a big family and spent a lot of my life around kids, kids, and more kids."

She looked into a remembered past as the water on the lake glinted and sparkled, making her squint. "Several divorces. The kids always thought the divorces were their fault, even when the parents had been arguing and yelling for years. Like if they washed the dishes without being asked it would have been different."

Eddie nodded. "When Aurora took the kids and moved back to her place, I could tell Alex and Matty were trying to put it all back together. So maybe they thought they had something to do with the breakup. But truthfully it was a grown-up problem. She hates politics and didn't want to be my wife if I was going to pursue that."

Ruth explained that there might still be a loss of security when you have to find a gun and take it to the police to be tested. "I bet he's worried that something is going to happen to you. That would be enough to scare any kid. Dad's a hero, he's Superman. If it turns out he has feet of clay, that's scary."

Eddie looked distracted, like he was having a hard time concentrating.

"Are you worried that Alex might know something about who killed Jimmy?" I asked slowly.

He looked at me and nodded while he said, "Not exactly, no, but I realize now that he has a different point of view on everything. He has always been a clinger. Even when he was little he would hold onto my leg and refuse to let go. He's okay with his mom and me living in different places. Maybe not so okay with me marrying Jimmy, or with his mom someday being with another guy."

"So, you're worried about yourself, like you might lose him," Ruth said.

He touched his finger to his nose then pointed it at her, like a game of Charades.

"And," he added portentously, "I worry that he's afraid he is losing his dad in some way."

"Have you told him that you and Jimmy were basically just very good friends?"

He just stared at me, then said, "What does that mean, when you say we were just very good friends?"

"Well, you told us there was no physical side to the relationship."

"Is that what it's all about?"

I didn't respond. Neither did Ruth.

"Jimmy was compromising by accepting me because he had given his whole heart to Raul. It didn't work for them. I gave my love to Aurora, and she broke it off over something that came flying in from the wings. I just wasn't expecting that kind of blind hit. Jimmy and I were marrying because we were both making the best out of being second-best for each other. Like they say, making chicken salad out of chicken shit. But we loved each other in a very special way. Maybe even more important, we trusted each other implicitly and explicitly. It wasn't impossible, I guess, that someday the sex part would have happened. It just wasn't what we were thinking about when we were getting ready to say our vows."

Ruth put her hands up and covered her mouth, as though she might have said something, but didn't want to.

"What?" Eddie asked her. "What?"

She took her hands away from her face and looked at Eddie. "I just never looked at it that way, that's all." She paused, then took a breath that I could hear have heard down a hallway, maybe with a strangled tear in it. "Of course, I wouldn't have. I didn't know what you just told us."

He looked at his hands.

"Is it possible that Alex doesn't know that either?"

He looked wounded as he nodded. "Maybe," he whispered.

"I got something to say," I volunteered. "You may not know it, but Gabriele and I are like you and Jimmy. Not because our hearts have been broken by someone else, but because we had both given up hope that we might ever find someone to be with. We're both afraid we might never stop being alone. That can be a very bleak thing to wake up to or to fall asleep with at night, and you're right, we love each other. I can't imagine what the pain would be like if he wasn't there. I can't see us getting married or wanting to have a sexual relationship, but after what you said, it makes more sense now than it did a few minutes ago."

He stood up, reached over and hugged me. "My heart is broken and I feel the pain again every day. I may miss Jimmy more than I ever missed Aurora, because he was my last port in a storm. Sometimes I feel like I might as well move into a cave, dress in animal pelts, and start memorizing the Bible."

"Okay," Ruth said, with actual tears running down her cheeks. "I am goddamn ordering another round, and we'll all drink to Murray this time because as it turns out we have all found ourselves alone and hopeless in one way or another. So, we're not as alone as we thought, and you, Mr. Hall, are too young to sound so defeated."

She looked at me and pointed. "And you," she said, "you, I'm gonna dance at your wedding."

"What is this? A Kleenex commercial?" It was Mike, smiling sympathetically.

"How did you know where we were?" I wiped my brow and eyes with my napkin. "Hot in here."

"You're getting old, Hugo. You sent me a text."

I pulled a vacant chair up to the table and Mike sat down. The waiter came over and asked Mike if he wanted a drink. He ordered ginger ale.

"We're drinking real drinks, Mike," I said.

"You're not on duty," he said.

"But you are?"

"I am," he said. "I wanted to bring you up to date on some things we've found out."

"All ears," Eddie said.

Mike explained that the forensic tests had been repeated, and this time it came back very unlikely that Eddie's gun fired the bullet that killed Jimmy van Gelsen. "Not a final negative result, but enough for us."

Eddie smiled and pulled out his phone, started typing with his thumbs. "Sending a text to Alex," he said,

"Like. I. Told. You," he said to nobody in particular as he typed.

"So that means we're back to square one?" Ruth screwed up her face in distaste.

"Not exactly, no," Mike said. "We've eliminated a lot of what seemed like possibilities."

"And we all know what Sherlock Holmes said about that," I pronounced pontifically.

"Once you eliminate the impossible, whatever remains, however improbable, must be the truth," Mike said. "Problem is we still have not narrowed the possibilities down to one, so we have more work to do."

"What have you eliminated?" Eddie sounded like he was questioning a witness.

Mike enumerated that we know Jimmy didn't kill himself, that he didn't hire a hitman, that Eddie didn't shoot anyone from his hospital bed, and that Eddie's gun, which was at Aurora's place, was most likely not the murder weapon. "We also eliminated robbery and random shooting by a stranger."

"How about a stray bullet?" Ruth put the knuckles of her right hand under her chin with her elbow on the bar.

"Probably also eliminated because of the precision of the shot. A stray bullet or a ricochet would most likely have come from an angle."

"And why have you not been able to totally determine whether my gun was or was not used?"

"Good question. It was clearly fired from a Ruger Security-Six or Speed-Six, and that's what your gun was. It was a thirty-eight slug, which was what you used in your gun. The markings were indicative of the type of gun, but didn't match the slug that killed Mr. van Gelsen to a large enough degree."

"So, whoever shot him was using a gun like Eddie's gun, but most likely a different gun," Ruth said. "Right?"

Mike nodded. "That weapon was marketed almost exclusively to law enforcement, but it was available for self-defense and was relatively easy to conceal."

"Could you buy one at a gun fair these days?" Eddie asked.

"Possibly, but gun fairs have different vendors with different weapons for sale, so you might not be able to find one at just any gun fair, and it would not be feasible to try to find out which gun fairs had Ruger Special-Six guns for sale. Even if it was possible, it would be like looking for a needle in a haystack."

"O O O O that Shakespeherian rag, it's so elegant, so intelligent," Ruth said, as though it made sense.

"What?"

"It's a poem," she said. "I just like it, has to do with things like needles in haystacks."

Eddie clinked his glass with a spoon. "So, if I can try to extract some sense from what we've been talking about, the parts of the world that we have not eliminated starts with Jimmy's neighbors, his family, anybody who owed him money, or anybody that hated fags."

Mike nodded slightly. "And it may be worth remembering that the attack on Jimmy happened within twenty-four hours of your car accident upstate."

"You mean somebody might have been trying to kill both of us?"

"Not meaning anything in particular, just that you frequently can't trust coincidences. It could have just happened that way, like the principles of the *I Ching*. There is a number combination that would combine the two things, just the same as there would be a number combination that would combine the shooting with a comet passing overhead."

"And you thought I was being abstruse when I quoted T.S. Eliot," she said.

"Forget it," Mike said. "*I Ching* is an ancient Chinese divination text, seems completely at random, but tries to help make sense out of unconnected things. All I meant was that when two incidents happen so close to each other, you don't want to dismiss that out of hand. That's all."

Eddie was shaking his head like he had water in his ear.

"I hadn't thought of it being somebody that wanted to kill a fag," I said. "Seems like something that wouldn't happen in Greenwich Village." I was casting around in my mind for other possibilities. "And how about my two thugs, or people like them from political protests who would have resented Eddie for his politics?"

"Are you trying to connect the two events?" Mike asked. "Because if you are, it may be more likely to happen in Greenwich Village than in other places."

"Why?"

"Lots of reasons, but keep in mind that whoever pulled the trigger may not have been from Greenwich Village."

"You mean if you want to hunt fags, you go someplace where fags live?"

Mike exhaled heavily. "Not to put too fine a point on it."

"And my thugs? Or other thugs with a grudge?"

He shrugged. *How should I know?* Clearly being tolerant and exercising patience.

Chapter Thirty-eight

On a hunch, I went on a real estate website to see what places were for sale in the West Village area where Jimmy had lived. I thought maybe I would see something that Jimmy might have been looking at. We knew he was looking at a new place to live in with Eddie, and we also knew he had been on the verge of making an offer on it at one point. I also was curious to know the value of Jimmy's place, to see what Eddie had given back to the family, apparently without even thinking about it. Jimmy's will had left virtually everything to Eddie in anticipation of their wedding. Odd that they both had full-floor apartments in townhouses—Jimmy in the West Village and Eddie in Park Slope.

I hadn't ever been in Jimmy's apartment, but I had found a video tour of it online from a charity event that took place a few years back. I looked it up online when Mike first asked Ruth and me to have a look at the murder. It was a ground-floor and garden apartment that also included a semi-basement that was probably originally used for a live-in servant. I was impressed by the art, which included two **suggestive but sketchy and abstract mostly** red-colored Susan Rothenberg paintings and otherwise was very contemporary, and the structure itself, which had oak-planked flooring clearly dating from the 1800's. It had sleek modern furnishings, a dream kitchen and a general feeling of openness in a relatively old building. Beautiful manicured garden with two mature trees.

There were lots of places. I recalled that Bud or Eddie told me the place Jimmy was looking at was much larger than the place where he was living. I couldn't recall what the online video tour said about how big Jimmy's place was, but I had the general feeling that there was a master bedroom on the ground floor, and probably one or two bedrooms in the below-stairs part of the apartment. So, I decided to look for places in the West Village or SoHo that were two thousand square feet and up, guessing

Jimmy's place was around fifteen hundred square feet. No way to be more precise, especially since I didn't know exactly what I was after.

There were a lot of places to read about, most of them in new high rises. I excluded the steel-and-glass places, thinking that from what I knew of Jimmy van Gelsen, he would want character instead of glitz. That tended to push me inland from the Hudson River, not far, obviously, because Manhattan is a narrow island but to areas with tree-lined streets in the Village or cast-iron facades in SoHo. In general the West Village homes are primarily late eighteenth to early nineteenth centuries, and SoHo is from about 1850 to World War I. Easy to see when you walk the streets of both areas that the Industrial Revolution happened after the elegant Federal-period Village, and before SoHo was built out using the cast-iron that fell out of vogue after the Eiffel Tower was built in Paris using wrought iron, which is stronger. Then wrought iron gave way to steel.

So, when I eliminated the new buildings, or any building with more than five stories, the selection dropped by at least half, but the prices were surprisingly the same. I thought I remembered that Bud said Jimmy was looking at a place in SoHo, so I ditched the Village places. I could always go back if I wanted to.

Several of the places I looked at online seemed to me to fit the little I knew about Jimmy's taste. From looking at his art and the general style of his apartment, it seemed to me that he would have liked the high-ceilinged open spaces of SoHo buildings, which in the places I looked at had surprisingly few architectural obstructions like columns even in factory-sized spaces and the huge expanses of windows—no plate glass but hundreds of panes set in metal latticework that would flood a home with sunlight in a city that lived largely without it, due to the sun-blocking height of buildings. Many Manhattan streets are in shadow at street level except at mid-day.

Basically, Jimmy could buy shell space in a SoHo building built one hundred and twenty-five years earlier, the size of a bowling alley or a couple of indoor basketball courts then partition it off, or not, however he wanted. That meant he could have big open rooms. He could also have no walls inside at all if that's what he thought would set off his art best. As I looked at some of them, I envisioned very tall bookcases creating rooms, but I also saw photos of apartments with views from one end to the other without much in between other than furniture groupings. Seemed to me like privacy would be impossible if you did that.

It was the prices that were the biggest surprise. The places in the West Village that seemed to be similar to what I had seen online of Jimmy's apartment were in the range of four million dollars to six million dollars. Places with comparable square footage in old SoHo buildings ranged up to fifteen million dollars. That meant if Jimmy was serious about buying a place in SoHo, he would be taking a huge step up in cost, and if he was looking at places that were appreciably bigger, the delta could be even greater. I had no idea at all what Jimmy's net worth was, but even a wealthy guy might have to think twice about that.

I saved the searches I had been doing, and called Mike to give him a briefing on what I found out.

"Why do you think the cost of a new apartment would help us figure out what happened?" he asked me.

"I don't know, but it could tell us why, for instance, he bought an almost-shabby vacation house in the Caribbean."

"Okay?"

"And if he was over-extended, he might have had some dealings we haven't yet found out about."

"Well, I don't know what Mr. van Gelsen's resources were, but I know that most purchases of that size aren't done with a mortgage," he said. "Most of them are cash purchases."

I asked if his forensic accounting people would have an idea of Jimmy's net worth. He said they might, or probably might. They had kept copies of all the documents they used in determining what kinds of transactions Jimmy had engaged in.

"If he was on shaky ground financially, that might mean somebody in his family might be upset, or even might be exposed to problems themselves. I think there were a lot of shared properties between the van Gelsen family and don't I recall that Jimmy had inherited more than some of the others?"

Mike said his tendency was to want to investigate Jimmy's brothers and Eddie's ex-wife, Aurora Carter Hall.

"I thought women classically use different weapons to kill people, not guns."

He said there was a time when you assumed that if the killer was a woman, the murder would be a knifing or **poisoning**. "But there are so many handguns now that anything can happen."

"And motive?"

"For Mrs. Hall? Jealousy? Embarrassment? Just plain pissed off? Hard to tell why a spouse kills a spouse. Like it's hard to tell why they got married in the first place when they're in divorce court."

I told Mike that if he wanted to know the inside scoop on the van Gelsen family, I thought he should talk to Christopher. He had seemed to me to be the closest to Jimmy, and maybe also the most well-off, due to his being an investment banker.

"I thought you told me Bud was probably the wealthiest brother."

"If I did, that was probably before I met Kip. You know there's a sister too, right? **But she's** developmentally disabled in some way and lives in a nursing home upstate someplace. I wonder if she inherited money too."

Mike made a noncommittal noise that indicated he heard me but had nothing to say.

"If you talk to him, say hi for Ruth and me," I said. "Oh, and his nickname is Kip."

"Do you think Kip might have a grudge against Jimmy?"

I didn't have that impression. "**But** he lives in San Francisco, so if he was there when Jimmy was shot, he would have had to fly in, stay in a hotel, and fly home, so that might be easy to check."

After Mike signed off, I texted Gabriele, who popped back at me quickly.

Where are you
Brooklyn
Busy?
I come you appartamento
CU

I'm addicted to peanut butter. I found a box of water crackers with rosemary and took out five of them, put a smear of fake butter on each one, and then a dab of peanut butter. I grew up mixing butter and peanut butter, which made the peanut butter smoother and, I suppose, a little oilier. I poured a glass of wine and turned on the television to CNN.

There was a commercial with a man-on-the-street format. Attractive young and middle-aged people saying things like "He cares about my friends and neighbors" and "It's time for a change." Turned out to be a campaign spot for Eddie Hall.

I switched to one of the other networks and found a local news program. A fire in the Bronx. A car that ran up on a sidewalk in Crown Heights. A child missing on the Lower East Side. I ate my crackers and peanut butter and sipped on the wine, which was a bottle of *aglianico del vulture* that I had opened and re-corked a couple of nights before. Chewy and comforting.

I got a notification on my cellphone that someone was on his way up from the lobby. *Gabriele.*

He was looking as perfect as perfect can be in a pink polo shirt with a Brooks Brothers Golden Fleece insignia on the pocket, a pair of 501's and black Nikes. I looked at his small waist and thought about the larger belt size I was wearing. I pushed aside the remaining two peanut butter crackers.

I told him about the conversation at the Boathouse, the real estate cyber-tours I had of the West Village and SoHo, and my talk with Mike.

I offered him a drink. He looked at the wine bottle on the pass-through and said yes, so I poured him a glass. I don't use stemware for red wine, just low-ball glasses, or sometimes one of the old crystal juice glasses that had been in my grandmother's house in Westchester. I handed him a low-ball glass and the bottle of *aglianico*.

I wanted his thoughts on where the case stood, and whether Mike was right about the van Gelsen family and Aurora Hall being suspects.

"I no meet Signora Hall," he said, but he added that if Eddie's gun was not the murder weapon, it would be possible to check to see if she had bought a gun herself. "Jimmy brothers I only see at lunch, and one in Ora di Pranzo."

"What do you think about the brothers you met?"

"Not help find who kill Jimmy."

I said I thought they were anxious to help, and didn't seem to be concealing anything.

"Lawyer brother that come to Ora di Pranzo, maybe not tell what he know."

"Bud?"

"Si, Bud."

"Well, he was taking care of Jimmy's finances, so he knew a lot about what Jimmy was spending money on, but he didn't tell us much about that. We didn't really ask him much about that."

"But police take records, no?"

"Some records, yes. The records of Jimmy's credit card and bank statements, so they could analyze what Jimmy had been spending his money on."

He shrugged, as though he didn't understand what I was saying.

"They only took some records. They didn't take his brokerage records or his tax returns, for instance."

"And not take Bud records?"

"Bud's own records? His personal records? No, not as far as I know."

"Bud know all what Jimmy is doing."

I nodded. "His brother, and Bud is a lawyer. He was helping Jimmy keep track of his credit cards and banking."

"And know how much money Jimmy have?"

"Maybe, I don't know. I don't know who did Jimmy's taxes."

"I think money good reason to kill, *anche gelosia* is good reason to kill."

Money and also jealousy. I picked up the wine to pour some more. He covered his glass with his hand. I poured some more in my glass and drank it in a couple of swallows. I stared at Gabriele, and for once I didn't see a handsome man. I saw a very smart man who was waiting for me to figure out what he was telling me.

He stood up and walked over to my CD shelves, picked one out, and slipped it into the Bose stereo on an old glass-topped side table that was in a corner of the room. It was a tenor singing '*Cielo e mar*', from *La Gioconda*, an opera about jealousy and potentially suicide that is seldom done because it has a reputation for ruining the voices of everyone in the cast. This tenor was Luciano Pavarotti, and he sounded glorious, but strained. Gabriele opened the sliding door to the balcony and stepped outside with his back to me.

The long, high aria built and built. *Vieni, o donna, vieni al bacio. Della vita e dell'amor...Ah! vien!* The full-throated last note was a B flat, but it sounded stratospheric. Music like that helps me relax, oddly enough. It's like going to church for Midnight Mass on Christmas Eve—completely transporting.

He turned around and looked at me then walked back into the apartment, picked up his glass and poured two fingers of wine into it. He retrieved the CD and put it back in its sleeve. He walked over to me with his glass held out to clink mine. I picked mine up and stood up. He lightly touched my glass with his and they made a very brief, silvery sound. He drank his wine in a single gulp and put the glass back on the pass-through next to the wine bottle. Then he sat down on the couch and picked up the remote control, turning the television to CNN.

A story on Washington DC concentrating on members of the President's cabinet charging first-class airplane tickets to the government.

"See? Is money make everybody *arrabiato.*"

Angry, money makes everybody angry, like red sauce with lots of red pepper flakes in it makes your mouth sting.

I called Mike on the speaker phone. He answered.

"Mike, I'm on the speaker here, and Gabriele is with me, but nobody else. I wanted him to be able to join the conversation."

"Okay."

"I think you're right. You should be looking at Mrs. Hall and Bud van Gelsen." I looked at Gabriele, who smiled a bit but said nothing, and he shook his head. He didn't want to say anything.

"*Ciao,* Gabriele," Mike said.

"*Ciao, Michele, come va?*"

"*Va bene, grazie. E lei?*"

Gabriele grinned because Mike was using a very formal phrase that didn't fit the situation. In formal Italian, if you address somebody, you use the third person. Mike had said "*e lei?*" instead of "*e tu?*" If you translate that directly, he was asking "and him?" instead of "and you?"

"*Molto bene, grazie.*"

"So why Bud instead of the other brothers?" Mike sounded puzzled. "He helped us before, you know."

"Bud had full access to Jimmy's records, so if there was something going on, he would know, and I think all he did was to box up the records you asked for."

"What would be going on?"

"The only way to know that is to go through Jimmy's records completely, instead of just looking at a bank statement and some credit-card bills. First of all, maybe he had more than one bank account or other credit cards. I told you the difference in valuations of apartments in the West Village and in SoHo. It would be even more expensive in TriBeCa. He could have been setting himself up for a fall. Look at his taxes, look at his brokerage statements, check his safe deposit box for bearer bonds. See if he had any gold coins. I don't know. Everything. See if he was spending himself into the poor house."

"And the search warrant? What would we tell the judge?"

"Tell the judge the truth. You think Jimmy may have been in financial trouble and you want to find out the extent of it."

"And that would lead where?"

"Maybe it wouldn't lead anywhere if it turns out that Jimmy was in good shape financially. But if he was setting himself up to be on the edge of disaster, it could have had an effect on the other people in the family, and Bud was probably aware of everything that was going on. I bet Bud also handles the estate of the sister in a nursing home upstate."

"And why did you come to this conclusion?"

"Gabriele said something to me that made me look at things a different way. He said money is a reason to kill and jealousy is a reason to kill. I had been going off in different directions, but of course what he said is right. They're not the only reasons to kill, but they're common reasons to kill, and I had been ignoring that."

"Sherlock Holmes you're not, in other words."

"Very funny."

"Truth is, I was up against a brick wall myself. I had my nose up against the bricks and I couldn't see anything else."

My God, he's telling me my idea is a good one.

"Like I said, Mike, it was something Gabriele said, not something I thought of by myself."

"*Gabriele, ci sei?*" He was asking if Gabriele was there on the phone.

"Si, Signor Mike."

"*Sono in debito con te. Mille grazie.*" ("I owe you")

"No, Signor Mike. *Non in debito con me.* Is right thing for me. I want be real American. And you my friend, Signor Mike. You come to Ora di Pranzo and I cook for you. I go in kitchen and cook for you."

"I want to see that," I said, but not loud enough for Mike to hear me.

Gabriele gave me a thumbs up, then flexed his biceps like Jack LaLanne, and flashed me a silly grin.

What's not to love?

Chapter Thirty-nine

Mike was already ahead of us. He was checking everyone in both families for gun licenses. Nothing for Aurora Hall or Aurora Carter or Aurora Carter Hall. He couldn't check Kip, who lived in California, but there was nothing for John or Gus. There was a concealed-carry permit for Ragnar, as well as a New York State Pistol Permit and a registration for a Special-Six handgun from Ruger. Bingo.

The NYPD raided Bud's office and home with a search warrant issued by a midtown judge, and hauled away boxes of documents, several computers and two cellphones. They also searched Jimmy's apartment on the same search warrant to take any tax records or other financial records. The Manhattan DA's office obtained a court order that authorized the police to confiscate Bud's passport and that forbade Bud to leave New York City without permission. Things moved fast. The media got wind of the search warrant and had footage of cops walking out of the apartment with boxes, the evening news broke the story the same day, and it was covered in the newspapers the next morning.

Two days later, Gabriele, Ruth and I were at Mike's office for a briefing. Mike brought us up to date. They had the gun. The ballistics test said it could be the murder weapon, and the slug matched test bullets fired into water canisters at the forensic lab. There was also text message evidence that Bud had been a go-between for the supposed alt-right demonstrators in Prospect Park and later downtown during the Million Woman March. The Boston fiasco was still up in the air, but there was some indication that the marchers were basically actors, not political demonstrators.

There was no evidence that tied Bud to the stolen Bentley that had been the cause of Eddie's nearly disastrous car accident on the New York State Thruway.

Bud had hidden or at least withheld several bank accounts when the NYPD wanted to investigate the financial status of Jimmy van Gelsen's estate and had apparently gutted the estate of his sister, Alana, at the nursing home upstate. The other three brothers then chipped in to cover her needs, and to assure that she could stay at the place she had been most of her life, and that she considered home.

"Do you remember how Bud chased those two goons away when we met him, Gus and John at Joe Allen on 46th Street for lunch?" I asked rhetorically. "He didn't even say anything to them, just waved them away. They knew him. He told them where we were having lunch. Then he told them to scram. He was helping pay for everything they were doing. I guess he was even in on that night they grabbed me at Dominie's Hoek in Long Island City and dragged me down the street before Mike sent a car to save me. Very elaborate hoax. He might have been a lot better off if he just shut up, but he wanted to get Eddie. Maybe he also wanted to get me, but I doubt it. He just wanted to invent an opposition to keep Eddie from being elected."

The DA secured an indictment from the Grand Jury for aggravated assault with a deadly weapon, and Bud was arrested, over the objections of bigwigs at his law firm protesting that it was all a mistake. Bud was then charged with several counts of financial malfeasance as well as assault, with the likelihood of a murder indictment coming down the pike. He made bail easily, but was ordered to wear an electronic bracelet to track his comings and goings.

"If we're right, it's very clear why Jimmy was not afraid of his assailant," Mike said. "As far as we can tell, he had no idea that Bud was stealing money from him, so he died without ever finding out. He may not even have realized that the gun Bud was holding was real. So, his end may have come very fast. There's no evidence that he ducked or even put his hand up. He probably went from living to dead in the space of a second."

I was surprised when Kip van Gelsen called me from San Francisco to thank me for my part in finding out what happened. He said he was flying into New York and would like to see me, along with his brothers, Johnny and Gus. "And then there were three," he said sadly.

He didn't mention Bud's name then or ever in my hearing, but it was clear that he was twice heart-broken. We agreed to meet at the Oyster Bar at Grand Central to lift a glass to Jimmy. I asked if it was okay for Eddie to join us. Yes, that would be ideal. I told them I wanted to bring Ruth and Gabriele along too, since they were part of what we did throughout this puzzling case. Of course, that would be okay.

"We are devastated at what happened to Jimmy, and the three surviving brothers want to do everything we can do to help Jimmy's friends and loved ones."

He said they were putting together a one hundred and fifty thousand dollar donation to Housing Works, which Jimmy always talked about and considered a 'second home'- to him. They had decided to turn down Eddie's offer to give Jimmy's estate back to the family. "In spite of the fact that Jimmy owned the family home on the North Fork, we want it to go to Eddie as it would have if Jimmy had lived."

I knew Eddie would put the quietus on the idea of taking anything from Jimmy's estate, but I didn't say anything.

We met the next afternoon at two o'clock as we had agreed, at the old Oyster Bar in the lower level of Grand Central. Gus arrived with two jereboams (the equivalent of nine liters total) of a fifteen-year-old Chateau Latour, and had arranged with the restaurant to have a small section of the dining room roped off. The Oyster Bar is such a popular and well-trod place that the checkered tablecloths and banquet-style wood and vinyl chairs didn't even look out of place with the breathtakingly expensive gigantic bottles of wine. I stared at them and wondered how they could possibly be uncorked.

As it happened, Gus pulled out an Ah-So from a paper bag. It's a tool that has two thin metal prongs extending out from it. One prong is inserted between the cork and the bottle, and then the other is inserted diametrically opposite the first one, also between the cork and the bottle. The waiter who did it gently rocked the tool back and forth and twisted it slightly and *voila,* the cork slid up and out of the huge bottle in one piece— no broken pieces, no dried-cork problems. We all clapped and cheered, and the waiter took a theatrical bow before pouring the wine into five service decanters that he set around the big round table where we would be sitting.

Kip bowed his head and prayed for God to bless the wine and the food that we would share, and to accept the soul of his brother Jimmy into eternal life. "We know he's already up there in heaven," he said, "but we miss him so horribly and we want him to be happy. He was an innocent soul, never wanted anything but the best for everyone he knew."

"Even Raul," Johnny said.

"Especially Raul," Gus said.

"No, especially Eddie," Kip said.

Everyone nodded.

"Good bye, brother of mine. We hardly knew ya, you were with us such a short time. We thought we would grow old together."

There wasn't a dry eye anywhere. Eddie was jerking with silent sobs. He had brought Alex, who was staring wide-eyed at the whole scene, tearing up, wiping his nose with his hand. Eddie put his arm around Alex's shoulder and squeezed him gently.

Gabriele walked around the table pulling chairs out, and pushed Ruth's chair in as she sat down. We all sat down. *How smooth he is, how kind and good.* Eddie managed a weak smile as he looked at Gabriele being a mother hen to everyone at the table.

Then a huge tower of raw seafood arrived. There must have been fifteen different types: oysters, cherrystone and little-neck clams, and little cockles. There were also some boiled or steamed shrimp. We helped ourselves. I grabbed some fresh horseradish. Gabriele watched me do it, and then did the same. He was sitting to my left, and leaned in to me slightly with a puppy dog look in his eyes.

"You're a fine young man," Kip said, smiling at Gabriele. "I'm happy that you're one of us, that we're all in the same family."

Eddie stood up and clinked a knife against his wine glass.

"Hear, hear," the table said and echoed.

Mike di Saronno walked in. "Sorry to miss the benediction," he said. "I never had the pleasure of meeting your brother, Jimmy. I think I'm the only one here who didn't meet him." I raised my hand and shook my head that I had never met him either. "Oh," he said, "and Hugo Miller, my strong right hand in figuring out what happened, and I see Gabriele Cortese, a fine gentleman who runs the best Italian restaurant in the whole damn city." He walked around the table to Ruth. "And Ruth Jensen, without whom we might have given up halfway." She beamed at him through some tears.

Mike found an empty wine glass and poured a couple of fingers into it. "Here's to healing," he said, lifting the glass high and then sipped it. "May all of us remember how to smile when we think of Jimmy. I didn't know him, but from what people tell me, the very last thing he would want is for you to sit here with long faces and cry. He died young, but he made a lot of people happy, I believe. I give you Jimmy van Gelsen, everyone."

We all drained our glasses. Mike did not sit down. He excused himself and left.

It was Eddie's turn.

He stood up again and looked up at the tiled ceiling. "Hey, Jimmy," he said with a slight wave like you would wave at an airplane that was flying over. Alex started to stand up, and Eddie gently pushed him back into his chair.

"I'm a politician," he said. "I'm supposed to be able to make a speech at the drop of a hat." He crossed his arms over his chest like he was having an argument with someone. "Here's what I'm afraid of. I'm afraid that without Jimmy I will be alone for the rest of my life." He looked down at the table, made a feint toward the wine glass, then decided against it.

"No, that's not what I meant. I didn't look to Jimmy to keep me from being alone." He looked around the largely empty restaurant and then scanned the faces at the table with a faraway gaze. "Something we have in common, most of us. I loved Jimmy. I know you did too," he said, looking from Kip to John to Gus. "You probably miss him more than you think I do," he said, looking at the brothers, "since you knew him all of your life or all of his life. I only knew him for a few years."

He kept glancing up at the ceiling. "Isn't it strange than when somebody dies, we think of them as up in the sky? Jimmy's not up in the sky, and I don't think I will be up in the sky when I die. When I was a kid, I thought heaven was in the heavens, but frankly with NASA and all, we know too much about the sky for that to make sense." He shook his head like his hair was wet.

"I'm the Johnny-come-lately where Jimmy is concerned." He uncrossed his arms and stuck his hands in his pants pockets, which pushed his shoulders up a little, like he was hunching over. "But here's the thing. Jimmy and I shared something that only the two of us shared, that you never shared with him." He looked around and smiled. "No, not that. In fact, we never shared that, and probably never would have."

He gestured upward. "We shared a broken heart. Jimmy had been in love with Raul, and he told me he felt like his heart was dead. We spoke the same language where that was concerned, because I have had a broken heart since Aurora left." He reached to his son and ran his hand through Alex's hair. Alex began to cry.

"We decided to get married, Jimmy and I, because what we shared was so intimate that no one else could ever understand it, and we fell in love with each other either before or after. Not the normal kind of married love, but a kind of love that is based on accepting each other with all our warts.

"I was older than Jimmy. We talked about how he would probably have to nurse me when I got old and sick, and we laughed about that. Strange, I guess. Now there's nobody left for me to live with and love. So maybe Jimmy was the lucky one, you know? Only God knows how long I will live, but as long as that is, I will never again meet anyone like Jimmy, just like there will never be anyone like Aurora.

"There was an Elizabethan poet named Chidiock Tichborne. Well, he was going to have his head cut off for some reason and he was in prison waiting. I memorized the poem that he wrote the night before he died. Part of it went like this:

My tale was heard, and yet it was not told,
My fruit is fallen, and yet my leaves are green,
My youth is spent, and yet I am not old,
I saw the world, and yet I was not seen:
My thread is cut, and yet it is not spun,
And now I live, and now my life is done.

"There was more, but along the same lines. That's Jimmy, you know; I live and now my life is done.

"Alex, I'm sorry to put you through this. You know I love you and Matty and your mom, but I'm afraid that what you will never know is how much I loved Jimmy and how much I needed him just to keep going."

He took his hands out of his pockets and straightened up.

"So, here's what I have to say. My name is Eddie Hall and I'm running for congress. I promise that if I am elected, I will try to be as fine a person as Jimmy van Gelsen."

There were audible sobs around the table.

"I'm gonna push for all the things that Jimmy and I talked about. The rights of the downtrodden, a good life for my children, your children, the waiter's children, and the kids who drop out of school. The kids who don't speak English. The kids who take drugs and the ones who get scholarships to Harvard. All of them. All of them. All I have to do is think of Jimmy and I will know what to do next.

"I love Aurora with all my heart, but oh, I am so bereft without Jimmy. He and I would have been the best married couple who ever lived, if he had lived."

He cleared his throat and looked around like he was thinking of running out of the restaurant. Then he looked at each person one at a time, and said, "Vote for me and I make that promise to you, and I thank you with all my heart for being here with me today." He sat down to silence around the table.

The waiter brought in a cart with two big platters of fried fish and a huge basket of french fries. He served plates one by one and put them in front of each person at the table. "Bon appetite," he said, "and I was eavesdropping a little, I'm sorry. But I'm gonna vote for you, Mr. Hall. I was going to before today, but for sure now."

We started to eat in silence then Johnny said, "I'm with you, brother."

There was a chorus of "Me too." Smiles on faces.

"Since you're gonna support me, I'll tell you what my tag line is. All my posters are going to say 'A More Perfect Union.' I've been thinking about that for a long time. It's a phrase from the Preamble to the Constitution, of course. I had to memorize it in grammar school. You probably did too.

We the People of the United States, in Order to form a more perfect Union, establish Justice, insure domestic Tranquility, provide for the common defence, promote the general Welfare, and secure the Blessings of

Liberty to ourselves and our Posterity, do ordain and establish this Constitution for the United States of America.

"It's also what Jimmy and I wanted to build for each other, and with each other. It's a goal to aspire to as we climb up to the city on the hill." He pointed up at the ceiling.

Silence.

"That's it," Ruth said loudly. "I'm gonna register to vote in Brooklyn. I own my parents' apartment not far from Park Slope and I'm gonna re-register there and vote for Eddie Hall for congress.

"I'm a member of your club, too, Eddie. My heart is broken. I'm a widow, and Hugo and I have been hauling my husband's ashes around for quite a while because I know where I want to scatter him up in Woodstock. We were on our way there when you had an accident on the Thruway and we saw it happen and stopped to help. I asked Murray if he minded waiting and he didn't say no, so I took him home with me and he's sitting on the mantel. Hugo and I will be taking Murray up to the Catskills one of these days. Like Jimmy is at the right hand of God, so is Murray. Only for right now he's spending a lot of time with Janis and Bobby McGee."

Epilogue

A few days after the lunch at the Oyster Bar, Ruth and I headed north on the Thruway again. A little way north of New Paltz, we took an exit from the Thruway and got on the old Kings Highway. We took a left on the Glasco Turnpike and drove to Woodstock.

I was feeling good because Mike had persuaded the NYPD to appoint me a Civilian Criminalist. Normally that's a real job with a desk and hours, but in my case, it gives me a badge and lets me work with Mike officially. It seems like a real accomplishment for someone who's been at sixes and sevens for the last several years, and I've been thinking about how important Gabriele is to me. I guess Eddie said it all and I don't need to go over it again.

There was a beautiful high-steepled church in Woodstock, but it had a cross on top, so probably not the right place for Murray. We kept going and finally ended up on the north end of the Ashokan Reservoir, which is one of the principal sources of drinking water for New York City.

Ruth flung the ashes into the water's edge.

"I'll race you home, Murray then I'm going to have a drink. Love ya, man, always will."

About the Author

Born in Houston, I spent most of my life in southern California, grew up in Palos Verdes and went to UCLA, studied Latin, Greek and literature. I wrote several nonfiction books when I was young, and gave it up when my children were born and I couldn't support them as a writer. The last of those was *SANDCASTLES: The Uses of Enchantment*, which was a Doubleday Dolphin book in 1981. Married for forty-five years, two grown children, two granddaughters. I started a small investor relations company in 1981 and ran it for thirty-six years. I did a reverse migration in 1998 and moved from California to New York.

I like writing. I write short stories but seldom send them to anyone, the same way I do pushups, to keep in shape. Like my characters, I love to cook. I love theater and classical music. My mind is like the bottom of a birdcage, where everything falls in no particular order.

I don't eat red meat and am a bit of a gym rat. I'm afraid of black ice on roads and sometimes I have a hard time looking down from heights. I like flying and I like going to new places. I 'collect' cathedrals, and have been to more than two-thirds of the cathedrals in England. Of course, you can't count the cathedrals in France or Italy, but I've been to a lot there too. Something about them soars. Christmas carols make me cry; not sad, but tears nonetheless.

I like paintings and family heirlooms. Also, vodka and aggressive red wine.

Also by the Author
at
Rogue Phoenix Press

The Hanging Man

When wealthy investment banker Luigi's body is found hanging from the crossbars of the George Washington Bridge, it is immediately thought to be a Mafia hit. Is it? Not according to a Catholic bishop with a diplomatic errand from the Vatican and an out-of-control Twitter account. As the truth unfolds, the reader meets a mad dwarf who eats insects and small rodents, a long-dead candidate for canonization, a deceased gangster who owned The Cotton Club in Harlem, and a tribe of mis-shapen males whose lives have been spent in tunnels under Hell's Kitchen.

Explosions, whispers coming from walls, mysterious billionaires from Grand Cayman, Luigi's terrified young wife with a suckling baby at her breast, treasure-hunters looking for buried gold in the basement provide a frightening backdrop to a mystery that literally goes deeper and deeper into Manhattan as the story develops.

Hugo Miller, Ruth the Sleuth, handsome Gabriele Cortese and stalwart NYPD detective Mike di Saronno pool their considerable resources to solve a series of crimes that may hark back as far as seventy-five or one hundred years.

Chapter One

Nobody wanted to go for a bike ride.

Too hot, too much traffic, what if you got a flat tire? I explained to each one I called that there is a bike path that goes all the way up the west side of Manhattan between the West Side Highway and the Hudson River.

There are no places where you have to cross a street once you get on the path. It's paved and there are lots of people skating, running and biking on it all day every day, even when you'd assume most people would be at work. It's that kind of city. You don't have to worry about being by yourself and running into thugs.

Still, nobody would go with me. I really had my mind set on exploring that afternoon with a buddy. My trusty roommate, Carl, was, not unusually, out of town, up in Montreal. Finally, I tried Gabriele Cortese, whom I had met as part of a murder investigation that I was partly involved in solving with my friend Mike di Saronno, a detective in the Midtown West Police Precinct. Gabriele was originally a suspect, but he had nothing to do with the crime. He was totally innocent.

Gabriele lives all the way in Brooklyn Heights, and I had no real hope he would be willing to schlep into town and then ride all the way up to Fort Washington Park, which was what I wanted to do. I had never seen the little red lighthouse that sits under the George Washington Bridge. Very few people have seen it, comparatively speaking, because you have to wander out under the bridge to see it. There are no vantage points in Manhattan where it is visible. One of those hidden treasures of New York—and there are a lot of those.

"*Ciao, Ugo,*" he said when he picked the phone up, clearly with a caller ID.

I told him what my idea was, and he said yes right away, without even thinking about it. Woo hoo! He said he was going to take the subway to Times Square, which is where I lived, because his bike folds up so he can carry it on the train. So, there was no chance he would fink out after riding all the way from Brooklyn Heights. Perfect.

He's from the Isle of Capri and speaks English with a slight Italian lilt most of the time, but with pronounced 'foreigner' grammar when the mood comes upon him, so to speak. He's startlingly handsome and I have learned to be amused by the looks on faces and the craned necks when he walks into a room. He had also been a sex worker at one point.

Yes, the truth is that like most people, I find him handsome. We actually met because, although we were not exactly neighbors, I thought we were neighbors because, well, the area where I lived, which is the theater district in New York, is thick with sex workers. Even someone who looked like a movie star, as Gabriele does, would have fewer takers where he lives in Brooklyn Heights than where he used to hang out around Times Square, which is choked with hotels, bars and horny travelers. These days he is the respectable host of a white-tablecloth restaurant near Gramercy Park that he and his cousin, Dante, own together. Dante is the chef; Gabriele is the matinee idol. The food is to die for.

No, we aren't involved, and I don't see how that could ever change. When I first met him, I thought he was trying to kill me. Fortunately, I was mistaken. Maybe that's why we are close friends; we'd been to the mat together, so to speak. There's just too much clutter in our lives to toss it all aside and try to change everything in one swell swoop. It's worth pointing out that I'm twenty years older than he is, which makes him young and me middle-aged. Okay, later middle-aged. Okay, senior. Besides, I have kids, even though I seldom see them because they live on the other side of the country, in La-La-Land. You know that old *New Yorker* cover that shows a New Yorker's view looking west? Well, way at the far side, before Japan. Nuff said.

I am very fortunate because I started a consulting company about twenty years ago and was able to work there and increase the value of it, and then to sell it to a bigger company in the same business for an ongoing percentage of the profits. I have some duties there, but mostly I am on my own, with enough income to pay my bills and a decent-sized—not princely—net worth.

And just to be clear, if I were going to throw everything over for someone, it would be Ruth. Luckily for me, she's happily married—so we are happily 'friended' rather than anything else. She suspects that I'm gay even though she knows I would do her in a heartbeat. (Women like knowing that, especially when they think the stud is gay.) Forget that, not in a heartbeat. I don't want her husband, Murray, coming after me with a cleaver—ugh! Ruth and I have known each other for decades, when she was working for a hedge fund manager who made a run for the mayoralty of New York (and lost). Before she married Murray, we used to go to the theater together, or dinner sometimes, but we never so much as kissed romantically. It's still more or less the same—I am her regular 'date' because Murray does not like opera, concerts, musicals or Shakespeare— and apparently, he can snore pretty loud even in a sitting-up position. I like

Murray; we're friends.

So, there we were, starting out from my place at 48th Street and 8th Avenue at about one o'clock, heading for the GW Bridge on bicycles. It was Sunday and it was September, and it was still drippy summer humid, so we took bottled water in the saddlebags. Dehydration is not part of my plan for myself. It being hot, the population on the bike trail was not as heavy as it would be in better weather. On weekends in hot weather, by the way, the great and the good are not in town—they're still out east (in the Hamptons), or down the shore (the beachfront towns in New Jersey), or maybe at some lake upstate if they can't afford either of the first two places. Still, there were rollerbladers, runners, sweaty walkers, and helmeted bikers like Gabriele and me. We dismounted at the Boat Basin at 79th Street and polished off a full bottle of Poland Spring water each then refilled the bottles from a water fountain next to the restaurant there. Then we were back at it, pedaling and staring at the people on parade.

Gabriele wanted to stop at Riverbank State Park, which is a place that could only happen in New York. It's a real park, like thirty acres of real park, built on top of, *literally on top of*, a sewage treatment plant. No, it doesn't smell bad. The bridge was looming in front of us, but I still couldn't see the little red lighthouse. There is actually a kids' book called *The Little Red Lighthouse*. I saw one in a used bookstore one time and actually that is what caused me to look it up in Wikipedia and decide it was being added to my bucket list. There is actually a Little Red Lighthouse swim every year, but the thought of submerging myself in the Hudson River with God knows what kind of vermin or ancient industrial toxins is far too grim to consider.

I kept thinking we would see the lighthouse, but it is really obscured by the trees, and as you get closer, it is hidden on the river side of the huge aluminum-colored erector-set pylons that hold the bridge up. Originally, the bridge was to have looked more like the Brooklyn Bridge, with the metal skeleton covered by stone or cement. They never got around to doing the all-clad chiseled stone exterior during the Depression because it was too expensive. But the distinctive girders filled with x-shaped struts have been admired over the decades by artists and architects almost universally. One famous French architect said it was the most beautiful bridge in the world, and that was while he was designing the General Assembly building at the United Nations. Finally, there was a branch of the bike path to the left and the little red lighthouse was there in front of us, where the main path continued on north.

We walked up the cast-iron staircase inside the lighthouse to the lantern, which has been restored as a lighthouse, even though its light is ridiculously overwhelmed by the millions of lights on the bridge that towers over it. Needless to say, the lighthouse predated the bridge by more than forty years, so there was a navigational purpose to it when it was built. We admired, it then walked over toward the base of the bridge to see how the structure was raised that is the busiest vehicle bridge in the world.

Italians are very much into beautiful things, and Gabriele is no exception. He was very taken by the bridge itself, from the completely unaccustomed angle and viewpoint we had. The gigantism of the bridge is more evident from beneath it than it is driving across it. Like the Great Pyramid at Giza, the simplicity of its shape makes it look smaller than it is in real life. The bridge is basically what has been called an inverted arch where the suspension cables are the defining aspect of its appearance. He was busily taking photo after photo on his smartphone, looking across the river toward the stunning vista of the Palisades on the New Jersey side of the river.

I walked over to the pylons to look up and started taking some cellphone photos myself. I have to admit that my distance vision, even with my glasses on, is not 20-20, especially when the lighting is not great, but as I looked up, I saw what I thought must have been a big bird's nest in a corner up about sixty or seventy feet. The sun was in front of me as I looked up, and it obscured the nest, which I thought must be the abode of bald eagles, because there are certainly bald eagles all over and their whole diet is fish. If you drive along the Hudson River on a cold winter day, you can see the bald eagles sitting on ice floes waiting for a foolish fish to be visible—and then they dive straight into the water and come up with a meal. I was determined to get a picture.

Then it moved. Or swayed. I thought maybe I was getting dizzy, and looked down, put my hand out to a tree to steady myself. When I looked back up, the nest was quite different looking from what I had thought before. The sunlight was very dazzling, almost blinding me so I couldn't make out anything for sure. I walked back over to the water's edge and grabbed Gabriele's arm.

"Come over here," I said. "There's something I can't really see very well, and I want to know what it is."

I pointed up inside the pylon and said, "I thought there was an eagle's nest up there, but now I don't think that's what it is. Can you see what I'm pointing at?"

He nodded and took out a pair of dark sunglasses from his backpack and put them on. "There are two large black birds. No, maybe three."

"Black? Are you sure? They must be crows. That's disappointing, I was hoping they were eagles."

"I can't tell what they're doing, but they're flapping their wings like they are trying to hold onto something," he said.

Just as he said that, the birds let go of what they were holding onto and flew up to a girder. What they were sitting on was a black lump that was actually swaying like a streetlight in a high wind.

Then without warning it started to fall, and as it fell, we could both see that it was not a nest, but something with a black piece of cloth waving as it fell. As it fell, we both knew what it was. It was a body, a human body, and it had been hanging from a rope. It hit the ground with a squishy thud. Gabriele stared at it; I ran over to the lighthouse and interrupted a uniformed woman who obviously worked there.

"I'm sorry, miss, officer," I said. "There's an emergency over here." I ran ahead of her to where Gabriele was standing and as I ran up to him, he turned and vomited all over the ground. When the body hit the ground, the birds returned and started to eat again. It was also immediately obvious why the body had fallen—the head had become detached from the body and had landed a few feet away. There was a ferocious smell.

I thought the woman was going to faint, but she didn't. She called in an alarm to someone, and there were sirens almost immediately.

Gabriele, who has the darker skin of a Mediterranean, was as pale as a sheet. I walked him down the slight incline toward the lighthouse and sat him on a bench. I pushed his legs up so that the knees were bent in front of him.

"Put your head between your knees," I said in as authoritative a voice as I could summon while feeling fairly sure I was going to be sick myself. We had moved away from the sight and smell of the cadaver and the birds, and there were firemen in full regalia, and paramedics running by us toward the pylon. I sank down on the bench next to Gabriele and put my arm around his shoulder. I was still wearing my backpack and I reached inside and pulled out a fresh bottle of water, opened it, and handed it to him.

"Just a little. Don't drink much. It'll make you sick."

He sat up, sweaty but with his color returning. His hand shook as he lifted the bottle to his mouth.

"The Bridge is the most common location for suicide anywhere in the whole region," I said. "Although most people jump off into the river. Hanging yourself seems like a much worse way to die than just smacking into the water."

He looked at me quizzically. "Nobody would kill himself like that," he said.

There was a used-car lot melee of yellow crime scene tape being strung from every vertical to every other vertical, and two plain-clothes detectives arrived within minutes. One stopped and said, "You found the body?"

We nodded.

"Stay here," he said. "I'll be right back."

I did not feel faint, but I had the inevitable reaction after a tidal wave of adrenalin had rushed through my body: too weak to stand up, or to hold my head erect on my neck. I looked down at my legs, at the black-and-yellow bike pants and the cross-trainer shoes I chose to wear instead of bike shoes. I could feel myself shaking, especially my head and my jaw.

The detective came back. "Okay if I ask you some questions?"

We told him the whole thing. How I thought it was eagles but couldn't see over the glare from the sunlight. The birds scattering, the fall. "I guess you saw how it all landed," I said. "Did he kill himself?"

"No way to tell. The M.E. will have to rule on that. Can you tell me how you happened to be here today?"

I told him that we came to see the lighthouse, rode our bikes. Gabriele said nothing, just stared at the ground between his feet. The detective asked to see identification. He took photos of the two driver's licenses with his cellphone, thanked us and handed each of us his card. Then he turned to walk off toward the pylon.

"Excuse me, detective?"

He turned back to me.

"I don't think we're going to be up to riding our bikes one hundred and forty blocks back to Times Square. Any chance you could give us a lift? We have two bikes with us."

"Wait here," he said. "I'll see what I can do."

I pulled out my smartphone and called Ruth.

"Hey, sweetie," she said.

"Hey yourself. I'm up at the GW Bridge, under it, actually. Gabriele and I found a dead body, or it found us. The cops are here. We need to be picked up, because we rode our bikes up here and we're both just wrecked, never make it back on the bikes. And I don't have an Uber account. Can you come and get us? We have two bikes, so it has to be a car with plenty of room in back, or a pickup or something like that."

"What do you mean, a body?"

"Can I tell you later? A body. A dead man, dead for a while, being eaten by birds. The cops are working on it. We just have to get out of here. Both of us are ready to blow our stomachs. Gabriele already did."

"Murray has an Escalade. I'll bring that. Where are you?"

"Fort Washington Park, near the little red lighthouse if you know where that is."

"I'll figure it out. Or GPS will figure it out. Be there as soon as I can get the car out of the garage and drive up there. I'm a sight, not gonna get pretty before I leave. A body! Cripes. You are a magnet for mayhem, Hugo Miller."

FOR THE FULL INVENTORY
OF QUALITY BOOKS:
http://www.roguephoenixpress.com

Rogue Phoenix Press
Representing Excellence in Publishing

Quality trade paperbacks and downloads
in multiple formats,
in genres ranging from historical to contemporary romance, mystery
and science fiction.
Visit the website then bookmark it.
We add new titles each month!

www.ingramcontent.com/pod-product-compliance
Lightning Source LLC
Chambersburg PA
CBHW051414170626

46809CB00006B/2157